# Goddess

## Book Seven

*USA Today* Bestselling Author

# Ednah Walters

NEIL HELLMAN LIBRARY
COLLEGE OF SAINT ROSE
ALBANY, NY

813.6
W2353g

POPULAR
FIC
Wal

## COPYRIGHTS

Reproducing this book without permission
from the author or the publisher is an infringement
of its copyright. This book is a work of fiction. The names
characters, places, and incidents are products of the
author's imagination and are not to be construed as real.
Any resemblance to any actual events or persons,
living or dead, actual events, locale or
organizations is entirely coincidental

Copyright © 2017 Ednah Walters
All rights reserved.
ISBN: 1-943053-41-3
ISBN-13: 978-1-943053-41-4

Edited by Kelly Hashway
Cover Design by Cora Graphics. All Rights Reserved.
Front Matter Design and Formatting by Carolina Silva. All Rights
Reserved. No part of this book may be used or reproduced in any
manner whatsoever without permission, except in the case of brief
Quotations embodied in critical articles and reviews.

First Firetrail Publishing publication: Feb 2017
www.ednahwalters.com

FIRETRAIL PUBLISHING

EDNAH WALTERS

## ALSO BY EDNAH WALTERS:

The Runes Series:
Runes (book 1)
Immortals (book 2)
Grimnirs (book 3)
Seeress (book 4)
Souls (book 5)
Witches (book 6)
Demons (Book 7)
Heroes (book 8)
Gods (book 9)
Goddess (book 10)

The Guardian Legacy Series:
Awakened (prequel)
Betrayed (book one)
Hunted (book two)
Forgotten (book three)
Vindicated – Coming 2018

The Phantom Islanders Series:
Storm – Coming May 2nd 2017
Storm Revealed – Coming May 30th 2017
Storm Unleashed – Coming June 27th 2017

## WRITING AS E. B. WALTERS:

The Fitzgerald Family series
Slow Burn (book 1)
Mine Until Dawn (book 2)
Kiss Me Crazy (book 3)
Dangerous Love (book 4)
Forever Hers (book 5)
Surrender to Temptation (book 6)

The Infinitus Billionaires series
Impulse (book 1)
Indulge (book 2)
Intrigue (book 3)

## TABLE OF CONTENTS

## DEDICATION

To my fans…
For hanging with me from the beginning to the end.

## ACKNOWLEDGMENTS

As always, I'm grateful for the amazing members of my support team. My editor, Kelly Bradley Hashway, thanks for streamlining the book and weeding out the verbiage. Cora of Cora Graphics, your covers are stunning as always. To Carolina Silva, thank you for combing through this and weeding out the inconsistencies, taking my finished product, and formatting it so perfectly, and for being such an amazing PA and friend. I'm in awe of you, woman. Love you, lady. To Melissa Haag, best author buddy ever. Thanks for giving it to me right between the eyes. Your honesty, bluntness, and fresh eyes are so welcomed. To Irina Wolpers and Jeanette Conkling, thank you for finding those pesky typos and missing words. Your meticulousness never fails to humble me. You two are the best Omega-readers ever. To my Beta Reader Meghan Johnson & my launch team, you guys rock. Your keen eyes didn't miss a damn thing. You guys are the best. To my family, as always, thank you for your love and support. I love you, guys.

## TRADEMARK LIST:

Elantra
Twizzlers
Supernatural
Vikings
History Channel
Warner Bros
Starbucks
The Flash CWTV
ABC.COM
Marvel
The Fifa World Cup
DC Comics

# GLOSSARY

*Mon gyhrá geal* **(GHRAH gyal):** Gaelic for my bright love.

*Mon mhuirnín* **(WUR-neen):** Gaelic for my darling.

*Mon rúnsearc* **(ROON-shark):** Gaelic for my secret love/beloved.

*Mon stór* (stohr): My treasure.

**Aesir Court:** The court made of the twelve main gods led by Odin. Freyr (Vanir god) is part of this court though not counted among the twelve.

**Artavo:** Plural of artavus.

**Artavus:** Magical knife or dagger used to etch runes.

**Asgard:** Home of the *Aesir* gods.

*Ástin mín:* My darling.

*Ásynjur* **(ah-sin-yoor) Court:** The court made of the twelve goddesses led by Frigg. Freya (Vanir goddess and Freyr's sister) is part of this court, though not accounted among the twelve. She answers to Odin, not Frigg.

*Dýrr:* Dear.

**Eljudnir (El-yud-nir/near):** The hall of Goddess Hel.

*Elskr mín:* My beloved.

**Fensalir:** The hall of Goddess Frigg.

**Fólkvangr:** "Army field" for slain warriors belonging to Goddess Freya.

**Frigg:** Odin's wife, the patron of marriage and motherhood

**Freya:** The poetry-loving goddess of love and fertility; the other half of the dead warriors/soldiers/athletes go to her hall in Falkvang.

**Garm:** Hel's hound.

**Gargan:** Snake in old Norse.

**Gladsheim:** The hall in Asgard where all the gods have their high seats.

**Grimnirs:** Reapers for Hel.

**Hel:** The Goddess Hel in charge of the dead. She is sometimes called Hela.

**Hel:** Home of Goddess Hel, dead criminals, those dead from Illness, and those dead from old age.

**Helheim:** The realm where Hel's Hall is located.

**Himinbjörg**: Heimdall's home in Asgard.

**Hlidskialf**: The high seat of Odin, where he can see the whole Universe.

**Idun**: Norse Goddess of spring.

**Idun-Grimnir**: A wise Grimnir given the power to recruit other Grimnirs.

**Idun-Valkyrie**: A wise Valkyrie given the power to recruit other Valkyries.

**Immortals**: Humans who stop aging and self-heal. because of the magical runes etched on their skin.

**Jötnar**: Plural of giants in Norse Mythology.

**Jötun/Jötunn**: A giant in Norse Mythology.

**Jötunheim**: Home of the Giants in Norse Mythology.

**Meinfretr**: Stinkfart

**Midgard**: Earth in Norse Mythology.

**Mjornir (Myawl-nir/near)**: Thor's hammer.

**Nastraad/Corpse Strand**: The island in Hel for criminals. and evil Mortals, where their souls are tortured.

**Norns**: Deities who control destinies of men and gods.

**Nornsgard**: Norns' Hall.

**Nwyfre**: The life force in Druidic

**Odin**: An *Aesir* god, the father and ruler of all gods and men; Half of the dead soldiers/warriors/athletes go to live in his hall in Valhalla.

**Ragnarok**: The end of the world war between the gods and the Fire Giants.

**Sessrúmnir**: Goddess Freya's hall in Asgard.

**Seidr**: An old Norse term referring to a magical practice by Scandinavians. It includes act of divination or prophecy performed while in a trance.

**Stillo**: A type of artavus.

*Stjärna mín*: My star.

**Svartelfheim**: The realm of the Dwarves.

**Utgard**: Famous city in Jötunheim.

**Valaskialf**: Odin's hall in Asgard.

**Valknut**: The rune formed by three interlocked triangles.

**Valkyries**: Immortals who collect fallen warriors/soldiers/fighters/athletes and take them to Valhalla and Falkvang.

**Vingolf**: The hall of the *Ásynjur* where all the goddesses have high seats.

**Völur**: A group of Seeresses.

**Yggdrasil**: The tree of life or tree of knowledge that connects the nine realms of Norse cosmology.

# CHAPTER 1. ARE YOU DYING

Standing before the girls' bathroom mirror, I ignored my audience and stared at my reflection as medium runes coiled and spread up my arms and neck. I tried not to cringe. They crept up my cheeks and head, my scalp tingling. If circus freaks or mutants were in, I would be their poster girl.

"You look hot," Andris said. He was seated on the edge of the counter, arms crossed and a cup of caramel macchiato in his hand.

Of course, he would think a freak was hot. I rolled my eyes and shook my head. I was busy trying to focus on engaging the right runes.

"Maybe not as hot as him,"—Andris angled his head and did a slow trek down and then up the guy behind me—"but you know me. I like variety."

I met Syn's eyes in the mirror and tried not to laugh. Most guys would have been insulted that Andris was coming on to them, but not Syn. The Grimnir was so comfortable in his masculinity he tended to ignore Andris. This was not the first time they were hanging out with me in this bathroom on the top floor of my school. Sometimes Echo was around to make sure the souls behaved, and other times it was just Syn. On the Valkyries' side, it was usually Andris. I was an equal opportunity medium since prom night when souls needing closure had come to our aid and helped us with their evil brothers and sisters.

"You can't handle me, Valkyrie," Syn said in his smooth sexy voice.

Andris shrugged. "You have no idea what I can handle or dish out, Grimnir. I once had this Nubian lover who taught me amazing tricks that could rock anyone's world. She—"

1

"Shhh. Stop showing off. She's ready," Syn warned.

I'd already put on my gloves and opened the notebook. I picked up the pen and glanced to my right at the line of souls. They stared at me as though I was their last hope, and I guess I was. They didn't see the runes the way Mortals and Immortals did. To them, the black runes glowed and dazzled, drawing them to me the same way runes on a reaper's scythe drew them. The difference was reapers could turn their scythe into a weapon and disintegrate a soul. I'd never hurt them.

A year ago, I was just another ordinary high school girl vlogging about hot guys when a jealous Immortal etched medium runes on me and turned me into a magnet for the dead. Fear had landed me in a psych ward, but I grew stronger after that. Now that I knew how to use the runes to stabilize possession, I could listen to a soul's last request without fainting.

The short balding guy first in line was dressed in custom-made gym clothes. His shoes were designer and even the class rings on his fingers said he'd belonged to some exclusive secret society before he died. He looked like he was in his sixties, yet he had the body of a thirty-something, which meant he was bound for Asgard, where souls of athletes and soldiers resided.

Behind him stood a girl in silk pajamas and a bad perm, her eyes flashing with rage. She was so thin and emaciated she must have been ill before she died, which meant she was bound for Helheim, home of the souls of the sickly and those dead from old age. I wanted to hear her story, but I had a rule I lived by. I treated all the souls the same. Young or old, rich or poor, whatever the race, it was a first-come-first-serve basis. Word had spread about what I could do, so now I dealt with long lines during each session. Today, the bathroom was packed.

I smiled at Baldy and extended my hands toward him. He stepped forward and blended with me. A shiver crawled up my spine as my body adjusted to the invasion. The medium runes made the possession easier, but they didn't completely stop my stomach from roiling or the slow energy drain. Souls sucked on energy of those they possessed, even mediums like me.

*Are you dying?*

I blinked when the question drifted into my psyche. Souls rarely asked me personal questions. They tended to be self-absorbed.

*No.*

*You are not going to stop helping us?*

*Of course not. Whatever gave you that idea?*

Silence.

*Who told you I was dying?* I asked.

Instead of explaining why he'd asked, he started talking about what he wanted me to do. Sighing, I wrote. Sometimes souls conveyed their thoughts so fast I had to tell them to slow down so I could catch up. Others were hesitant to share their intimate moments, and I either had to reassure them or scold them. A few times, I cried for the ones with painful pasts. Whatever the case, I validated their feelings, justified or not.

Baldy had instructions for his lawyer, his girlfriend—I didn't judge—and his three children: two daughters and one son. I didn't do wills, but I could help with the rest of what he'd requested.

He moved out of me, and I studied the letters—one for his children, one for his girlfriend and soon-to-be-born son, and the last for his lawyer. It turned out his wife had died and his girlfriend was expecting. His squiggly handwriting was barely intelligible, though. I might have written down his thoughts, but the handwriting wasn't mine. Even the signature at the bottom was his. Any forensic expert would not prove he hadn't written the letters.

I passed them to Andris, who shoved them into envelopes and wrote the names on the outside. He didn't bother to wear gloves like I. He didn't care if they tried to find where the letters came from and found his fingerprints. Soul reapers were hundreds of years old, Immortal, and used runic magic. He had no problem making people forget things, including him. I, on the other hand, couldn't afford to leave evidence behind. I didn't deliver the letters either, not after that first time. People asked way too many questions.

"Over here, Dunbar." Andris waved at the empty stalls. "When

Cora is done, you're leaving with me." He glanced at the remaining souls in line, his eyes narrowing on a woman. "I promised to take her with me. She's Svana's, and so is the dude in the ill-fitting suit. How many can you do now?"

"Twelve. Maybe fifteen." Surprise flashed on his face while Syn frowned. I usually only managed to help half that number of souls during lunch. "I'm skipping first period after this."

"Why?" Syn asked, straightening.

"We have a substitute teacher this week. A total creep. Plus, it's a writing class, and I'm done with my piece."

"Creep how?" Andris asked.

"What has he done to you?" Syn added.

"Down, boys. He hasn't done anything to me or I would have dealt with him by now." I hadn't learned cool runes only to have them fight my battles. Besides, Ockleberry hadn't done anything to deserve letting these two loose on him. He just liked staring at cleavage a little too much. I wasn't sure what runes to use on him yet, but he was going to wish he never did that again.

"You have the addresses?"

Andris looked at the letters. "No, but I know where to find his people. I'll be invisible, so they won't see me coming or going."

I focused on the skinny girl and gave her a smile, but her expression didn't change. Most souls looked confused right after death, but these weren't recently departed. They were runners hoping to communicate with their relatives one last time and were usually angry. Before I started helping them find closure, they'd try to fix things their own way with little results.

I allowed her to possess me. The first emotion to hit me was rage. It was more than usual. I waited until the runes dampened the effect of her emotions.

*What's wrong with you? You don't look sick or like you're dying,* drifted into my thoughts.

*No, I'm not sick. Jeez, why do you souls think I'm dying?*

*Rumors. I hope they are mistaken, because I need your help, and I'm not leaving until my killers are exposed and stopped.*

Her name was Jenny, and she was fifteen, not as young as I'd thought, and she had a lot to say. The more she talked, the more pissed I got. I didn't realize I was crying until a tear fell on the book. I'd written several pages of everything that had happened to her, including the names and the addresses of the girls responsible.

*Anything else?* I let the thought drift through my head.

*Tell my reaper I would have possessed those bitches and driven them crazy, but I chose to work with you because I knew you'd help me. I'm counting on you, Medium. I want them stopped before they do to other girls what they did to me.*

Jenny was bossy, but I forgave her because she'd been through a lot. She and I separated.

"What happened to her?" Andris jumped off the counter and offered me a handkerchief. Only Andris would accessorize his outfit with a handkerchief. Syn was in the process of pulling wads of tissue and stopped.

I wiped at my cheeks. "Jenny was a student at an elite boarding school. Unlike the other girls, she was on scholarship, not one of the paying girls or children of the founding fathers, who bullied her constantly. They called her fat, so she tried to fit in. First, she became bulimic. Then, she ended up being"—I waved toward the skinny girl—"anorexic. All to fit in. They mocked her hair, so she changed it. Or tried to. Her clothes. Everything about her was just never good enough. The bitches did it at school and online. There's a website where these private prep schools socialize. They posted her pictures there and basically terrorized her. When she thought she was in and started dating a boy at a neighboring school, it turned out it was all a bet to see if he could get her in the sack. He posted intimate pictures of her online."

"Punk," Syn ground out.

"The bitches paid him, Syn. They are just as responsible for Jenny starving herself and the prank that ended her life. They locked her in an old building as part of some stupid initiation into a society and left her there for two days. When she tried to escape and found the stairs, she tripped and fell to her death." From her expression, Jenny was following our conversation. "Jenny said the leader of the pack is a senior and the daughter of one of the founding fathers. The girl keeps an online diary chronicling the things she and her friends do to the undesirables like Jenny, girls who don't belong in their school." I gave Syn the pages. "That's the log-in information. I hate bullies. If Raine were here, we would visit the girls and make them pay."

"I'll take care of this," Syn snarled, folding the papers. He was usually an easygoing guy, so seeing this side of him was interesting.

"I'm going with you, Grimnir," Andris said. "Making Mortals squirm is my specialty."

"Jenny doesn't want to be reaped until this is over," I said.

Syn looked ready to argue. He beckoned Jenny forward and peered into her face. "We'll get them, Jenny. Today. And you'll watch."

Jenny nodded.

"Just don't do anything to them that attracts the attention of the Norns," I said. "I don't want to be on their radar. Ever."

"You won't," Syn said. "I like computers. There's so much damage I can do with them."

"I knew there was a reason I liked you, Nubian," Andris piped in. "You know, other than the obvious. Life around here had gotten boring since Torin got hitched and we dispatched the dark souls."

"Uh, that was last week," I reminded him.

"So it's been a boring few days. I need to be stimulated. You and I, Nubian, will be vigilante reapers. Blondie can find us victims—or should I call them the perps?—and we'll finish them off."

"First, don't call me blondie. I hate it." Eirik had used it whenever he wanted to piss me off. "Second, you are not allowed to kill Mortals."

"I was speaking metaphorically," Andris said. "We'll punish them. Make them confess and fix things. Any thoughts on how we can do this, Grimnir?"

"I have plenty."

While they plotted mayhem, I moved on to the next soul. Halfway through, Andris opened the jar of Twizzlers and offered me some. I munched as I worked.

"That's enough for now," I said when I reached the fifteenth soul. Andris had his three while Syn had the rest. "We'll continue this evening. Tell your friends I'm not quitting," I reminded the ones I hadn't helped. Syn and Andris looked at me questioningly. "Almost all of them asked me if I was sick or dying. Strange."

The Grimnir placed the bag with my lunch and ice tea bottle on the counter.

"Echo said that's your favorite brand," he said.

"Thanks, Syn."

"It's no problem." He reached inside his trench coat and pulled out a small sickle. The second he lifted it, runes appeared on his arm, hands, and fingers, and connected to the ones on the sickle. It elongated into a scythe. The souls I'd helped stared at the blade with morbid fascination while the ones who still needed my help disappeared quickly.

Andris stared at the scythe and rolled his eyes without reaching for his artavus. The Valkyries' artavo had the same effect as a scythe when the light from it was used to control or disperse a soul, but I was finally seeing why Grimnirs used the bigger scythe. They reaped and controlled ten times the number of souls as the Valkyries. Their targets included criminals, who tended to run from reapers. I'd listened to enough of them to know their reason for running was always revenge. I opened the lid of the ice tea and chugged.

"How can you stand eating in here?" Andris asked, looking around.

"I don't intend to. I'm going to the beach house. Besides, no one dares to use this bathroom anymore."

"Ah, there are rumors going around your school that it's haunted. Flickering lights and electronics acting crazy. One even reported a voice on her phone asking her personal questions."

I grinned. Dev tended to get carried away. "How did you hear about it? Are you dating a student again?"

Andris grinned. "Are you and Dev having fun?"

"Always. Dating a student?"

"Several. Like I said, variety spices life." He glanced at Syn and sighed. "Fine, sour face. Let's go cause some mayhem. Like Blondie, I hate bullies." He threw his coffee cup in the garbage. "Will let you know how it goes. Come along, souls."

They opened a portal and disappeared through it, Syn leading the way with Jenny and his group of souls following, while Andris took the rear. A few souls wandered into the bathroom while I collected my things, but I shook my head. They understood what that meant, yet they still lingered and watched me. Their presence no longer bothered me. They were here when I arrived and would stay when I left, sometimes refusing to give up their places in line. The smart ones headed to the mansion, where I helped them after school. A few times, I helped some at my farm by the apple trees. It all depended on my mood.

I opened a portal to Echo's beach house in Miami and waved to the souls staring at me with woeful expressions. The students were right about that bathroom. It was haunted. I headed to the pool deck and lifted my face to the sky. It was going on three, the weather perfect for being outdoors. I settled on a lounge and ate my food. Alone.

I missed Raine. I would have gone to the mansion for lunch if she weren't on her honeymoon, or we would have come here if she hadn't quit school. I hated the Norns for forcing her to quit school and to get married secretly. At least they hadn't come after me.

I had a feeling Echo was responsible for that. He'd shielded me from them so well I was invisible, and I wanted it to stay that way. He was my protector, the one constant person in my life now. Someone I could count on no matter what. I could count on Mom and Dad, too, but they were my parents and keeping an eye on me was their innate responsibility. Echo chose me and adored me despite all my imperfections. It was time my parents knew the truth about him.

~*~

"Later, Cora," Kicker called out, and I waved without looking.

Kicker and I had been on the swim team together since freshman year, but we'd become closer the last few months. I wondered what she would say when she learned I didn't plan to finish my senior year at Kayville High. She'd probably demand to know why and where I was headed, which I couldn't tell her. She would never know I led a double life as a regular student during school and a medium for the dead whenever I could. Or how my friends and I saved the students from possession by evil souls during prom last weekend, or that our school had souls drifting through the walls and loitering on every floor and classroom. Sometimes I worried about the angry ones possessing students. After all, they were here because of me.

I grabbed my backpack and headed for the foyer, passing a few along the way. Did Raine ever worry about things the way I did, or did she just face one problem at a time and keep going? She'd just gotten married to her soul mate and was planning to finish her senior year at Mystic Academy, a private school for people with gifts like her. Witches and Immortals. I wanted to go with her, but I needed to deal with a few problems before I could commit.

First, my parents didn't know I wanted to switch schools. Heck, I hadn't told them I could see the dead. Second, Echo and I wanted to get married, and I still hadn't told my parents our plans. Mom adored him, and Dad respected him, but my stomach churned with dread just imagining how they'd react to what I planned to tell them. Everything. Including what he was. I couldn't do half-truths with my parents.

Students in the foyer stepped out of my way to let me pass. When their gazes went outside, I knew Echo was around. He had that effect on people. They tended to try to stay out of his line of vision while studying him on the sly. Some even tried to imitate his Grimnir style, but no one had the guts to ask me who he was. They just knew he was my boyfriend. The souls standing by the windows and staring outside knew he was a reaper, and I was the only one stopping him from reaping them.

I stepped outside and saw him by his SUV. He'd bought a car just so he could pick me up and drop me off at school. Classic rock vibrated the windows and pulsed through the air. From the lack of reaction from the other students, no one could hear the music except me, thanks to the dampening runes covering the black exterior.

Echo's wolfish eyes stayed locked on me, so I knew he wasn't really listening to the music. My stomach flip-flopped as I got closer, and my heart picked up speed. Even after dating him for almost a year, I still got flustered when he looked at me like I stole his breath away and he couldn't wait to have me in his arms.

"Cora-mia," he whispered and opened his arms.

I stopped and crossed my arms. "Stop being mean to Dev."

He growled. "Now I can't even get a hug because of him?"

"Oh, you'll get your hug. I just want you to be nice to him. Turn off the music."

"He talks too much, sings like a toad, and"—he pinned me with narrowed eyes—"I hate that he's permanently a part of our lives."

He sounded so frustrated my instinct to ease his dark mood kicked in. I closed the gap between us and kissed him. He let me initiate it, but took over, showing me he was in charge until he was all I breathed and tasted.

He lifted his head and smiled. "Want to open a portal, ditch the car, and go to our cottage?"

"Don't you mean ditch Dev? No, hun. We can't. He and I are going to the hospital." After I talked to my parents. "Did the furniture arrive?"

"Every last piece you ordered. I spent the afternoon making the cottage perfect."

He'd bought a house at the edge of town so we had a local place where we could entertain our friends.

"I want to see it, but I have a promise to keep." I reached around him and lowered the volume of the radio. "Hey, Dev."

"*A rún mo chroí*, how was school?" he answered through the car speakers.

He'd just called me a secret of his heart. Echo growled at the endearment, but I ignored him. As long as he kept reacting like that,

Dev would keep flirting with me. They were like two dogs with a bone. Echo might be the love of my life, but he had to learn to share me. Dev was my charge, a soul searching for redemption, and I was his only hope.

"I can't wait for the semester to be over. You okay in there, Dev?" I asked.

"Good. Do we still have a date?"

Echo stiffened beside me, and I sighed. I pulled him away to the hood of the car so Dev wouldn't hear us.

"He's supposed to help anchor the soul of a coma patient so the man can wake up and talk to his family. Remember Mr. Reeds from Moonbeam Terrace?"

"The old man who'd flirt with you or the captain?"

"The flirt. He had a heart attack and slipped into a coma. I need Dev to anchor his soul and give his family closure."

"He doesn't need you to anchor a soul," Echo griped, then pulled me into his arms and rested his forehead on mine. A sigh escaped him. "He's been doing this soul-cleansing thing on his own for weeks."

"And struggling. But he doesn't know who Mr. Reeds is." I lowered my voice as I continued. "Dev cannot slip back, Echo. The longer he stays inside a person, the stronger the urge to take over completely. He needs me to draw him out if that happens, and nothing works on souls like my medium runes." There was something off about Echo. He seemed restless. "You okay?"

"Couldn't be better. The golden dragon is in Asgard, and things are back to normal in the hall."

I frowned. He rarely discussed Helheim, the realm of the dead, or the goddess he served. "Golden dragon? As in a real golden dragon?"

"Yep. You should see him. He can be a real pain, and we've gone on some really amazing adventures the last few weeks, but"—he scowled—"he's in Asgard now and things are back to normal. That's a good thing."

I reached up and stroked his cheek. His voice and his words didn't match. "You miss him."

"Hel's Mist no. He's a pain in my ass. The adventures were nice, but that was not who I am. I'm a reaper."

He was so cute when he tried to act indifferent. "Are you sure you should be telling me this? You said you can't share things that take place over there."

"I know." He pressed a kiss on my temple. "I hate not sharing everything with you."

I hated it, too. I planned to marry him and had to accept that I'd only see him when he was on Earth. If something were to happen when he was in Hel, I wouldn't know about it unless another reaper told me, and I wouldn't be able to visit him.

"Do you think after we marry the goddess might be more accommodating? After all, you are her favorite reaper."

He grinned. "We'll see. She's changed because of the dragon, so she might change her mind about reapers bringing their Immortal wives to Eljudnir. I plan to talk to her after we set a date, which means—"

"Telling my parents the truth." Something I wasn't looking forward to. I glanced at my watch. I needed to get home and get it done. "Are you driving or am I?"

"I am." Grinning, he scooped me up and walked around to the front passenger seat. "That way you can distract me."

I laughed and kissed his chin. Instead of closing the door, he tilted my chin and studied my face, his smile fading.

"If the goddess says yes, would you be willing to spend time there with me? My quarters are spacious, and you'd never have to see her."

Panic coursed through me. The little I knew about Goddess Hel said she was not a nice person. She had the power and the authority to detain anyone who entered her realm, dead or alive. What if she insisted I stay there forever? Even Raine, who'd adored her father, was reluctant to visit Hel's Hall to see him.

"Of course, you don't have to," Echo said and pressed his lips against mine. It was a featherlight kiss, filled with love and patience, which made me feel terrible. Echo loved me, yet I couldn't agree to a simple request out of fear. He would protect me.

I created space between us. For Echo, I would face anything and anyone.

"Yes, the place has been your home for hundreds of years, so yes, I'd love to visit if she's okay with it."

This time, he crushed my lips with his, letting his passion show. He was volatile and unpredictable, but he felt things deeply. Having me with him meant everything to him, but would his boss think so, too? Grinning, he closed the door and moved around the hood, his leather trench coat flying behind him.

"I'm happy you agreed," Dev said from the car radio. He sounded serious, which was unusual. "I could feel his soul shrivel with every second you stayed silent. If you'd like, I can come with you and watch your back."

I chuckled. "If you can, why not? Just remember, there's nothing you can do that Echo can't."

"I'm a soul, doll-face. I could slip in and out of places he could only dream about."

Echo caught the last part of Dev's sentence when he opened the car door. "Out of my stereo," he barked.

"What did I do this time?" Dev asked, sounding bewildered.

"Out. Now."

Dev slithered out, sat on the hood of the car, arms and legs crossed like a genie, and neatly blocked Echo's view.

"He thinks he's funny. That's the last time you try to seduce my girl behind my back, you bodiless smog."

*Oh brother.* I placed my hand on Echo's arm. "We were talking about visiting Hel's Hall. He offered to come with me and keep an eye on things. I told him there was nothing he can do that you can't do."

"Damn straight." He peered at Dev. "What you don't know, Casanova, is that in Helheim, you will become solid and Goddess Hel knows everything that goes on there, including the presence of unwelcomed visitors. And who said you can go with us?"

Dev pointed at me with two fingers and smirked. He was such a goofball.

"He can come, right?"

"No, he can't. You are Earth-bound, Dev. Get out of here. I need a moment with my girl without you butting in."

Dev lay across the hood as though he planned to stay there forever and gave Echo the finger. I laughed.

Echo cursed. "Fine," he snarled. "Go to the cottage and find something to do there."

Dev grinned. He loved the place. It was spacious with a lot of land and very few neighbors. He could sing along with the radio without starting a neighborhood riot. There was something about hearing his own voice that kept him sane, he'd told me. We also had a smart TV with enough online movie channels to keep him busy.

"Behave while there, or you will be uninvited indefinitely," Echo added.

Dev floated upward until he was standing on the hood and saluted Echo. Funny how dark and formless he'd looked when we first met. Now I could see his features, and the smoke clinging to his form was growing thinner with each person he helped. He had a long way to go, but I was determined to see him redeem himself.

"I'll come get you when it's time to go to the hospital." He nodded and floated away. Echo smirked. I didn't understand his relationship with Dev. He cared about him, but he was always being mean to him, which Dev ignored or responded with a finger. "Why can't you try to be nice to him?"

"That was me being nice." Echo nudged me closer until my head rested on his shoulder. He started the car and eased out of the parking lot. The smile disappeared from his face. "He can never go to Hel, Cora. The portal is one directional for souls."

"Oh. I didn't know that." I sighed. "Dev needs a purpose, Echo."

"Once Mystic Academy begins, he'll be okay."

Dev wanted to teach there, but how could he without a body? He'd have to use electronics. "He needs a body, but that's impossible."

Echo laughed. "Actually, it's possible. I knew Druids who could bring the dead back to life if a body was still fresh and the soul hadn't moved on."

"Really? That's awesome. So we need to find a fresh body for Dev?"

"No, we don't. Rhys kept his body and preserved it using magic. All we need is someone with the ability to anchor a soul to a body."

"Can my runes work? Medium runes make it easy for souls to possess a body."

"And that's because you have a life force, which souls borrow. That's why you always feel drained after a possession. A dead body has zero life force. We need a healer, a life force manipulator. Unfortunately, I haven't met a Witch with ergokinetic abilities in the last several centuries. And even if they have it, they wouldn't tell anyone. It is a powerful and rare gift, which can be exploited by both magical and non-magical people. Those who have it guard it and keep it a secret." He sighed. "At least one good thing will come out of starting Mystic Academy. We'll know who has what powers. We might get lucky and find someone who can help him."

I wanted to go to that school so badly I could taste it. I hoped there would be people like me who weren't born with abilities, but were willing to acquire them through runes. I'd love to mentor future mediums. I had to talk to my parents. Today. I also wanted to go to Hel for Echo, no matter how scared I was.

"I'll talk to my parents before I go to the hospital, and you should talk to the goddess about us. No more secrets. What do you think?"

"I'm on board." He glanced at me and grinned. "Distract me."

I kissed his neck and slipped a hand under his shirt to caress his chest.

"You can do better than that," he challenged.

I could and did. He veered off the road and almost crashed through the fence into the Melbecks' vineyard. Luckily, we were closer to the farm and traffic was low. I was still laughing when we parked outside our house. Mom's truck was parked beside Dad's SUV and my Elantra, which meant they were both home.

"Well?" I teased.

He kissed me. "You are an evil woman."

"You issued a challenge, and I accepted it. What did I get in return? You almost crashed the car."

He laughed. "I'm crazy about you, Cora-mia."

"Good, because I'm crazy about you, too." God, I hoped my parents would be okay with what he was.

"What is it?" Echo asked.

"I'm still worried about Mom. Something is off with her." Her erratic behavior had started on Saturday, the day of our high school prom. She'd looked like she'd been crying while I'd slept off an energy drain from a possession. Then she'd burst into tears the second she'd seen me. Mom was not the crying type. Dad had to take our prom pictures instead of her, and he kind of sucked at it.

"Have you tried talking to her?"

"Several times, but she keeps saying she's okay. Do you think she knows about my abilities? I've caught her staring at me with a weird expression."

"I don't know, Cora-mia, but if you want me there while you talk to them, I can come inside."

"No, I'll be fine. If they need further proof of your world, I'll show them. I mean, I can do everything you do."

He scoffed at the idea.

"Hey." I smacked his arm. "I can move fast now that I have speed runes, become invisible, open portals, and talk to a soul better than you. You yell and threaten them, while I just stand there like a saint. No, like an angel, and they flock to me. I might not have a size-changing runic scythe, but my body is a magnet for souls, so we are even."

Laughing, he leaned in and stole a kiss. "I have almost a thousand years on you, sweet cheeks. Now get your lovely ass out of my car before I open a portal to my bedroom and show you who can do things better."

"You have a one-track mind."

"Yet you still love me."

"Like I said, I'm a saint."

He laughed. "Sweetheart, you may have the face of an angel, but sainthood is not for you."

"And who corrupted me?" I got out of the car. "A certain reaper who won't be getting any."

His door swung open, and his head appeared on the other side of the hood. "You can't be serious."

"Bye." I wiggled my fingers and laughed when he growled. He was still staring at me with a lost puppy expression when I reached the patio. I blew him a kiss and disappeared inside. The playfulness disappeared when I saw my parents.

Mom's eyes were red, again. And Dad wore a helpless look as he cleaned his glasses, something he did when he got emotional. I dropped my books on the table with a thud and moved closer to his writing nook where they stood, worry and anger colliding inside me.

## CHAPTER 2. THE TRUTH

"What's going on? And no more hedging or telling me it's nothing." My eyes volleyed between them. "You'd better not be getting a divorce because I will drag you guys to the nearest marriage counselor first."

"Oh, honey," Mom whispered, her voice shaking.

No. Not a divorce. My throat closed up, and my eyes smarted. Their unwavering love for each other was another constant in my life. So much had changed the last year that if they got divorced now, it would rip my world apart.

"You always said family came first and we stick together through thick and thin, so whatever it is, I need to know."

Mom pulled me into her arms, tears racing down her face. "Of course, we're not getting a divorce. Your father would be lost without us." She chuckled through her tears.

She was joking now? I wiggled free from her arms and studied her tear-stained face.

"Then what is it? You taught me to always face new challenges no matter how daunting. I've never seen you cry... except when you dropped me off at the middle school that first time. I saw you through the window, so I cried, too." Then another thought occurred to me. "You're not sick, are you? You would tell me instead of hiding it like Raine's parents did, right?" My eyes flew to my father. "Dad?"

"No one is sick, but there's something we need to tell you."

No divorce and no illness, then it couldn't be bad. "Okay. Let's sit down. Mom, would you like tea?"

"Yes, dear."

I kissed her cheek and touched Dad's arm. "Dad?"

"Something soothing would be nice."

I went into the kitchen while they settled on the couch. While I waited for the water to boil, I munched on a banana. I placed organic chamomile teabags in three mugs. One mug had two definitions of a mother.

*Mom: A hero that does whatever it takes to get things done.*

*Mom: One who is never wrong about anything.*

The other said Dad's Memorable Moments:

*Unforgettable: December 16th*

*Memorable: July 29th*

The first was my birthday and the second their anniversary. Both were gifts from me. Mom wasn't big on processed foods, so I added honey to our drinks. I was starting to act like her. Echo had a sweet tooth, so I could see us in the future, me with my healthy, homemade non-fat yogurt while he binged on some cream-filled pastries packed with empty calories. I'd probably join him. He had a way of making me do things I was unsure about and love them. Nah, I doubted I'd ever go completely healthy. I loved Twizzlers, especially after a possession.

I glanced over at my parents and found Mom wringing her hands. Dad had disappeared. I opened my mouth to ask her where he was when he appeared on the stairs. He was carrying a green cloth. Mom took it and folded it on her lap.

My mother was the strongest woman I knew. She would not break down like this over nothing. Whatever this was, we would work on it together.

I gave them their drinks. On a different day, they would have chuckled over my choice of mugs. This wasn't the first time I'd used cocoa or tea in mugs with pithy words to smooth over a squabble. Something was definitely different this time. My parents wore stricken expressions.

"You guys are really scaring me now. What's going on?"

Mom put her drink down without sipping it and reached for Dad's hand, forcing him to relinquish his mug. He patted her hand. Since I was on the adjacent chair and closest to her, she reached for my hand, too, and squeezed it gently.

"First, we want you to know that we love you very much," Dad said.

A hollow feeling settled in my stomach.

"I know, Dad."

"I remember the first time I saw you." He shook his head and chuckled. "You had lungs on you. You didn't just lie in your crib and coo like other children. You demanded attention and caught ours. Your mother took one look at you and knew you were the one for us."

Confused, my eyes volleyed between them. "What are you talking about?"

"The day we adopted you. We knew you were the one for us from the moment we entered the nursery and heard you scream."

The pit in my stomach widened. "I'm adopted?"

They nodded. Stunned, I stared at them. No, this couldn't be happening. They were Mom and Dad. My parents. Everything I knew about them zipped through my head.

"No," I whispered.

Mom inched closer. "Honey, I know it's a shock."

"Why?" I stared at her, my brain in shambles as I tried to think up words to deny what they were saying.

"Why did we adopt you?" Mom asked. "Because—"

"Not that. Why didn't you tell me this before?"

They looked at each other, and Mom sighed. "Because it didn't matter. You were our daughter."

"Were?"

"You still are, but things have changed. The reason you see souls is connected with who your biological parents are"—Mom started to sniffle—"and where you came from."

Blood drained from my head. The damn pit was now a black hole. "You know I see souls?"

"Yes," they said in unison.

"When you were young, you called them your invisible friends," Mom added. "It was part of the reason we decided to homeschool you. We weren't sure whether the runes we used would block your ability."

I pulled my hand from Mom's and sunk deep into my seat. "Runes?

You know about runes? Wait. Did you say you used runes to block my ability? And I'd seen souls as a child?" What about Maliina and the medium runes she'd etched on me? She was the reason I saw souls, wasn't she? "I don't understand."

"I think we should start from the beginning, dear," Dad said and glanced at Mom. She reached for my hand again, but I shook my head and crossed my arms, hugging myself, my heart pounding so hard it hurt.

"We are Immortals, Cora. We came to this country from Ireland in the early seventeen hundreds, moved around the country as most Immortals do, and reinvented ourselves over and over again. Because we had to do that, we never had children of our own. Fifty years ago, we decided we'd lived a rich and fulfilling life and it was time to age gracefully. We stopped adding more healing runes, and without them repairing our cells, we started to age. We'd heard about a special adoption among Immortals, but we never thought to pursue it until we moved to Kayville and found a thriving community of Immortals here."

"There are other Immortals like you?" I asked in a tiny voice. I knew about Svana and her friends, as well as Blaine, Lavania, Ingrid, and the Sevilles. That was it.

Mom nodded. "Yes. The Immortals here protected the orphans from those who would hurt them and supported each other, so we joined them. We got in touch with a representative of the adoption agency and told them we were interested in adopting a baby. So when the new ones arrived, someone got in touch with us."

I was drowning in nowhere land, every breath I took hurting. "Arrived from where?"

"Other realms. We didn't know who brought them here until recently. We just knew they were orphans from other realms."

"Were you ever going to tell me the truth?"

Their faces said they weren't.

"What changed? Why are you confessing now?"

"We wanted to keep you safe."

"From what?" I snapped.

"There was a group of evil Immortals searching for the orphans from other realms. The Immortals were like us, born here on earth and turned by runes. They felt they deserved to move between realms and visit the gods because of the way they've defended humanity over the years."

"Are you talking about Lord Worthington and the Immortals Raine and the others fought?" I asked, astonished. Did they know everything?

"Yes. Before they came here after Raine, they targeted the other orphans, those who have the right to move between realms. Children like you. It took Eirik weeks to find the Immortals and rescue the children."

I blinked. "Eirik Seville?"

"Yes. He goes by Eirik Baldurson now because he is the son of Goddess Hel and God Baldur."

"I know who his parents are," I yelled. "And I don't want to discuss him or the other orphans. You lied to me. Everything about our life is a lie."

"Cora," Mom and Dad said in unison. Mom reached for my arm, and I jumped up.

"Don't. Do you have any idea how much I've agonized over telling you the truth about Echo and my ability to see souls. Oh God. You've known Echo was a reaper all this time?"

"Yes. At first we thought he was an Immortal, but..." Mom glanced at Dad. "Yes, we know he is a reaper."

The past zipped through my head: Echo kissing me right in front of them during breakfast. Echo standing behind me and saying naughty things while Dad stood in the doorway of my bedroom. Everything we'd ever done while thinking they couldn't see us...

"You overheard and saw everything. The runes on my car after I met him, when he'd come to my room and even in here, you knew, yet you acted like he wasn't there. How could you?"

"Pumpkin," Dad said.

"Cora," Mom muttered at the same time and extended her hand toward me. I took a step back.

"How could you know and not say anything? Everything about you, me, us is a sham. We are a mockery of a family. Let me guess, the psych ward you took me to was not really a nuthouse, was it?" They didn't have to admit it. It was written on their faces. "You tried to fix me again so I wouldn't see souls and you could continue lying to me."

Tears swam in Mom's eyes. "We thought it was for the best, honey."

"Best for whom, Mom? Obviously not for me. Why now? And don't lie to me. Just once, tell me the truth."

"Your parents want to meet you," Mom said and lifted the green cloth on her lap. "This blanket is yours. They didn't give you away. You were stolen from them, and they've been searching for you for a very long time."

I was too hurt to feel pity for imaginary people.

"Screw them."

"Cora!" my parents snapped.

"Exactly. Cora. That's who I am. I'm not meeting some strangers who didn't watch me closely enough eighteen years ago. I'm not walking away from the life I have. The life I'm meant to live." Tears threatened to spill. I turned and yanked the door open.

"Where are you going, Cora?" Mom yelled in a pleading tone.

"Far away from you. Don't bother coming after me because I will not come back." I engaged my speed runes and took off.

~*~

I ran until my chest and feet hurt. My high-heeled boots weren't built for speed, and I'd lost one heel somewhere along the forest. Giant trees whispered and swayed as though to soothe my pain. I dropped to my knees, and the banana I'd eaten spewed from my mouth until nothing was left in my stomach. I staggered back and sat on a log. I wanted to curl up right there and waste away.

Strong arms lifted me and cradled me close.

"Tell me who hurt you, Cora-mia," Echo said soothingly, but his body was taut with anger.

Hearing his voice only made things worse. I couldn't talk, so I clung to him. He opened a portal, walked across the main bedroom of the cottage to the large bed, and held me while I cried. We stayed there until I was rung out.

"Who hurt you? Is it Raine?" He sounded like he would take on my best friend, who would never knowingly hurt me.

"They knew, Echo," I mumbled in his chest. "All this time, they've known about you and about me seeing souls, and they never said a thing. Even when you visited my house and spent the night in my room, they knew."

"Your parents?"

"Yes. They lied to me. Everything about them is a lie. My whole life is… is a lie."

"Why would they lie? And how do they know about me?"

I leaned back to see his confused expression. "They are Immortals."

Shock flashed in his eyes. Then a frown chased it.

I told him everything and ended with, "They said my biological parents want to meet me. I don't care. I never want to meet them."

Echo sighed and ran his knuckles up and down my arms. Usually his touch soothed me, but not this time.

"I'm so sorry, baby. Keeping such a big secret was a terrible thing to do to you, and you have every right to be angry. How could I not have known about them being Immortals?"

"They stopped using runes fifty years ago."

"I still should have known. There is a bright side to this," he said softly. "Since you are one of the orphans, I can share things from the other realms with you."

"I don't want to know."

"But it might help clarify things for you. I helped Eirik find the other orphans. Most of them didn't know they were originally from the other realms either. They were scared, confused, and just wanted to come back home to Earth. To the Immortal parents who'd adopted them, and to the only homes they'd ever known."

"Did their parents lie to them about who they were, or had they always known?"

A thoughtful expression settled on his face.

"Did they lie?"

"No."

"Mine did."

"The other orphans knew they were adopted, and that bad Immortals were after them. They spent their lives moving from place to place, never staying anywhere for long. Your parents and the Immortals here worked hard together to hide you and the other children and keep you safe."

I glared at him. "Are you siding with them?"

"No, Cora-mia. I'm on your side. They were wrong to hide the truth from you."

"Damn right. They've lost every right to call me their daughter or be my parents."

"You may think so now—"

I scooted to the edge of the bed and glared at him. "I don't think. I know so."

He sighed. "Would you like to talk to the other orphans? I know one in New Orleans."

"No."

"Eirik?"

"Why would I want to talk to Eirik?"

"You were both raised here, and he went through what you are going through right now."

"The. Sevilles. Did. Not. Lie. To. Him." I got up and paced. "He always knew he was adopted. And when he found out, I wasn't even there to see how he dealt with it because the Jemisons had taken me to a damn psych ward. A fake psych ward where they tried to fix my ability to see souls. *The Jemisons*. It felt weird calling them that, yet I couldn't bring myself to say my parents. Not anymore. At least not right now. "Do you know I used to see souls when I was little? I guess Maliina's runes didn't give me the ability to see souls. They did. My birth father and mother. Maliina just gave me medium runes so she could use me as a suit." I sat down, and Echo shifted closer and pulled me against him.

He pressed a kiss on my shoulder and then nuzzled my neck. "What do you want to do?" he asked.

"Crawl into bed and never leave." I did exactly that and pulled the covers over my head. I wanted to lock out the world and wallow in self-pity. I couldn't believe what the Jemison's had done.

Echo lifted the covers. "Cora-mia…"

"Please, go away." The last word came out in a wail. I wanted him gone so I could cry. Instead of leaving, he stroked my hair.

"Don't cry, Cora-mia. It breaks my heart to see you like this."

"I'm not crying," I shot back even as my eyes brimmed. I pulled the blanket over my head again. "Just go."

"I'll be back."

I heard his voice in the other room. I wasn't sure whether he was talking to Dev or my parents. No, the Jemisons. My parents were the faceless couple that had given me the ability to see souls. My entire life was falling apart right before my eyes, and I was helpless to do anything about it. This was worse than when I'd found out I could see the dead. Then I had my family to fall back on. Now, I had nothing.

I relived everything my parents had ever told me, getting more and more angry. How could they lie to me like that? They taught me values, and at the top of that list was staying true to myself. Mom taught me how a woman carried herself, and Dad taught me how a man should love. He was the standard I used to measure every man that ever waltzed through my life, and most had failed, until Echo. How could all of that be based on a lie?

The bedside radio alarm turned on, and an old tune started to play. I winced. Dev could not hold a tune.

I lowered the covers. "Not now, Dev."

"I was just trying to cheer you up."

"You can't. This is one of those things I have to deal with on my own. Could you just go to the hospital without me and see how Mr. Reeds is doing? If his family is there…"

"I'll anchor his soul and make him talk to them. I promise not to push him out and replace his soul."

Why was I concerning myself with others? I needed to focus on me for a change. Then Dev's words registered.

"Can you really do that? Replace his soul?"

"More like dominate his, but without a life force, I can't stay anchored to his body for long. When a soul leaves a body, it does because the person's life force is too low to tether it. When I was possessing living things, I'd share their life force, which quickened their death if they were sick. The longer I stayed, the faster they died after I left. If they were not sick, they'd act crazy."

"Are you still sharing their life force?"

"No. Now I give them some of my energy, such as it is."

"No wonder you are always weak and sleepy afterward."

"Exactly. If I stay too long, I might be tempted to take theirs, and that's why I like having you there. You yell at me to get out."

"I can't deal with anyone tonight, Dev. I'm sorry."

"But Mr. Reeds could die tonight."

"I know. Well, you win some…" I pulled the covers over my head and focused on my pain.

"That doesn't sound like you, doll-face," Dev reprimanded.

I didn't care what he thought. I was done giving and being Ms. Nice. Then Mr. Reeds's face flashed through my head, and I sighed. I'd liked talking to him and Captain G at the nursing home. I pulled down the covers.

"Help him, please."

"Without you?" Dev asked. "Are you sure?"

"Yes. I trust you and know you will not fail me because I can't deal with any more bad news, Dev. Go and make me proud."

There was silence, then, "Thank you, doll-face."

I frowned. "For what?"

"Trusting me."

"I don't see it as lack of trust, Dev. I see it as working together as a team. You do it before they die, and I do it afterward. If I'm not there, you work without me. If you're not there, I do my part. We are a team."

"So you don't mind if I help others? The cancer ward at Kayville Memorial has a few coma patients that could use my help."

"Then do it. Help as many as you can. Just be careful and report to me when you're done."

Once he left, I continued to wallow in misery until Echo returned with food from his favorite restaurant in Miami. He tried to entertain me with stories about the newbie reapers he was training. I only half listened. When he got up and disappeared inside the bathroom, I didn't ask him what he was doing. The sound of running water followed. When I could have crawled back under the covers and continued wallowing, he scooped me up and carried me to the bathroom. The scene brought a rush of tears.

Scented candles covered most surfaces. Lavender, rose geranium, and jasmine. He knew exactly what I needed to relax. He'd also added jasmine bath salt to the water.

"Forget about everything except us and the fact that I love you." He lowered me to the floor and peered at me, his eyes troubled.

"I'll be fine," I mumbled.

"I know, but I got your back. Every step of the way." He started unbuttoning my top and pushed it off my shoulders. Then he gripped the waistband of my skirt and pulled it down. There was nothing sexual about the way he undressed me. His touch was gentle, his focus on what I needed. Even when his eyes heated as he removed my bra, he didn't reach for me or try to kiss me.

"I'm going to put your hair up so we can wash it later."

More tears fell. He knew me so well. I had specific shampoo and conditioner for my hair and never just dunked it in my bath water.

Completely naked, I stepped into the churning water and slid in. The warmth surrounded me, the water massaging my skin. Echo sat on the floor and rested his arm along the ridge of the tub. He scooped water with his hand and poured it on my shoulder.

"Do you want your lingerie or just shorts and a tank top?"

My lingerie was lacy, silky, and sexy. Looking sexy was the last thing on my mind. "Shorts and a tank top."

He pressed a kiss on my forehead and left the room. I leaned back against the bath pillow, closed my eyes, and tried to let the aromatic scents soothe my senses, but I couldn't relax. The scents weren't enough.

Echo returned and checked on me. "How are you feeling?"

"Like crap."

He frowned. "I bought a new massage oil—"

"Join me." I extended my hand to him. "I need you, not a massage. Help me drown out their voices from my head. I keep hearing them."

*You were adopted. Your birth parents want to meet you. You were...*

He'd never undressed so fast. Echo was such a beautiful man, body and soul, and he was mine. I scooted forward and created space behind me, but the second he sat down, I turned and faced him, wedging my knees between his and the tub so I straddled his thighs.

"Cora-mia," he whispered.

"I need you now." I stared into his eyes and scooted closer. "I need to forget."

"I'm yours, always," he whispered, voice husky. "Tell me what you want."

"I want to get lost in you." I scooted closer and reached up to cup his face.

The kiss I gave him wasn't tentative. I wasn't the innocent girl he'd met a year ago. I was a woman now, his woman, and I knew how to love him just as he knew what I loved.

I nipped on his lower lip, and a groan rumbled through his chest. Pushing my tongue between the seam of his lips, I swept it across his, inviting him to play. He did, but he didn't take over. This was what I needed now. To be in control of something. Everything else was falling apart.

I savored the taste and texture of him as I moved along his jawline to his neck. His muscles leaped as my nails dug into his chest, and another groan escaped him. It wasn't enough. I wanted him to beg me to stop torturing him.

I pushed him back, so he was partially reclined on the tub, his head resting on the bath pillow. I kissed down his chest, nipping him here and there and feeling him tremble. He completely submitted to my exploration. A few times, he smothered a curse, but he didn't stop me. He often turned the tables on me when I pushed him too far. Not this time.

His hands caressed my back, one moving up to sink into my hair to grip the strands. He was close to losing it, his body taut with tension. I moved up and shuffled closer. He stared at me with half-closed eyelids, the amber in his eyes burning with love and need.

I reached down, and without breaking eye contact, I guided him, and a sigh of bliss escaped me when we were one. He gripped the edges of the tub, his jaw taught with tension. I wasn't being fair, but I needed this. When I lowered my head and kissed him, his hips rose.

"Don't move, please," I begged him. I wrapped my arms around him and went back to kissing him, pouring all my love into it. His hands left the edges to stroke my back, my side, and my face.

Then slowly, I loved him at my own pace until we reached that point where the sensations became magnified, a sum of his and mine. When the crest swept us, he was there with me, shouting my name and his love.

I rested my head on his shoulder and closed my eyes. The rest of the world could crumble into pieces, but my Echo would always stay the same. He was my anchor. He steadied me when I could have fallen. I didn't want reality to intrude, but the thoughts wouldn't let me go.

"Did you go to the farm?" I asked, speaking against his neck.

"Yes. I knew they'd be worried about you."

I rolled my eyes.

"They love you, and no matter what you decide to do, they'll support you. You can stay here for as long as you want."

"They have no say in what I do with my life anymore. I'm eighteen."

He didn't argue. "Do you want to watch something after this? Go to the hospital with Dev? Swing by Raine's?"

"Dev already left, and Raine is on her honeymoon. Besides, what does she know about this?" If Raine knew... I leaned back and studied Echo's face. "Does she know?"

"I don't think Eirik talked to anyone about the orphans, except to the people in Helheim. Those kids had a shitty life, running and hiding, always looking over their shoulders. It's not a life I would have wanted for you."

"You are forgetting one thing. They all knew they were adopted. I didn't. They probably knew about their parents being Immortal. I didn't. My parents knew I could see souls when I was young, and they blocked it. So drop it." When he sighed, my frustration shot up. "Are you reaping tonight?"

"Syn is covering for me."

"Maybe you should join him."

He chuckled. "Am I annoying you?"

"Yes. For someone who hates being betrayed, you are excusing my parents' betrayal so quickly. Why?"

"I'm not, Cora-mia." He stroked my shoulder. "I see possibilities. If you are from the other realm, you could visit..."

I growled.

"I guess this is not the time to discuss that."

"No."

"Okay." He studied me, his eyes shifting to my lips. "Can I make love to you now?"

"Only if you promise not to discuss my parents or other realms."

He was more than eager to make up for annoying me, and I forgave him. How could I not? He loved me and knew how to make me happy. Knew how to make me fly and fall apart, because he was also there to catch me.

The water was cold when we moved to the shower. He washed my hair, wrapped a towel around it, and cocooned me in a thick robe. Echo had always taken care of me, and it didn't cross my mind once to complain that he was babying me. When we left the bathroom, I paid more attention to the décor.

He'd done a good job with the furniture we'd ordered. He'd asked me where I wanted everything and had followed my instructions. The paneled rooms were smaller and cozier than those in his house in La Gorce, Miami. The fireplace dominated the living room, and facing it was a burgundy leather sectional. A giant smart TV was in the family room by the kitchen. There was another sectional there, too.

He fussed with the remote until I took pity on him. He usually showed no interest in watching TV. News bored him, and the inaccuracy of action movies drove him nuts. He solved most detective series way before the TV cops did, and according to him, documentaries were so rife with inaccuracies he refused to watch them.

We curled in front of the TV, and he didn't complain when I found my favorite demon-hunting brothers. I fell asleep after binge watching for a couple of hours.

When I woke up, it was morning and I was in bed. Echo was tinkering in the kitchen. He didn't say anything when I told him I was skipping school.

"I won't be able to focus," I said.

"I'll keep you company."

"No." I shook my head. "Go reap. I'll be fine."

"I need to be here for you, babe."

"Whether you are here or reaping, I know I can count on you, Echo. Go. I'll feel guilty if you don't. I like Syn, and I don't want him thinking I'm this helpless Immortal you have to baby just because… because…" My parents had lied to me. Just thinking about them hurt too much. I was going to dull my senses with TV. "I plan to binge watch something. I've been meaning to watch a new series, and this is the perfect time. Have you seen or heard from Dev since last night? He went to help Mr. Reeds and mentioned swinging by the cancer ward."

"To do what?"

"Help coma patients find closure."

Echo frowned. "I hope he didn't fall off the wagon." He gave me a long kiss that would have easily translated into something else if I hadn't pushed him away. "Your father said he'd call the school and excuse your absence."

"What does it matter? I'm going to Lavania's school with Raine in the fall. They can't stop me now."

## CHAPTER 3. ANOTHER ORPHAN

My parents sent text messages, but I didn't respond. I was taking a bathroom break when Dev floated in. He crawled into my phone and mumbled, "No school?"

"What do you think?"

"You're in a nasty mood. I feel your pain, doll-face, so I'm here if you need to vent. And FYI, I helped about twenty people in the last twelve hours, including your friend. I don't understand Mortals. They are so vicious with each other. You'd think when people are about to die they'd mellow out. Nope. All the nastiness just kept pouring out. There were a few I wish I hadn't helped." There was silence before he added, "You're not responding."

"That's because I don't care." I went back to watching TV, and he stopped bothering me. I presumed he went to sleep.

Echo brought lunch and left after we ate. Dev mumbled something a few hours later and must have left because he wasn't in my phone when I tried to talk to him.

Days blurred. Pain and anger with a large dose of self-pity ruled my waking hours. Poor Echo did his best to take my mind off things, but for once he wasn't enough.

On Friday evening, I was trying to decide what to order for dinner when a portal opened and Raine walked in. She was so radiant it hurt to look at her. Her hug was exuberant and long until she realized I wasn't responding. She leaned back and studied me.

"What's wrong? You mad at me?"

"I'm attending Mystic Academy next year."

She frowned. "That's great, so why the long face? Your parents said no?"

"I haven't told them."

"Okay." She looked even more confused. "I know you were worried about how they'd react to your abilities and to Echo. Did that not go well?"

"I really don't want to discuss them now. I'm so angry I haven't seen or spoken to them since Tuesday."

Anger flashed in her eyes. "Just a sec." Raine walked to the living room.

"You staying or leaving?" I asked. "Maybe you can help me decide between pasta and pizza." I didn't pay her much attention and continued to scrutinize the two menus.

"Mr. and Mrs. Jemison, I hope you don't mind the intrusion, but we need to talk."

Crap! I should have known she'd open a portal to confront my parents. I ran to the living room mirror portal, and sure enough, she was in the middle of my parents' living room.

"Raine!" I walked through the portal and grabbed her arm.

"Do not blame Cora for keeping her abilities a secret or helping souls. She wanted to tell you for a long time. She is truly gifted, and she's helped so many find closure. Her runes might draw them to her, but her kindness and selflessness is why she does it."

"You don't need to explain anything to them. Come on."

"But I'm not done. They must know how you're working with Dev to help people before they die, too. And Echo is an amazing guy."

"They don't care about that," I snapped, pushing her toward the portal, my strength runes engaged.

"Cora, we care, and we are so proud of you," Mom called out. "Please, talk to us."

Ignoring my parents, I pushed Raine back into the cottage. "What's wrong with you? Since when did you become such a buttinsky?"

The portal closed behind us.

"What's going on?" She scowled at me. "They don't like you dating Echo?"

I scoffed at the idea. They loved him. "I'm not ready to talk about my parents. God, I wish I could rip them from my head and my heart.

Such hypocrites."

Shock flashed in Raine's eyes.

"Please, don't push. I'll explain when I'm ready. Right now, tell me what to order for dinner, or go home to your husband."

"Okay. Pizza." Her eyes went to the TV, where a ship was frozen on the screen. "*Vikings?*"

"Don't judge."

"Never. Get brownies, too."

"I'll get more of everything in case the guys decide to join us."

"Torin might. He's checking in on his first recruit, a future Valkyrie."

"Is he excited?" I asked, trying to focus on someone else rather than me.

Raine made a face. "You know him. He's taking it seriously. I'm more worried about Andris. They've been together for centuries, and now he'll be getting a new reaping partner. Maybe he should be reassigned to Lavania's school. He'd make an amazing teacher."

I scoffed. "Teaching what? Seduction 101?"

"Immortality: How to Piss Off the Norns. How to rune a woman just so you can have a playmate."

"Make Mortals fall in love with you before they die," I added. "Do you think they have an Andris Support Group in Valhalla for those he seduced and reaped?"

"Probably. Worse, they see him every time he brings in a new soul. 'Hi, my name is Sarai. It's been twenty hours since I last saw Andris. I still love and hate him.' He is terrible."

"He's such an amazing guy I wish he'd be serious about something or someone."

Having Raine around made me forget about my problems. We talked just like the old days. The food arrived first, then Torin and Echo. The fact that they came together didn't escape us. They might not be best friends, but they were learning to tolerate each other. Raine flew into her husband's arms like she hadn't seen him in days, instead of hours. Echo lifted me up, took over the couch, and set me on his lap.

"Should we offer them the guest room?" he asked when Raine and Torin continued to kiss.

"Guest bedroom is that way, guys," I called out.

Torin scooped her up. "Thanks, luv, but ours is a portal away. See you tomorrow."

"No, see you in two hours," Raine corrected as he engaged runes and the mirror in the living room responded. They disappeared inside their castle, and the portal closed.

"So what were you and Torin doing before you came home?" I asked.

"Who said...?" His voice trailed off when I lifted my head and gave him a do-not-lie-to-me look. "I wanted to know what Lord Worthington was up to. He was the leader of the group that went after orphans. I didn't want him coming after you."

"I thought his organization was destroyed."

"It doesn't mean he's stopped. Torin took me to his club, and we had a little chat."

"Is the club still standing?"

Echo chuckled. "Unfortunately. He was so cordial I wanted to punch his nose. Our talk lasted fifteen seconds."

"Let me see. It probably went like this. 'If you come after Cora, I will kill you and hide your body in an unmarked grave, then haul your worthless soul to Corpse Strand.' Am I right?"

"You forgot I was with Torin. I told him his son would hide his body, and while in Corpse Strand, I'd make sure he fights the dragon every day. Being charbroiled at least once a week is the least he deserves."

I laughed. "No, you didn't."

He flashed his famous I-did-it-and-enjoyed-every-second-of-it grin.

"And Torin did nothing?"

"He smirked the entire time. He hates the bastard but can't kill him. I won't have that problem if he ever hurts you."

Something else occurred to me. "You didn't mention me by name, did you? I haven't told Raine what's going on."

"No, sweetheart. I wouldn't mention you by name. That would be telling him my weakness. Men like him always find a man's Achilles' heel, and you"—he pressed a kiss on my forehead—"are mine. I warned him against going after other orphans because I have a vetted interest in their well-being."

That was my man. He would raze the earth to the ground for me. I was lucky that way.

"Are all the orphans Immortal?"

He nodded. "Most were runed by their parents when they were young."

Would my life have turned out differently if my parents had done that? We would never know. Torin and Raine rejoined us hours later and sat through two episodes of *Vikings* without complaining. I wasn't sure whether it was historically accurate or if they were just being supportive of our weird habits.

"Want to come to a soccer game in California tomorrow?" Raine asked before they left.

I made a face and glanced at Torin. "Your club soccer team is playing?"

He shook his head. "World Cup, Uruguay versus USA."

Soccer didn't interest me. "I'll pass, but we could hang out later."

"Great!" Raine glanced at Torin, and he cocked an eyebrow. "Not after the game, Cora. We're celebrating Torin's birthday. Belated birthday party. Just the two of us. We could meet on Sunday. The women want us to hang out."

Damn. I was hoping I could talk to her alone. "Women?"

"Lavania, Mom, Ingrid, and Femi, but we could ditch them. They want to share news about Mystic Academy. Don't know what the big deal is. I know Monday is school for you, and I don't want to keep you."

"I'm going to miss school next week, too."

Raine looked ready to ask more questions.

"Just count me in. Now go," I said. "I need time alone with my man, or you won't be invited to the wedding." She winced. I knew I was hitting below the belt, but I didn't want to explain my messed-up life. "Go. Love you."

We hugged. "I'm so sorry about the wedding. I will make it up to you some day. I promise." I waited until she left before saying, "That was mean of me. I know she did it to protect me, but still…"

"Cora-mia, there's so much you don't know," Echo said mysteriously.

I didn't understand what that had to do with missing Raine's wedding, but he was right. I didn't want to meet my biological parents yet, but I should still learn about what Mom and Dad had protected me from.

"Can you introduce me to an orphan? I was hoping to talk to Raine about Eirik and how he dealt with things, but our experiences are different. He was summoned to Asgard right away, and when he returned, his mother wanted to see him." I shivered.

I hoped my parents, whoever they were, weren't powerful. The last thing I needed was an army of guards from some god summoning me. I had no interest in visiting other realms, except Hel. But that was for Echo.

"Maybe I'll talk to Eirik next, but for now, I want to meet an Earthbound orphan."

"We'll go tomorrow morning."

~*~

The next morning, we appeared inside a store with everything a Witch could possibly need. Shelves of grimoires, cauldrons, crystals, candles, and ointments. The store didn't appear busy, but the few browsers inside were stocking up on things.

"Where are we?" I asked.

"Windfall, a small town outside New Orleans. Tammy adopted Hayden, though both of them were orphans. Tammy remembers being in Jötunheim, but Hayden was brought here as a baby and doesn't remember much."

Hayden? It was a unique name, yet it sounded familiar. Where had I heard it before? We reached the front of the store, and I stared at the displayed athames and Wiccan jewelry. Racks of cloaks and T-shirts with cute sayings were to the right of the entrance. A woman in her early-to-mid thirties was ringing up a customer's purchases and looked up. Her face paled when she saw us.

"She's scared of you. What did you do?" I whispered.

Echo made a face. "Nothing. I'm the good guy here. I helped rescue the orphans. That's Tammy." He looked around. "Hayden should be here somewhere."

I went to check out the T-shirts and smiled at some of the writings while Echo walked to Tammy. Raine might like them. I chose two and glanced over my shoulder to find Echo with Tammy. He was talking to her, while she studied me with a weird expression.

A door to my right opened, and a girl with flawless brown skin and curly hair with natural blonde highlights stepped out. A memory teased me and disappeared. Her eyes lit up when she saw Echo. How exactly did they know each other?

I moved closer, feeling a little jealous. I frowned. The perfume she wore was familiar, too, and her eyes lit up as though she was happy to see me.

"Hi, Cora," she said.

"Hi. Have we met before?" I asked.

Something flickered in her eyes, but it disappeared so fast I couldn't tell what it was. "I've heard so much about you and Raine."

"From?"

"Celestia."

I rubbed my temple. Another name that sounded familiar. Maybe Raine had mentioned them in passing. "Who is Celestia?"

She frowned and glanced at Echo. "Eirik's girlfriend and my best friend," she said, speaking slowly as though regretting mentioning them.

"Eirik has a girlfriend?" I punched Echo on the arm. "Why didn't you tell me? No, don't answer that. Whatever happens in Helheim stays in Helheim. Stupid rule. Nice to meet you, Hayden, and you too, Tammy." The older woman smiled, but her eyes were still wary. My habit of always carrying an ID and a credit card paid off. "Can I buy these?"

"Take them," Tammy said.

I tried to protest.

"Don't bother," Hayden said. "Once she makes up her mind, there's no changing it. You haven't spoken to Eirik?"

I shook my head. "I haven't seen him in months. Well, except on Saturday when he sent his pet hound to help us get rid of dark souls."

"Garm?"

"Yes. He's become very secretive. I doubt he's told Raine about Celestia or I'd know. "

Hayden pursed her lips and narrowed her eyes at Echo. "So you haven't spoken to Eirik either since last week?"

"No. When we returned to Eljudnir, they packed up and left for Asgard. I have no idea when they'll be back."

Hayden blew out a breath. "Okay. Mom said you wanted to talk. Um, we could use our back office or go upstairs to our apartment."

"I have a better idea," Echo said. "We can go to our place. I promised to listen to Dev's ramblings while you two talk. Can we use your back office to open a portal?"

Hayden nodded. "Sure. This way."

"Pass my regards to your mother, Cora," Tammy said. "She was very nice to me when I was recovering." I stared at her for a brief moment, too shocked to react. Of course, she'd know the Jemisons. They were all Immortals.

I nodded and followed Hayden into a room with a round table. Echo opened a portal to the cottage. Dev was pacing impatiently when we entered the room and stopped. There was something different about him. He spread his arms and turned around.

"What's going on?" I asked.

He palmed his face and slithered into the TV. It flickered on, and his image appeared on the screen in front of the logos. His eyes went to Hayden and stayed on her.

"It's rude to stare, Dev," I said.

"Sorry, but she is exquisite, and I never forget a face. Have we met?"

"No, you haven't. Let's go, smokey," Echo said rudely. "They want to be alone."

"Sometimes I wonder what Cora sees in you, Brother. You are an ass on a good day and a piss poor excuse for a Druid on a bad day. Introduce us."

Echo shot Dev a venomous look. Echo was proud of his heritage, and for anyone to question it was like waving a red flag to a bull.

"You will be taking that back before the day is over, Brother," Echo said, imitating Dev's beautiful Irish accent. Then he gave us his heart-melting smile. "What do you ladies want to drink? I can mix something at the bar or head to the nearest Starbucks."

"Water is fine," Hayden said. She was still staring at Dev. "I'm Hayden Ferrand."

"Devyn Graenenson, but everyone calls me Dev."

"Do you only possess electronics, Dev?"

"No. I possess people too, but I'm one of the good guys, so don't frown. I help the dying or those in comas. I possess them and give them some of my energy so they can communicate with their families, which is why I look this amazing. Notice anything different about me, doll-face?" he asked, glancing at me. He spread his arms, and his small image turned a circle on the screen.

"Your energy is clearer," I said. "How many people have you helped this week?"

"A lot. I lost count after the woman who cursed her sons for faking sadness and told them she made a new will so they weren't getting a dime. Then there was the man who confused his wife of forty years for his mistress. Did I mention that Mortals are horrible beings? They made me wish I'd never volunteered to help them. I'll leave you two ladies so I can talk to my brother before heading out again. I have a personal deadline." He winked at us and floated out of the TV.

Echo brought us drinks—water for Hayden and root beer for me—then joined Dev. He closed the door behind him.

"You must lead quite an interesting life," Hayden said.

"It's been quite a ride, but with Echo by my side, nothing seems impossible. He and Dev go way back to their childhood."

"I didn't know reapers could deliberately not reap souls."

"Usually souls who don't want to be reaped run, which is what Dev did. When he came to me, he was a mass of smoke with barely any shape, but then I learned about his history with Echo and that he was redeeming himself by helping the dying, and I chose to help him." I glanced toward the closed door.

I returned to studying her, the feeling of déjà vu growing stronger. Everything about her—her mannerism, her voice, even the riotous curls with blond highlights—was familiar.

"So what's going on?" Hayden asked. "Echo said you want to know more about my life. Instead, you are staring and frowning."

"Sorry. You look so familiar, and not knowing where we've met is driving me crazy."

"Maybe our paths crossed when we were young. You heard Mom. She knows your mother. We moved around a lot. That was our life, and the life of other orphans I knew. Mom took odd jobs here and there, got us a place to stay until the Immortals after us were sighted. Then, one of the parents took the kids into hiding while the rest acted as decoys."

"That's so sad. Did you ever have friends growing up?"

"No. Even though we moved a lot, we didn't live together as a group. The combined magical energy would have attracted the attention of the Immortals after us. A very evil giantess marked some of us, so we were always aware of each other. I could go to a new school and pick out the orphans based on that connection. So no, I never made lasting relationships until Mom opened TC in Windfall and I met Celestia."

"What is this connection?"

"A thread of energy connecting us."

I wondered if I had it. "Did you always know you were adopted?"

"Yes, and it's not because I'm biracial," she added, grinning. "Mom told me when a kid in kindergarten pointed out my skin and said it was different from Mom's, and that I must be someone else's baby. I went home crying. Mom likes to say I chose her. She'd tell me how most kids don't get to choose their parents, but I took one look at her and smiled, and"—Hayden chuckled—"she knew she was meant to be my mother. She took me home and never looked back once." Hayden twisted the lid off her bottle and sipped the water. "And I'd never trade her for another."

My parents' faces flashed in my head. They'd chosen me among all the other children, and that meant something. I tried to imagine my life with somebody else, but I couldn't.

"But constantly moving must have been hard," I said.

"It sucked. But when we weren't moving, we had fun. Things just got crazy the last few months with the evil Immortals." The light in her eyes dimmed. "The evil giantess who marked us was powerful, and some of us were weak and fell prey to her grandiose plans. Yet here we are."

Just like Maliina had marked me, and I survived her evil ass. "Did you always know you were different?"

She laughed. "I'm a Witch, Cora. Even though I'm Immortal now, I'll always be a Witch. And yes, I've always known I was different. Tammy encouraged me to embrace my abilities when they first appeared and helped me master them. Embrace who you are and you won't have anything to fear, she often said."

If only my parents had felt that way. "What are your abilities?"

"Power of persuasion. I can get inside your head and make you do and say things. Mess with your memories, so you forget them."

"Like Norns?"

She grimaced. "I'm not at their level, unless I work with another mind controller. Then I can give the Norns serious competition. Alone, I just mess with teachers and difficult customers."

I liked her. Something about her reminded me of Raine. "Do you ever wonder about your biological parents?"

She made a face. "Not anymore. I used to, but now I have no interest in meeting them. They lost their chance when they let me go."

"Let you go?"

"Not all Orphans lost their parents. Sometimes they were given away."

I knew that wasn't the case for me. I almost wished it was.

"We were in Jötunheim and Svartelfheim, and word spread fast that some of the orphans were back. I didn't see a crowd of parents beating down the doors, trying to claim them. Your boyfriend, Eirik, Celestia, and a bunch of us claimed them instead." She bit her lower lip and scrunched her face. Despite her nonchalant attitude, she was hurt by their indifference. "So, no, I have zero interest in meeting mine. So why the interest in orphans?"

I hesitated. I'd wanted to tell Raine first. "I'm like you. I came from the other realm and was adopted."

She didn't look surprised. "When did you find out?"

"Earlier this week. I'm still processing. On top of that, my biological parents want to meet me. I'm not sure I want to." I shook my head. "My life was perfect until now." That wasn't exactly true, but I'd accepted my ability to see souls and why. That was no longer true. "I used to see souls when I was younger. I guess that's my special ability, but my adopted parents wanted to spare me, so they used runes to block it and homeschooled me for a while. When I started seeing the souls again a year ago, they tried to block my ability again. It didn't work the second time, so here we are. Do I have that energy you mentioned, the one connecting the orphans?"

Hayden shook her head. "No, or I would have felt it the second we met." A weird expression settled on her face. "So you really don't want to meet your parents?"

"Nope. I have no interest in Immortals beyond Echo and my friends. Echo hopes to appeal to Goddess Hel so I can visit his home, and that's about as far as I planned to go. From the stories I've heard, she's not nice. I try not to say anything about her to Echo because he's loyal to her, but I'm scared of visiting her hall. What if she decides not to let me go? What if she comes between us? I've heard she's very petty."

"Oh, crap," Hayden muttered.

"What?"

"I think you need to stop listening to anything anyone says about her. Don't watch movies or read comics about her. She's nothing like that. She's tough, yet willing to compromise. Firm, but loving. Ohmigod, you should see her with Celestia and Eirik. She even took in one of the orphans no one wanted and adopted her. And your, uh, her husband, Eirik's father, is so amazing. Every time I visit, he insists on giving me hugs and warming me. He is a god, yet he's not pompous or pretentious. You'll love them."

Somehow I doubted it. "How often do you visit?"

"A lot. Celestia got hurt and stayed there for a while, so her father and I would visit her. Even Zack came with us. He is Celestia's cousin." Something in her voice said Celestia's cousin meant something to her. "I love it there so much I'm hoping I become a Grimnir some day."

Maybe the place wasn't as bad as I'd thought. "What's Celestia like?"

Hayden grinned. "She's the best, and the craziest Witch I've ever met."

No wonder Eirik was chummy with Witches. "Crazy how?"

"She's very proud of her powers. She can astral project to places before or after something happens. Her father is the police chief of our town, and she helps him solve crimes. When you meet her, ask her how she and Eirik met."

"How?"

Hayden grinned. "I love the story, but it's hers to tell, not mine. But she and Eirik are amazing together. He took her to Asgard to meet his grandparents. That's where they are now."

"Now, that's one place I wouldn't mind visiting. I've heard great stories about it."

"Me too." She glanced at her watch. "I gotta go. I promised my mother I'd watch the store while she and some of her friends went to a soccer game in California. If you need to know anything else about the other orphans, or if you want to meet more, let me know. We're keeping in touch now that the threat is gone. My mother and other parents are trying to help the ones who've been kept in special homes for years because their parents couldn't cope with their abilities."

Like me. So my parents weren't the only ones who couldn't cope with my powers. Maybe I was being hard on them.

"A group of local Immortals are starting a special school, Mystic Academy, so hopefully they'll find a place there."

Hayden laughed. "So it's true about the school. Eirik had mentioned a special place for Witches and Immortals, but we didn't think it would happen so soon."

"It's happening. They've already selected a location and are renovating the rooms." I stood. "I'll be in touch if I have questions."

"Anytime. Now that I'm not being forced to go to school, I'll be at the shop a lot, unless I sneak off to visit Celestia in Eljudnir."

She made it seem like it was nothing, yet despite all her positive comments, the thought of visiting the realm still filled me with dread.

"I can't wait to meet her."

"She's awesome." She opened a portal to the room with the large table and turned, a frown on her face. "Could you tell Echo to swing by the store? We've had a couple of Idun-Grimnirs visit us for no reason. Mom's really spooked because we don't know if someone is about to die or if they're shopping for new robes. They never talk."

"Idun-Grimnirs? Raine's husband is one, but for Valkyries."

"Oh, these are nothing like Torin. They are old and ancient."

"Okay. I'll tell him." I waited until the portal closed before I went looking for Echo. He wasn't in the kitchen, and neither was Dev.

I pulled out my phone and texted Raine. "Where r u?"

"StubHub @soccer game," she texted back.

Was that where Hayden's mother and her friends were headed? Wait a second. Hayden had mentioned Torin. How did she know him?

"Do you know a Hayden Ferrand?"

"No. Who is she?"

"An Immortal girl I just met. So what's happening? Soccer or something Witchy?"

"Both, but I have it covered," she texted back, adding emojis.

"K. Let me know if you need me." When I'd had problems with dark souls, Raine, the Valkyries, Grimnirs, Immortals, and even the souls had all stepped up to help. We were like one giant family, so I knew she'd call if she needed me. The way the souls had rallied for me during the prom had shown everyone I had loyal followers. I might not have a special ability to hurt someone with a wave of my hand or an artavus, but I had them and they'd do anything for me.

I turned off the phone and opened a portal to the farm. My room was in total darkness, and right by my bed was a woman in a cloak.

## CHAPTER 4. MY BROTHER

*I do not want to deal with a soul right now.* Souls were not supposed to come into my house.

"Get out!"

The soul didn't even look at me. That was the first sign I was dealing with a very unusual soul. She moved closer to my bed, and all three drawers on my nightstand opened with each step she took. I couldn't even explain how I knew it was a she. I couldn't see her face under the cloak, but her shoulders were slender. She raised a gloved hand, and something floated from my drawer to her hand.

"Hey," I yelled and stepped forward, or tried to, but I was frozen in place. I looked down and attempted to lift my leg. Once again, nothing happened. It was as though I was glued to the floor. Who was this soul? And how was she doing this?

"You!"

Ignoring me, she brought the cloth to her nose and inhaled. What in Hel's Mist? I recognized the baby blanket my parents had shown me.

"That's mine! Put it back."

She turned and faced me. I was sure I'd see her face, but the cloak made it impossible. Dark souls were like that. Amorphous with no features. But something was different about this one. I couldn't see her face, yet her robe was normal. And she had opened my drawer telepathically and taken my blanket.

"Listen here, you piece of smog. Put that back right this instant or I'll never help another soul again."

She disappeared. One second she was there with my blanket, and the next, she was gone and the drawers were closed. This time, when I tried to step forward, I could move. What in Hel's Mist just happened?

I opened the drawers, but the baby blanket was gone. That thing had taken it. I couldn't hear sounds from downstairs, but I knew Dad was in his cave. He had a deadline. Mom was probably in the chicken coop. I stood at the window and studied the barn. They'd hurt me by keeping secrets from me, but they were still my parents. Talking to Hayden had helped me see things clearly.

I headed downstairs. Dad left his nook and stood at the bottom of the stairs before I reached the bottom. He watched me with worried eyes.

"I'm fine," I said. The door opened, and Mom rushed in. Dad must have called and told her I was home. "I'm still angry with you guys for not telling me the truth."

"We know, sweetheart," Mom murmured, moving closer. Usually, she would have hugged me. Both of them would have, but now they hesitated. I wasn't ready to close that gap either. "We are so sorry," she continued. "We thought we were doing what was best for you."

"I know. It still doesn't make it right. I was coming to ask you for my baby blanket, but I think a soul just stole it from my room."

My parents looked at each other and frowned.

"Are you sure?" Mom asked. "We kept it in our bedroom, not yours."

"But I just saw a soul in my room and she…" I shook my head. "The whole incident was weird."

"Weird how?" Mom asked.

I opened my mouth to tell her, then remembered the lies. "It's nothing."

Hurt crunched her face, but I pretended not to notice. Dad went upstairs to get the blanket while Mom tried to feed me. She needed to reconnect with me, and food was her way of doing it. I accepted the slice of cherry pie. I knew she'd baked it specifically for me because I hated apple pie. Dad brought back the blanket.

I could have sworn that creepy soul had stolen it. On the other hand, the whole encounter had been weird. Maybe I'd imagined it.

"Thank you. I'll be in my room if you need me."

Upstairs, I spread the baby blanket on the bed, sat in my chair, and stared at it while I ate. Some of the runes were familiar. Love runes. Protection runes. I was still learning about runes, so I wasn't surprised I didn't know all of them. I got a piece of paper and sketched the unknown ones. Lavania would know them.

After a while, I couldn't stand it. I had to touch it. I picked it up and pressed it against my cheek. The material was soft like nothing I've ever felt before. I checked the finish along the edges. The embroidery was gorgeous. Tears rushed to my eyes. Someone had taken her time making it. For me.

"Who am I?"

"You are the woman I adore," Echo answered from behind me, and I glanced over my shoulder. He grinned, coming to stand behind me. "Why are you questioning who you are?"

"Because I don't know anymore. Last year, I was sure I knew exactly who I was—the only daughter of a loving, overprotective couple who homeschooled me to give me the best education. Then I started seeing souls, and they rushed me to the nearest psych ward, and I met you. Then I became the girl who could see souls, and the reasons for that were clear. An evil Immortal etched runes on me. I embraced my new gifts because I had you by my side. Without you telling the souls to behave, I may never have had the courage to help them."

He walked around, sat on the edge of the bed, and pulled my chair closer so I was between his legs, but I didn't give him a chance to speak.

"And just when I've accepted that I'm a medium, life throws me another curveball. My parents are not really my parents, and Maliina's runes are not the reason souls are attracted to me." I dropped my forehead on his chest. "I want my life to be normal again, Echo. Don't say it," I added. "Our normal is different from an average Mortal. You are a reaper, and I am a medium. I'm okay with that. I just want my parents to be normal and Mortal."

Echo chuckled, and I sat back. The smile disappeared from his face when he realized I meant it. "First of all, you didn't need me to become the amazing medium you are. You were helping souls before I inserted myself in the midst of it and decided to referee. Two, the Jemisons will always be your parents. They might not have given birth to you, but they raised you, loved you, and gave you everything you ever needed. They are not perfect. Even though they are Immortals, they have the same failings as Mortals."

"Why can't they be like you? You are perfect. You are honest and blunt. You don't play games or have hidden agendas."

He laughed. "I'm far from perfect. I had a big fight with Rhys a few weeks ago and learned I can be a jackass."

"Oh, I know that, but you're still perfect." I sat on his lap and leaned against his chest. "Tell me why you finally realized you can be a jackass?"

"It happened outside the hall the morning I learned he's been keeping Dev's body all these years. I gave up on Dev because I believed he'd betrayed us, but Rhys never did. He never believed Dev would do such a thing to us. His family. I tend to jump to conclusions fast and go with my gut. Now, I'm trying to weigh the consequences of each action before I act. Think things through. It's hard, but I'm trying."

"Oh, Echo." I studied his face. From his expression, he meant it. "Your passion and spontaneity are part of what make you unique. Don't go changing just because of one mistake."

"My mind is made up." He kissed me as though to shut me up.

"Then I'll make sure I unmake it for you. Look at this." I spread the green blanket on my lap. "This is the blanket that was wrapped around baby-me when I was brought to the orphanage where Mom and Dad found me. They think it might lead to my biological parents." Echo stiffened, and I glanced at him. "What is it?"

"These are protection runes, but mixed with them are bind runes I've seen before." He stood and deposited me on the bed. He spread out the blanket and studied the runes. "There's a slight variation, but some of these are locator runes. And this one here"—he tapped the corner of the blanket—"is Goddess Hel's rune."

"What does that mean?"

"It means that your parents considered Goddess Hel their

protector. That means you are from Helheim."

I grinned. "Looks like you are going to get your wish. That is, if I agree to visit."

He was still staring at the blanket and frowning.

I folded it and slipped it under my pillow. "You need to work on your goddess while I gather the courage to meet her. Hayden said she is nice." Aware that he was now staring at where I'd put the baby blanket, I shifted and blocked his line of vision. "What is it?"

He dragged his attention back to me. "You had a good conversation with Hayden?"

I had a feeling that was not what he was thinking about. "Yep. She wants you to stop by their store. Something about a couple of Idun-Grimnirs visiting them. She's worried they want to reap them or something. You're not listening to me." I pulled out the blanket. "What is it about this that has you scowling so hard?"

"Can I borrow it for a few days?"

"No," I said it quickly and frowned. The thought of giving it away filled me with a fear I couldn't explain. Maybe it was the figure I'd seen stealing it or something else. I couldn't explain it.

Echo stood, his eyes not leaving me. "I promise to bring it back."

"I can't."

"Sweetheart, I know it's the only thing you have that connects you with them, but—"

"That's not it. I told you I'm not ready to meet them, whoever they are. If you took it, you'd find them like that"—I snapped my fingers—"and come back with some sob story about how destitute they were and how they were forced to give me up or watch me starve to death."

His lips twitched.

"Or how devastated they were after searching for me all these years and couldn't find me. I'll only feel bad and forgive them when they don't deserve my forgiveness. So the answer is no. You can't have it or try to find them until I'm ready."

He smiled. "Okay. I won't say anything until you're ready to hear it."

Which meant he planned to find out who my parents were anyway. If my parents were in Helheim, he would have an excuse to make me go with him. I wasn't ready to face them. Maybe I'd never be ready to face them.

~*~

"Come on. We gotta go," Raine said, entering my bedroom. "They are discussing Mystic Academy, and I don't want to miss a thing."

"Nice to see you, too." I pulled on a swimsuit skirt and fixed the waist.

Raine grinned, watching me.

"What?"

"I love the outfit. I still can't decide whether I hate you or love you. You can make any two piece look classy, despite the boobs."

"They are the bane of my existence, so love me."

"You know I do." She sighed. "You know how evil Norns are behind natural disasters? I stopped a plane from crashing and pissed them off yesterday during the soccer game, so be careful around souls. I'm afraid the hags might send them after us again. They pulled that move a week ago and sent evil souls to possess bears. Ingrid and I were sprinting through the forest when the bears attacked us. All because the hags want my dagger."

"Damn. We just got rid of the last horde."

"I know. Be careful. Tell Dev to be on alert, too."

I studied her. She didn't seem worried. "A bear attack? Why is it I always hear things after they've happened?"

"Because I don't plan them." She plopped on my bed and kicked off her flip-flops. She was wearing a sexy one-piece swimsuit with large openings on the sides. The Raine of before would have worn a cover. It was nice to see Torin's influence on her wardrobe. "But if you feel left out, I'll open a portal in the middle of an attack and pull you in the foray."

Raine was all talk. She would jump in front of a bear and kick ass to protect me. She was a powerful Witch with elemental powers, while I had no fighting ability. On the other hand, I had speed and strength runes now, so I could wrestle a bear.

"Do that next time. Friends should laugh and fight together. Why do the evil Norns want your dagger?"

"I have no idea. All I know is they are scared of it, the good and the evil Norns. And since they want it, I'm keeping it." She sat up. "I need to talk to Eirik about that. He told Onyx to hide it in case they got inside my head and learned where I hid it."

"When did you last see him?"

"Hmm, during my wedding. Stop glaring at me. I feel guilty about that already."

I dismissed it with a wave. "Did you know Eirik has a girlfriend? Celestia."

Raine sat up. "Really? No, I didn't. How do you know?"

"Ha! I know something you don't."

She made a face. "Hardy har har. Have you met her?"

"No, but I met her best friend, Hayden Ferrand. Golden-brown skin, blond highlights, drop-dead gorgeous. Ring a bell?"

Raine frowned. "No."

"Hmm, she looks familiar. Even her name is familiar. Her perfume. I know we've met. Just don't know where. Okay, I'm ready."

"Why were you meeting with her?" Raine asked as the mirror responded to her runes and turned into a portal.

"Echo wanted me to." I felt bad lying to her, but I couldn't explain Hayden without mentioning my parents being Immortals. "I guess he's been working with Eirik."

"Yeah, Eirik's been busy. He's been working with Witches around the world. Some from New Orleans helped me stop the plane from crashing in the stadium yesterday."

I grabbed my phone, half listening to her. Could Hayden's mother have gone to help Raine? I needed to be in the loop on what was going on. I started to follow her when she stopped suddenly.

"Your parents." Raine glanced at the door and then me. "Do they—

?"

"Know that I'm heading to the mansion to hang out or that I can open portals and run like *The Flash* without becoming a human torch because runes protect me? Yes. Let's talk later."

She frowned. "Do you want me to talk to them? Or Mom could. She's at the mansion."

"Not yet." I followed her to the foyer at the mansion, using one of the hallway mirror portals. We followed laughter to the pool room where the women—Svana, Raine's mother, and her best friend, Femi, along with Ingrid and Lavania—lounged on chairs and sipped on cocktails while Dev entertained them from Lavania's phone.

"Come here, Cora," Svana said. I wondered whether she'd always known about me. I hugged her and bit my tongue. "I'm so sorry, hun, but I'm happy you finally know everything now."

And there was my answer. I had questions. Lots of them. Like how many more knew? My eyes met Femi's. She blew me a kiss.

"Hey, doll," Femi said. She called everyone doll. Just how many Immortals were in town?

For the next several hours, I listened to the discussion about Mystic Academy and who would teach what. Lavania was already sending out invitations. They still refused to tell us the location. I drifted away, hearing them without listening.

"What is it?" Raine asked, bumping me on the shoulder.

"I'll race you. We'll start with backstroke."

She laughed. "That's your best stroke."

"I know. I need to feel good, and winning does that." I didn't give her a chance to argue. I left the hot tub and dove into the pool. I won backstroke, but she trounced me at breaststroke. When we pulled out, the others were standing in a group and Dev was out of Lavania's phone. The expression on his face was one I'd never seen before. Pure terror. I engaged my speed runes and was beside them in a beat.

"What's going on?" I asked.

"Mom?" Raine asked at the same time. She'd raced with me.

"Idun-Grimnirs are outside the house," Svana said and shivered.

"What do they want?"

"Idun-Grimnirs don't just train future Grimnirs," Svana explained. "Goddess Hel often sends them to find souls where her reapers fail. They could be after Dev."

He should have been reaped centuries ago. "They can't have him."

Dev nodded.

I engaged my medium runes. "Blend with me now."

No one spoke as he floated and meshed with my body. The cold and the suffocating feeling didn't last long.

"I'll see what they want," Svana said. "Lie down and keep him trapped."

I moved to the nearest lounge while Svana and Lavania hurried out of the room. Raine pulled on a robe and dragged a chair closer to me. Her eyes didn't leave my face.

"Quit worrying," I told her. "I'm fine. After the initial icky feeling, it's not so bad." I shivered, the cold coming from within. She grabbed an extra robe and covered me.

"He will come out when it's time, right?" she asked, frowning.

"Yes. He's been helping coma patients the last week and has become very good at disengaging. Why do they want him?"

"I don't know. Do you want me to find Echo? He could tell them to get lost."

"No, it's okay. You and I need to talk." I glanced at Ingrid and Femi. They were near the door to the pool room as though keeping guard. They were too far to hear us.

"You don't have to say anything. Conserve your energy. In fact, I'll go get Twizzlers for later."

I grabbed her wrist. "I need to talk so I can stop thinking about Dev prowling around inside me like a caged animal. Dev, calm the hell down. No one is taking you anywhere. If I have to follow you to Helheim, I will. Get it?"

*Aye, love.*

"Good. Raine, do not interrupt, okay?"

She nodded.

I glanced at the other two women before saying, "My parents have lied to me all my life about who they are. They are Immortals, Raine."

Her jaw dropped, eyes widening. "What? How?"

"Oh, thank God you weren't in on it. I swear if I'd found out you knew, I would have disowned your sorry ass. Mom's been acting strange since the night of the prom. A few times I came home to find her with red eyes. Finally, I insisted on answers." I told Raine everything, and when I was done, she just sat there. Then she hugged me until I said, "Your mother knew."

Raine leaned back. "Really? Do you think that's why they've always pushed our friendship? You, me, and… Eirik?"

I followed her eyes to see Eirik enter the pool. He was dressed like an Asgardian in skin-tight pants made of some weird material, knee-length boots, arm braces, and even a cloak. The boy I'd known before was gone. Instead, there was a buff guy with an angular face and muscles. The pants and the vest hugged every inch of his body. Despite the outfit or the change in his physique, I didn't have that innate need to get his approval or get his attention like I used to. Whatever hang-ups I'd had about him had long since disappeared.

Raine jumped up to hug him, but he studied me over her shoulder with a weird expression. Eirik planted a kiss on Raine's temple, and the two walked toward me.

"Get out of her, Dev," he ordered. Even his voice had changed. I wasn't surprised when Dev obeyed. He disappeared fast. "The reapers are gone, and they weren't after you."

The relief of not having a soul hitching a ride inside me was sweet. I disengaged my runes and sat up. Dizziness washed over me, but I knew it would pass. Standing was out of the question. I would fall flat on my face.

"Am I getting a hug, Blondie?" Eirik asked.

I wrinkled my nose. "You know I hate that name."

Raine laughed. "I'll get you some Twizzlers. She needs the sugar after a possession," she added for Eirik's benefit and walked away.

Eirik sat on the lounge beside me and placed an arm around my shoulder. "I thought your runes helped with possession."

"They make it less traumatic. What are you doing here?"

"I came to see you."

"Me?"

"Don't sound surprised. Could we go somewhere private and talk?"

"About?" I asked, wariness creeping in. He had a girlfriend now, so he couldn't still be into me.

"Something I need to discuss with you." His eyes were on Raine, who'd returned to the pool deck with a jar of the stringy sweets. Since I did most of my after school closure in the mansion, they had a whole cupboard of them. "Alone," Eirik added in a low voice.

A year ago, I would have been thrilled at the idea. He had paid Raine more attention while treating me like his bratty younger sister. Now I was just irritated. I had enough on my plate without adding him.

"What is this about, Eirik?" I asked, not hiding my irritation.

"No need to be snippy, Blondie. Eat your Twizzlers first. Then we'll talk. And if you want Echo to hold your hand while we do it, text him. Actually, it might be nice to have him there. I'm going to eat something in the kitchen." He jumped up and walked away, grinning.

I glared after him.

"What's going on?" Raine asked.

"I'd forgotten how easily he pushes my buttons."

She frowned. "Really? Even now?"

"More so now because he's so damn bossy." I took the jar from her and grabbed two of the Twizzlers. "I can't explain it."

"Me neither." She sat beside me and grabbed a couple of Twizzlers too. "I thought he did that before because you were into him."

"I thought so too, but that's not it. He's just so… Eirik. Always having the last word. Where are the others?"

"Kitchen. Talking. When I walked in, they clammed up, but I'd heard them. I told them I knew about your parents and they didn't need to pretend anymore. You should have seen their faces. I told them they should be ashamed of themselves even though it wasn't their place to tell you the truth. I can't believe Mom knew all these years. On the other hand, she had hidden stuff from me, too." She stood and pulled me up. "Can you walk on your own if I let go?"

"No. Carry me." I gave her a lost puppy expression.

"In your dreams."

"I wonder how many people we know are Immortals." I picked up my phone and looked around. "Dev?"

"He's gone. Let's go hear what other secrets they've been keeping from us."

"Actually, Eirik wants to talk to me, so I won't stay. But you can eat lunch with me tomorrow."

I left her with the other women in the kitchen and opened a portal to the cottage. Eirik followed and looked around with interest. "This is not your farm."

"Echo bought it for me. Do you want something to drink?" I headed to the kitchen, and he followed, frowning. "Oh, I heard about Celestia. Where have you been hiding her? And when do we meet her?"

"Anytime. You and Echo are playing house already?"

I bristled at the censure in his voice. "I'm eighteen, smarty-pants. I can play house with the guy I love. Not that it's any of your business."

He raised his hands. "I'm not complaining." He grabbed a stool and watched me open the fridge. "I'll have whatever you're having. Is that leftover pizza?"

I piled the slices on a plate and warmed them in the microwave. I gave him a can of iced tea, which he gulped while eyeing the microwave. It was amazing how much he'd changed, yet stayed the same. I waited as he demolished the slices and chugged iced tea.

"Don't they feed you in Hel's Hall?"

He chuckled. "Maera would be insulted to hear that."

"Who is Maera?"

"The cook and housekeeper at Eljudnir. She loves to ply us with heaps of food and gets insulted when we don't finish. I never disappoint her. In fact, I'm her favorite." He pushed the empty plate aside and checked his watch. "What's taking Echo so long?"

"He's not coming. You said you wanted to talk to me, so talk."

He scratched his forehead and chuckled. "Easier said than done. Celestia is better at these things. I should have brought her."

"Why are you hiding her from us?"

He grinned. "No one hides Celestia. By the time I finish explaining, you'll understand why. You'll like her."

I rolled my eyes. It was obvious he was in love, and I was happy for him. "Is she the reason you want to talk? Because I'd rather just meet her and get to know her on my own without you being in the equation."

"Ah, but I'm part of the equation. I'm her other half." He blew out air. "Okay, I'll start with me. A little over eighteen years ago, my parents had me. My grandmother was living with them at the time." He stopped and scowled. "No, I'll start with Crazy Granny. What do you know about Goddess Hel?"

"Is that a trick question? She is your mother, so I can't say anything mean."

Eirik grinned. "Hit me with all you've heard."

"Really?"

"Yep." He nodded.

"She is mean as hell, cold as her realm, hard as nails, uncompromising, half-mummified, and has morose-looking servants who follow her around, doing her bidding." By the time I finished, Eirik was laughing hard. Only he would find what I'd said funny. It was part of his charm, I supposed. He found humor even in insults. "I also learned yesterday that she's none of the above."

Laughter disappeared from his face. "Echo talked?"

"Hayden."

He blinked. "You talked to Hayden?"

"I needed to talk to one of the orphans from the other realms after I learned that my parents are Immortals and I was adopted. Echo took me to her." Eirik didn't react to my announcement. "You know about me and my parents?"

He nodded. "What did Hayden tell you?"

"That they moved around a lot and I was better off here in Kayville shielded from the evil Immortals." I ran a finger around the edge of my unopened can of iced tea. "We didn't talk much about anything else. Oh, and she mentioned visiting Hel's Hall when Celestia was sick or hurt or something along those lines and how your mother was nice. I wanted to know how you and Celestia met, but she wouldn't tell me."

He smiled, visibly relaxing.

"What did you think she told me?"

"About Mom, she is the daughter of Loki and a Jötun woman, Angrboda. Grandma Angrboda is crazy, vengeful, and mean. In fact, everything you've heard about Mom could be applied to Crazy Granny. Mom just hides her sweetness behind a cold exterior. Because Odin took Mom and her brothers away, Crazy Granny hates all Asgardians. So when I was born, she saw me as a weapon to use against Asgard."

"How?"

"She is a shifter, like Onyx, Raine's mouthy pet. Yeah, we've met," he added when I laughed. Raine's cat didn't like me for reasons I couldn't explain. "Quite a number of Jötuns are shifters. Wolves. Serpents. Ravens. Cats. Dragons. Granny is a dragon shifter, which is rare. When I was born with the same ability, she thought she had a weapon to destroy Asgard." Eirik grinned. "Don't look at me like that."

"Dragon shifter? You?"

His grin turned cocky. "Yep. That's why I eat a lot and have the big guns." He raised his arms and flexed his biceps. "Shifting back and forth does that to you."

"Holy crap. It explains a lot. Does Raine know?"

He shook his head. "No, you are the first to know. I'll show you later. Anyway, Granny wanted to use me to destroy Asgard. Dad and Mom found out, and booted her out of Eljudnir. She became obsessed with hurting them. Fearing for my safety, Dad talked to the Norns and handed me over to them for safekeeping. They brought me to Earth. He didn't tell Mom he'd colluded with the Norns to keep me safe from Crazy Granny. She thought the Norns did this to her out of spite."

"Jeez, what is it with people keeping secrets? Don't they get that secrets hurt? I swear if Echo ever pulled that shit on me, I'd kill him."

"That's my attitude, too. Celestia and I swore to never try to shield each other that way. If I did, she would kill me, bring me back to life, and do it again. She's amazing."

Wow, she sounded powerful. "Can she really do that?"

"Oh, yes. She can manipulate her life force, but we are digressing. Mom had Grimnirs searching for me. She even sent her Idun-Grimnirs with little results. The Immortals in this town are very good at hiding. Meanwhile, Dad got weekly reports on how I was doing from two loyal Grimnirs, Rhys and Nara."

"Those two?"

"I guess you've met them. They are very loyal to my family. After I was taken, they decided to have a second child. They had a girl. This time, Mom made sure she etched locator runes on her in case she was taken. After a few days, she was told the child had died and was given a body to bury."

"Oh man. That must have been tough on her."

"Very. On top of losing me, she'd also lost her baby girl. She shut everyone out, including Dad. Losing my sister and me did something to her. It turned her mean, uncompromising, and cold. Then Maliina saw me and told her."

"She must have been happy to see you," I said, feeling sorry for the woman. Betrayed by her husband and the Norns, then losing her second child. No one should have to go through something like that. I couldn't even imagine her pain.

"She was and she wasn't, but we worked out our issues. There's more. Can I have another drink?"

I got him a third can of iced tea and waited as he chugged it. This time I was sure he was deliberately procrastinating. "What is it, Eirik?"

"My sister didn't die."

"What happened to her?"

"Crazy Granny happened. She grabbed Einmyria, hoping she had the dragon strain too. When she learned that the baby didn't, Granny left her in Jötunheim. The Norns found her and brought her to Earth with the other orphans. Dad found out the truth, and started searching for her without telling Mom."

"I know he's your father, but he has a lot to learn about relationships," I said.

"I know, and he has learned. Their relationship was so unusual he was never sure how Mom would react to anything. She's very unpredictable. But the one thing he knew was her temper. He knew she would have started a war if she'd found out Einmyria was alive."

"Really?"

"Oh, yeah. She would have come to Earth herself to find her and probably would have jumpstarted Ragnarok because the Asgardians would have come down to defend the people. So he kept it a secret and kept searching for my sister relentlessly. Finding my sister was the first task he gave me when I arrived in Eljudnir." Eirik drained his drink and shot me a furtive glance. He was acting weird. "It took me weeks of searching among the orphans here on Earth before I finally found her. Having Celestia helped."

He told me about Celestia. The more I heard about her, the more I was amazed by what she could do. He talked about fighting Crazy Granny, the kidnapping of the orphans, and finally locking Granny up. He made it sound like it was nothing, but I now understood why Echo missed what he called their adventures. They were heroes. Not just to the orphans, but to their parents. For once, Eirik didn't paint himself as the star of every adventure. He gave everyone his or her dues. The Eirik I'd known would have made sure he was the hero.

"No wonder you've been gone forever. You've been busy. Finding orphans, searching for your sister. And FYI, your grandmother deserves to be hanged."

He chuckled. "She'll stay locked up in Corpse Strand, until Ragnarok. Celestia's mom too."

"Imagine if you hadn't gone home. You would never have found your sister and your mother would still be thinking she was dead."

"Mom mourned her death for seventeen years. She wore black and covered the halls and paintings with black linens, every year on

Einmyria's birthday. She wasn't the only one grieving for my sister, the whole castle grieved with her. They all felt her anguish. The pain she repressed inside almost tore her apart. She even kept the nursery the same way it was before my sister died, her baby clothes, blankets, and decor. It was part of her mourning, a reminder of the loss she'd suffered, and she wouldn't let herself forget. Now that I found my sister, she has hope again. She's vowed to celebrate and throw balls in her honor."

It was hard to imagine a ball in a place so cold Echo often arrived frozen whenever he came from there. "I bet she threw a huge one when Einmyria came home. I love that name. It's unique like yours. Anyway, Hayden told me most of the orphans you rescued chose to return to Earth to be with their Immortal parents."

"That's true. None of them met their birth parents. They weren't as lucky. There hasn't been a celebration for us yet, but maybe we can have it soon. I'm hoping Einmyria will want to meet Mom."

Confused, I shook my head. "They haven't met yet?"

"Not yet, but they will soon." He leaned closer. "Give me your hand."

I frowned. "Why?"

"Because I asked."

"Dumb answer, bonehead."

He groaned. "Man, I'd forgotten what a pain you can be. Just give me your hand." I did, narrowing my eyes at him. He was acting really weird. He studied my pink polished nails. "Remember I told you Mom drew locator runes on my sister?"

I nodded.

"Mom has the same runes, and now so do I." Eirik rolled back his sleeve and stretched his arm toward mine. I instantly recognized the runes that began appearing on his skin. They were the same ones I'd seen on the green baby blanket at home. Before I could ask him what was going on, the same runes appeared on my skin. I jumped up and stepped away from him, my eyes volleying between his arm and mine.

"What are these?" I rubbed my arm, but the runes stayed.

"The locator runes Mother etched on you respond to mine and hers. Cora, you are Einmyria."

I shook my head. "No, I'm not. I can't be."

"That was my reaction too. In fact, it took me a while to connect the dots because your parents and the Immortals in this town protected us so well we didn't even know we were different. Your blanket and those runes are the proof I needed to confirm you are my sister. I would have told you last week when I found out, but I decided to talk to your parents first. They wanted to be the ones to tell you about them and your adoption."

"You're wrong, Eirik." I shook my head. "We look nothing alike."

"I look like Dad and you…" He studied me and frowned. "Damn."

"What?"

"You'll have to see for yourself, little sis."

"Don't call me that." I moved away as though putting some distance between us would nullify his confession. "I'm not your sister."

"You think I wanted this? I thought I had a crush on you, my baby sis."

"Do *not* call me that, Eirik. I'm eighteen, and your sister is seventeen."

"The ages given by the orphanages were wrong. You are seventeen, not eighteen, Cora. Your birthday was a couple of weeks ago, not in December like you were raised to believe. You just turned seventeen. Listen, it took me a long time to find you, and it never crossed my mind you were Einmyria. Unless we engage them, the locator runes can only be seen by souls. They are the reason souls are drawn to you, just like they are drawn to Mom. And me now."

This was insane. Eirik could not be my brother. "Maybe it is a coincidence."

"Ask your parents if souls were drawn to you when you were young and before Maliina marked you with medium runes. Medium runes stabilize possession, while locator runes can be detected by souls and Idun-Grimnirs because they are ancient. Locator runes also help our family find each other. Crazy Granny etched them on Mom, too. Ask your parents about the baby blanket you were wrapped in," Eirik added. "It has our mother's runes at the corners and locator runes all over it. She never thought you were alive, or she would have moved every obstacle to find you. She tried with me, but she was broken after she lost you. She became angry and bitter. Consumed by her pain. She's not anymore." Eirik sighed. "She knows who you are, Cora, because I told her, and that's why the two Idun-Grimnirs were here. They were looking for you. I didn't tell her where you were because I promised the Jemisons I'd give them time to talk to you first."

A wave of dizziness washed over me, and I realized I was holding my breath. I sucked in air and exhaled. I needed to look at the blanket again. Talk to my parents. No, they'd lied to me before. I needed to talk to Echo. Everything Eirik said pointed at me being his sister.

"What do you want from me?" I asked.

"To come to Eljudnir and meet Mom and Dad."

I cringed. I didn't need another set of parents. "When?"

"Now would be nice. The Grimnirs will tell Mom they found you, and she'll expect me to bring you home. She won't force you or anything like that," he added quickly. "But she's suffered enough, Cora. Knowing you are alive and don't even want to meet her is going to hurt her even more."

Crap! "I need time to catch my breath and process all this. This is too much." I still didn't want to believe it. "This week, I learned Mom and Dad are not my biological parents. Today, you are telling me I'm your sister and our grandmother is not only crazy, she is responsible for the attack on the other kids like me. Why would I want to go to Eljudnir with you?"

"Because you belong there." Eirik rubbed his nape and sighed. "I know it's a lot to process, but Mom deserves to meet and know you, her only daughter. She deserves to be happy, Cora, because she's been unhappy for a very long time. And visiting Eljudnir will give her the same closure you give souls. It's what you do. How can you give so much to them and deny your own mother?"

"Eirik…"

"And it's not just for her. There's our father, who's known you were alive and has been searching for you for seventeen years. He deserves to know you. Then there are our grandparents, Odin and Frigg. They deserve to know they have another grandchild."

"I didn't mean I wasn't going to go. It's just too much." I covered my face, wanting to crawl back in bed and shut out the world again. "It's been five days, and I still can't look at my parents without feeling betrayed and hurt. And now this?"

"You will forgive the Jemisons because they are your parents, too. Even though you don't have biological ties with them, they've loved you and provided for you physically, mentally, and emotionally as though you were their flesh and blood. That's something no one can or will ever take away from you. If it weren't for them, you'd not be the person you are today."

I blinked. I'd expected him to say the Jemisons weren't my parents, period. The changes in him weren't just physical. Eirik had grown mentally, too.

"Thank you for saying that," I said. "You are right. Despite the secrets and the lies, they are my parents."

"That's how I feel toward Raine's family and the Seville's. But getting to know Mom and Dad filled something in me I didn't even know was missing. I found who I really am because of them, especially Mom. She has this amazing ability to see things and guide you to your fullest potential. She's tough, and her methods can be unorthodox, but she comes from a place of love. She and I knocked heads, but in the end, I embraced who I am." A grin lifted his lips. "Because of her, I found Celestia. When she astral projected into my room and got trapped, Mom knew exactly what she was and never once hinted or kicked her out. It gave me a chance to get to know Celestia and fall in love. I don't think I would have found her if it weren't for Mom. You are more than a medium, Cora. She can help you find out who you really are."

She sounded larger than life. Scary. "I need time to process all this and be in the right place, mentally and emotionally, before I can meet them."

Disappointment flashed on Eirik's face, and I felt terrible, but all he said was, "Okay. I'll talk to Mom." He stood. "That was a lot to dump on you, but I wanted you to know the truth. All of it. Secrets nearly destroyed our family, and I want us to heal. All of us."

It was surreal, but it was slowly sinking in. "I agree. Secrets destroy, and that was a lot to dump on me. I was still trying to imagine you as a dragon, then *bam*... you're my brother. Next time give me a few days in between to process."

"So you don't want to hear about Jessica? She's the girl who pretended to be you, and is now part of our family because Mom and Dad didn't have the heart to kick her out after I exposed her."

I gave him a tiny smile. "Not today, but I'd love to meet Celestia."

"I left her in Asgard when I saw the Idun-Grimnirs outside the mansion. I knew they'd probably scare you, so I left her behind and raced here. I'll bring her to meet you."

"You saw them from Asgard?"

He smiled, the brief sadness caused by my reluctance to meet our parents right away gone. His boyish grin hadn't changed. "From Odin's high chair. I'll show you when we visit. Best place to spy on people in different realms."

And I once wished to visit the place. My grandparents ruled it. The bed was calling me.

"I'd better head back and take Celestia home. We'll stop by in a couple of days for the two of you to meet." He got up and walked around the counter. He opened his arms. "I'm happy you are my baby sister, Blondie, and that you didn't freak out on me."

I was freaking out on the inside. I hugged him, then pinched his side. I let "baby sister" slide this time. "Stop calling me Blondie."

His iris narrowed like a reptile's, and I stepped back.

"Your eyes. They were like a lizard's. Did you just shift?"

He laughed and showed me his arm. Golden scales appeared on the surface of his skin, and then they disappeared. "Nah, that's something my body does to protect me. When I shift, you'll know, baby sister."

Damn it. Now I had to object. "Until an hour ago, I was older than you in here." I tapped my head. "So ease up on the 'baby sister' crap."

He smirked. Yeah, he wasn't going to stop. Trust me to get the bane of my existence as my big brother. I sighed, the past rushing through my head.

"You had a crush on me, big brother. Gag on that."

He laughed. "I did until I started seeing it for what it was—a connection we didn't understand. We explained it the only way we could, a crush. Now that I know you are my sister, the feelings make perfect sense. I hated seeing you date losers, flirt with stupid jocks who didn't see beyond your looks, and it annoyed the crap out of me whenever you acted dumb, which you are not."

That was a nice explanation. "I hated math."

"Yet you never failed it. Like I said, you acted like a dumb blonde."

I made a face. He was right. "Echo is either going to like this or hate it."

"Why? He is getting a goddess as a mate. Because that's what you are, Cora." He pressed a kiss on my forehead. "A goddess."

"Oh, shit!"

## CHAPTER 5. A GODDESS

Eirik walked through the portal and flashing rainbow colors swirled around him. He turned and smirked before the portal closed. I was still standing in the same spot when Echo arrived.

"What's wrong?"

Echo often claimed he could tell when I needed him. I never believed him because I thought I had no magic in me. What if locator runes were the reason he could feel me from afar? They attracted souls just like his scythe. If Goddess Hel was really my mother, I came from a line of magical people. Loki. Frigg. Odin. According to Lavania, all of them had magic in them. A tingle of excitement coursed through me.

"I'm a goddess," I said, trying it on for size.

Echo grinned and closed the space between us. "I know that. *My* goddess."

Oh, he was so cute, and he was going to love my news. "I want to tell you everything, but first let's get the blanket." I opened a portal to my room and grabbed his hand.

"Why?"

"Because it explains everything." I had thrown it in one of my drawers after studying it last night. "I just had a long talk with Eirik, and what he told me answered all my questions. My ability to see souls as a baby, my relationship with him, you always knowing when I need you." I laughed when Echo scowled. "It's kind of hard to explain without showing you the runes on the blanket." I let go of his hand, went to the drawer, and opened it.

The blanket wasn't there. Weird. I checked the drawer under it. Nothing. Could I have moved it? I checked under my pillows. I glanced at Echo.

"I put the blanket right here, and now it's missing. Did you take it?"

"No, sweetheart. You told me not to, and I respected your wishes. What did Eirik tell you?"

I walked to where he stood in the middle of my room and took his hands. "Brace yourself. The Idun-Grimnirs came to the mansion, and Eirik rushed from Asgard to stop them."

"Why?"

"Because they were looking for me. Me, Echo. We panicked thinking they'd come for Dev. They'd come for me because Goddess Hel had sent them. Eirik told me I'm his sister. Can you believe it?" I paused, giving him a chance to process. Echo winced, but something in his eyes gave him away. "You knew?"

"I suspected it when I saw the blanket. I needed to confirm it."

Where was the excitement? I'd expected him to bring up me visiting Eljudnir. Instead, I was getting strange vibes from him. He wasn't taking this well.

"Let me check with my parents first and see if they took it back. Then we'll talk."

I raced downstairs and didn't realize Echo was behind me until Dad looked up and said, "Cora? Echo? What's going on?"

"It's missing, Dad. The baby blanket you gave me is gone. "

"I haven't seen it since we gave it to you last night. Ask your mother. She brought your laundry upstairs this afternoon and might have moved it. She's in the barn."

Beginning to panic, I engaged speed runes and was inside the barn seconds later. The chickens reacted to the rush of air and squawked.

Mom scowled when she looked up, but her face cleared when she saw me. "Hey, honey. Grab this for me." She handed me a basket of eggs. "We'll need a new set of rules around here now that you can be yourself. At the top of the list is no super speeding around the chickens or they'll become more neurotic than they already are." She chuckled. "What is it?" she added when I didn't laugh at her joke.

Furrows appeared on her forehead. I used to search her face for a resemblance between us and had concluded I favored her because of our hair color. Dad had a mop of brown hair, but Mom had blond hair, hers lighter than mine. So I'd reached my own conclusions. One, I'd inherited her hair, but our features were different because she was older. And two, I favored my grandparents or some relative down the line. If Eirik were right, I should see myself in his parents. My birth parents.

"What's going on? You're staring at me with a peculiar expression."

"Did you take the baby blanket you gave me? I can't find it."

"No, I didn't. I just took your laundry upstairs, but I placed the hamper on your bed and didn't touch anything. Weren't you in your room about half an hour ago? I came up when I heard you, but you were gone by the time I got upstairs. I closed the drawers you'd left open."

"That wasn't me." My voice rose in panic. "Oh. Mom? I thought I saw a soul in my room taking it, but she didn't."

She reached out and gripped my hand. "Easy now, honey. Tell me what you saw."

I explained what I'd seen, how I couldn't move, and how the cloaked woman had disappeared with the blanket.

"I think you had a vision. You saw the person who took the blanket *before* she did it."

I shook my head. "What?"

"If you knew who your parents are, you'd see that this makes perfect sense. You come from magical people, so being clairvoyant should come naturally for you."

Clairvoyant? Me? "I know everything, Mom. Eirik and I have been talking for the past hour." Why would anyone take the blanket? "I don't want to believe him."

"Believe him." She closed the second coop and opened the last one. "That young man went through a lot to find you and saved a lot of orphans from a very crazy woman along the way."

Yeah, his grandmother. *My* grandmother. Yikes.

Mom put the eggs in the second basket and turned to face me. "You don't need the blanket to prove Eirik is your brother, Cora. He is. We checked everything he told us, and the runes on the blanket are the goddess' special runes. And you are clairvoyant." She laughed, then sobered up. "If we hadn't used warding and dampening runes on you, your ability would have manifested itself years ago. For that I'm sorry. Next time you see a vision, just analyze it. Don't panic. You are your father's daughter and Frigg's granddaughter. Both are powerful clairvoyants."

I didn't know what I'd expected to hear. When they'd told me my biological parents wanted to meet me, I'd fought it without knowing anything about them. Talking to Eirik had helped. And now I might have abilities because of them. I put the basket of eggs down and closed the distance between us. I hugged Mom.

A soft *oomph* left her, followed by a chuckle. "Why are you squeezing me to death?" She lifted my chin. "Tears? From my tough medium?"

"I love you, Mom."

"I know, hun. Dad and I love you so much, and we always will. Now." She pressed a kiss on my forehead and nudged me away from her. "How many people knew about your blanket?"

"You, Dad, Raine, Echo, and Eirik. None of you have a reason to steal it."

"Hmm. That's strange. Come on. Let's find out what's going on. We'll look everywhere."

Echo and Dad were talking quietly by Dad's writing cave when we entered the house.

"Mom didn't take it, and she says someone was in my room about half an hour ago and left drawers open. I kind of saw the person who took it." I explained my vision.

"A clairvoyant, that's my girl." Dad hugged me. He always acted like he was responsible for anything I accomplished.

"We don't know for sure, Dad."

Echo was frowning.

"What is it, grouch?"

"Most souls cannot move objects."

"Even dark ones? I couldn't see her face at all, even when she looked at me."

"Maybe she wasn't a soul," Echo said.

"I agree." Mom started upstairs.

"Maybe she was an Immortal loyal to Lord Worthington," Dad piped in, following her.

Echo and I exchanged a glance.

"Why would Immortals come after me? She smelled the blanket. That was creepy. Are you coming?"

Echo hadn't moved.

I followed my parents upstairs. On any given day, I'd have been embarrassed to have my parents go through my drawers and look through my things, but there was no time for embarrassment now. I had a mystery to solve.

The blanket was not in the room. I looked at the faces of the three most important people in my life and said, "If she's an Immortal, they know who I am. You talked to Warlock Worthington and then this happened."

"I'll pay him another visit," Echo vowed.

"You talked to Lord Worthington?" Dad asked. Even Mom stopped pacing to stare at Echo.

"The second I found out Cora was an orphan, I paid him a visit. I didn't mention Cora by name, but he knows all the reapers, Grimnirs, and Valkyries are watching them. His crazy followers will not use Cora to cross realms. He and I need to have another chat."

"Let's not jump to hasty conclusions," Mom said. "We need someone who can connect with energies and locate the person who was in here."

"People can do that?" I asked.

"Oh, yes." Mom smiled. "In my days before we learned runic magic, we had Witches who could find a thread of energy and follow it anywhere like a bloodhound with a scent."

"Unfortunately, most Immortals around here are like us," Dad said, frowning. "We haven't connected with our inner magic for centuries because we relied on runes. And even those we've used sparingly in the last fifty years."

"Celestia Deveraux can find traces of energy anywhere and follow it," Echo chimed in. "She helped Eirik find traces of Crazy Granny—uh, Angrboda and the orphans." Echo shot me an apologetic look.

"Eirik told me about her."

"Did he tell you she can also astral project anywhere in the future, past, or present. That's how she helps her father and his department solve crimes," Echo added.

"We met her when she came here with Eirik. Such an amazing young woman," Mom said.

"Extraordinary orator," Dad mumbled. "I wonder if she's ever thought of being a writer."

I just shook my head. Dad was weird like that. He always tied everything he saw or heard to writing.

I inched closer to Echo until I could feel his warmth. My worries eased a bit. Being close to him often did that. And he usually rested his hand on my back or took my hand as though he needed to connect with me physically. He didn't reach for me. Was he standoffish because my parents knew about him?

"I'll ask her when she returns from Asgard," he said.

Eirik had said he'd bring her to meet me in a couple of days, but that might be too late. My eyes volleyed between my parents. "Uh, about visiting Helheim, I'm still thinking about it. I'll go back to school and finish the term, but I want to discuss something with you guys."

My parents looked at each other and nodded.

"I'd rather finish at Mystic Academy, the school Lavania is starting. I don't know if you've heard about it. Raine is going and… What?" I asked when they exchanged another look.

"We've heard about the academy, but we didn't think you'd care about school after what you learned from Eirik," Mom said.

"We thought you'd want to visit Helheim and stay there for a while to get to know your other family," Dad added.

"Really? I know these two amazing people who taught me to always see things through, no matter how unpleasant or boring. And believe me, school without Raine is boring. Shame on you for thinking I'd just up and quit."

They grinned. Even Echo chuckled.

"About Mystic Academy, they'll offer regular classes for those who plan to continue on to college and get regular jobs. I'm not sure whether that's what I want. It depends on how I feel and my future plans. If I'm really clairvoyant, I'm going to need help mastering it, and Mystic Academy is the only place to do that. Is that okay?"

"That's perfectly fine," Dad said, his grin so wide you'd think he'd won a Pulitzer.

"Yes, dear," Mom chimed in. "It's okay with us."

"Then if you'll excuse us, I'd like to discuss a few things with Echo."

"We did right, didn't we?" I overheard Mom say as they disappeared into the hallway.

"Yes, love. She's a chip off the old block."

Except I wasn't a chip off them. However, they'd influenced me. They'd taught me to believe in myself and to work hard at whatever I did. Dad encouraged me to follow my passion, no matter what people thought. He'd been my number one supporter when I'd vlogged even though he never watched any of my videos. Mom had and commented. I had no idea what other professions Dad had to reinvent himself in his lifetime, but in mine, he'd quit teaching to become an author and was damn successful at it.

Mom appreciated little things in life, whether it was watching the chickens act silly, mucking the soil, or tending her precious prized organic plants. She taught me to appreciate the mundane and to be patient. I wondered if she'd always done organic farming. I had so many questions about their past lives. What special abilities did they have before runic magic? Were they rich? According to Echo, most Immortals were loaded.

I closed the door and turned to face Echo. He stood in the middle of my room—duster, boots, fingerless gloves, and a frown on his face.

"Do you remember when we agreed we wouldn't keep secrets from each other?" I asked, and his expression stayed unreadable. Anger licked at me, but I pushed it away. "Listen, I'm going through a lot right now, and the one person I know I can count on through good and bad times is you, Echo. Instead, I can feel you distancing yourself from me. Why?"

"I'm not," he said.

"Yes, you are."

"Someone was in your room, Cora. That's enough to make me break out in a cold sweat. They stole from you. Another cause for alarm. I'm thinking of who I need to beat up to find answers."

I didn't buy his response. Yes, he tended to be passionate about my safety, but he'd arrived in a funky mood and that was before he knew about my missing blanket. I removed the hamper of clothes from my bed and sat. Instead of sitting beside me, or lifting me and pulling me onto his lap as he often did, he took the chair and scooted close until his knees bracketed mine. He took my hands and threaded our fingers.

He sighed. "If anything ever happened to you—"

"You'd level the Earth, I know. What is really bothering you, Echo?"

He studied me intently then smiled. "You can always see through my bullshit."

"Damn right."

"Which is impressive for someone so young."

I frowned. "Is my age an issue now?"

"No." He sighed. "You are Goddess Hel's daughter, Cora. Odin and Frigg's granddaughter. Eirik's sister. He's a dragon with an attitude and so much power I'm surprised he can contain it."

"We haven't exactly proven I'm his sister."

"There's nothing to prove. When you showed me that blanket yesterday, I had my suspicions. So I asked Maera to show me baby Einmyria's things. Goddess Hel finally moved them from the nursery when she converted the room into a bedroom for Jessica, but she kept everything. The blanket and the runes are the same as hers. You are Einmyria."

"Okay, let's say that it's true. So what? I'm still me, the girl you fell in love with."

"And slept with when she was only sixteen. You just turned

seventeen."

I growled and fell onto my back. "Seriously? My age is a problem now? It never was before."

"I know. I, uh, I feel..." He stood and scrubbed his face. He studied me with an expression filled with pain and frustration. He was struggling with something big. Something beyond what he was saying. "I think we should slow things down a bit. Take a step back."

"What do you mean?" I asked, sitting up, my chest squeezing.

He scrubbed his face again. "We should ease up on intimate stuff until all this is settled."

Anger swallowed my patience. I was pissed and wanted to hit him. "Oh gee, Echo. You know that's all you are to me. Someone I go to for *intimate stuff*. Why don't you say what's really bothering you? When I was a scared nobody who needed you, you couldn't wait to step up and be my hero. Now there's a possibility that I'm more, and you think I don't need you. Or maybe you think you're not good enough for me."

"That's not it." His eyes went to the ring on my finger.

The Druidic engagement ring didn't have a rock, but it was priceless. He'd given it to me with my parents' approval months ago. As far as I was concerned, it symbolized something greater than a promise ring and an engagement rock combined. It meant something to him. A hollow settled in my stomach, and I couldn't breathe.

"Do you want your ring back?"

He paled, his eyes flying to mine. "No. Not that."

"Then what?"

"You have your entire life ahead of you and a chance to be more powerful than you've ever dreamed. Your brother is a dragon, your father comes from powerful people, and your mother is a—"

"Shut up." I threw a pillow at him. "I don't care about being powerful. I care about you, Echo. From the moment I met you and you told those souls to leave me alone or whatever it is you yelled, you've been mine. You'd take on anyone who looks at me wrong and let no one stand in your way."

His eyes went wolfish in seconds.

"I don't care how powerful Eirik is, how powerful my parents are, or if my grandparents run Asgard. You and I are a couple. We complete each other. So whatever crawled up your butt—"

One second I was glaring at him, the next I was on my back with him on top of me, reminding me of the first time he'd appeared in my room.

"You don't talk about my ass," he growled.

"When it belongs to me, I do," I shot back. "When you're being a shithead, I do. When you are pushing me away and hurting me until it hurts to breathe, I fucking do."

"Hel's Mist." Then his mouth was on mine. He kissed me as though to swallow me whole. Whatever he was going through was screwing with his head.

I wrapped my arms and legs around him, wanting to get as close to him as humanly possible and help him chase away his demons, whatever they were. He jumped off the bed, scooped me up, and started for the portal, runes blazing. The portal responded, opening into the bedroom of the house in La Gorce, not the cottage. I had a feeling he wanted to be as far away from Kayville as possible.

He wasn't gentle when he pulled his clothes off, but that changed the moment he joined me. I still wore the two-piece swimsuit and the robe I'd thrown over it. He removed the robe while raining kisses along my neck and down my arm.

"My favorite swim suit," he murmured, unhooking the top.

"You bought it. Along with several more."

"You can never wear them in Eljudnir," he murmured and nuzzled my neck.

I couldn't imagine a pool in Hel's Hall and really didn't care as he transported me to that special place where we spoke our language, the language of love, sensual bliss, and perfect unity. Who my parents were didn't matter there. We were two people in love and passionate about each other. Each touch was filled with shared memories, each kiss with promises of our future, and when he looked into my eyes, I knew that nothing could ever take away what we had. Not my family, not my insecurities or fears of the unknown, and certainly not his demons, whatever they were.

"You are mine, Cora-mia," he whispered.

"Always," was my response. Whether it penetrated his thick skull was another story. When we crashed, we stayed wrapped in each other's arms until I bit into his shoulder to get his attention. "I love you, Echo. Whatever is bothering you, we'll work through it. We have to because I'd be lost without you."

"No, Cora-mia. I'd be lost without you. There's no version of my life without you in it."

He was worried about losing me. How silly. Just because I was acquiring a new, powerful family didn't mean he would be on the outside. I'd just have to show him until he accepted that he was my family, too.

"Tell me about Helheim."

"I don't want to talk about Helheim." He rolled us over, so I was on top. "Show me how you own my ass."

I did until his beautiful, scarred body trembled in my arms.

~*~

Monday and Tuesday came and went. I helped souls during lunch with Rhys and Nara to escort them. In the evening, I helped the ones at the farm under my parents' watchful eyes. Dev continued to help coma patients wherever he could find them, and his soul buddies continued to keep an eye on me even though I kept telling them I didn't need it. The Idun-Grimnirs searching for me were the ones who'd scared the souls and made them believe I was dying.

Echo was gone a lot more than usual. At first, I thought it was because he was working on his issues, until I had a chat with Dev on Wednesday morning.

"He said someone was in your room and something went missing. Finding the person seems to be his first priority right now."

We were in my car outside my school. For once, Echo hadn't driven me. "Where is he looking for answers?"

"Among the Immortals. He's convinced an evil Immortal was involved. Don't worry. He'll find the person who robbed you. He has ways of finding people, Mortal or Immortal."

"He didn't find you."

"I'm a soul, doll-face, even though you tend to forget it. I also happen to know how your man thinks. And"—he stretched out the word—"I believe he knew exactly where I was, but chose to leave me alone. He told me to ask around and see if anyone met with the two ancient Grimnirs who were at the mansion. Souls can't outrun them, but for once they weren't interested in us. They were after a missing girl."

I laughed. "They were after me, Dev."

"You? Why?"

"Remember I told Raine I was adopted?"

"Yes, but… Do you feel that?"

"Feel what?"

"A presence. It's so powerful I can feel the pull from inside this radio."

I glanced outside. "There's no one out there but students."

"Someone is here. Someone powerful. I'm coming out and standing guard in case it's the evil Immortal. Then I want to know why the ancients are after you."

"Were," I corrected him.

"Are. Were. It doesn't matter. They are not touching you. Right now, I need to locate the person emitting that energy. It's potent." He slithered from the radio and stayed with me when I stepped out of the car. Runes erupted on my arms. I recognized them right away. Locator runes.

What was going on? I looked around but didn't see anything unusual. I didn't even get the creepy feeling I often associated with someone watching me. Frowning, I indicated for Dev to walk closer. He floated around me and acted like a ninja, moving stealthily, throwing punches and flying kicks. He looked ridiculous.

"Don't hurt yourself, Dev," I warned and faked a cough when a few students walked past and glanced my way.

Dev entered my phone the second I entered the school building. "It's still there, yet I can't see where it's coming from. Maybe you should skip school."

I raised the phone to my lips and faked a conversation. "It might be Eirik watching us from Odin's high chair."

"The Boy Scout at the mansion?"

Nice description. "Yes. And that Boy Scout is my brother. I didn't know he was even though we grew up together. He was watching me from Odin's chair when he saw the ancients."

"Why would the ancients be...? Whoa, Odin's chair?"

"Let's talk later. I have a class in two minutes, and you need to help the dying and redeem your soul."

"Forget my soul. I'm not leaving you until I know what we're dealing with here. If anything happened to you, I'd never forgive myself. Your brother goes to Asgard? What is he?"

"A dragon." I turned off the phone, grabbed my books, and hurried toward class. Dev insisted the presence was in my class and refused to leave for three periods. In between classes, he grilled me on Eirik and my biological parents. Just before lunch, he claimed the presence was gone. I had my suspicions about the person responsible.

The second I stepped out of math class, I spotted several souls in the hallway. They smiled, but didn't approach me. They often headed upstairs to the bathroom to wait for me. These didn't look like they wanted my help, so I ignored them. I got a text before I reached the lockers.

"Come to the mansion for lunch," her text said.

The souls followed me upstairs and floated through the wall before I went inside. Usually, they lined up outside and waited until I went ahead of them. I told them there would be no lunch session, and it didn't seem to bother them. I tried reassuring them that no one was after me, but they just stared. Raine was waiting when I arrived at the mansion, along with Andris, Torin, and Ingrid.

"What's going on?"

"Torin made lunch," Raine said, hugging me. "I told you we should do lunch."

"That was Monday, and you stood me up," I said and pinched her.

She pinched me right back. "Just because you are a goddess doesn't mean you get to abuse me."

The others laughed.

"We added more protection runes around your school after Dev stopped by and told us about something stalking you, *Goddess*," Ingrid added. "We'll see what gets trapped inside."

I loved that soul, but he was such a worrywart. "Thanks for the runes, guys. He also left souls on guard duty." I pointed at Ingrid and snarled, "Stop messing with me, Blondie."

"I can't, Goddess Blondie," Ingrid said and curtseyed. "Your royal deity-ness."

I shook my head. "Clown."

"Own your goddess-ship," Andris whispered, sliding beside me. "You already have the bearing and the fashion sense." He removed imaginary lint from my top. "Now all you need is the chair. Come sit beside me so I can find ways to replace Echo in your heart. I've always wanted a chair."

I planted a kiss on his cheek. "You couldn't handle me, Casanova, and no one can ever replace Echo. How did things go with Jenny?"

"The bullies were forced to go to the principal and confessed everything after we hacked the diary of the head bitch and posted its contents online. They were expelled after they apologized for what they'd done to Jenny and the others in front of the entire school. I made sure the students had their phones ready, and the apology has gone viral. While you've been busy discovering your brother, social media made their apologies and humiliation trend."

"The principal expelled legacy children?"

"Every last one of them. How did he put it? The school had to show the students, the staff, the board, and the alumni that bullying would not be tolerated at McLane Prep. He had no choice because we made an insane donation in Jenny's name. Her parents have been invited to a gala at the school."

"Wow. Awesome."

"Thank you." He grinned and glanced at the others. From their expressions, he'd told them the story. "I told Syn we were awesome. He disagreed. He wanted the principal to resign for not doing his job. I told him we needed the man at that school where we could keep an eye on him. Syn wasn't happy, but I can be very persuasive. So now I owe him."

"Was Jenny happy?"

"As a clam."

"Thanks, Andris. And you too, Torin." He'd just placed a steaming plate of stir-fry in front of me. I gave him a hug.

"You okay?" he asked.

"Yeah. Dev worries too much." I couldn't tell them my suspicions.

"We can hang around the school until we figure out this new threat."

"It's okay. Honestly, I don't feel threatened at all. Even when Dev mentioned it, I didn't feel scared."

"Ah, *noblesse oblige*?" Andris said.

The others laughed while Torin shook his head and went to join Raine. They fed each other. Marriage agreed with them. She glowed. He was content. I wanted what they had, not all this drama with my birth parents.

"What is *noblesse oblige*?" I asked.

"It's French for nobility doesn't fear anything," Andris said. "They boldly face all sorts of danger because it's in their blood to do so. If you are of a noble birth like Sir Anal over here"—Andris indicated Torin with a nod—"or of godly birth like you, you are invincible."

Ingrid flicked water at him. "Don't listen to him, Cora. *Noblesse oblige* means there are certain expectations and responsibilities required of you when you are of noble birth. Not feeling threatened has nothing to do with it, which begs the question, what could Dev have felt."

I explained about Eirik and Odin's chair. "He could still be up there watching us. Did you guys know he is a dragon shifter?"

"A what?" echoed around the kitchen.

"A dragon shifter," I said, grinning at the expression on Raine and Ingrid's faces.

"That explains it," Ingrid said and high-fived Raine.

"Explains what, Freckles?" Torin asked.

"The muscles." Raine lifted her arms and flexed hers while Torin scowled.

"He visited a couple of weeks ago. Raine and I found him asleep on her bed and got an eyeful," Ingrid said. "I'm not complaining. I was tempted to see if he felt as good as he looked. I mean, the guy is seriously packing." She kept throwing Torin and Andris side-glances. It was obvious she was deliberately baiting them.

"An eyeful of what?" Torin growled, and Raine shut him up with a kiss.

"I wonder if he was the golden dragon we saw flying around Asgard last week," Andris said. "He even fought with the *Einherjar.*"

"What's that?" I asked.

"The warriors preparing for Ragnarok," Andris explained, and I wondered if Goddess Hel had warriors preparing, too. I was starting to wonder about her and how she treated her reapers. Did she mingle with them, or were they like her servants?

"Do Valkyries mingle with the gods?"

Andris laughed and explained in detail how life was in Asgard. The more I heard about their interaction with the gods, the more I worried about my future with Echo. If Goddess Hel didn't encourage interaction between her hall and the Grimnirs', I'd never see Echo.

## CHAPTER 6. CELESTIA KNOWS

Echo was waiting by my car when school got out. I studied his face. He smiled. He seemed to be back to his usual self. Since the car was off, I assumed Dev wasn't around.

"Are they all waiting for you?" He indicated the souls, and I turned to study them. They no longer hid the fact that they were guarding me.

"Guarding me. Dev asked them to keep an eye on me."

A frown creased Echo's forehead. "Why would he do that?"

"He thought I was in danger."

"Danger?" Echo was by my side before the words stopped echoing in the air. He cupped my face and searched it. "What danger? Why didn't he tell me?"

"It's nothing. He insisted something powerful was around the school on yesterday, but he couldn't see it and neither could I. He insisted on hanging around, even when I told him to leave, until he felt the presence disappear. They've been hovering since." I glanced around. "And now they're leaving. See? You are my hero, and they know it." I patted Echo's chest and gave him a big smile. "Let's go, handsome."

I took one step, and he pulled me into his arms.

"Are you forgetting something?" He didn't wait for an answer, just kissed me until my head started to spin. He lifted his head and smiled. "I needed that."

So did I, but I couldn't help teasing him. "I thought we were laying off the intimate stuff."

"I'm an idiot."

"I know."

He chuckled and pressed his forehead against mine. "I cannot stand seeing you hurt."

"Good. Then stay glued to me forever. Come on, let's go."

He still palmed my face and didn't let me go. "Promise me you'll be careful."

"Always."

"Even when I'm not there."

My smile almost slipped. "You'd better be around, mister, or I'll come find you." I waited until he pulled out of the parking lot before I said, "Tell me about Hel's Hall."

"What do you want to know?"

"Where's Grimnirs Hall, and how far is it from Eirik's and his parents'? Do you guys eat together? Party together? Are you guys buddies?"

He laughed.

"I mean it. I want to know everything. Does she treat you guys like servants or part of the household? After listening to Andris, I'm scared I'll never see you when I visit."

"Helheim is cold and filled with magic. There are different halls within Hel's Hall, including Eljudnir—which is the goddess' hall. There is a Waiting Hall, a Throne Hall, the Guest Halls, Grimnirs Hall, Staff Hall, and Eternal Resting Halls, which some people call Eternal Hall or just Resting Hall." He talked about Trudy and her family. "Maera is the housekeeper and head of the kitchen. Her staff cooks for everyone, including the goddess' household. Her husband, Oskrud, ferries damned souls to Corpse Strand, and their oldest daughter Modgud guards the gates with Garm. The goddess and Baldur don't eat with us, but Eirik does." Echo chuckled. "He eats all the time. I'm not sure if that's because the kitchen and Grimnirs Hall is open 24/7 or if he needs to feed his dragon. He works out and spars with us when not practicing with your mother's warriors. For whatever reason, he bugs me with senseless questions whenever I'm in Ejudnir."

"Wait a second. When you talked about a dragon leaving, you meant Eirik." I grinned. "Ha! So you two are buddies now."

"No, we're not. We went on a few adventures. That's all. Whenever the goddess throws a party, we are usually invited." He talked about how Helheim had become a home to all of the Grimnirs. "Your mother treats us like members of her family, Cora. She took Trudy under her wing and treats her like her charge. Trudy and Celestia are tight. Then there's Jessica, the girl who pretended to be you. Even though she knew from the moment Jessica arrived that she wasn't you, she didn't throw her out."

He drove slower than usual as he talked about the goddess, a string of emotions playing on his face. They'd known about her missing son and dead daughter, saw how it had changed her, and grieved with her.

"She feels things deeply and maybe she's a bit melodramatic like some people I know." He pressed a kiss on my forehead. "But she is loved by everyone who knows her because she is an amazing person."

"How is she melodramatic?"

"Every year, on your birthday, she covered every painting, mural, and figurine, disappeared into the nursery, and smashed everything. The Golden One was never allowed to enter the room until she was done grieving and putting the nursery back together. She did that for seventeen years, and each time lasted three days to mark when you were born and when you died. Sometimes she started early, so the mourning period lasted longer."

Tears filled my eyes.

Echo kissed my knuckles. "She never made it a decree, but everyone wears black on those days. Staff. Grimnirs. Her guards. No color of any kind. The lights are dimmed, and the noise level in all the halls drops out of respect to her."

"That's not being melodramatic, Echo. That's grieving."

"I know." He lifted my chin and wiped my cheeks. "Don't cry."

"You are the melodramatic one in this relationship," I mumbled.

"I know that, too. She loved you as a baby, Cora, and she will love the woman you've become."

"You think so?"

"I know so." He kissed my cheek. "What else do you want to know?"

"Eirik's dragon."

"It's huge." He shook his head. "You have to see it to appreciate him."

"Celestia? What?" I asked when he grinned.

"The little Druidess is a pint-sized Witch with a mouth and an attitude, but she grows on you." He talked about the first time they'd met at some club in her hometown because the goddess had sent him to find her. I laughed as he explained her reaction. She sounded like someone I'd enjoy knowing. "I see her as a blend of you and Raine. Like you, she looks delicate on the outside but has an amazing inner strength. Like Raine, she goes headfirst into situations, acting first and thinking about the consequences later, which can drive a person insane."

That sounded like him, something I loved about him. He was spontaneous while I tended to weigh the pros and cons before acting. He never regretted his actions before, yet he did regret the way he'd treated Dev. Was this constant worrying about my other family part of the new Echo? Man, I hoped not because I needed him to be his usual cocky self when I visited Helheim.

He pulled up outside the farmhouse then parked beside Dad's truck and turned to study me with a serious expression. "It is important that everything at the hall stays the same for everyone, Cora."

I nodded. "I get that."

"Centuries ago, I forced my brothers and sisters to follow me and they helped turn our Druidic sisters and brothers into Immortals. Because of that, they were kicked out of Asgard and condemned to a lifetime of serving Goddess Hel in Helheim."

"I know the story, Echo. I think it's ridiculous for them to hold a grudge this long."

"That's just it. They're not angry. We may not be buddies, but like I told you, they've found a home in Helheim and are happy. I do not want that to change."

I frowned. "You think if they find out we are dating, they'd hate you again?"

A smile tugged the corner of his mouth. "Every Grimnir knows about my medium girlfriend who helps souls, sweetheart. What they don't know is your connection with the goddess."

"We can tell them the truth when I come to visit."

Echo pressed his forehead against mine and sighed. "It's not them I'm worried about, sweetheart. I don't know how your mother and father will react to our relationship. If they feel I've crossed the line by dating their daughter, they might change how they treat Grimnirs."

"Why should they care about our relationship? We fell in love before we knew who I was. And our relationship has nothing to do with the other Grimnirs."

Echo leaned back and stroked my arm absentmindedly. "Centuries ago, it was a social taboo for a woman of noble birth to marry beneath her station. You are their daughter, a goddess in your own right. I'm just her reaper. She might have a problem with us being together."

I didn't like this. "Then I don't want to be her daughter."

"You can't reject who you are. We should not mention anything about us to the goddess right away."

This was not what I'd expected to hear after he mentioned taking things slowly. "Are you saying we should hide our relationship from them?"

"Yes, until we know how she'll react."

So he was more worried about Goddess Hel's reaction than Baldur's. "And if she disapproves?"

"We'll decide our next move if that happens."

"I can't hide how I feel about you, Echo. We gravitate toward each other when we are in the same room. Only an idiot wouldn't realize there's something between us."

He smiled. "I'm asking for time, Cora-mia. Time to assess the situation and study your parents. Time for you to get to know them without our relationship being thrown in the middle of things. I don't want all the Grimnirs to suffer because I didn't think through my next course of action."

*Think things through.* I was beginning to hate that expression. I wanted my spontaneous Echo back. I understood his concern for his reaper friends, but what about me. Why was he putting them ahead of us? I didn't know how to pretend I didn't love him.

"How do I explain this?" I showed him the ring.

He swallowed. "That stays." Did he realize how contradictory his behavior was?

"Okay."

He smiled with approval.

"If I have to pretend I don't love you, I'm not going."

A scowl replaced his smile. "You are going."

"You can't make me."

"You are being childish."

"Childish? Really?" I glared at him. "Fine. Let's go ahead and hide our feelings while you think things through, Echo. If you see me, pretend you don't know me, and I'll pretend I don't know you."

"I didn't mean it like that."

"There's no other way to pretend. We either come clean right off the bat or fake it. If they ask where I got the ring, I'll tell them a friend gave it to me. A friend, not the man I love." I slammed the door. He was beside me in a fraction of a second, but my front door opened at the same time and Eirik stepped out. He frowned at us. "Ooh, look! There's my all powerful dragon brother now. Let's use him as a guinea pig and see if we can pull off this pretend crap."

I waved to Eirik and started toward him when a petite girl in ripped jeans, ankle boots, and a Boho top followed him outside. She had wavy brown hair, piercing blue eyes, and dimples that flashed on her cheeks when she smiled. A feeling of déjà vu washed over me. I knew her. Echo's hand came to rest on my back, but my focus stayed on Eirik's girlfriend. Where had I seen her?

"Celestia?" I asked.

"Yes, and you are Cora." She gave me a hug.

Because I was on the steps and she was on the porch, we were at the same height level. She leaned back, still grinning. For a brief moment, everything faded. Then other images of her superimposed on her grinning face. I shook my head, and the images disappeared. What the hell?

"It's so nice to finally meet you," Celestia said. "Sorry it took us forever to get back. Alfadir insisted on throwing us a going-away party, then Frigg and her court insisted on another. It's ridiculous how often they party. When we came back to Helheim, one of the guards' wives was having a difficult pregnancy and I went to stabilize it. I was still working on her when more sick arrived. Before I knew it, I had a roomful of people with ailments their healer couldn't help. There's only one healer in Eastern Gjöll Pass, which is a village not far from the hall."

Eirik chuckled, tucking her against his side. "She talks a lot, but eventually she'll get to the point. What she's trying to say is she spent the whole day treating the sick. Went back the next day to treat more. If I hadn't dragged her away, she would still be there, but she's done the impossible. She made the southern clans sit and talk without trying to kill each other. Now she wants to open a clinic in Chief Skevnir's town and Eastern Gjöll Pass." Eirik kissed her.

"The healers must agree first, Eirik," Celestia said.

The entire time they talked, I kept staring at her, trying to remember when I'd seen her. Her voice, face, and those dimples were all familiar.

"We've met," I said.

The smile disappeared from her face.

"Don't deny it, please. Either I'm going crazy or the Norns erased my memories. At first, your name sounded familiar. Hayden's too. Then I had flashes of memories of the two of you at my school, yet I don't remember anything beyond that. Oh, and there was a third girl. A redhead."

Celestia looked at Eirik and then Echo. "You two are not saying anything?"

"Celestia," Eirik said.

"No, Eirik. She needs to know. You"—Celestia pointed at him—"are telling her the truth." A frown skidded across her face. "Echo, do not leave. You know what happened, too."

"Celestia," Eirik growled.

"If the Norns still want to flex their muscles, they'll have to go through you, right?" She grabbed his sleeve, pulled him down, and planted a kiss on his lips. "Love you, my dragon." Then she turned to me. "Echo said someone stole something from your room. Do you still want to know who did it?"

I nodded, but I was thoroughly confused. What did the images I was seeing have to do with Eirik and Echo? I shot them a questioning glance. Echo was grinning while Eirik shot Celestia a look that said he was resigned to doing whatever she'd asked.

"Come on, Cora. Let's find out who dared to mess with you. Have they met Echo? He's going to rip them apart."

"Wow, you're the first girl to make Eirik shut up," I said. "You just barreled right through him. I wish Raine had seen that."

"He's used to getting his way, so whenever I get the upper hand, I milk it. We argued about you on our way here. You are his sister, so there's no need for him to worry about the Norns messing with you. Between him, Echo, and the goddess, those hags wouldn't stand a chance."

My parents were in the living room and watched us head upstairs without batting an eyelid. It was nice to be able to have my friends over without worrying about one of them doing or saying something and giving themselves away.

"I'm looking forward to meeting Raine," Celestia said. "I hope we'll get together and get to know each other once her honeymoon is over." She glanced over her shoulder at me, and she faded. Another image of her flashed right before my eyes then disappeared.

"I just saw another memory of you comforting me," I said.

She stopped and turned. "Everything will all come back once Eirik explains. He wanted the two of you to be together, and typical of him, he made it happen. It's one of the things I love about him. Nothing stops him." She glanced behind me. "You will explain everything. Won't you, guys?"

Echo and Eirik had caught up with us. They nodded. Celestia might be pint-sized, as Echo had called her, but she had a way of commanding attention. And she talked a lot.

"If Raine were here, she'd hear the story, too," she added and gave

Eirik a toothy grin.

"It's almost midnight in England, Dimples," Eirik said. "I'm not waking them up."

"Oh. Too bad." She continued to lead the way, then stopped outside my bedroom.

"How do you know that's my bedroom?" I asked.

"We came here the day of your prom, but you were asleep up here after a possession. Eirik wanted to show your parents how your locator runes responded to his." She stepped aside to let me enter first, but I shook my head.

"No, after you," I insisted. "I don't want to mess with your mojo."

She entered the room and looked around. "I love your room. Are you attending Mystic Academy next year?"

"Yep. Are you?"

"I haven't decided yet. I'm supposed to be graduating in a few weeks, but I don't see that happening. I'd love to learn how to control my astral projection better." She looked around and rubbed her arms. "There's a very strong energy here. It's familiar, but it's not yours, your parents', or Echo's."

I exchanged a glance with Echo. He moved toward me, but I moved away. Annoyance flashed in his eyes. He couldn't possibly be getting angry with me now. He was the one who wanted us to pretend not to be a couple.

"Maybe it's Dev's," I said from the other side of the bed.

"I recognized his already. It's concentrated on your electronics. This is different yet familiar." She frowned.

"You know Dev?"

"We met once." She glanced at Eirik again and sighed. "It will make sense once they explain." She walked to the window, then walked around the room. "The energy is all over the room, like the person moved around, touching things. I've encountered it before. I just don't know where." She went to stand in front of the mirror. "I was sure it would be concentrated here, but it's not. The person didn't use the mirror."

"Air portal?" I asked.

"Most likely." Celestia's frown deepened. "May I use your bed?"

"Sure. Are you going to astral project?"

Celestia nodded. "Yes, and follow the energy. Most of the time it happens when I least expect it, but at times, I get lucky. That's how Eirik and I met." She glanced at him and grinned.

"She thought I was a lamb shifter," he said, walking to her side as she settled against the pillows. "Showed you, didn't I?"

"Show-off. When he's in his dragon form, he acts like he owns the freaking world." She closed her eyes. Eirik's gaze didn't leave her face. "Stop worrying. I can feel it pouring out of you."

"No, you can't. I'm the dragon, the all seer, smeller, and hearer of things, not you. And I can scent when you are lying. You know who stole her blanket, don't you?"

Celestia sighed. "I'm trying to concentrate, Eirik."

"You do know." His voice was accusatory.

Her eyelids lifted, and I inched closer. "No, I don't, but I have a theory."

"Care to share it before you float away?"

"No." She reached for his hand, gripped it, and closed her eyes again. My frustrations with Echo shot up as I watched them. His concerns made no sense. If Goddess Hel was okay with her only son being with Celestia, I didn't see why she would object to me being with Echo.

My jaw dropped when Celestia's astral self separated from her body. Laughing, she saluted us and disappeared into the ceiling.

Eirik shook his head. "She treats going to AP like it's nothing, while I think of all things that could possibly go wrong. It's one thing when she helps her father catch criminals and quite another when dealing with the supernatural world. She doesn't get it."

He sounded like Echo. "How long has she known she is a Witch?"

"Since she was a child." His eyes volleyed between Echo and me. "What's wrong with you two?"

"What do you mean?" I asked, feigning ignorance.

"He's over there, and you are over here. I'm getting bad vibes." He angled his head. "Your heartbeat just spiked, and Echo reeks of frustration. You two fought?"

"No," I said while Echo stayed quiet. "We have a new understanding, which I think will work great for us. You can hear heartbeats?"

"Yes, and scents, which change with moods, and I can see from far. What did you do, reaper?"

Echo growled something then left the room. I stared at the door, wishing I could yell at him or something.

"What's going on?" Eirik asked.

"Nothing I can't handle. You once told Raine you were a seer."

"Because I can see from far."

I rolled my eyes. "Seers, Einstein, are what Celestia and Raine are." What I might be. "They see into the past or the future, not things from miles away. It's not the same."

He shrugged indifferently, his focus on Celestia.

I sat on the other side of the bed and studied her charm bracelets, the layered necklace, and matching earrings. She wore a beautiful ornate ring on her finger. It had runes on the band and a big clear stone in the middle. It looked like a wedding ring. "Raine and I tried to imagine what she looked like. She's beautiful."

"Breathtaking." He stroked Celestia's cheek. "She is feisty, stubborn, and talks a lot."

"I noticed. She bullies you around."

"I allow her to bully me around. Not the same thing. Asgard officially accepted her as my mate, and Mom is planning our wedding. Trudy, Maera, Hayden, and Jessica are helping and trying to keep it a secret from her, but I have a feeling Celestia already knows."

"So that's not a wedding ring she's wearing?"

Eirik chuckled. "It is and it's not. Our grandmother Frigg gave it to me, and I gave it to Celestia as a symbol of our commitment to each other. To my parents and grandparents, we've chosen each other, and she is my consort. But her father expects a wedding, and I want her to have one."

"Where will it take place?"

"Eljudnir. I hope you and your parents can come. What happened between you and Echo?" Voices outside the door caught his attention and saved me from lying again.

Raine peered inside the room. She was wearing a robe over her pajamas. Torin had on a T-shirt, sweatpants, and loafers.

"What are you guys doing here?" I went to hug her.

"Echo said you needed me," she said. "I didn't hear the rest of what he told Torin, except a stolen baby blanket."

My eyes locked with Echo's. If this was his way of apologizing, it might buy him a few points, but not enough to make me see things his way.

"It doesn't make sense, though. Why would she not want me to have it? Was it to stop me from proving I'm the goddess' daughter? The funny thing is I don't need the blanket to prove anything anymore."

"She?"

"Or he," I improvised. I wasn't ready to tell them about what I'd seen.

"Or they," Raine added. "Maybe it was Norns. Is that Celestia?" Raine's eyes were on the bed.

"Yep." We moved closer. "She can find energies and astral project at will."

"Lucky, girl. I'm still working on mine. She's gorgeous," she whispered.

I grinned. "She orders Eirik around. It's so cute how she has him wrapped around her finger."

"I heard that," Eirik said. He, Echo, and Torin were talking in low voices by the door, but he kept glancing at Celestia.

"I've met her before, Raine," I whispered. "I keep having these flashbacks that don't make sense. She's in them and so is her best friend, Hayden, and a redhead." I glanced at the guys. "Celestia insisted Eirik tell me everything, and she suggested you should be here. I hope

Echo didn't drag you out of bed."

"We weren't ready for bed yet, so I don't mind. Besides, he said you needed me. He's never said that before, so I knew it was something he couldn't handle."

Or the fact that I wasn't talking to his sorry ass. A knock on the door, and Mom peered inside my room. "Anyone want a drink or pie?"

There was a chorus of "yes." Mom's pies were a favorite among my friends. She came back with a tray full of slices of apple pie and one cherry, utensils, and forks. Dad followed her with a pitcher of lemonade and glasses.

I took the pitcher from Dad and served drinks while Mom handed out pies. Eirik grabbed two slices and went to sit by Celestia. I only had two chairs in my room, and Torin grabbed one for him and Raine, while Echo brought me the other one and stayed close. I gave him kudos for trying to be his usual attentive self, but that wasn't what I needed. He was either with me one hundred percent or he was not. I went to sit on the bed opposite Eirik. He studied me with narrowed eyes.

"How's she doing?" Mom asked from behind me.

Eirik studied Celestia's face. "Good. I'll know when she's in trouble. Her heartbeat will shoot up and fear will sour her scent."

"Dragon senses," I explained to Raine.

"We were in the audience the night you spoke to the Immortals," Mom said. "We infiltrated the club and reported to the other parents here. That's how we kept the orphans in Kayville and Portland area safe. You did a good thing that evening."

Eirik shrugged. "It didn't stop them from coming here."

"But some of their members chickened out, so when they arrived here, there were a lot fewer. They lost because of you." Dad swept the room with a glance. "All of you and your friends. No matter what happens, you should all know we feel a lot safer because you dismantled Lord Worthington's movement."

I glanced at Torin. He was listening without speaking, but I knew he heard every word. This could not be a fun conversation for him.

Even Eirik kept glancing at him. My parents continued to talk, completely clueless about the connection between Lord Worthington and Torin.

"We'll continue to keep a close eye on them." Eirik touched Celestia's cheek and frowned. "What's going on, Dimples? Come back now. Can you hear me?"

"Is she okay?" I asked, moving closer. The others flocked around the bed, too.

"Her heartbeat spiked. She's panicking. Come on, Dimples. Come back."

The words barely left his mouth when she whooshed into the room so fast she was a blur and rejoined her body. She sat up and launched herself into Eirik's arms.

"It's okay, Dimples. I got you. I got you." He hugged her and rubbed her back. Our eyes met. "She's shaking." He leaned back and studied her face. "What happened?"

"I don't know. I was coming back when I felt a menacing energy. They chased me back."

"They?"

"I don't know how many there were, but there was more than one. I didn't look back, but I heard snickering and felt them."

"Do you need a pen and a paper? Did you see anything?" He looked at me. "She sketches whatever she sees in the AP."

"No, there's no need. I saw a woman wearing a cloak, but before I could see her face, she used an air portal and disappeared with the blanket. I don't think she means any harm."

My eyes went to Echo. I was sure we were thinking the same thing. She'd seen exactly what I'd described. Should I tell them now or wait? Maybe the vision was a fluke and I'd look stupid claiming clairvoyance.

"So she wasn't a soul?" Raine asked.

Celestia shook her head. "No. Flesh and blood. I think she was attracted to the runes on the blanket. I followed her to other places around Kayville."

"Was she at my school?"

Celestia nodded. "Yes."

The goddess. It had to be. I wondered why she'd taken my blanket. Why she was stalking me. Did Celestia know?

"Okay, forget about her," I said.

Raine didn't mask her surprise and traded glances with Torin. Echo wore an unreadable expression. Celestia was busy whispering something to Eirik. Then she rested her head against Eirik's chest while he rubbed his cheek against the side of her head. They looked so cute together the green monster reared its ugly head again inside me. That had been Echo and me a week ago.

"I want to know how I met you, Hayden, and the redhead. So someone needs to start talking," I said.

"The redhead is Trudy," Celestia said.

"Wait? You know who took your blanket, don't you? Both of you." Raine pointed at me, then Celestia. Smart girl. I could never hide anything from her.

"No, I don't," Celestia said quickly and shook her head. "The energy is familiar, but I couldn't see anything under the cloak."

Oh, she knew. I bet she'd recognized the goddess. Probably known all along. I wondered why she didn't want to admit it. I followed her lead.

"I don't, but I'm not going to stress about it," I said. "Blanket or no blanket, I believe everything Eirik told me. If the person hopes to stop me from going to Helheim, they are in for a huge surprise because I plan to go." Raine still looked suspicious, but I was done worrying about the goddess' motives. "Okay, Eirik. Talk."

"It started with Torin," Eirik said, and Raine who was getting comfortable in her man's arms turned her head and looked at him. "I stopped by his place and found him in a shitty mood because he had to surprise Raine with a wedding and Cora couldn't be there," Eirik continued. "He knew Raine would not go for it and would always feel guilty if her best friend didn't stand by her side."

I hadn't expected this. From Raine's expression, she hadn't either.

"Torin suggested Cora should attend the wedding then hide in

Helheim with Echo until the Norns learned Raine was bonded with Torin and beyond their reach. Mother would have known the second she appeared in the realm."

Celestia nudged him and whispered, "The story."

"I'm getting there, love," he whispered back before adding in a louder voice, "So I went to Celestia and suggested that she, Hayden, and Trudy get dressed, stop by Kayville High to pick up Cora, and take her to the wedding."

"What?" I asked, my eyes flying from Eirik to Celestia to Raine, who was also sitting up in shock.

Eirik grinned at our reaction. "Look at their faces. Man, I wish I had brought my camera. Priceless. Celestia was at school, but since she's such a sweetheart and crazy about me"—she rolled her eyes—"she agreed to help. She and Hayden left school, picked up Trudy, who was already at her house, and opened a portal to a certain Kayville High bathroom. Hayden and Trudy are amazing at mind control, so..." He kissed Celestia's temple. "Your turn."

"The girls did their mind control on the students and your attendance lady, who paged you, Cora. You were convinced we were Norns and refused to come with us. Trudy wanted to zap you. She gets very impatient. I told you everything I knew about you from Eirik, but you kept saying the Norns would know all that. I think Hayden was contemplating getting inside your head and forcing you to come with us when I dropped the magic word. Raine. I told you Raine was getting married and she needed you."

"I was there?" I asked, my voice squeaking.

"She was there?" Raine asked at the same time.

"Yes. You were there." Celestia glanced at Raine. "And she cried the entire time."

This was confusing. "Why can't I remember anything except the flashes of memories I've been getting? Who messed with my memories?"

"Hayden and Trudy suppressed them, but they can be retrieved," Celestia explained. "You watched her walk down the steps to the foyer and took pictures with Raine and her parents. I met Dev that day, too. Raine's father wasn't going to make it down the aisle on his own, so you released Dev from your phone and asked him to help Mr. Cooper. He possessed him and anchored his soul all the way to the altar."

I didn't realize I was crying until Raine hugged me. She was crying, too. Memories of moments we'd been there for each other flashed through my head, starting with the awkward hug Raine had given me in the girls' bathroom when we'd first met.

"Thank you," Raine whispered. "For being the best friend in the world. I wanted you by my side, but I was so scared for you. I kept thinking the Norns might go after you if you supported my deception, and I wouldn't be around to stop them from hurting you. But you were there, and without you, Dad would not have fulfilled his promise."

"I can now stop threatening not to invite you to my wedding." We laughed. "And we have a new sister to thank for making everything possible." She knew exactly who I meant. We went to Celestia and gave her a hug.

"Thank you, Sis," I whispered.

"Welcome to the family. I'm claiming you, too," Raine said.

The guys watched us with such smugness I had to ask, "When did Echo learn about it?" He and Eirik exchanged glances. "What?"

"Do you want to tell her?" Eirik asked.

Echo shook his head. "No, you do it."

"The day of the wedding, he heard you weren't there and was ready to fight me for excluding you, so I told him the truth," Eirik explained. "I made him swear not to tell you until it was safe."

Echo and I swore never to keep secrets from each other, but this time, I forgave him. As though he knew I needed a hug, he left his position by my dresser and walked to where I stood. For a moment, our little disagreement was forgotten.

"Why didn't I see Cora?" Raine asked. "Did you mess with my memories, too?"

Celestia chuckled. "No. Cora used my invisibility cloak the entire time she was there. It was a gift from the goddess for putting up with her difficult son."

"You love me, woman," Eirik told her.

I got comfortable in Echo's arms, my annoyance with him pushed aside. "When do I get back my memories, Celestia? I want to know everything."

"We need Hayden and Trudy to retrieve them. They work better together. You walked with Raine and her father all the way to the altar and stayed there while the vows were exchanged. You witnessed everything."

I was tearing up again and laughing.

"We have a couple of pictures with you, too," Eirik added.

"Really? How?"

"You lowered the hood of the cloak at hyper speed, and Celestia took pictures."

She chuckled. "I was so scared Raine had seen you when you did that. But Mr. Cooper knew because in one of the pictures, I caught him looking directly at you. We'll show you the pictures when you come to Helheim."

Was I ready to meet my biological parents? What if they were disappointed in me? Maybe I should ease in slowly. Go on Friday after school, spend a few hours with them, then come back to my safety zone—the farm. Next time, stay overnight. If we didn't click, I'd only visit when something big was happening.

"Will Hayden be there?" I asked.

"I'll make sure she's there," Celestia promised.

Raine yawned, and Torin suggested they head home. She didn't argue. They were on England time, so I knew she was exhausted. She made me promise to let her know once I figured out the identity of the hooded kleptomaniac and when I planned to visit Helheim. I nodded and made promises I had no intention of keeping. She'd been there for me on numerous occasions. I wasn't dragging her to Helheim until I knew the situation there.

The portal closed behind them, and I turned to find Celestia and Eirik standing. Echo was stretched out on my bed with his hands behind his head as though he wasn't leaving. I just shook my head.

"You're leaving, too?" I asked Eirik and Celestia.

"Yes, I'm feeling a little tired, but before we go, we have some news." Celestia glanced at Eirik. "Can I tell her?"

"I'm starting to think it's not such a good idea," he grumbled. "You look tired."

She punched him. "I'm not. Besides, you suggested it, you big oaf. He deserves a second chance, you said. Without him, Mr. Cooper would not have given Raine away and Cora would not have known about Maliina and the attack by the dark souls. You didn't just say it once. You said it three—"

"Okay, fine," Eirik mumbled and covered her mouth. "She talks too much."

Celestia pushed his hand away and smacked him on the chest. "Watch it, jackass."

He winked at her. "I love you, Dimples."

She made a face.

"Are you talking about Dev?" I asked, interrupting their little spat.

"Yes," Eirik said. "But Celestia must stop after forty-eight hours. Goddess Eir's orders. Nod if you agree."

Celestia glowered.

"Baldurson," Echo called out. "I'd like some time alone with my girl, so let the Little Druidess explain and leave."

Eirik studied Echo. "You looking for a fight?"

"No. I want to be alone with Cora."

"I hope she makes you grovel." Eirik released Celestia. "I hate anything that puts your life in danger, Dimples."

"I know, but I promise I'll be careful and do exactly as Goddess Eir showed me." She waited until he nodded before focusing on me. "I can manipulate my life force and anchor a soul to a body. I did it for Hayden's mother, and I can do it for Dev. We just need his soul and his body in one place, and time so I can give him some of my life force."

My jaw dropped. "You can?"

Celestia nodded. "Yes."

"Ohmigod, Echo mentioned it and said he's never met anyone who could do it." Our eyes met. "You knew all along she could."

He sat up. "Eirik beat me to it. I was going to ask them, but it's such a sacrifice I wasn't sure she'd do it."

"She must take her time so she doesn't hurt herself," Eirik cut in. "She gave Tammy too much and ended up in a coma for weeks."

Shock and awe washed over me as I stared at Celestia. "Yet you are willing to do this for Dev, a stranger?"

"I see it as doing it for you and Raine. Don't be fooled by Eirik's scowling either. He also thinks Dev has done so much for you guys and deserves this."

I could feel the waterworks threatening again. This was even better than the first news. I'd understood Raine's reason for shielding me against the Norns. It had come from the heart. But Dev was special.

"This could really happen," I whispered, glancing at Echo. He'd left the bed and was by my side.

"Yes. You saw Hayden's mother," he said. "She looks healthy and normal. Celestia can give Dev the same chance." He glanced at her with gratitude. "Whatever reason you give doesn't explain your selflessness and generosity. *O m 'anam, tha mi' toirt taing dhut,*" he added in Gaelic. I understood that. He'd started teaching me the language. "My brothers and I will owe you a debt that can never be repaid."

"Dev will be linked to me when I'm done," Celestia said. "I hope he won't mind."

I laughed. "He won't care as long as he's whole again."

"I'll have Rhys bring his body to our place in Miami," Echo said.

I hugged Celestia, squeezing her tightly until she laughed and wiggled. I waited for the portal to close before turning to Echo. Even though I was mad at him for his stupid suggestion to hide our relationship, I loved him.

"Let's find Dev and give him the news," I said.

# GODDESS

## CHAPTER 7. MY PARENTS AND THE PAST

"No, we need to talk. Just the two of us." He reached for me, but I engaged speed runes and evaded his hands. By the time he caught on, I was on the other side of the bed.

"We are going to find Dev," I insisted.

"It doesn't matter whether we tell him today or tomorrow. Celestia is not performing the ceremony tonight." He walked to the bed and extended a hand toward me. "Come with me. We'll get some food and talk about the future."

"Which future is that? The one where we pretend we don't know each other? For how long? What if the goddess says I'm too high up the social ladder for her favorite reaper? What then, Grimnir?"

He groaned. "Hel's Mist, you are stubborn."

"That's funny coming from you. You know exactly how I feel, so no matter what you say, I won't change my mind. You are either all in or not. As for dinner, I'm eating with my parents here on the farm and you are not invited."

He laughed, and for a beat I just stared at him, my insides melting. He was such a beautiful man. The next second, he'd engaged his speed runes. I did too, but I was too late. My heartbeat spiked as he looped one arm around my waist and gripped the back of my head with the other. His eyes dropped to my lips.

"I told you there were things I'm still better at than you," he whispered.

"Like what?" I challenged, and flames leaped into his eyes, making them glow.

"Like this." I expected a possessive kiss, but he pulled a full seduction, taking his time and savoring my response. I was still mad at him, but he knew what I loved. When he lifted me and lowered me onto the bed, I was surprised. I'd been sure he'd head for the portal.

He settled beside me, still giving me slow, sweet kisses, his hand running down the side of my body until it closed on my knee. He lifted my leg aside and settled in the space. I loved the weight and the feel of him. He lifted his head and studied me.

"You ran away from me," he said.

"So? You were being a douche. In fact, every time you open your mouth, you piss me off. Can we just kiss and not talk?" I leaned up and captured his lips. He laughed but stopped when I nipped his lower lip.

Our fight was forgotten as I slipped a hand under his shirt and caressed his skin. I sighed with pleasure at the rippling muscles, the solid feel of his pecs. I moved my fingers to his chest, loving the way his body responded to my touch.

He rolled over and pulled me on top, breaking off the kiss in the process. I liked to be on top. He nibbled his way along my jaw to my neck. When he reached my shoulder, he took a nip and stopped.

I glanced at him. "You okay?"

"Yes, but we have an audience and I'm not in the mood to be nice to them, so I'll let you deal with them."

I glanced over my shoulder at the soul peering at us through the window. She must have died in her twenties and at some club because she was wearing a tube top that left her mid-section bare and dark hair framed a heavily madeup face. Souls knew better than to come this close to my house.

I scooted off the bed and walked to the window. "No. You can't come inside."

She nodded and beckoned me. I glanced at Echo. "She wants something."

"Tell her to get lost. I need you more."

"I'll be back before you know it." I stepped back and reached for my shoe.

Echo sighed.

"You don't have to come. I just want to know what she wants."

He snickered and watched me with a long-suffering expression. "If only I could believe that. One will become two, then three."

Despite his annoyance, I knew he respected what I did too much to dismiss it. Before, he would have pulled out his scythe and used the glow from the runes to dissipate the souls.

"Is that why you send Syn to my school during my lunch sessions? I've noticed he tends to be overly protective. Usually, he starts to scowl by my fifth soul. A few times, I've caught him glaring at them."

"I have no idea what you are talking about. Where exactly did he and Andris disappear to last week? He was very vague about it."

"A pack of bullies from a private school needed to be taught a lesson." I grabbed a journal and a pen, then started for the door. He followed. "Jenny needed closure."

Echo snagged my wrist and pulled me to his side. "You're asking my people to become vigilantes?"

"Nope. They decided on their own. I even warned them to be careful. Besides, Andris is not a Grimnir."

"Thank the gods. But you have Grimnirs and Valakyries working together now. That's never happened since the beginning of this world."

"About time. When all is said and done, you are all reapers, regardless of the final destination of the souls. If Raine were around, she and I would have handled the bullies. We've discussed pooling our resources. She helps the living while I help the dead, but our fields are starting to cross." Dad looked up when we reached downstairs.

"You're not leaving, are you?" he asked.

"No, a few lost souls need my help outside," I said. It felt nice to say that instead of pretending the pen and paper in my hands were for homework.

"Dinner will be ready in an hour, so don't let them detain you for too long," Mom called from the kitchen. "Echo, make sure she doesn't overdo it."

Echo grinned. "Always, ma'am. If that's an invitation to join you for dinner, I accept."

Mom grinned. "You are always welcome here."

"Thank you, Mrs. Jemison. I have an open invitation," Echo

whispered, and I shot him a wide smile for the sake of my parents, who were watching us. I pushed open the door and dragged him outside, then pulled my hand free from his grip.

"Don't get too comfortable. When we start pretending for real, the farm will be off-limits to you."

"You know you can't resist me," he said. When he reached for my hand, I engaged my runes and took off. His laughter followed me.

The woman was by the apple trees, but as I got closer, more souls appeared. I settled on a bench while Echo leaned against an apple tree. The trees were in full bloom, white and pink flowers on every branch. Spring was my favorite time of the year, but I stopped admiring the blossoms when the woman looked at me impatiently. Souls were always impatient. The second we bonded, her thoughts drifted to me.

*My name is Caridee Williams, and I'm here to pledge my support to you, young medium. We heard about the bounty hunters. We will not let them reap you.*

*Bounty hunters?*

*The ancient reapers,* she said impatiently. *The others said not to say anything, just stay around and be ready to fight and defend you, but I had to say something. Being naïve got me killed, so I don't want you to die just because you are too trusting.*

I smiled. *That's so sweet of you, Caridee, but they were not here to reap me.*

*Yes, they are. They pretend to be nice, but when you let your guard down, they pounce and you find yourself tethered to them. Then there's the other one. The one no one can see, but we've felt its presence at your school and here at the farm. It was even inside your room. You see all these friends of mine?* She waved at the souls surrounding us. Quite a few of them were dressed like her. *They're not going to let anyone hurt you or take you away.*

I was touched. *Thank you for watching over me, but I don't want you guys to fight anyone on my behalf. The ancients had a message for me, but they're gone now. As for the second presence you can't see, she is a friend.*

*What kind of friend hides?*

A snooping mother. *A special one, but I'm happy you guys are watching over me. So what can I do for you?*

*I want the same justice you got Jenny before I can leave with a reaper.*

I wrote down everything she wanted. When she eased out of me, she stopped to say something to the next several souls before taking off.

*You are not alone, Medium,* the next one said.

*Thank you.*

For the next hour, I heard the same reassuring words before each and every soul shared their problem.

"That was strange," I said once we ended the session. Echo pushed away from the tree and came toward the bench, where I still sat. I explained what had happened, and he grinned.

"That's because they love you." He took the book and flipped through it, groaning every few minutes.

"What?"

"They all want to see justice served before being reaped," he grumbled.

I grinned. "Sorry."

"No, you're not. I'll pass this around to the others. This one belongs in Asgard," he added, pointing at a page. "And this one, too."

"Swing by the mansion and give them to Andris."

"Do I have to? Svana could reap them."

"Andris gets equal share. Besides, you two should bury the hatchet if you plan to continue working with me to help souls find closure."

Mom appeared on the patio. "Dinner is ready."

"About what we discussed earlier," Echo started.

"We didn't discuss anything. You decided what we should do, and I'm supposed to go along with it. So unless you plan to *discuss* it with me and listen to my opinions and take them into consideration, I'm not interested." When he didn't speak, I got up and went into the house. He followed without saying a word.

Mom studied us with a frown as we settled around the table. I didn't know what her gift was before she switched to runic magic, but I wouldn't be surprised if it was mind reading. She always knew things before I said them. She and Dad talked about Immortal families in the valley during dinner.

"The Tolberts arrived here after we did."

"The Tolberts are Immortal? Does that mean Jaeden and Nate were orphans?"

Dad chuckled at my reaction. "Yes."

The two were juniors in college now, but in high school, one had played football while the other had swum. Their family owned one of the largest vineyards in Kayville, their land bordering ours. "Do they know who they are?"

"They both chose to use runes. It is a choice most Immortals give the orphans. Some parents tell them early, while others wait until they're eighteen. Some kids decide to start using some runes early."

"Didn't runes give the Tolberts unfair advantage in sports."

Dad nodded. "It would have. That's why they stopped participating in sports as soon as they chose to use runes. We have a strict code when it comes to runes."

"Any other Immortals I know of?" I asked.

My jaw dropped as they listed more people around town. Storeowners Mom did business with, local businessmen, more farmers with vineyards. Some were kids who'd gone to my school and left for college, while others were still students at Kayville High or the other local high schools.

"What percent of the town is Immortal?"

"About twenty percent?" Dad looked at Mom for affirmation.

"Close to thirty, dear," Mom said. "Whenever we reinvent ourselves, we tend to stay in touch, so if one person finds the perfect location, the others join them. Those who love the anonymity of urban areas move from city to city, while we rural folks move from small town to small town. We usually prefer struggling or dying towns, so we pour our resources into rebuilding them. We buy the farms and businesses, encourage growth, and boost local economy. We even donate money to fix the schools and offer scholarships to local students. Within a year of taking over a town, we are usually the majority. As the towns do better, more Mortals move back or come looking for jobs, marry, and have babies. Before you know it, we become the minority."

"Do they realize you never age?"

Mom chuckled. "We move on before they do and reinvent ourselves elsewhere. How long do you think we have here, dear?" She glanced at Dad.

My stomach dropped as my imagination went into overdrive. I imagined coming home from school to finding the farm empty.

"For those who don't age, another ten years," Dad said. "But for those like us, we can hang in here for a little bit longer. Maybe another twenty."

Good. I didn't want them to move. This was my home. "Don't you get tired of moving?"

Mom shook her head. "As long as we have a purpose, we don't. We've helped rebuild communities, countries, and civilizations from ravages of wars for centuries. Heck, some of us even fight for our chosen countries, but what we help with is reconstruction after the devastation. We try not to interfere or change the course of history, which is why you don't see any of our kind in the limelight. We keep to the background. Do you ever see your father go on a book tour?" He had the same picture in the dust jackets of all his books. It must have been taken thirty years ago.

I helped Mom clean up the kitchen and continued our conversation.

"So since you are ancient, does that mean we are rich?" I asked.

Mom chuckled. "We have enough to get by," she said. "When you live as long as we do, you tend to use several banks in several countries and move your money around according to the shift in political stability."

"So how come I get a puny allowance and do chores like wash dishes when we can afford a maid?" I asked, dead serious. I hated washing dishes. I was okay with picking apples or collecting eggs from the coop, but dishes were the bane of my existence.

Dad laughed. "I'll let your mother answer that."

"Washing dishes creates character."

My jaw dropped while Echo tried hard not to laugh. "You're so not funny."

Mom chuckled. "Appearance, sweetheart. We can anonymously give out scholarships to struggling students, but when it comes to how we live, we have to maintain appearances. How would it look if we send you off to expensive holidays and buy you designer clothes when your father and I are simple organic farmers and bakers of apple pies?"

"But Dad is a successful author," I whined. "No one will know I'm wearing a couture. I could say they're knockoffs." My parents laughed. Somehow, I didn't think they'd sympathize with my obsession with fashion. "Can I at least have an increase in my allowance?"

"You walk around with a priceless ring on your finger and you own a cottage before your eighteenth birthday. What more could you possibly want?" Mom asked.

I didn't know they knew Echo had put my name on the title deed of the cottage. I stopped pushing. Echo left to reap and pass on closure notes to Rhys and Nara while I went to bed. Dev still hadn't come back.

Echo crawled into my bed just before I fell asleep, and I didn't have the heart to kick him out. He was cold and needed me to warm him. Love had turned me into a total pushover. I wasn't feeling so charitable in the morning.

"Are we no longer pretending?"

He sighed and gave me the lost puppy look. I resisted.

"Maybe you shouldn't sleep over here anymore. I'm planning on going to Helheim next weekend, so we might as well get mentally ready for the separation."

"Okay."

I gawked at him. He wasn't even willing to fight for us? What was wrong with him? I picked up a pillow and hit him with it. He caught and gently placed it on my bed without showing any emotions. If he'd shown he was tortured about his decision, I would have forgiven him.

It wasn't until he left that I noticed my baby blanket had been returned.

~*~

I drove my Elantra since Echo had taken his SUV to the cottage the night before. I noticed the increased number of souls the second I stepped out of the house. There were even more in the school's parking lot. Obviously, reassuring them I wasn't in danger hadn't worked. Maybe Echo should talk to them.

Kicker met me by the entrance and yapped on about some TV program while I looked around and tried to find Immortal kids. Kenzie Sinclair and Caesar Alvarez were seniors and orphans according to Mom. Did they know about me? Maybe we should have a huge get-to-know-you party and invite every Immortal in town and their children.

I was happy when we reached our lockers and Kicker went to hers. I checked my phone, but Dev wasn't in it. The whole day I kept hoping he'd appear. The one time I needed to talk to him and he pulled a disappearing act.

Just before lunch, I got a text from Raine, so I joined her at the mansion for lunch and told her about the blanket. "I'm happy she returned it, but I don't like the idea that she can waltz in and out of my home whenever she likes."

"And despite the protection runes around the farm," Raine added. "She could be an evil Immortal."

"Maybe she's not, Cora," Lavania called out from the table, where she, Femi, and Ingrid were busy shoving letters in envelopes. They were sending out invitations to more potential teachers.

"What do you mean?" I asked.

"She could be your mother, the goddess. The Idun-Grimnirs probably told her about finding you, and she came to see if you actually are real," Lavania said.

"If I heard my daughter was alive and another had lied about being her, I'd want proof, too," Femi added. "The blanket was it."

"And she gave Celestia an invisibility cloak," Raine added. "Chances are she owns a special one, too."

I didn't comment on their conclusion even though I agreed with them. I wasn't ready to confess about my clairvoyance or accuse a mother I'd never met of stalking me. After all, she'd returned the blanket. Had she seen Echo asleep beside me? I hoped so.

"I hope you guys get to meet Celestia," I called out to the other women. "She is perfect for Eirik."

"I hope she comes to Mystic Academy," Raine said. "We could have some fun. Astral projecting to places. Driving the guys crazy."

"We should invite her and Hayden for a girls' night out," I suggested.

"And Trudy, too. They could retrieve your memories."

"Maybe after Celestia helps Dev, who is still MIA."

"Help Dev? How?"

I explained what Celestia planned to do while Raine stared at me with wide eyes. "We need to find him and give him the good news, but he's on a cleansing binge."

"I'll help look for him. Torin is working on his next recruit, so I'm free. I might drag Ingrid from academy stuff." She glanced over her shoulder at Ingrid, Femi, and Lavania. "She knows where reapers and Immortals hang out."

"Talking of Immortals, did you know the Tolberts are Immortals?" By the time I finished naming all the Immortals around town, we both agreed we should have a meet-and-greet. "The reapers can come, too. I'd have to drag Echo, though."

"Not Torin. He's all about recruits now. Mystic Academy is going to be a mining field for him. They'll have students from ages ten to twenty plus."

"How many classes?"

"Three for juniors: ages ten and eleven combined, twelve and thirteen, and fourteen and fifteen. Sixteen and up will be senior classes, and those will depend on levels, not age." She looked at her watch. "You better go unless you want to be late."

"I'm skipping first period after lunch. Ockleberry is still subbing for Mr. Holland."

Raine made a face. "He's still staring at girls' boobs?"

"Yep. I'm thinking of ways to make him squirm. I wish there were runes for that."

"The perv. I have an idea. I should come with you, stay invisible, and poke him every time he peeks at someone's cleavage."

"Poke him where?"

"His ass or nuts. Somewhere he'd be embarrassed to scratch."

Imagining Ockleberry twitching, I laughed. "You are evil. I was going to let Dev mess with him, but whatever. Let's have some fun."

We slipped into the room undetected and laughed while torturing Mr. Ockleberry. When he decided to stay behind his desk, Raine saluted me and left. I couldn't wait until we were at Mystic Academy together.

~*~

Echo was by my car after school and acted like everything was normal between us. I wanted to punch him in the nose. The problem was I loved his nose. Who was I kidding? I loved every inch of him.

"Rhys already brought the body to Miami. Have you heard from Dev?"

"No. I'm starting to worry. Raine promised to try to find him."

"I'll look for him after this." The drive home was awkward, a first for us. Even when he'd hounded me after our first meeting, he often made our drive to and from school fun. "About what I *suggested* yesterday," he said when we pulled up outside my house. "Do you want to discuss it?"

"Yes."

"What would you have us do?"

"Tell them we are together from the get-go."

"How? When?" he asked, and I almost forgot I loved him. He was bringing up unnecessary obstacles. "The first time they meet you, they won't care about who your best friend is or the identity of the person you are dating. They'll want to know about you, Cora, their long-lost daughter. Your likes and dislikes. They'll want to show you off to their friends, introduce you to their people. There's no room to steer the conversation to me."

He didn't know me very well if he thought I couldn't do that. "Sounds like you know exactly what they are going to do and how I'm going to behave."

"Damn it, Cora."

I engaged my speed runes and was out of the Elantra before he realized it. He caught up with me by the door but couldn't do anything because Mom came around the house with empty containers of pyrethrum, the organic pesticide she used on the farm, and he went to help her.

"Are you two fighting again?" Mom asked.

Surprised, I didn't respond. Echo also clammed up. Inside the house, I remembered a question I'd been meaning to ask since Echo came up with his stupid proposal.

"Mom, how did you and Dad meet? And did your parents approve of your relationship?"

Mom studied me then glanced at Echo. "Well, I don't know if I can say they approved." Dad snorted, and Mom threw him a quick glance. "Things were different then."

"Different how?"

"Who you married mattered. Class mattered."

Echo threw me a triumphant look.

"I met your father at a Winter Solstice festival in Kilkenny and recognized a kindred spirit. He had magic in him, and I felt it right away. He wrote beautiful poetry and was reading one of his poems sprinkled with Irish charm when he looked up and our eyes met. I'd never met a man like him before. His words touched my heart and made me dream of the impossible. Love. Adventures in far away lands."

My jaw dropped. I'd never heard Mom talk like that before. Dad chuckled and left his desk to join us.

"I thought my emaciated body was the reason you took pity on me and invited me home. They owned a farm, and she claimed they were short of hands. So I helped her father on the farm, and they gave me room and board."

"And at night, he played his fiddle and sang catchy tunes. He always added funny lines to popular tunes and made us laugh."

Ignoring Echo, I sat on the nearest stool. "Then you fell in love?"

"I did." Dad slid next to Mom and placed his arm around her shoulder. "I didn't know how your mother felt. She was very good at hiding her feelings then until she found out what her father had planned for her."

My eyes volleyed between their faces. "What?"

"Sit down, Son," Dad ordered Echo, who stood a few feet away, before looking at me. "I'll let your mother tell the story."

"No, honey, you are the one with the gift of gab," Mom said.

"Her father wanted her to marry Eoin, the only son of a neighboring farmer. A strapping lad with beefy arms and a mean right hook. I'd seen him leer at her at the marketplace. Whenever he came to the farm, I made sure I was close by. I wasn't letting your mother near the cad."

I laughed. "You took on a strapping lad with beefy arms and a mean hook?"

"Yes, he did. One day, Eoin cornered me at the marketplace and tried to force himself on me. Your father pulled him off me and socked him in the face."

I grinned. "How chivalrous. I hope you knocked him out."

"By the time the local butcher and his men came to help, I couldn't see your father's bloodied face and he couldn't breathe."

My jaw dropped. "What happened?"

"Eion was out cold on top of me," Dad said.

She patted his cheek and smiled. "But I couldn't pretend I didn't love him anymore. I went home and told my parents how I felt."

"So Dad won?"

"Yes, he did. With a rock."

Dad chuckled. "I remember it differently. I landed one punch because I caught Eoin by surprise. Then he turned on me. He would have broken every bone in my body if your mother hadn't intervened. She found the biggest stone her tiny hands could carry and hit Eoin on the head. It took me weeks to heal, but that boy was never the same."

"And what did your parents say when you told them how you felt?" I asked.

"They knew and had been wondering when we would stop hiding it. By the end of the year, we were married."

I looked at Echo and smiled. "Yep, you should have told them right off the bat that you loved each other."

"That's true," Mom said. "I think your father taking on a bully on my behalf helped his case. My father wasn't an easy man to please, and he didn't think your father was the right suitor for me. In those days, a man had to be able to protect his family and he thought your father was too much of a romantic, a dreamer, and not a fighter. Your father proved him wrong."

"Let me guess. They didn't know Mom hit the village bully with the rock. They thought you did, Dad."

"Yes, they did. I wanted to tell them the truth, but your mother flat out forbade it. We packed up and moved to America, and your mother remained the unsung hero of that incident."

"Hardly a hero," Mom insisted, but something in her voice told me differently.

It wasn't until later, after dinner when I got Mom alone, that I asked, "They knew you did it?"

She smiled and nodded. "My father told me I defended the man I loved when he needed me and that was how it was supposed to be. A family that stands up for each other survives. Then he warned me to never tell your father he knew the truth because his ego would have been hurt."

I sighed. "He was a very wise person."

"He was. Now why are you fighting with Echo?"

"It's stupid."

"I understand stupid," she said.

"No, you don't. Everything you do turns out right. How old were you when you married Dad?"

"Seventeen."

"Ha, you told me you got married when you were in your thirties. Uh, thirty-two."

Her grin became sheepish. "I couldn't very well tell you I was your age when we married and had barely turned fifteen when Eoin asked my father for my hand."

"Eew. I would have had him for a father." I shuddered while she chuckled. "When did you become Immortal?"

"At twenty-four. And I was twenty-four for a very long time." She gripped my chin and peered at me. "About your fight with Echo, remember what your grandfather said. A family that stands up for each other..."

"Survives," I finished.

"However, fighting each other only leads to heartache. Remember that."

My parents spent the rest of the evening talking about growing up in Ireland and their trip to America. Mom often gravitated toward farming because she grew up on a farm, and Dad gravitated to creative writing whenever they started a new life.

Echo was quiet most of the evening. Then he kissed me goodnight and disappeared. I had no idea where he went, whether he'd gone reaping or to find Dev. Wherever he was, I hoped he was thinking about my parents' story.

## CHAPTER 8. DEV'S RESURGENCE

I was on my way to my third hour on Friday when Dev appeared. He wore a broad grin on his face, and I saw why. He had shed his gray energy. Instead of going to class, I hurried to the nearest bathroom and ordered him to enter my phone.

"Where have you been?"

"Following a lead about the thing outside your school when not doing my purification."

"Forget about her. We found someone to anchor your soul to your body."

Silence followed.

"Dev?"

"The only way someone can help me is if they can manipulate people's life force. They must take another's to give it to me. I do not want someone else to die in order for me to live." He was so noble.

"What if she shares hers?"

"That gift is rare, and those with it never perform that ceremony unless it involves their loved ones."

Dev was loved. He just didn't know it.

"Then you haven't met Celestia. She's going to share her life force. She said it might take days and she'll need to rest in between sessions, but she offered to do it. She hoped you wouldn't mind that the two of you would be linked forever."

This time the silence was longer.

"Dev?"

A string of Gaelic was all I got. He sounded choked up. I grinned. Families who worked together freaking survived together, and he was part of mine.

He disappeared again until I was grabbing my things from my locker. Looking solemn, he floated through the wall and stood silently beside me. I lifted my phone and silently invited him to enter, but he shook his head. Instead, he walked beside me as I headed toward the front of the school.

"So how many Mortals did you help?" I asked.

He flashed his fingers several times.

"You lost me at twenty-five. You need to talk to me." A few students walking by stared at me strangely. My phone was back in my pocket. I pulled it out. "Please."

He indicated talking and tears. He was so melodramatic.

"You do know I won't see you cry through the phone."

He pressed his hands together, mouthed, "Thank you," and blew me a kiss.

"I have nothing to do with this. Eirik and Celestia came up with the idea because you're now a member of our family."

He palmed his face.

"Seriously, talk to me, Dev. And no you're not going to cry," I added when he peered at me. "Souls don't feel emotions," I teased, messing with him.

He dropped his hand and glared at me.

I grinned. Souls experienced a wide range of emotions. I'd seen them happy, sad, frustrated, vengeful, bitter, and pissed off.

"Why didn't you tell me about Raine's wedding and the part you played?"

He pretended to zip his lips and throw away the key.

"Who told you to keep it a secret?"

He pursed his lips in a silent whistle and looked at the ceiling. Students walked through him, a few shuddering and frowning at the sudden chill. I'd heard Dad use the expression, "Someone walked over my grave" whenever he felt a sudden chill. I'd bet souls were responsible for that.

"Okay, Charlie Chaplin. Keep your secrets." Dev did the Chaplin walk while I laughed. I was going to miss hanging out with him. He always cracked me up.

We reached the foyer, and I could see Echo waiting by my Elantra. I stopped by the window and studied him. I loved that man, but he was driving me crazy.

"Echo is being an ass," I said.

Dev slithered into my phone so fast I swear I felt a displacement of air. "Why?"

"Now you want to talk?"

"Anything that makes you unhappy concerns me. What did he do?"

"I'm planning on visiting Helheim, and he wants to hide our relationship from my biological parents."

"Why?"

"Thank you. That's the problem. Maybe you can talk some sense into him."

"I agree with you. He's an ass. The smarter move is to claim you before some god from another realm begs your mother for your hand in marriage. I've heard about Goddess Hel. No one likes her, so she could use you to form an alliance with other gods. Anything to stick it to Asgard."

I winced. "Do not judge her based on what people say, Dev. From what I've heard, she's changed. I know that sounds hypocritical, but I'm talking about what Eirik, Celestia, and even Hayden have said about her. If one person had said it, I would have been skeptical. But three people and Echo's loyalty says she must be an exceptional woman. So please, wait until you get to know her first."

"Yes, ma'am. May I say something?"

"Sure."

"Now that my knee-jerk reaction to be your champion has passed, I can say Echo is not an ass. He's doing this for you."

I opened my mouth to interrupt.

"No, hear me out, doll-face. Echo loves you so much he's willing to step back and give you room to grow. Going to see your other parents means being exposed to a different world with different rules. You are no longer the daughter of a farmer. You are a young goddess. Your grandparents are rulers of Asgard. Your mother is the one and only Goddess Hel. He's not scared of losing you. He knows you love him, and he loves you. He is giving you room to blossom and become the woman he's always known you'd become, but he'll be waiting for you to come back to him. Because at the end of the day, after you've traveled all over the realms and been shown off by your parents and grandparents, you know that no one could ever love you as selflessly and deeply as he does."

My eyes smarted. "Do you really think so?"

"I know so. He's my brother, and I've known him a lot longer than you have. The man would do anything for you, including standing aside so you can shine."

"Why couldn't he explain himself the way you just did?"

"Because I'm the poet, doll-face," he bragged. "Echo is the action man. He's more likely to kiss you than explain what he is feeling deep inside. Or attempt to explain it and make a mess of things. Believe me, he wants what's best for you."

"Maybe that was why he mentioned my age."

"There you go. You are on the verge of becoming a woman, and he wants that for you even though it's probably killing him right now. Heck, he might even be worried about it, but he's bottling it inside because this is about you, not him. Look at him already panicking because most students have left the building and you're not one of them."

Echo was staring at the school building with narrowed eyes, but he kept shifting.

"We better go before he goes full manic." I hurried to the door.

Echo had started toward the building but stopped when he saw me.

I studied the souls milling outside. "Could you tell them the presence they felt here and at the farm doesn't mean me any harm? I've told them, but they don't seem to listen. She even returned my blanket."

"I'll be back in a few." Dev slithered out of my phone.

I crossed the street and walked straight into Echo's arms. After what Dev had said, I was done giving Echo a hard time.

He lifted my chin. "I was beginning to worry."

"I was talking to Dev, but I'm here now." I went to my toes and kissed him, then turned my head to search for Dev. He was surrounded by souls. I had no idea how souls communicated with each other. Heck, I had no idea they could, but Dev was holding court.

"What is he doing?" Echo asked impatiently.

"Reassuring them I'm safe. That no mysterious figure wants to hurt me."

He winced, and I was sure he'd tell me not to joke about it. Instead, he cupped my face and kissed me but kept it brief. He'd been stingy with his kisses since I told him he couldn't sleep over. If it was his way of punishing me, he'd succeeded. I felt terrible, especially after what Dev had just told me.

"Did you know it was the goddess checking me out? She's the one who took my blanket." The surprise on his face wasn't feigned. "At least that's the consensus among the women in my life."

"Who?"

"Femi, Lavania, Ingrid, and Raine. They figured since the other girl pretended to be me, the goddess decided to check me out. It explains the souls inability to see her. She probably wore a cloak like the one she gifted Celestia, and I have a feeling Celestia knew it. She recognized her energy before she astral projected."

"Ask her when we get Dev to Miami. Before you ask the goddess," he added and opened the car door. "I don't want you two starting off on the wrong foot."

I hated seeing him so standoffish. I really hoped Dev was right. Not wanting to share the limelight with me was better than the alternative.

"I miss you," I said before he closed the door.

He frowned. "I'm here, sweetheart. Always."

"I miss sleeping in your arms."

He stroked my cheek and, for one brief moment, flames leaped in his eyes. Then he closed the door. By the time he walked to the driver's side, Dev was heading back and the souls were gone. He slid inside the car stereo.

"Thanks, Dev."

"Anything for you."

Instead of going to the farm, we drove to the cottage and opened a portal from there to Miami. Rhys and Nara were already waiting in the guest bedroom. There were two queen beds in the room, and Dev's body, dressed in a long white robe, was in the middle of one. Tall, masculine with defined jawline, and a shadow on his chin, he was beautiful. What was his eye color? He could rock any eye color. His light-brown wavy hair was shorter on the side, but longer at the top, his eyebrows delicately arched. His ridiculous thick and long eyelashes formed canopies on his cheekbones. Physically, I'd say he was almost as tall as Echo, but was a little on the slender side. He was barefoot and wore triskelion anklets similar to the talismans around his neck. They were similar to Echo's rings. The rings on his fingers and charms on his wrists also had druidic symbols. A set of artavo was on the nightstand.

He looked as though he was asleep, but his hand was cold to the touch. Since the others were seated on one side of the bed, I grabbed one of the empty chairs on the opposite side and placed my phone on the bed.

"Did you bring him?" Nara asked.

"I'm here," Dev said, sounding glum.

Everyone in the room looked worried. Was I the only optimist here? I was excited.

"Thank you for preserving my body, Brother," Dev continued. "When Echo told me, I couldn't believe you'd do such a thing."

"Why not? Remember our pact," Rhys said.

"In life and in death, brothers forever," Dev finished.

"And sister," Nara added.

"You joined us after the pact," Rhys reminded her.

"I know, but Echo said I was one of you."

"He made you an honorary brother," Dev said and chuckled. "You didn't have boobs then and looked like a boy."

"Thanks for the reminder, bonehead. Are you ready for this?"

"I'm waiting to meet her first. Celestia. What is she like?"

"I'll get them," Echo said. "Does he need more talismans and runic rings? I have some in that drawer. I bought them from a collector who didn't understand the value of what he had."

"We'll add more," Nara said.

Echo nodded and left. I stared after him. He was worried. I could feel it.

"Why does he need more?"

"Magical objects help our young healer channel her powers better," Dev explained.

I went back to studying Dev's body and partially listened to Nara, Rhys, and Dev discuss their past to cover their nervousness. They added charm bracelets around his ankles and chains around his neck. They were still at it when Echo came back with Celestia and Eirik. Eirik looked worried while Celestia looked tired. I hoped she hadn't been healing people in the other realms. The Druids created room for her, and Eirik hovered protectively behind her.

Her eyes went to my phone. "He's in there?"

I nodded. "He wanted to meet you first."

Dev slithered from the phone and moved closer to Celestia until they were only a few inches apart. She closed her eyes, and Dev did the same. It was as though they were speaking in a language none of us understood. Her eyelids lifted as did his.

"You have good energy, Dev," she said. "I'm happy to share with you some of my life force." Dev touched his chest and bowed, then blended with his body. Celestia moved closer to the bed and spread her hands above his body. Then she placed her left hand on the crown of his head and her right on his chest. I reached for Dev's hand and watched his face.

An hour later, Celestia stopped, her skin pale and her breathing heavy. "His soul is settled in, but not sealed. For his heart to beat, it must be sealed."

~*~

"He has a heartbeat," Nara whispered. I was curled up on Echo's lap on the other side of the bed and lifted my head. It was after midnight, and Echo was fast asleep.

Nara held a small mirror near Dev's nose and gave me a wobbly smile. Then she hurried out of the room. I was sure she was going to cry and didn't want anyone to see her. Nara might act like she was one of the guys, but from her expression, her feelings for Dev were deeper and more personal than the others. She and Rhys had chosen couches in the living room, and I could hear Rhys' snores.

I gripped Dev's hand and studied his face under the yellow light from the bedside lamp. Celestia had made it clear that if his heart didn't start to pump, he wouldn't make it. I kind of liked that she hadn't sugarcoated anything.

I glanced at the other bed, where she slept in Eirik's arms. I didn't wake her up to give her the good news. She needed her rest. Every time she'd shared her life force with Dev and grown pale and weak, guilt had chewed my insides. Part of me had wanted to tell her to stop. I was happy I hadn't. Now there was hope.

"Go back to sleep," Echo urged and tugged me against him. He tucked the blanket around us. "He'll be fine."

"Do you really think so?" I asked even though I knew he was in no position to guarantee anything. I just needed to know he believed in what we were doing.

"Yes," Echo said with such conviction I believed him. I reached for Dev's hand and sighed.

When Echo had marched into the room with a blanket and lifted me up, I'd protested, thinking he meant to carry me to bed. Instead, he'd sat with me on his lap and covered us with the blanket. It didn't matter that he was conflicted about what to do when I visited Helheim. He'd known I needed him. Sinking into his chest, I closed my eyes and fell asleep surrounded by his warmth.

The next day, I woke up to find him gone. I showered and changed, then went back to the other bedroom. I continued to keep vigil as Celestia worked, ate, rested, and worked some more. She was determined to help Dev. Eirik had even brought a pitcher of special apple juice just for her, pouring her some whenever she needed it.

Dev's body warmed up, but his temperature was below normal and his heartbeat stayed low. We covered him with a blanket to keep him warm, but that didn't help. Outside the bedroom, people visited to check on Celestia. She had some serious friends. Two Grimnirs—one cowboy and his Japanese reaper buddy—dropped by a few times as did Hayden, Jessica, and Trudy. I didn't get to talk to them, and they didn't interrupt Celestia. In fact, I doubted she noticed them. She was focused on Dev and when not with him, she ate and slept. Everyone was not just rooting for her to succeed. They were worried about her, too. That night I thought I heard Echo snarl, "Damn it, Dev. Fight to live. Celestia can't help you if you don't fight."

Sunday brought more people. Andris, Ingrid, Lavania, Femi, and Raine's mother, Svana. "Why didn't you tell Raine about this?" Svana asked.

"I didn't want to interrupt her honeymoon."

She dismissed my words with a flick of her hand.

"She'd want to be here for you and Dev." When she left, I knew she was going to tell Raine what was happening. People continued to stream in—the cowboy and his partner, Trudy and her blond friend. I supplied Celestia with juice and Eirik made sure she ate, but the process was taking a toll on her. By evening, despair hung in the air and tempers frayed.

"How is he doing?" Rhys asked Celestia.

"Leave her alone," Echo snarled from behind him, and I groaned. He needed to go reap or swim or something. Sleeping on the chair with me at night and being cooped up in the house was not helping his crazy mood.

"You're not the only one worried about him, so back off," Rhys shot back.

"The way you two are behaving, you'd think you hadn't cursed him out the last several centuries," Nara cut in.

Celestia sighed. I could tell their bickering was irritating her, but she was too exhausted to reprimand them. Eirik must have felt her frustration because he appeared. His eyes became slits, and scales covered his arms. He looked scary.

"Out or I'm ripping heads off. All of you. Yes, even you, Echo. Go outside and snap each other's necks for all I care. Just let Celestia work. You are messing with her concentration."

The three filed out, and Celestia smiled at Eirik. "Thank you."

She was still working when Torin and Raine arrived. Raine hurried to my side.

"How's he doing?" Raine asked. She sat on the arm of my chair and rubbed my back.

"Not so good. Celestia's been great, but he's still not waking up. He has more color in his cheeks, though."

"Yes, he does." Celestia placed a hand on his forehead.

"His skin is warmer, too," I said, squeezing his hand.

"I'll feed him a few more times. Then he should have enough life force to open his eyes," Celestia said. "His heartbeat is steady, and his soul is sealed in."

"Really?" I searched her face. She looked like she could faint at any second.

"Yes. I can feel it. I'll be right back." She staggered out of the room, where Eirik was waiting for her.

"She looks terrible," Raine whispered.

"I know. I feel bad because I know she's doing this for me."

"For Dev." Raine touched Dev's forehead. "If you want to lie down and rest, I can keep an eye on him."

"No. I'm okay." I wanted to be there when he opened his eyes. I knew it was only a matter of time. I could feel it.

Raine sighed. "Why didn't you tell me you were helping him this weekend? I would have been here with you."

"You are on your honeymoon, silly. I wouldn't want you to interrupt mine either."

She smiled. "I'm a portal away. If you are about to do something this big, get me."

She had a point. "Then you should know I'm going to Helheim

after this."

Her eyes widened. "Okay. Count me in."

I shook my head. "I'd love to have you there, but not this time. I want to do this on my own." Just like Echo had said. I needed to know my mother without others or my relationship with them coming into the equation.

Thoughts about Helheim became secondary as I inched closer to Dev. His breathing was shallow as though he was struggling for air. Suddenly, his skin grew clammy and pale.

"No, no, please. Don't die, Dev. Fight," I begged, gripping his hand. "Please. Celestia!" She rushed back with Eirik behind her. The others followed. I didn't realize I was crying until Echo put his arms around me. Raine went to Torin while Nara and Rhys stood at the foot of the bed.

I touched Dev's face. "He's getting cold. What's happening?"

Celestia touched his neck, checking his pulse, and frowned. "I don't know, but I think we might be losing him. The life force is leaving his body. It's like it is not holding anymore. Like he doesn't want to come back."

"But you can fix him, right? Please, Celestia. Help him." My voice caught on a sob, and Echo muttered a curse under his breath. Celestia looked at Eirik, but he shook his head.

"You are too weak already," he said. "You need to rest, *Stjärna mín*."

She gripped his hand. "One last time. I promise."

"But what if…?"

She silenced him with a kiss. "Then you'll catch me," she said, looking into his eyes, love and understanding passing between them. Then she turned around and moved closer to Dev. A worried Eirik stayed by her side.

"Now you listen to me carefully, Dev," Celestia said. "I have spent the last three days here with you, giving you my life force when I could have spent them with Eirik, so you better wake up because I'm not letting you go. Do you hear me? You and I are linked now, and anyone with my life force in them isn't a quitter. They're fighters. Tammy fought and won. Merle did. And you damn well better, or I swear I'm going to personally make sure Eirik drags your soul to Corpse Strand for a week before you're allowed in a Resting Hall."

I stared at her, hoping for a miracle. She placed her hands on his chest.

"And if you didn't already know," Celestia continued, "Cora hasn't left your side or slept in a bed since Friday. She's been holding your hand and urging you to wake up every night. She's fought so hard to help you, fought so you can be back with your Druid family, so now it's your turn to fight to live. Fight like you've never fought, Dev. Echo is here, too. He hasn't reaped in three days, and although I'm sure he won't admit he's worried about you, he is. He's driving me crazy with his grouchiness and constant pacing." She was weakening. Her lips lost color and her eyes glazed. She slurred her words as she continued. "Then there's Rhys…" I didn't hear what she said about Rhys because her voice grew weak. Slowly, she whispered, "Nara, tell him how you feel."

"I'm not going to cry over you, you insufferable, arrogant bastard," Nara said, tears swimming in her eyes. "You'd better fight and get up so I can knock you on your ass again. Don't think I've forgotten our last fight."

"He's warmer," I said, feeling his forehead and cheeks. "And his color is improving."

"Keep talking," Celestia urged.

"Come on, Dev," I said. "Fight. Students at Mystic Academy will need you in the fall."

"Damn it, Dev," Nara added, moving closer to the bed. "You are a fighter, so stop dragging your feet. I have souls to reap instead of cheering for you to reach the freaking finish line."

"I didn't keep your body in that tomb for a thousand years so you can quit, pal," Rhys added. "Fight!"

"Listen to me, you waste of space," Echo snarled. "I didn't want your sorry ass back anyway because of one thing and one thing only. I'd have to apologize to you, and I don't do apologies. Now I'm pissed off at the way you've made Cora cry. You want an apology? You got it. I'm sorry I overreacted and killed you. I was an ass and said terrible things before that and afterward. You and Rhys are my brothers. Always have been and always will be. And Nara, when she's not being a pain, could pass for my sister. Now, get your sorry ass back to them, or I swear I will keep your soul tethered to me for the next millennium for the tears Cora has shed over you."

Color returned to Dev's face, and his breathing became regular. I don't know how long it was before his eyes moved behind the closed lids, then fluttered open.

"You did it. You brought him back," I cried out. I touched Dev's cheek. "Dev. You are back. She brought you back."

He stared straight up and kept blinking as though he was trying to clear his vision. Slowly, he turned his head to look at me.

I stared into his gorgeous aquamarine eyes. "Hey, handsome."

He blinked, his eyes bright. His mouth opened and closed, but not a word came out. I was sure his voice was rusty from lack of use and his mouth too dry for speech.

"He's really back," Nara said in awe.

"She did it," Rhys said.

"How do you feel? You want to sit up?" I asked.

He nodded, and we helped him sit up, propping him against pillows.

"You still glow, *mon stór*," he whispered in a rough and rusty voice. I loved his beautiful Irish accent.

"I have no idea what that means, but I love it, Dev." I hugged him. His body was frail but solid. No more ghost body passing through me and filling me with a cold, creepy feeling. Then I noticed Eirik headed for the door with Celestia.

"Don't leave, Eirik. Dev, I want to introduce you to the person who brought you back. My amazing sister, Celestia. She's my, uh, brother Eirik's chosen mate." Eirik walked back to the bed and lowered Celestia so Dev could see her.

"Is she going to be okay?" Dev asked, talking haltingly.

"Yes. She needs to rest now and rejuvenate. Thank her later," Eirik said impatiently.

"Celestia," Dev whispered her name and pressed a kiss on her cheek. "Take a piece of my heart with you until we meet again, *mo mhuirnín*. I'm forever your humble servant."

"Damn," Eirik muttered as he moved away from the bed. "Another person you share a bond with and it has to be Mr. Suave. If he calls you darling again, I'll kill him."

"He didn't mean that," I reassured Dev, patting his arm. "I need to talk to him before he leaves. I'll be right back."

I hurried out of the room to find Eirik had already opened a portal. A cold draft filled the room, and Echo hurried forward to tuck a blanket around Celestia. They didn't see me, but I overheard Eirik say, "Fix whatever is broken between you and Cora, man. I don't want to be involved, so just take care of it."

Echo didn't like that. Eyes flashing, he disappeared into his bedroom. Eirik was already acting like my big brother, and I didn't know how I felt about that. He and I needed to set some boundaries. He started for the portal.

"Eirik, wait up," I called. I stopped beside them and studied Celestia. She looked really bad. I hoped she'd recover quickly. "I'm so sorry helping Dev did this to Celestia. I know I pushed her. Will she be okay?"

Eirik chuckled. "My Celestia is a lot tougher than she looks." He pressed a kiss on my forehead. "Besides, she knows I'd hound her in the astral plane if she disappeared for too long, and she has an army of goddesses who will be pissed if she doesn't wake up. I hope you heard that, *Stjärna mín*. I will contact the *Åsynjur Court* if you don't wake up in the next six hours."

I wanted what they had without my man worrying about my parents and what they'd say or do. Seeing the two of them renewed my hope.

"You really love her."

Eirik smiled. "With every breath in my body. Just like Echo loves you."

"I know." I sighed. "But sometimes it takes more than love." *It takes believing that everything will be okay, no matter what fate throws your way.* "Do you think they're ready to, uh, meet me?"

"Mom and Dad?" Eirik asked and grinned. "They were ready the moment I told them about you. No, the moment they learned you were still alive. They've been giving you space because I told them you needed it."

Space? Right. I didn't bother to correct him. Whatever doubts the goddess might have had about me, I hoped they were gone now. I didn't want to visit her while she had doubts about my identity.

"I'm ready to meet them." Having said it, I felt both relieved and apprehensive. "Will you and Celestia be there? I'll need the support."

"Of course, we'll be there, but you won't need us. They're pretty awesome as far as parents go." He looked down and frowned. "Okay, I need to take Celestia home now, but I'll be back for you."

"Thanks, Eirik. It's weird thinking of you as my brother, but it just seems right at the same time."

"I don't know. More weird than right," he said, laughter in his voice.

"Thanks, Celestia." I kissed her cheek. "I look forward to getting to know you. Later, Eirik."

I waited until the portal closed, then walked back to join the others. Echo, Torin, and Raine were by the doorway while Nara and Rhys were busy monopolizing Dev's time. I slipped my hand through Echo's, and he tugged me closer.

"Sip slowly," Nara said, giving Dev water through a straw. "You'll have to start with fluids and work up to pureed foods."

"Disgusting," Rhys said, making a face. I'd never seen him this playful. "She'll treat you like a baby if you let her. We need to hit a bar and party. Beer, burgers, and women. And not necessarily in that order."

"That's disgusting," Nara retorted.

"Where is he going to stay?" Torin asked.

Echo shrugged. "Here, though I won't be around to help him adjust."

"He could stay at the mansion in Kayville," Raine suggested. "He already knows Ingrid, Femi, and Lavania. Blaine could show him around, and Ingrid could take him shopping." She looked at me and cocked her eyebrow.

"I agree. He won't be lonely there." I glanced at Echo and caught him scowling at me. "You and the others can visit him whenever you like." That didn't seem to placate him. "Or not."

"I don't care where he stays. I'll make sure he has an account and a credit card," Echo said. He glanced at Torin. "Can Andris get him an ID?"

Torin chuckled. "He'll consider it a challenge. Country of origin?"

"Ireland. Our people moved there before they ran us out." Echo studied Dev and scowled harder. "He looks ridiculous in that gown. I'll get him some clothes." He left.

"Thank you for suggesting the mansion," I whispered to Raine. "It is much more convenient despite Mr. Grouch's attitude."

"What's wrong with him?"

"Nothing that a knock on his thick head wouldn't fix. I don't know how to convince him nothing has changed between us because of my biological parents."

"Oh, man," Raine said on a sigh while Torin chuckled. She glared at him. "It's not funny."

"Sorry, Freckles, but it's bloody hilarious. He has a dragon for a future brother-in-law. If he steps out of line, he gets barbecued. And he's in love with his boss's daughter. He steps out of line and it's Corpse Strand for a few hours."

I punched Torin's arm. "Stop being mean. Everything will be fine once we are in Helheim."

"When are you going?" Torin asked.

"Whenever. Depends on when Eirik comes for me."

"Do you want us there?" Torin asked. "We can postpone the honeymoon if you do."

I shook my head. "No, I need to do this on my own."

"Are you nervous?" Raine asked.

"Petrified, but I'll be okay," as long as Echo was by my side.

"If you need us, send for us," Raine said.

"Okay." I indicated Dev with a nod and whispered to Raine, "Did you see his eyes? He is going to be everyone's favorite teacher at the academy."

"I noticed. Aquamarine. Gorgeous," Raine glanced at Torin. "I love yours better."

He laughed.

I left them, and approached the bed. Rhys and Nara gave me room, and Dev took my hands. For a beat, we grinned at each other. I loved this man. I might have just discovered that Eirik was my biological brother, but Dev was my adopted brother. It didn't matter that he was about two millennia old. He'd always be my responsibility.

"You are coming back to Kayville with us to stay at the mansion with Lavania, Ingrid, and Blaine. You can discuss Mystic Academy to your heart's content."

He grinned.

"Ingrid?" Rhys asked and tried to keep his expression clear of emotions, but his eyes brightened.

"You two can visit him there anytime," I said.

"And you?" Dev asked, lacing our fingers.

"I'll be there every day." He grinned like I'd told him I'd be moving in. "The students are going to love you, Dev. You may have to walk around with a baseball bat to fend off the girls."

"Can I date them?"

"No-ooo," Rhys and Nara said in unison.

"Hundreds of years without a body and you still haven't changed," Echo muttered, entering the room with some of his clothes. "Feel free to use this place whenever you feel the urge to escape Kayville. Just stay out of my bedroom and my closet. These are loaners." He dropped the clothes on the bed and glanced at our joined hands, his eyes narrowing. "He doesn't need you to help him change, does he?" Then he walked out.

I stared after him and sighed. I wanted to hurl something at his head. The look on Dev's face said he was going to have a thing or two to say to his brother before the week was over.

"Moron," Rhys said.

"I second that." Nara looked at me. "If you want me to kick his ass for you, let me know. He doesn't like to hit girls, which puts him at a disadvantage."

It looked like battle lines were being drawn and Echo's people were on my side. I had to find a way to get them to his side. Not just these three. All his Druid family in Helheim, too.

## CHAPTER 9. A NEW REALM, A NEW LIFE

We took Dev to the mansion and made sure he was settled in Blaine's old room since the Immortal had taken Eirik's bigger unit. Echo went back to work while I headed home to pack and wait for Eirik.

I rummaged through my closet for anything I could wear in Helheim and found very little. Winters in Kayville were mild, so I didn't have heavy-duty outfits for extreme cold. I got online, ordered new winter clothes, and expedited the shipping.

Eirik didn't come for me that night. The next day came and went. I figured he was busy with Celestia, so I didn't complain. She might need a day or two to recover. I spent time at the mansion with Dev. He was eating well and resting well. We talked when I wasn't helping souls. When Eirik was a no-show on Tuesday, I tried to get answers from my moody boyfriend.

"I haven't seen him or Celestia since Sunday. I'll check with Maera."

I was brushing my teeth and wearing one of my silk lingerie, his favorite, but he refused to look at me. He leaned against the door, arms crossed and eyes on my shower curtain. There was nothing interesting about that damn curtain.

The second I started for the door, he stepped back, his focus shifting to the boxes piled in my closet. "Shopping?"

"For Helheim. Those arrived today. Want to see?" I kneeled on the floor and opened the first box. Inside were fur-lined boots. The heels were low, which was unusual for my footwear. I preferred high-heeled boots. I glanced up at Echo and caught his expression before he could hide it. "What is it?"

"I miss sleeping with you in my arms, too."

"Are you spending the night?"

"No, I can't out of respect to your parents. They know when I open a portal or when I'm in the house. I plan to continue coming through the front door or using the mirror downstairs."

"Okay," I said. That explained why he'd left after dinner the last three days and didn't return. I couldn't fault him for respecting my parents.

"I'll let you know what I find out about Eirik." He dropped a kiss on my forehead and headed downstairs.

I grabbed a robe and opened a portal to the foyer of the mansion. Voices came from the library upstairs, but I went straight to Dev's room and knocked. There was no answer. A door to my right opened, and Blaine stepped into the hallway.

"Hey, Blaine. Just checking on him before bed."

He sauntered toward me. "You just missed him." He joined me and opened the door. The lights were on, and Dev was fast asleep, covers flung to the side. He appeared agitated, tossing and turning.

"Is that normal?"

"Honestly? We don't know. Lavania and Ingrid have been keeping an eye on him, and Femi checks his aura and energy daily. He is healthy magically and physically, but he's tormented by something. I plan to start him on a workout regiment next week. Maybe that might help steady him." Dev turned again, almost falling off the bed, but Blaine engaged speed runes and was by his side in a fraction of a second. He pulled him back to the center of the bed without waking him. "This restlessness is new."

Wednesday, I snapped at Kicker at school and felt terrible afterward. When I stopped at the mansion, a pale Dev greeted me at the door. My stomach dropped when I saw his aquamarine eyes. They were clouded.

"What is it?" I asked, studying his face. "Are you in pain?"

"No, but something is terribly wrong with Celestia. At first I wasn't sure what I was feeling. I couldn't sleep, and when awake, I felt troubled and weak, so I tried to contact Tammy since Celestia brought her back, too, but their shop is closed. Celestia is in trouble."

I left my car at the mansion, opened a portal, and went in search of Echo. He wasn't in Miami or at the cottage. My parents picked up on my mood the second I entered the house, and they asked what was going on.

I explained who Dev was and how Celestia had helped him. "He told me she is not well. I need Echo to confirm it, but I can't find him—"

A portal opened, and he walked in, his eyes flying to me. Ignoring my parents, he closed the gap between us. "What is it? Are you okay?"

"Is Celestia okay?"

"I thought you were hurt or sick." He shook his head to clear it. "I tried talking to Maera, but I got nothing. They are getting ready for a grand celebration to celebrate your arrival. Sorry, it was supposed to be a surprise."

"I don't want a party." My voice shook. "You know how Dev has a connection with Celestia? He said something is terribly wrong. I need to know that she is okay."

"I'll be right back." Echo disappeared, leaving a blast of cold air behind.

I ran upstairs to change, then packed. I threw everything I'd bought into a suitcase. Some still had tags on. I added everything I believed I could possibly need, including hair products and an overnight makeup bag. I was almost done when Echo returned. The expression on his face had panic igniting in my core. I jumped to my feet.

"What is it?"

"Come here."

I shook my head. "No. Just tell me."

He closed the gap between us and pulled me into his arms. "Celestia hasn't recovered since Sunday. She slipped into a coma and hasn't come out of it."

Blood rushed from my head. If Echo weren't holding me, I would have keeled over. "This is my fault."

"No, it isn't."

"It is. They offered to help him because of me. If I hadn't helped Dev, he would not have helped Raine's father and Eirik would not have felt we owe him." Feeling a little sick, I wiggled out of his arms and went to my closet to grab my new winter coat. Eirik probably blamed me. "I'm coming with you."

Echo shook his head. "Cora—"

"I'm coming with you, Echo, or I'll find another Grimnir to take me." I stood taller and stared down at him from the tip of my nose. I knew I wasn't being fair to him, but I needed to see Celestia and be there for Eirik. There must be something I could do to help. "No one will dare refuse me once they know who I am."

Echo's eyebrows shot up. "Playing the daughter of the goddess card?"

"Yes, I am. I can't just stay here and do nothing. I want to help him take care of her. And please, don't tell Dev. He would be devastated."

Annoyance crossed Echo's face. I would deal with his groundless jealousy later. Right now, Celestia needed me.

"They're not ready for you, Cora."

"I don't care. I need to be there." I was the cause of their pain. I'd been looking forward to visiting, and now this. What if they didn't want to meet me now? I'd put Ceelstia's life in danger to help a friend. Tears rushed to my eyes.

"Hey. Don't cry," Echo said. "I'll take you."

I turned and went to get my things.

Echo's eyes volleyed between the suitcase and me. "How long are you planning on staying?"

"For as long as they need me. Why? You think I should bring more?"

"No," he said quickly. "If you need anything, I'll bring it."

I frowned. "You wouldn't know where to look."

"I know everything you've ever worn and how you organize your closet, Cora-mia. If it's new, I'll find it. I'm very observant when it comes to everything you do."

Gah, I loved this man. "Okay, you win. We'll bring only the suitcase."

He lifted it and removed his runic knife.

The portal was starting to form when I remembered my parents.

"Just a second."

I ran downstairs and found them talking in the kitchen.

"Celestia hasn't recovered since she helped Dev," I whispered, my throat closing. "It's my fault."

"Sweetheart, don't," Mom said, hugging me. I held on to her tightly.

"If she doesn't recover, I'll always blame myself."

"No," she said firmly and leaned back to peer into my face. "Look at me. Sometimes things happen beyond our control, okay? That's just life."

"But she wanted to give up, and I begged her not to. She used all her life force, and now she's in a coma."

"You will not do this to yourself, Cora." Mom hugged me again. "You tend to blame yourself for things beyond your control. Even as a child. You care about Dev and wanted him whole. I'm sure Celestia and Eirik don't believe it's your fault."

For one brief second, I wanted to stay in the comfort of her arms and push away the world, but I knew I couldn't. She was also not an enabler. She was the first to peel me away from her.

"Go. Celestia needs you. Your brother and mother need you."

"You are my mother," I mumbled a tad rebelliously.

"So I am, but I didn't carry you in my womb or nurse you for those first three days. She did. I didn't cover every figurine, mural, and mirror in the house every year for seventeen years to remember your birthday and the day you were taken from me. She did. I'm the mother letting you go because I love you so much and want to see you reach your full potential. You, my daughter, are meant to be much more than a medium, so I'm handing the torch to the goddess, the mother meant to guide you the rest of the way. She loved you even when she thought you were gone, and she'll love you even more now. Go to your other family. Dad and I are not going anywhere."

Tears raced down my face, but I felt a little better. Surely, the woman who'd mourned me for seventeen years would not be angry that I came home unexpectedly.

"I'm so sorry for the way I behaved when I found out about you and the adoption," I said.

"You were hurting," Mom said, cupping my face. "We are the ones who should apologize. We shouldn't have kept the truth from you."

"Or tried to block your abilities," Dad added.

I hugged them. "I love you guys so much. Always. I don't know when I'll be back."

"It's okay," Dad said.

"We'll take care of things at school," Mom added.

School had ceased to matter the second I heard about Celestia. Echo opened a portal, causing a chill to fill the air, and reached for my hand. His expression was hard to read. I'd always been able to figure him out, but lately, his mood was all over the place. Yet I needed his support now more than ever. I was about to close a chapter in my life and start another. I glanced back at my parents one last time. Then the portal closed behind us.

~*~

The room we entered was huge with crystals smooth as mirrors covering the walls and rough ones on the ceiling. It was a cave. I couldn't tell how big it was because it was wide and curved to our left and right.

Portals appeared on the walls as Grimnirs entered with souls. Some nodded at Echo, and others ignored him. But all studied me curiously. The souls looked sad and pale and followed the reapers as though tethered to them.

"Ready?" Echo asked.

"No." I had no idea what to expect.

He studied my face, then lowered my suitcase to the floor, cupped the back of my fur-lined hoodie covered head, and laid a brief kiss on me. "I love you, Cora-mia. No matter what happens after this, I'm yours."

"I know. And just so you know, I'm yours, too, so I expect you to rescue me from whatever situation I get myself into while here."

He chuckled. "I think you will rescue yourself while I cheer from the sideline." Then his smile disappeared. "But I have your back. Always."

"Okay. Now I'm ready." He gripped my hand firmly and led me to the exit of the cave.

The landscape was covered with snow. There were no visible trees or buildings, only mountains. If the sun was in the sky, the mist hid it. I took a deep breath and frowned. I really hoped this wasn't a mistake.

"You okay?" Echo asked.

"Yes. The magic here is strong."

"Very."

It was hard to describe. It was like waking up on the first day of summer and knowing school was out. I felt happy and relieved. Although why I should be happy or relieved boggled my mind. My reason for being here unannounced and unexpected was heartbreaking. If Celestia didn't recover, I'd never forgive myself. I wasn't sure what I could do to help. I just knew I needed to be here.

Grimnirs passed us with souls while others headed out. Some were in groups of twos while others moved as a group, talking and laughing. We got more nods and stares than smiles. It was obvious I wasn't a soul because they wore whatever they'd died in—hospital-issued gowns, robes, or regular clothes—while I wore a fur-lined coat, gloves, and boots.

"Do you know the other reapers?"

"Yes. Some have been around as long as I have, while others I trained."

The cold was crawling under my pants. Maybe I should have worn snow pants. I'd let fashion dictate my attire. My fur-lined white boots had heels, and my hooded coat was chic and cinched at the waist. Its gold buttons matched the long-sleeved wool sweater underneath it. I had layered the tops and worn a black silk shirt, but the cold in this realm crept everywhere. I should have gone for long-sleeved thermal underwear. Echo didn't appear bothered by the cold, but I'd warmed him often enough when he returned from reaping to know he felt it.

The sound of rushing water reached my ears before I saw the bridge. Echo had told me about the bridge and Modgie, the giant guarding it. I didn't see anyone when we approached it. The roof of the bridge appeared to be made of gold, and the river rushing under it had snakes and razor-sharp icicles visible from where we were. Anyone stupid enough to fall into it would die. Everything was like Echo had described it.

I moved closer to him and wrapped both my arms around his. The cold air stung my face, but I didn't dare warm it on his coat. It was frozen.

"You cold?" he asked.

"Freezing."

"I'll carry you as soon as we pass the gate. Modgie usually locks it." He peered ahead. "I'm not sure where she is. I didn't see her earlier either."

Below us was a boat moored on the banks of the river. Some Grimnirs were standing by the boat with souls.

"Those are damned souls heading to Corpse Strand. They're waiting for Trudy's father," Echo explained.

We stepped off the bridge, and something dark and huge loomed ahead. As we drew closer, I realized it was the gate. It was open, and no one was guarding it. That couldn't be a good sign.

"Do you think Celestia has gotten worse?" I asked.

"No. If she had, Eirik would be in the air destroying everything in his path." Echo scooped me up and went into hyper speed. I buried my face in his neck to block the biting wind. Going at a hyper speed didn't bother me anymore. The first time had been scary.

Just before we reached the building, something huge appeared as though spat by the air. Echo stopped and cursed as snow flew around us. When the flying flakes cleared, a giantess with wavy blond hair visible under her hat peered at us. Man, she was huge.

"Out of the way, Modgie," Echo snapped, not intimidated by her.

"That's not a soul you have there, Grimnir," she said in a deep, smooth voice. "You know the rules about bringing girlfriends to this realm, you rascal."

"This is Einmyria."

Modgie studied me as though trying to see past the hood covering my head. "I don't believe you."

"Damn it, Modgie. She is freezing. How will you explain that to the goddess?"

"It's okay," I said. I wiggled until Echo lowered me to the ground. I didn't dare remove the glove to shake the giant's hand because my fingers were frozen, but I looked up and smiled. "I'm Cora, but people here know me as Einmyria. You must be Trudy's sister, Modgud."

The giantess frowned and continued to peer at me. Then she put four fingers inside her mouth and let out a deafening whistle. The ground shook and icicles fell from the turrets. I knew what was coming and braced myself. Echo planted himself between the hound and me, but I didn't escape being showered by fresh snow. The hound wagged a tail as big as a tree branch, his breath steaming the air. He sniffed Echo, then licked him.

"What the...?" Echo muttered.

The hound moved his massive head and continued to sniff as though determined to find me. I shivered, cold and fear colliding inside me. He nudged Echo, knocking him sideways. I froze as four eyes stared at me and hot breath fanned my face. Then he did something strange. He lay down on the snow and made mewling noises, his tail slapping the snow.

"It's okay," Modgie said, stepping out of the way. "Garm can tell you are Einmyria."

"How?" Echo asked, not masking his annoyance.

"Her essence is similar to the goddess'."

"He's been unfriendly the past year, and now he's licking me." Echo put his arms around me and headed for the entrance. "Crazy hound."

"How long have you known Einmyria, Grimnir?" Modgud asked.

"None of your business, Modgie," Echo retorted.

Man, he didn't even try to be nice. "About a year, but he didn't know who I was," I said.

"You are the reason Garm's been growling at Echo whenever he returns from Midgard," Modgud called out. "The hound recognized your essence on him."

I didn't care why the hound had been mean to Echo. I wanted to get out of the cold and stop my man from making an enemy of everyone. Someone opened the front entrance of the hall, and Echo ushered me inside. He undid his coat and pulled me close, pressing my face on his chest. It was cute how he was trying to warm me. Usually, I was the one who warmed him. I turned my head to the side of his neck and sought the warmth there.

"Creed, find Maera," Echo ordered. "Tell her Einmyria is home."

I turned to see the person he was talking to, and my gaze met the guard, who stared at me with wide eyes. I was too cold to smile or speak. He bowed before a portal appeared, voices reaching me before it fully formed. He turned and hurried through it. The other guards lined up and bowed. I glanced at Echo, but he wasn't paying them any attention. Warming me was his focus. He removed his gloves and cupped my face. Usually, he wore fingerless gloves. Not this time. My cheeks tingled as circulation returned to them.

"The magic here doesn't use runes?" I asked.

"No. It responds to your thoughts," he said. "If you want to go somewhere, you visualize it, and the portal opens to that place."

Finding him was going to be easy. "Are you going to keep calling me Einmyria here?"

He studied me, a frown pulling his eyebrows down. "I'll call you whichever name you prefer, Cora-mia, but to the people of the hall, you are Einmyria. If you prefer Cora, that's okay, too."

"No, I'm okay with Einmyria." It was a beautiful name, and that way I could separate the person I was here from the one back at home.

The scent of freshly baked bread filled the air as the portal opened to reveal a pretty blond Dwarf. She stared at us, her hands clasped together on her bosom. Her chin started to tremble, and her eyes grew bright. I smiled tentatively, not sure whether I should say something.

"That's Maera," Echo whispered. "She took care of you as a baby, and was devastated when she thought you died."

Tears streamed down her face as other Dwarves appeared behind her. They gasped and smiled or turned to whisper to each other.

"Our baby is home," Maera whispered and walked through the portal, her arms stretched out. I went down on my knees and hugged her, fighting tears. I was a sympathetic crier. Behind her, the other Dwarves were either crying or fighting tears, too.

"She has the Golden One's hair," one of the Dwarves whispered.

"Her face. Look at her nose," another said excitedly.

"And her lips."

"They turn up the same way."

"She's the one."

Maera stepped back and wiped her eyes with the edge of her apron. "I'm sorry for breaking down, but it's a miracle to have you home." She glanced at the staff peering at us through the portal. "Of course, she's the one. Back to work everyone. The food will not cook itself. Astrid, come with me." One of the younger Dwarves with black hair and green eyes removed her apron and curtseyed when she joined us. Maera waited until the portal closed before saying, "Welcome home, young goddess. This is Astrid. She will be your maid. Any time you need anything, find her and she'll find me."

"Thank you. You are Trudy's mother."

"That's me, *dýrr mín.*" She turned to the guards and introduced them one by one. Each bowed before straightening up. I didn't catch their names. "Creed," she told the last guy. "Find Litr and bring him to me. Do not tell him Einmyria is home, or he will tell the Golden One. I want him and the goddess together when I give them the good news. Dagr, take the young goddess' suitcase to her chambers. Astrid, go with him and take care of the rest. The rest of you, don't say a word to anyone until I speak to the goddess." The entire time she spoke, her eyes didn't leave me and the smile didn't waver from her lips. "Will you excuse us, *dýrr mín?*" She waited until I nodded, then gave Echo a censuring glance. "Come with me, young man."

Echo followed her meekly. I had a feeling no one around here stood up to her. I couldn't help overhearing part of their conversation.

"Why didn't you warn us, you naughty boy? The Golden One wants a big welcome home party for Einmyria."

"She heard about Celestia and insisted on coming. Once Cora… Einmyria makes up her mind about something, there's no stopping her."

Maera chuckled. "Stubborn like her ma. Now I need to get everything ready for her. Her chambers, her…"

I tuned out their conversation and focused on my surroundings. The guards appeared to have doubled. Dressed in black pants, shirts, tabards, and cloaks, except for the green band around the sleeves of their shirts, they looked fierce. Most were taller than average, and none bothered to hide their interest as they stared at me. Weren't guards supposed to be stiff or at least pretend not to see people? These might not smile with their mouths, but their eyes said they were happy to see me.

Starting to sweat, I removed my gloves and shrugged off my coat. The room was interesting. It had giant black slate pillars with snakes, dragons, and wolves etched along the column. The top of the pillar continued to the ceiling, the details breathtaking. The floor was also made of black slate with shades of gray striations. The stained glass windows, depicting various battle scenes with men in armor, giants, wolves, snakes, and dragons were done in black and shades of gray, too. Because the windows were closed, beautiful sconces on the walls bathed the room with golden light. There was an understated elegance to the décor. Despite the lack of color, the place was warm and welcoming.

I stopped when I saw the throne. The seat was wide and black with snake carvings along the arms and the high back. Semicircular steps led to it. Several black cushions and pillows covered the seat. It could seat more than one person. To the right was a smaller chair that was not as elaborately decorated. Did Baldur share the throne with the goddess, or did he sit on the smaller chair?

I still didn't know what to call them. God and goddess seemed stiff and impersonal. Hel and Baldur were too presumptuous. And Mom and Dad were too personal. I already had those on Earth.

Maybe I should take my cues from Eirik. Poor Eirik. What he must be going through. I glanced back and realized I'd walked a lot farther than I'd thought. Echo and Maera were now talking to a male Dwarf with red hair and a bulbous nose. He grinned when our eyes met. The warm welcome from the staff made me feel a little less apprehensive. Were my parents going to be happy to see me, too?

I caught the eye of the nearest guard. I hoped they spoke English, too. "Where's Eirik?"

"The Shining Star's quarters are this way, young goddess," he said and pointed to a hallway.

"Can you take me to him, please?"

He bowed. "It would be my honor."

I followed him into a hallway with colorful murals and paintings of more battle scenes with giants, Dwarves, and Asgardians. I assumed the fighters with flowing robes were Elves. We reached the end of the hallway and entered a rotunda with huge marble statues and a gorgeous mural on the high ceiling. There were more guards in the room. Unlike the others, they wore green tabards and the inner lining of their cloaks was also green. They didn't smile, and the confusion on their faces when they saw me said they hadn't heard of my arrival. But something about me had them bowing.

"Don't bow, please."

"There you are," Echo said from behind me, and I turned. "We've been looking everywhere for you."

"The guard is taking me to Eirik. Is everything okay?"

"Maera wanted to know what you like to eat and drink, whether to put you in your parents' quarters"—he indicated the widest hallway off the rotunda—"or your personal quarters, which are not ready, or Eirik's." He indicated the second hallway. Both had guards.

"Yours," I said, and he scowled. Jeez, he needed to lighten up. "I don't care where I sleep, Echo."

"We need to wait for Maera and your parents in the Throne Hall."

"No. I want to see Celestia first," I said and started toward the hallway he'd indicated led to Eirik's quarters. The guards stepped aside and bowed, letting me pass.

"Damn it, Cora. Stop."

"We are already here, Echo. She would not be in a coma if it weren't for me. I don't care what anyone says. This happened because of Dev, and it's my fault."

"Tell them to let me pass," he said, and I glanced back to find the guards blocking his path. Echo looked thoroughly annoyed.

Surprised by the guards' actions, I walked back. "Let him through, please." The guards didn't hesitate. "Don't ever do that to him. He is with me." Confusion flashed in their eyes. Because of Echo's stupid stance, I couldn't tell them he was my boyfriend. "He is my personal bodyguard." They frowned. Bet that confused them even more. They were the guards while Echo was a Grimnir. Frustrated, I added, "Don't ever stop him when he comes looking for me, please."

"These quarters are private to your family. For security purposes, the guards have every right to stop anyone from entering them," Echo cut in before the guards could respond.

"I don't care. You get a free pass." I swept the guards' faces. "He is my…" *Soul mate. Love of my life. The other half of me who was refusing to claim me.* "Friend," I finished. Thoroughly annoyed I had to introduce him as a friend, I whipped around and marched to Eirik's quarters. The door was slightly open.

"Cora!"

"Don't! I hate that I can't claim you, so don't try to placate me with words. Allow me the right to be angry and frustrated with the situation." I glanced over my shoulder at him and wished I hadn't. There was so much frustration in his eyes I knew this wasn't easy for him either.

Sighing, I pushed the door open and entered a room with another beautifully done mural on its walls. There was something familiar about the landscape. On the other side was a sunset over the ocean, the waves and sand on the beach so detailed I expected the waves to actually sweep into the room.

An arched doorway led to a dining room, and the murals covered several doors, seamlessly blending them with the wall. I only realized they were doors when I noticed the knobs. One was partially open, and a voice filtered through it. Echo indicated it with a nod, and I headed that way. No one responded when I knocked, so I pushed it open. The room was huge, and ahead was a giant, canopy bed. Celestia lay in the middle, the covers pulled up to her neck.

She looked so fragile and just as pale as the last time I'd seen her. Guilt weighed heavily over my heart. Eirik sat on a chair by the bed, his eyes locked on her face. It was his voice I'd heard. He was still talking to her but stopped when he realized they were not alone and looked up. My chest squeezed, my guilt shooting through the roof. His eyes were glazed as though he was in pain, and he must not have shaved since Sunday because he had a scruffy beard.

"Cora? What are you doing here?" He sounded like crap, but at least he was coherent.

I moved closer. "I'm here to help. How is she doing?"

"The same. Was I supposed to pick you up, or did I already do it and just forgot?"

"It's okay. You are needed here." I touched his hair and immediately moved to his shoulder. His hair was greasy, and he smelled awful. When was the last time he'd bathed? I moved to the other side of the bed and felt Celestia's forehead. She was cool to the touch. Should they take her to the hospital? Was she getting enough fluids here?

"Eirik?"

"Father and Mother will be happy to see you," he mumbled without looking up. He went back to what he'd been doing—watching Celestia. "*Stjärna mín,*" he whispered, reaching out to touch her cheek. "Come back to me."

Listening to him was heartbreaking. I sat on the lounge on the other side of the bed and took Celestia's hand. I'd been around old and sickly people at the nursing home and could tell when someone was slipping away. Celestia was, and it was my fault. Her breathing was shallow and her heartbeat weak.

Echo slid beside me. Having him close steadied me, and I leaned against him. He rubbed my back, and for a moment, we stayed that way and listened to Eirik's pleas. Tears filled my eyes. Saving Dev did this. Had it been worth it? To lose a life to save another?

Then Echo stiffened.

"Einmyria," came from the doorway before I could find what caused his reaction. His arm dropped from my shoulder, and he jumped up. His reaction would have annoyed me if my focus weren't on the new arrival.

A blond man who could be in his mid-to-late forties stood in the doorway. Baldur. He was the spitting image of Eirik, except his hair. Eirik's was like Chex Mix, a blend of brown and blond. Baldur's was pure gold, like mine. I glanced at Echo. He nodded encouragingly. Swallowing, I stood on shaky legs.

"You can do this," Echo whispered. "I believe in you."

"Father?" I asked, not sure whether to hug him or curtsey.

Baldur laughed and opened his arms. "Yes, Einmyria. I'm your father. Come here, *elskr mín.*"

He met me halfway across the room. I closed my eyes and inhaled as we hugged. He smelled nice and was warm. I still wasn't sure how things worked in this realm, but he felt real. I'd inherited his hair color. Why had the Dwarves mentioned my face, nose, and mouth? They looked nothing like his.

I opened my eyes, and my gaze met hers.

The goddess.

My mother.

# CHAPTER 10. MOTHER

Half of her was covered with black runes, which zipped around. Her hair on that side was white and her eye black. Her other side was porcelain and flawless, and very much familiar. I recognized the arched eyebrow, pert nose, and even the slight upturned lips. I saw the same features whenever I looked in the mirror. Hers were more refined and defined, making me a pale copy of her, but I didn't care. I saw myself in her.

Her chin went up, the runes on her face moving faster. She was tall with a regal bearing, her green gown clinging to her curves. I had her body type, too. Hips, tiny waist, and some serious boobs. While Baldur had a presence that radiated warmth, she had an aura of cool, calm authority. She was the ruler of this realm and looked it. The scepter with a green crystal at the top and the black cloak all added to her presence.

"Go to her," Baldur whispered. "She needs to know you're not scared of her."

I wasn't. Echo had helped me take that first, difficult step toward embracing the new me, the daughter of a god. And now my father was asking me to take another. Claim my place as Goddess Hel's daughter. At least, that was how I saw it. With her, I had a feeling it was going to take a leap of faith. She could very well reject me if the blanket hadn't convinced her. Those shoulders, that regal bearing, and the way the cloak fell to the floor all said she was the woman in my vision.

I stepped away from Baldur and started toward her, expecting her to close the gap between us or meet me halfway. She didn't. She stayed on the exact spot, her hand gripping the scepter, eyes searching my face.

A girl already pretended to be me once, so she was probably being cautious. I glanced over my shoulder, and Baldur smiled. Eirik had inherited his personality. My eyes met Echo's. I saw the love in his eyes even though he was not ready to proclaim it to all the realms. Encouraged by it, I continued walking toward my biological mother.

I stopped an arm's length away and studied her, my heart racing. I knew it was up to me to break the silence, and I planned to do it my way. She could either laugh in my face, or accept me.

"For years, I'd stare at my reflection and wonder why I didn't look like my parents. I thought I was a changeling, a throwback to their parents or grandparents, except my hair. Mine is more golden than Mom's, but I chalked that up to old age. I insisted there were some similarities where there were none. Now I know why I look nothing like them."

"Why?" the goddess asked, her voice deep and commanding, nothing like Mom's.

"I inherited everything from you. Well, almost everything. I have your eyebrows," I said.

Hers shot up. "Really?"

Man, if I had zero confidence, that one question would have floored me. But I could hear my mother's voice telling me how the goddess had mourned me and loved me all these years. I was counting on that love even though my chest hurt and my stomach had a huge knot in it.

"Really," I said, lifting my chin, trying to imitate her regal bearing. I tapped the edges of my eyebrows. "I pluck the areas closer to my nose because I like to be flawless, but yours show me I should leave them alone."

Her lips twitched. "Anything else?"

"Our noses turn upward just a little." I grinned. "I think it's cute."

"Me too," she said, one blue eye twinkling, and if I wasn't mistaken, the runes on the other cheek were slowing down.

"I got your lips, too, though yours are more defined. Side by side, a blind person could tell I'm your daughter. You know, just in case you were thinking I'm an imposter. Although, I think the blanket must have removed whatever doubts you might have had."

Her lips twitched again.

"I've also been told I'm stubborn, opinionated, and driven. I hope

I can thank you or blame you for some of those."

Her blue eyes grew teary. "If I'd known you were alive, Einmyria, I would have done everything to find you and bring you home. I would have sent every reaper to scour Midgard the way I did with Eirik." A tear escaped and rolled down her cheek.

"Don't cry." Tears rushed to my eyes. "Please."

I wasn't sure who moved first, but I was finally in her arms. One hand pressed the back of my head to her chest as she hugged me close. My arms tightened around her. Something fell with a thud, and I knew she'd dropped her scepter.

"Welcome home, Daughter." Her voice shook. "To hold you in my arms again, feel your breath, and hear your heartbeat is more than I ever hoped for. Dreamed of. My baby is home."

And the dam broke. Mine.

It was a while before she leaned back and gently wiped the tears from my cheeks with a scented handkerchief, the gesture gentle.

"Look at you. You are everything I'd hoped for in a daughter. You are beautiful and poised, and yes, *elskr mín*, you get your stubbornness from me. Opinionated is just an impolite way of saying you refuse to be silenced because you have something important to say." She palmed my cheeks and pressed a kiss on my forehead. "As for being driven, that's something fostered. So you'll have to thank your parents in Midgard for that. I'd love to meet them and thank them for everything they've done for you."

She just called Mom and Dad my parents. The second surge of tears started. "They'd love that, too."

"We'll discuss it later. Right now, I want to look at you and know everything about you. It's okay to call you Einmyria or should I call you Cora?"

"Einmyria is perfect. It's a beautiful name."

"I chose it. It means ashes. How long can you stay?"

"For as long as you want me to." I glanced over my shoulder at where Eirik was keeping vigil. Baldur had joined him while Echo had disappeared. I focused on Eirik. "How's he doing?"

"Terribly. He's not eating or sleeping well. He hasn't exercised in days, and he needs to fly or he becomes impossible to deal with. Let me hold you one more time." She hugged me again. My eyes met Baldur, who watched us with a broad grin. When the goddess leaned back, she put an arm around my shoulder and lifted her hand. The scepter flew from the floor, returning to her.

"How did you do that?" I asked.

"Magic. I have so much to learn about you and to teach you. How did you know I took your baby blanket? You were not there when I visited." She led me to the dining room and pulled out a chair. She sat and indicated the adjacent one, watching me intently. "And when I returned it, you were fast asleep."

"I saw you in a vision," I said, maybe to make her proud of my ability or because I didn't want to hide anything from her. I was sure she knew about Echo and me anyway.

"You get visions?" She didn't hide the excitement in her voice.

"Just of you, the mysterious woman in a cloak. You were my first vision, so I can't say I get them. I know you were outside the school, too, even though I didn't see that in a vision, but the souls felt your presence and were drawn to you. They couldn't see you either."

"I hope you don't mind that I stalked you." She gripped my hands and studied my Druidic ring, but she didn't ask about it. "When Eirik sent the Idun-Grimnirs home and told them they'd scare you, they'd already visited the farm and your school. I left to find the blanket, and the next day I was outside the school when you arrived. I stayed and observed you in class. I thought it was my right for having missed every school play, recital, and softball game."

I laughed. "You didn't miss much. I was homeschooled, so no plays, recitals, or softball games, but like Eirik, I swam."

"I would have been on the stands with big signs, cheering you on. Are your parents proud of the young woman you've become?"

"I hope so."

"Hope so? They should be. I want to hear about your life. Everything you can remember. When did you start swimming? What's your favorite stroke?"

"Backstroke. I brought my laptop, and it has pictures and videos. I'm sorry I didn't come sooner."

She dismissed my words with a wave of her hand. "That's okay. Your father needed time anyway because he had big plans for your arrival. A homecoming party worthy of our daughter." A frown chased the smile away. "But Celestia needs us now."

I felt a little sick to my stomach and braced myself before saying, "I am responsible for her condition."

The goddess frowned. "Why do you say that?"

"She shared her life force with a friend of mine because of me. When she wanted to stop, I begged her to keep going. And now her life force is so low she's sunk into a coma. It's my fault."

"You're talking about Dev?"

"Yes. How did you know?"

"Celestia talked to me about him, and I thought it was a brave thing to do. But that should not have caused this problem. She is strong and powerful. Something else is stopping her from recovering. I need to figure out what it is." Concern furrowed her brow. "Not knowing is driving me crazy."

"Did she tell you that Dev was once a dark soul? He could have contaminated her energy."

The goddess shook her head. "From what I've been told, he redeemed himself by helping others, so her reaction has nothing to do with the fact that he was once a dark soul. I saw how he protected you outside your school when he felt my presence. All the souls are very protective of you." She peered at me. "Do not blame yourself, Einmyria. Celestia's situation is not your fault. I've seen her heal many people and recover, and I've called every healer in the realm, but they can't figure out what's wrong with her." Annoyance laced her words. "I just sent emissaries to Asgard to bring Eir today. We'll soon have answers."

The name was familiar. "Who is Eir?"

"The Goddess of Healing. She trained Celestia. I hope they realize how urgent the matter is. Asgardians tend to take their time when something doesn't involve war. They love to party or find a reason to celebrate." She shook her head. "I just want her awake. The hall always rings with laughter when she's around, which improves your brother's mood."

Love and frustration tinged her voice, and my guilt increased. Despite what she'd said, I knew it was my fault Celestia was in a coma. If only I hadn't accepted their offer. I should have said no. Stopped her when she'd become tired.

"What can I do to help?" I asked, desperate to do anything, however small.

"Not much, *dýrr mín*." Then a thoughtful expression crossed her face. "Unless you can convince your brother to eat."

"And shower," I added.

She chuckled. "Yes, he smells worse than Garm. He went flying a couple of days ago, and I doubt he showered afterward. I've tried everything. I've threatened. Scolded. Begged, but he just stares at me, then goes back to talking to her. It's breaking my heart."

And that was the woman everyone had told me about, not the one I'd read about. I had a feeling the face she'd shown me before the hugs and the tears was the one she showed the world. The face of a goddess, ruler of Helheim. The one who cried while she hugged me and was now begging me to help her son was the mother goddess. She really loved Eirik.

"I'll take care of him now."

"Good idea. Then we can sit down and talk." She stood, and I did, too. "You two have known each other for a long time?"

"Since elementary school," I said as we walked toward Eirik's bedroom. She took my arm as though she needed to be physically in contact with me to confirm I was really there. "Because my parents homeschooled me for years, I hated going to public school at first. Raine found me crying in the bathroom and took me under her wing." I glanced at the goddess. "I don't know if you know Raine."

"Svana and Tristan's daughter? Yes. I know about her friendship with Eirik and that the two of you are very close. I owe her family a lot for taking your brother in, and loving him."

"Raine is awesome. She introduced me to Eirik the same day during lunch." The main door opened, and Maera wheeled in a trolley with covered plates.

"Not yet, Maera. Take care of our guests first." She waited until Maera left before asking, "Have you met Celestia's family?"

"No, but I've met her best friend, Hayden, and Tammy. Are they here?"

"They arrived earlier. Richard—that's her father, her aunt, and her cousin are also here." She cupped my cheek and smiled. "I'm so happy you are home."

"Me too." Then I went on my toes despite the heels and kissed her runed cheek. I went to where Eirik sat and touched his shoulder. "Let me take over, Eirik."

"No. I need to be here when she wakes up."

"When she does, I'll call you."

"You don't understand," he snapped. "I have to be here. I want my face to be the first one she sees when she wakes up."

I leaned back to escape his stale breath. "So you want her to see you looking like a hobo when she wakes up? Or should I explain to you in detail what a girl finds unattractive in a man. Believe me, she won't think it's hot you are not eating or bathing. She'd be disgusted."

Eirik glared at me. "Celestia would never be disgusted by me."

"She's a girl, and I know how girls think. Believe me, a stinky, unshaven love of my life is not what I want to see when I wake up from a coma. I'd want my man to have his shit together and be ready to hold me and kiss me and tell me how much he's missed me, not blow stale breath in my face." I leaned back. "Not even a mint can save you, pal."

Frowning, he cupped his hand, blew in it, and sniffed. He made a face.

"See what I mean? That happens when you haven't brushed. The mouth has the most germs in your entire body. Dental hygiene 101.

Celestia will not want to smell that or kiss that when she wakes up. I don't feel her soul struggling to leave her body. She's just resting and building up the life force she gave up. Go. I'll watch over her."

"If she wakes up—"

"I'll get you. I promise."

He hesitated.

"I have strength runes, so if you are not done, I'll kick down the door and drag you out here, naked and wet. Since I have no interest in seeing you naked, you better hurry up."

He glowered. "Dang, I've forgotten how annoying you can be."

"You were just as annoying when you came to see me at the mansion, so call this payback. Go. You smell worse than dirty gym socks."

"I don't." He lifted his arm and sniffed his armpit. "Damn."

"Now imagine hugging Celestia."

"I'm going." His eyes went to Celestia and lingered. "You sure about her soul?"

"Yes, I am. Remember, they love me. If her soul wants to separate, I'd know." That wasn't really true, but he needed to hear it.

Sighing, he got up and disappeared through a door. My eyes met Baldur's across the bed. He smiled with approval. Sounds came from behind me, and I looked over my shoulder. The goddess was smiling, too. I hadn't realized she was still around.

"You have a way of talking to him that makes him listen," she said.

My cheeks warmed. I'd been unfeeling. "I know how guys at home think. Eirik has changed a lot, but in some ways he hasn't. I knew which buttons to push, and I'm afraid I wasn't nice about it."

"Is it true what you said about being able to see souls wanting to separate?" Baldur asked.

"Not really. Back at home, I'd see them once they started to separate, not before. I just wanted to reassure him."

"Well, I'm happy you did," he said and extended a hand toward the goddess. She joined him on the lounge and reached out to stroke Celestia's hand. "The poor sweetheart. I wish Eir could get here faster.

You think *he* is stopping her from leaving?" The way she said "he" told me she was referring to someone she thoroughly disliked.

"No, *elskr mín. Asynjur Court* is autonomous, and Alfadir would have no say on what the goddesses do," Baldur said. "On the other hand, it involves traveling here and they still fear you."

The goddess chuckled. "Then they are idiots. I've relaxed rules about visitors to my realm. All are welcome." Baldur laughed, and she threw him an annoyed look. "Eirik and Celestia visited them from here. Why wouldn't I be a gracious hostess?"

"Do you really want me to explain? They are terrified of you, *elskr mín.*" He lifted her hand to his lips. "Give them a few more days to gather courage."

She shook her head. "Like I said, they are idiots. If my emissaries are not back in a couple of days, I'm going to Asgard."

"I don't think that's a good idea, *dýrr mín,*" he said in a soothing tone.

"I think it's brilliant. A couple of days, Baldur, then I'm going. I will put up with their stares and distain to bring Celestia the help she needs."

"Of course, *dýrr,*" Baldur said and smiled.

"That's not going to work on me, so stop it," she whispered.

"I didn't do anything. I'm agreeing with you."

"That's what I'm concerned about."

The dynamics of their relationship were interesting. "How did you two meet? I mean, I know it was here. But how did you know you loved each other?"

Baldur chuckled while the goddess continued to stroke Celestia's hand. For a beat, I thought she wouldn't respond. Then she glanced at him. "Do you want to tell her?"

"No, you tell her." He kissed her on the lips. "I'm better at filling in the blanks."

She studied him with narrowed eyes. "Do you promise to behave and not sugarcoat anything?"

"Would I do that to you, my love?"

"Yes." She glanced at me. "He embellishes everything to make me look good. I wasn't. Not to him anyway. How much do you know about me?"

Watching them only made me want to learn more about how they met. "Everyone in Helheim loves you and is loyal to you because you are tough but just. You care about them and the souls you help. You grew up in Jötunheim, then went to Asgard before Odin gave you this realm to rule."

"She demanded a realm to rule because she deserved one, and Alfadir, your grandfather, gave her Helheim."

I looked at the goddess. "You demanded?"

"Asked. Like I said, your father embellishes things. When you feel you deserve something, you go for it and don't let anyone stop you or dissuade you. Things don't happen for those who wait or beg. What else do you know?"

"Your life in Asgard was not an easy one."

She grimaced. "It had its moments."

"Now you are being kind, *dýrr mín*," Baldur said. "I'm afraid some of my friends and family were very cruel to your mother as a child. No one, let alone a child, should ever be ridiculed for their looks. I was very annoyed and disappointed with their behavior."

The goddess chuckled. "He takes it very personal. The fact is being seen as different and treated a certain way is something I faced growing up. Some of the gods and goddesses were unkind, but I also found refuge with some. Frigg, your grandmother, for instance, is very compassionate. She would send for me for visits. Her hall is by a brook, and she has wild animals roaming her woods and meadows with flowers. I'd spend hours studying the birds and the animals. As I got older, she'd allow me to observe the proceeding in the *Ásynjur Court*."

"What's that? Father mentioned it before."

"The court of female goddesses. I learned a lot watching her, so when I overheard them discuss Helheim and how the god in charge no longer wanted the job and had disappeared, I knew exactly what to say to Odin to get this realm."

"That was before my father learned about the prophecy of what would happen during Ragnarok," Baldur chimed in. "He tried to change things, but Ragnarok is fated to happen. Once the Norns seal your fate, there's no changing it without consequences."

Raine had changed destinies, and so far, she was okay because she was supposed to be a Norn. What if Celestia's situation was the result of her changing Dev's destiny? I focused on what the goddess was saying, but my mind was racing with what could be wrong with Celestia. The Norns could be behind her condition.

"Your father is right. He had to die in order for you and Eirik to be born," the goddess said. "You both have an important role to play in the future."

"Like what?"

The goddess chuckled. "Your brother will be the next head of the *Æsir Court* in Asgard, and Celestia will head the *Ásynjur Court*. Now where were we? Yes, my relationship with your father."

She neatly avoided talking about me. Did that mean I had no future worth mentioning?

"I was running things here with my mother, who'd fueled my hatred for Asgardians for what they'd done to our family. When the reapers arrived from Asgard with Baldur, his wife Nanna, and Litr, I wanted payback." She glanced at Baldur and grimaced. "I was not very nice to you, *elskr mín*, was I?"

"You had every right to be angry and wanted revenge for the pain they'd caused you in Asgard," he said.

"It was more than that. There was this thing inside me I needed to ease, and I thought that having your father, Odin's favorite son, in my hall would do that. His wife just wanted to rest, so I sent her to an Eternal Resting Hall the moment they arrived, but I kept your father with me. When his brother came to plead for his return, I was more than happy to show him off."

"Her newly acquired pet," Baldur whispered.

She backhanded his chest. "Don't listen to him. He was never my pet, but I had him sit next to me on my throne as I told his brother

Asgard couldn't have him back because he belonged with me in Helheim." She sighed and glanced at him again. "I was horrible to you."

"Ah, but it was the beginning of our adventure," Baldur countered.

"You are being kind. You should have seen your father in Asgard, Einmyria. He was glorious."

"I'm still glorious," he countered, trying to look offended but failing miserably.

She smiled and continued to stroke Celestia's hand. "He was just. Kind. Charismatic. Envied by many and admired by all. Whenever I met him, he was always kind. I admired him greatly."

"Just admired?" he teased, and pink tinged the goddess' normal cheek while the runes on the other appeared to coil faster. "I think it was more than that."

"You had a crush on him?" I asked, grinning.

She scowled. "Explain this crush."

"Our daughter means you more than liked me, *dýrr mín*."

She sat upright and lifted her chin. "You were a married man and far older than I was."

"She had a *huge* crush on me." He whispered something in her ear, and she laughed softly, her eyes twinkling.

"Maybe a little," she conceded. "I admit I'd hide behind pillars and watch him. Everyone adored him."

"And now I adore your mother."

"That's because I wore you down. You had no choice but to love me."

He sighed melodramatically. "What a chore."

I laughed. Now I knew where Eirik got his wacky sense of humor. The goddess just shook her head, her eyes going to the bathroom door. The water had stopped running.

"Are you hungry?" she asked.

"A little, but I want to hear more of your story."

"Can you convince your brother to eat, too?"

"Oh, yes." I glanced at the closed bathroom door and hoped Eirik stayed a little longer and shaved. "So how did, uh, Mother wear you down?"

"She didn't. I wore her down. I reminded her every day she was a beautiful woman and I was devoted to her. She wanted me to talk to her while I wanted to kiss her, so I did both. And she rather liked it."

The goddess sighed. "You are impossible, Baldur."

"I'm telling our daughter the truth."

"She doesn't need to know every detail." She angled her head and said, "Yes, Maera. You can come in."

Sounds came from the living room. Then the housekeeper appeared in the doorway. She beamed. "Shall I set the table here or your quarters?"

"In here, and let me know when Einmyria's rooms are ready."

Maera left, and Baldur got to his feet. "I'll join you for dinner, but first I need to check on our guests. Don't forget to tell our daughter how hard you made me work to prove my love to you." He kissed her forehead and walked around the bed, dropping a kiss on my forehead and another on Celestia's. "Come back to us soon, little one."

The goddess watched him as he walked across the room. A sigh escaped her. "Your father is a wonderful man. I hope one day you meet someone like him."

I wanted to tell her I already had, but I held my tongue.

"Not once during those years did he complain about how I treated him. He didn't just take care of everything I asked of him, he made sure the guards did their duties, dressed properly, and learned court decorum. He ran drills for possible attacks, created a chain of command, and a duty schedule. I didn't ask him to do any of these things. My mother had trained the guards before he arrived here. She was an amazing strategist when it came to military attacks and counterattacks, but she didn't know anything about running a hall and dealing with visitors from other realms. Her solution was to attack anyone who entered our realm and ask questions later, and we did that for millennia. Baldur changed all that, and so the two of them didn't get along. It only grew worse with time. Maybe it was the fact that she hated him that caused me to seek his counsel more and more. The more time we spent together, the more he'd ask me personal questions about my past instead of discussing the realm. I kept telling him it was none of his business."

I laughed. "But he didn't stop?"

"No." She chuckled. "I think you might get your stubbornness from him, after all. Once he decides to pursue something, he never gives up. Ordering him to stop didn't work. Talking down to him didn't work either. Finally, I gave him a little information to test him. I told him terrible things about my childhood. Cruel stunts children played on me. He'd get angry. I even overheard him tell Litr he wanted to beat his uncles to a pulp for the things they'd said about my parents in my presence." She smiled while my heart broke for her. Tears rushed to my eyes. "I never realized how much pain I'd carried from those years until I saw things through your father's eyes. Oh, *dýrr mín*. Don't cry. This is all in the past."

"Doesn't make it right. I hate bullies, Mortal or gods. Only last week I had the Grimnirs punish the bullies who'd caused a girl's death.

The goddess smiled. "I want to hear the details of that story."

The sweet aroma of spices and freshly baked bread reached me before I heard sounds from the other room. Maera had arrived with dinner, and Eirik was still in the bathroom. My stomach growled, but I ignored it.

"When did you realize you loved him?"

"I think I always did. He is warm and kind, he makes me laugh, and there's nothing he can't accomplish when he sets his mind to it. Like you said, I had a crush on him as a child, but as a woman, I'd thought falling in love with him would only lead to heartache, so I fought it. I did what the others had done to me for millennia and judged him by his looks. I concluded that a god who looked like him would never see the real me, yet he did. He won me over with his love, kindness, and thoughtfulness."

Maera appeared in the doorway and announced that dinner was ready before bowing. The goddess stood up, and I followed. When she glanced at the bathroom door, I knew it was time.

"I'll get him." Eirik mumbled something when I knocked. "You okay in there? Do you want me to break down the door and rescue you?"

He opened the door, cut me an annoyed look, and pushed past me.

"Dinner is ready. Do you want a plate?" I asked.

"Not now," Eirik said, taking Celestia's hand and the chair I'd been using.

"I'll make you one anyway." When he didn't respond, I added, "You can eat while watching her."

"I'm not hungry," he grumbled.

"Of course you are. I can hear your stomach growling from here. If you'd like, I could feed you since your hands are occupied. It's not like I haven't done it before." He scowled and looked up. "Remember when you'd become ill and feverish like clockwork. Raine and I would take turns feeding you."

"No, you didn't."

"Did too, so one plate coming up. Be ready to open your mouth and chew with it closed." I was deliberately goading him so he'd agree to eat. The goddess followed me to the dining room. The table was set for four, and servants waited to serve us, including Astrid, the girl Maera had assigned to me. Once they pulled out our chairs, the goddess dismissed them.

"I hate people standing around while we eat," she said. "It's okay when we have guests, but I find it unnecessary when it's just our family. Litr can take care of us."

"Who is Litr?" I asked.

As though on cue, the Dwarf with red hair and a bulbous nose appeared with Baldur. The goddess introduced him as Litr. He bowed several times, then went to the covered plates and started serving.

"How are our guests doing?" the goddess asked.

"Settled in," Baldur said. "Richard promised me a game later this evening. He taught me how to play chess," he explained for my benefit. "Now I beat him."

"Or he allows you to win," the goddess teased.

"I'm insulted. You are supposed to be my champion, *ástin mín*."

"I am, but you love to win and you become a grouch when you don't. I'm sure Celestia told Richard to let you win."

Baldur sighed. "You see what I have to deal with? My own wife has no faith in me. Do you play chess, Daughter?"

"No. I could never sit down long enough to learn."

"Then I'll teach you."

The goddess groaned.

"Stay out of this, *dýrr*. This is between me and my daughter."

"Our daughter," she corrected him.

In some ways they reminded me of Mom and Dad. "I promised Eirik a plate."

"Litr will prepare him one," Baldur said. "How is Eirik doing?"

"He showered and shaved, and might even join us for dinner. I think he was ready to bite Einmyria's head off when she suggested feeding him."

"She never fed me," Eirik said from the doorway. "She just says stuff to annoy me." He walked to the side table, took the plate Litr had prepared for him, and walked out of the room again. Litr followed him with a tumbler and a glass. No one spoke until they disappeared inside the bedroom.

"At least he's eating," Baldur said.

Litr returned to serve us. Dinner was fun, listening to Baldur and the goddess talk about life in the hall, their work, how Eirik changed things. I asked questions, and they were more than willing to answer. I was, too, until they became personal.

"Do you have a special young man, Einmyria?" Baldur asked.

Echo's face flashed in my head, and I smiled. "Yes."

"I hope we get to meet him. We want to make sure he is worthy of you," he continued, and I stared at him with round eyes. He wasn't serious.

"Stop teasing the child. She is free to choose her consort without our consent."

"Our son can do that. Different rules apply to daughters." His expression was serious. The goddess groaned.

"He's been impossible ever since we learned you were alive. He wants to show you off, but no one is allowed to take you away from us. He made a list of potential suitors then burned it because none of them was good enough. He had no idea what you looked like or your taste in men, but he listed qualities of your future consort."

I stared at him with wide eyes. "He did?"

"Of course, I did. I'm your father. He must be handsome and honorable. He must come from a good stock. He must put your interest above his and all others. He must be willing to break every rule for you. He must be strong, smart, fast, and unstoppable when it comes to protecting you and your realm."

He'd just described Echo.

"Here, eat something." The goddess broke a piece of bread and placed it in his mouth, shutting him up. "And stop embarrassing our daughter. She doesn't need a man to protect her or the realm. She can do it all by herself."

Their open display of affection was sweet, but my mind was on what Baldur had said. My realm? What realm? I took a bite while my mind raced. The food was really good. The loaves flaky on the outside and moist on the inside. The meat was tasty. It was so good I temporarily forgot about *my realm* and the tumbler of apple juice Litr had poured.

I didn't get a chance to ask them what they meant because Maera entered the room and hurried to the goddess' side. She whispered in her ear. The expression on the goddess' face changed.

"Excuse us, Daughter," she said and stood. A portal opened beside her, and she swept through it.

Baldur followed, leaving me with Liltr and Maera. The two exchanged worried glances.

"What's going on?"

"It appears we have a visitor," Maera said, sounding angry.

"Is that bad?" I asked.

"Someone talked about your arrival. The visitor claims he is here to heal Celestia, but I know him, the self-opportunist Dwarf. He's heard about your arrival and, as usual, came bearing gifts. Unfortunately, he is Baldurson's friend, so the goddess cannot throw him out. If he corners you, kick him between the legs."

I tried not to grin. A Dwarf interested in me? Not sure how to respond, I left the dining room and went to join Eirik.

# CHAPTER 11. DWARVES, GRIMNIRS AND WARRIORS

Eirik looked so much better.

"Where are Father and Mother?" he asked.

"They went to meet a friend of yours, who's come bearing gifts. A Dwarf. Maera calls him an opportunist."

"Lavion. Can you stay with Celestia?"

I nodded, and he took off. I settled against the seat when voices reached me from the living room and the others arrived. I recognized Hayden and her mother. The other two—the redhead from my memories and the blonde—had visited Celestia while she was helping Dev in Miami. The other three were new, but I guessed the older man was Celestia's father, Richard. He had the same startling blue eyes. The other woman could be her mother. Something about her face reminded me of Celestia. The younger guy could be anyone, but the way he glanced at Celestia and went pale said he cared about her.

"When did you get here, Cora?" Hayden asked, pulling away from the others.

"A couple of hours ago." My eyes went to Trudy. "Hey, Trudy. Thanks for taking me to Raine's wedding. I would have missed it if it weren't for you, Hayden, and Celestia."

Everyone's gaze went to Celestia, and an awkward silence followed before Hayden broke it as she introduced the crew from Windfall. The woman was Celestia's aunt, and the guy was Celestia's cousin, Zack.

"Everyone, this is Eirik's sister, Cora." I got bows and curtsies until I told them to stop. I ignored the stares and focused on Celestia. A loud sound came from outside the hall, and everyone glanced at each other uneasily, but no one spoke. When it happened again, I knew something was wrong.

"What is that?"

"Garm," she said. "Did you meet him?"

"Yes. What's wrong with him?"

Trudy looked at Celestia. "He knows something is wrong. Dogs are very sensitive. Usually Eirik takes him out, and he hasn't since Saturday. Would you like to look around?"

"I promised Eirik I'd stay with Celestia until he returns."

"We'll watch over her," Tammy said, and Celestia's aunt nodded.

I glanced at the door, then Celestia. Eirik would never forgive me if anything happened to her while he was gone. I was saved from explaining when he entered with the flashiest Dwarf I'd ever seen. Litr was behind them, and from his expression, he didn't approve of Lavion either.

The Dwarf was dressed in a red and black cloak lined with fur, his hair reaching past his shoulders, tiny braids on his beard and the tips tied with gold beads. He looked like a stage performer. Gothic rings on his fingers and matching chains around his neck finished his outlandish outfit. I wasn't the only one staring. Trudy tried to hide behind Jessica.

Eirik introduced him to everyone, starting with the crew from Windfall before moving to me. "My sister, Einmyria."

The Dwarf kissed the back of my hand. "Welcome to Helheim, Einmyria. Baldurson deliberately forgot to tell me he had a sister. Now I see why. You are exquisite," he added, winking at me.

"And you are very handsome," I said.

He laughed. "I like your sister, Baldurson."

"And this is my other sister, Jessica."

Lavion didn't mask his confusion as his eyes volleyed between Jessica and me. "Another one? You've been holding out on me, man."

"They are both unavailable to you, Lavion," Eirik said.

"You wound me, my friend. I'm charming and rich. I could have them both as my consorts. No, three of them." He glanced at Trudy and grinned. "I haven't forgotten you, my lovely Trudnir." She made a face but didn't respond.

Not bothered by her indifference, he crossed his arms and levitated. When the people around the bed gasped, he bowed.

"Dwarf magic is the best there is," he explained. "My people make all the weapons used by the gods, Valkyries, and Grimnirs. Ask Baldurson. We make all artavo, his *gunnlogi*. I'm sure you've seen him wield it. Then there's Thor's *mjornir*, Odin's *gungnir*, and jewelry so beautiful the goddesses are willing to do anything to acquire it. I'll have to make something that rivals the beauty of the women of Eljudnir." He bowed and switched focus to Celestia, resting his hand on her forehead, then her chest. "Her energy is weak but not that faint."

My eyes met Eirik's, and guilt followed.

"She should be tired but still up and about. This is very strange. It's like nothing I've ever seen before." He glanced at Eirik. "I need to consult our head healer in Nidavellir and get back to you."

"Thanks, Lavion. Maera will prepare your quarters if you plan on spending the night."

"No, my friend," the Dwarf said, returning to the floor. "I'm going home posthaste to consult our healer. She might have answers. She's already heard about Celestia's healing abilities and how she's helped families in Eastern Gjöll Pass. Sleep ceases to matter when a young life is in danger. I'll come back with answers as soon as I can."

I was impressed. My watch said it was after six and it had to be dark outside, but he was willing to ignore his comfort for Celestia. That was loyalty. He and Eirik were headed to the door when Lavion stopped and glanced at me.

"I hope we meet again, Einmyria," he said, bowing.

"I'm not going anywhere," I said.

He chuckled. "I like her, Baldurson."

As soon as the door closed behind him, Trudy made a disgusted noise. "Do not let that Dwarf anywhere near you, Cora. He might be loyal to Eirik and Celestia, but he's a terrible man."

I didn't care. Loyalty like that could not be bought. "Have they been friends for long?"

"Since we visited Nidavallir while searching for the orphans. He helped us and later came to visit." She was still talking about their quest when Eirik returned with Maera. The Dwarf carried a pitcher of green liquid, which she placed by the bed.

"Out everyone. We need the room," Maera said. She noticed I kept looking at the pitcher. "Special brew. It will keep her hydrated and healthy."

"Can we show Einmyria around?" Trudy asked, looking at Eirik. He nodded, his focus already back on Celestia. We left and headed for the rotunda.

"They're still working on your room, but I promised the goddess I'd take you to her after we finish showing you around," Trudy said.

There seemed to be more guards around. Several of them followed us, but kept their distance. There were so many halls. We stopped by the Sorting Hall, where souls were waiting to be escorted to the Resting Halls.

"This is where they wait for the goddess," Trudy said, but I didn't hear the rest of her words. I entered the room, drawn to the souls, the need to comfort them so consuming I didn't stop to think. I stopped next to the first one, an old man in a hospital gown, and touched his hand. It was cold, like a dead person's.

"It's okay. There's no need to be afraid. Everything will be okay."

His eyes locked with mine. *Thank you.*

Surprised, I broke the contact. He gripped my wrist.

*I'd seen you from afar but lost hope of ever talking through you. The young ones are faster and a lot more aggressive.*

"Do you need my help with anything?"

*No, dear. Since you are here, I don't think you can help now.*

"But I can. I will be going back to Earth, so if you have a message for your loved ones, I can still pass it to them."

*I lived a happy and fulfilling life, and said my good-byes. I just wanted my Pauline to know that I'm okay and remind her never to forget Cabos.*

"I will." This was better than being possessed by a soul. "What is your address?"

He rattled off a town in San Diego. I moved to the next one, a woman also in her hospital gown, and took her hand. She'd had her closure, but my touch reassured her. I continued down the line. Most of them just appreciated a touch. At the end of the line was a young girl. She needed some closure. Her demands were so long I turned to ask Trudy for a pen and paper, and my eyes met the goddess. She, the three girls, and a group of Grimnirs were by the door, watching me. Warmth crept up my face, and I stepped back.

"Don't stop, please," the goddess said, entering the room. The green color on her dress leached out until it was white. Even the green crystal on her scepter became clear. She had serious powers. "What is she saying?"

I explained what I'd done and about the girl's request.

"This is how you help them on Earth?"

"Except I allow them to possess me and write down everything they need. Here, I just have to touch them for their thoughts to flow into mine. Most of them are happy to be here. They're just a little lost."

"Release more of your locator runes. The more runes you engage, the brighter they glow and the stronger their effect on souls." As though on cue, more runes appeared on her normal side. They were black like mine. "It calms them. Did you need something to write on?"

"Yes, please."

She lifted her hand and a leather book appeared in her palm. She handed it to me. "All you have to do is direct your thoughts for the words to appear on each page."

I lifted the leather cover to the first page. Despite being blank, I had a feeling the book was ancient. The pages were yellowed and thin, almost translucent like the books Lavania had given us to record the runes we etched on our skin.

*Paulina Paulsen, remember Cahos. From Benjamin Paulsen of La Jolla, San Diego.* The words appeared on the page. I recorded the girl's demands and glanced at the goddess.

"This is awesome," I said. "I wish I had one of these back at home."

"You can take it with you. I wasn't planning on starting lessons so soon, but when Maera told me you were in the Sorting Room talking to the souls, I had to come see."

"What is involved in sorting?"

"I welcome them, ease their fears, get their names and birthdays so they are sorted into the right hall, and then I wish them a peaceful rest and send them off with the guards. Usually, I do it twice a day. Three times if there're more deaths. When a natural disaster strikes, I'm in here day and night until your father insists I rest. I hate leaving them standing in here when they should be reliving their best memories in the halls."

"So they have private rooms?"

She chuckled. "In a way. They turn into pockets of energy, each unique. Sometimes when energies collide memories blend, so I tend to give the gods private rooms. Are you done here for now?"

"Do they always look so sad?"

"Until they see me—or you from their expressions." She smiled when a young man around my age reached out and touched my hand. I turned my palm up and gripped his hand. He smiled, and his thoughts drifted to me. "What is he saying?"

"He's flirting with me. He thinks I'm pretty."

She chuckled. "Which is why I don't touch them or listen to them. It slows me down, so I do the talking."

*Of course she does.* And she didn't apologize for it.

"You, on the other hand, give them closure, and I admire that. You'll find out that a lot of them don't need it because they've dealt with whatever problems they had while still alive. The ones that didn't must accept the consequences because usually I don't have the time to help them."

I caught a glimpse of the tough goddess everyone had told me about. Compassionate yet tough. "I guess if you gave them closure, you wouldn't have time to welcome all of them."

She smiled with approval. "Exactly."

"When are you going to send these ones off?"

"Later tonight."

"Can I watch?"

She chuckled. "You can stand right beside me if you want. Come on. I'll finish the tour Trudy started."

~*~

We visited the Resting Halls as they were often called. Some of the staff called them Eternal Halls instead of the more formal title Eternal Resting Halls, the goddess explained. She called forth a soul using their name and birth time narrowed down to the second they were born. Seeing people's memories was interesting. It was like a 3-D movie, only better. Like something happening in real time.

"Trudy sits outside halls for hours, watching memories. Now she has introduced Jessica to the same habit. They think I don't see them sneaking into the hallways at odd hours, but nothing goes on around the halls without my knowledge."

I guessed that meant I couldn't sneak into Echo's quarters. "Where's Raine's father?"

"Tristan is in one of the east halls reserved for the gods. It was the least I could do after he and Svana helped raise your brother. She came down to see me before Tristan died, and we had a very interesting chat about Eirik's childhood." She took my arm and led me down a hallway made of glass.

I could see the frozen tundra, and to our right was an arena of some kind. "Is that for winter sports?"

The goddess chuckled, but before she could answer, a portal opened and Baldur walked through it to join us. "What did I miss?" he asked.

"Einmyria would like to know if that's a sports arena."

"That, *dýrr mín*, is where your mother's warriors practice. Are you into sports?"

"Yes. Swimming, of course, and football and basketball because of Dad's influence." And I'd interview the jocks for my vlog. "He is not athletic, but he has his favorite teams."

"He must visit and watch the Grimnirs play. I'd like to meet him and his wife."

"I told her the same thing," the goddess said. "She brought pictures and videos."

Baldur rubbed his hands and grinned. "Then we can catch up on what we missed. What does your father like to do? Or should I call him Mr. Jemison? No, he must have a name. Something strong and manly."

The goddess was trying hard not to laugh. "Jeffrey is his name, *dýrr.*"

"Then Jeffrey and I must have a chance to enjoy a few games when he visits. Let me show you what I have in mind." He wedged himself between us and took the goddess' arm and mine. "So what happened in the Sorting Hall? I heard excited whispers."

The goddess and I exchanged glances.

"We talked to a few souls," she said.

"You had a conversation? You? What happened to 'There's no time for idle chatter?'"

"It hasn't changed, but our daughter has a knack for communicating with them. They wanted to touch her."

Baldur gave a mock shudder. "They are cold."

"Why aren't you?" I asked.

"Your mother warms me with her touch and love." He kissed her cheek and stopped outside a set of stairs. "Here we go."

We went up the stairs, and my jaw dropped when we reached the top. The setting was like an arena. There were seats on either side of the upstairs hallway, some facing what looked like ice hockey rinks, which were empty. We continued on and came to basketball courts, two of them occupied. The players were brutal with each other, all of them using runes for speed and strength, knocking each other. The boxing area was packed. It had a ring and punching bags. The dojo area had hand-to-hand combat training mats and a hard floor. On the walls were training sticks and swords, which didn't make sense until I remembered that these people came from different civilizations and some were more comfortable with swords than a basketball.

"Are all these Grimnirs, or are some of them warriors?" I asked.

Baldur chuckled. "These are Grimnirs. Your mother's warriors are in Corpse Strand. They come out every day to train and then go back. Ragnarok will give them a chance to redeem themselves and earn their freedom, if they survive."

Corpse Strand was for condemned souls, and Ragnarok was eons away. Not that I felt bad for the criminals, but I glanced at the goddess to see her reaction. She was busy studying one of the Grimnirs with a frown.

"I didn't set the rules on what criminals and oath-breakers must endure, but I enforce them," she said, and I wondered if she could read my thoughts. She sighed. "Echo is in one of his moods, *dýrr*. Do you think you should step in?"

My eyes flew to the men sparring with swords. My heart hurtled to my throat when I recognized Echo. He was wielding two swords and so was his opponent. They rushed each other, swords clanging as they parried left and right and attacked. I didn't realize I'd moved closer to the glass wall when a blade missed his chest by inches. Why was he fighting without a shirt or runes?

"He's been like that since the beginning of this week," Baldur said. "Something is bothering him." He glanced at the goddess. "Has he talked to you yet?"

"He asked for an audience last week, but I told him to wait. I'm not discussing Grimnir matters until this crisis with Celestia is over." The goddess smiled when Echo knocked the sword off his opponent's hand and nicked the man's neck. "He'll always be one of my finest fighters even though he abhors violence. It is the Druids' way," she added for my benefit.

I was still trying to wrap my head around what she'd said. Echo had asked to talk to her. He must have planned to tell them about us before I arrived in Helheim.

"What is he doing now?" the goddess asked sharply, and my eyes flew to the floor below. Echo was fighting two people.

"I kept hoping whatever was bothering him would pass," Baldur said. "Maybe you need to talk to him before he hurts someone, *dýrr*."

"He's more likely to get hurt. He's exhausted and is making mistakes. Look at that. He left himself wide open and would have gotten a blade in his gut. He doesn't even have his runes on. I don't know what's bothering him, but let him exhaust his demons. Eirik would stop this, but this is not the right time to ask our son to referee Grimnirs."

I didn't know anything about sword fights, but I could tell when a person fought like a drunken sailor. The goddess was right. Echo was exhausted. I winced when he got nicked on the thigh and then the arm. Even though he was bleeding, he still didn't engage any of his runes. His opponents backed up while he continued to swing. Thoroughly annoyed, I turned and faced my parents.

"Is it okay if I stop him?"

The goddess traded a look with Baldur and nodded. "Go ahead."

"Thank you." I must have engaged my speed runes, because I cleared those stairs like a sprinter. Through the glass wall, I could see Grimnirs working out, but I couldn't find the entrance to the damn gym. Luckily, the same two guards who'd stayed with us during the tour had followed me downstairs.

"Where's the entrance to the gym?" I asked them.

"You passed it back there, young goddess," one of the guards said.

"Show me."

We retraced our steps, and I entered the dojo area to find a crowd had formed around the fighters. Echo was still fighting, except his opponent was now Syn, his reaping buddy. I could tell Syn was toying with him, which only seemed to piss off Echo.

The person beside me noticed me first, and his eyes widened.

"Einmyria," he whispered, but the person next to him overheard him and looked back. They stepped aside to let me pass and tapped on the shoulders of those in front of them. In seconds, I had a path.

"Thanks," I said and marched forward, too furious to care that they were staring and whispering. Most of them probably knew about me and Echo.

I reached the front of the crowd and waited to catch Echo's eyes, but instead I caught Syn's. I shook my head, and he stepped back, ducking to evade Echo's blade. He dropped and swept his leg under Echo in an attempt to bring him down, but Echo jumped back, almost losing his balance. Yep, he was definitely exhausted. The Echo I knew was graceful. Syn sprung to his feet and joined me.

"I can't stop him today. He's been like this since last week and won't talk about whatever crawled up his ass. I had to snap his neck several times this week. This time, he was expecting it and nearly gutted me."

"Give me your sword."

Echo turned to face Syn but found me. I had no idea how to use a sword, but if he needed a target, he had one.

"Cora?" he asked, peering at me.

"Yep, it's me." I gripped the sword with both hands and widened my stance. "You want someone to fight, come and get me."

He frowned. "I'm not going to fight you."

"Why not?"

"Because…" He glanced around, surprise flickering on his face at the audience. He'd been so caught up in the fight he hadn't noticed the crowd. "I can't."

"Then drop the swords."

He dropped them and swayed on his feet. I wanted to run to him, hold him, scold him, and kiss him, but I fought the urge and passed the sword back to Syn. He looked puzzled by my behavior. I glanced at Echo, and once again fought the urge to rush to his side.

"Engage healing runes. You are bleeding."

He glanced down and frowned. He didn't engage his runes, and concern coursed through me. Did he think the goddess refused him a meeting because she knew about us and didn't approve? I glanced up at my parents. They waved.

Not caring what they thought, I stepped closer to Echo and looked into his eyes. They looked so tortured my heart cracked and my resolve not to touch him slipped a notch.

"Heal your wounds, Echo."

"She won't let me talk to her," he whispered. "I changed my mind. I was going to tell her everything and surprise you, but she won't listen to me."

And being Echo, he'd assumed the worst. Thank goodness his

thinking things through phase had passed. He might be impatient and melodramatic, but that was part of his charm.

"She will," I reassured him. "Her concern right now is Celestia. Please, heal your wounds."

"I need the pain until you are mine again. It keeps me from going crazy."

Gah, he could be such a baby.

"I am yours, silly. Always." I didn't care if the Grimnirs watching us heard my next words. I reached up and palmed Echo's cheek. "Seeing you like this breaks my heart, Echo. Please, heal yourself."

"Not yet."

"Fine. Suit yourself."

Even as the words left my lips, I wanted to wrap my arms around him and never let go. It took all my energy to drop my hand, turn, and walk away. The crowd parted. When I glanced back, he was looking at me with so much longing I almost ran back to him.

Shaking my head, I kept walking until I cleared the crowd. A glowering Nara was on the outskirts and fell in step with me. We'd moved from her dislike of me to grudging acceptance to some kind of sisterhood because of Dev. It looked like we were back at the beginning.

"Why didn't you tell us who you are?" Her voice dripped with ice.

I didn't need to explain myself to her. "Nice to see you again, Nara."

"He's hurting," she whispered, following me to the door.

"He'll be fine."

"He's been like this since last week. Coming here and challenging anyone who'd fight him."

All because the goddess had turned down his request? I glanced back, but Echo was now punching a bag as though to obliterate it. He was a hot mess over nothing. I wasn't sure what I'd do, but I needed him to get his act together.

"I can't help him. Not now." Rage flashed in Nara's eyes, but I didn't let it bother me. "Keep him out of trouble until Celestia gets better."

# GODDESS

## CHAPTER 12. MY ECHO IS BACK

"How is Echo doing?" the goddess asked when I joined them.

"Better. He is impossible and intense and tends to blow everything out of proportion." I realized what I'd just said and wondered if I'd given myself away. "I've known him for over a year now," I added.

My parents didn't comment, but unasked questions hung in the air. Part of me wanted to tell them the truth about us, but I remembered the story Mom had told me. Men had big, yet delicate egos. Dad would have been humiliated that his in-laws knew he hadn't defended her. Echo wanted to be the one to tell my parents about us, so I wasn't going behind his back and upstaging him.

We went back to their quarters, which had a gorgeous 3-D mural of a pillared hallway. It gave an illusion of a larger hall and a gorgeous sunset that seemed so real it was uncanny. My bedroom used to be a baby's room and still had a rainbow mural and gorgeous snowflakes on the wall, but instead of the crib, there was a large canopy bed. Jessica had used it, but now she had Eirik's old quarters.

"We are still working on your quarters," Baldur explained.

"This is fine. Tonight I'll probably stay up with Eirik anyway. Maybe even force him to sleep." Astrid had unpacked my things, putting my makeup and paraphernalia on the vanity by a full-length mirror and my clothes and shoes in the large walk-in closet. They barely covered half of one side. The rest of my toiletries were in the bathroom, which was pretty modern.

I grabbed my laptop and the external hard drive where I stored most of my videos and pictures and joined them in a cozy room with a fireplace and shelves of books.

I shared my childhood while answering their questions. They had many. I was happy when the goddess called a halt.

"You can show us more tomorrow. It's time to finish my duties in the Sorting Hall."

The Grimnirs crowded the doorways leading to the room as I took my place beside her. Black runes like mine appeared on her normal side, so I knew she was glowing.

"I know you are tired and scared, but everything is going to be okay," she told the hall of souls. "We have a place you can rest and be with your loved ones. You can talk and catch up, and stay with them as long as you like. When you are ready to be on your own, you can rest with your happiest memories. You decide which moment of your life to revisit and relive, who you'd like to join you there. Some of you can correct some of the wrongs you did or were done to you. The Eternal Resting Halls are meant to be happy and worry-free." She glanced at me and smiled. "Ready?"

I wasn't sure whether I was, but I nodded. A guard appeared beside me with the book the goddess had given me earlier. He turned it to a blank page. Several guards guided the souls to where we stood.

They passed me before going to her. The first one, a man, reached out and touched my hand. His thoughts flowed into mine, and from my thoughts into the book.

"Donovan Fuller, born October 1965 at 3:42:22 in Wichita, Kansas. Rest in peace," the goddess said. The guards took him and disappeared through a portal to the entrance of an Eternal Resting Hall. The whole process was surreal and seemed never-ending because Grimnirs kept arriving with more souls. Luckily for me, there were not a lot who needed closure. The majority just wanted to connect with someone.

When we stopped, I had a knot between my shoulders. I rotated them to remove the kinks. "You do this every day? It's only been"—I glanced at my watch—"an hour? It seemed longer."

"It's not bad once you learn to pace yourself." She ran a hand along my back and the knot disappeared. "If you get tired, you will it away or sit. There's a chair around here somewhere, and you can adjust it at will so you are at eye level with each soul."

The Grimnirs, who'd stayed and watched the whole process, stepped back as we left the room. I didn't realize more had arrived until I heard the buzz. The Throne Hall and the adjacent Waiting Hall were packed with reapers, guards, and the staff.

The goddess led me to her seat, but instead of sitting, she stayed standing until Baldur joined us. I had a feeling they'd planned this. He raised his hand, and silence spread through the halls. I tried to find Echo in the crowd, but there were so many reapers. I found the hooded ancients, or Idun-Grimnirs. There couldn't be more than a dozen. At the very front, along the stairs leading to the throne, were the goddess' private guards in their black and green cloaks. Behind them stood regular guards.

"I had planned to have a big welcome home party to make this announcement," Baldur started, "but we have to postpone it because our daughter Celestia is gravely ill. I'm sure you've noticed the lack of laughter in the hall the last week. We hope she'll recover soon. In the meantime, I want to introduce you to our long-lost daughter, Einmyria. Some of you know her as Cora Jemison, the courageous young Mortal who selflessly helps souls find closure. We thought she died as a baby, but that was not the case." He turned his head and smiled at me. "She was taken from this hall by Angrboda, left in Jötunheim, where the Norns collected her and took her to Earth with other orphans. She will be staying with us for a while, but her life is still back on Earth, where she was raised. Regardless of where she is, Einmyria is a young goddess, our daughter. Treat her with the same respect you give her mother and protect her with everything you've got."

The guards were the first to drop on one knee, bow their heads, and press their fists to their chests. The silent allegiance spread like a wave. Even the Idun-Grimnirs went on their knees and showed their loyalty.

My throat thickened with all sorts of emotions, part of me touched, but the other part worried about my future. Echo was somewhere in this crowd. What must he be feeling? An invisible line seemed to have been drawn between us.

"Rise," Baldur said, and the crowd did. Flanked by my parents, I gave tentative smiles and nods as they parted and we walked through them.

"That was daunting," I said when we reached the hallway to their private quarters.

"Why?" the goddess asked. "You are our daughter, and they needed to know that."

"A year ago I was a simple high school student. Then Maliina marked me. Last week, I was just an Immortal with the ability to help souls with my medium runes. And now I am…"

"A young goddess and future ruler of this realm," she finished, stopping.

"What?"

"*Elskr mín*," Baldur whispered. "It's too soon to be discussing such matters. It's her first day."

"But I'd rather get it out of the way," the goddess said firmly.

We were still in the hallway connecting the Throne Hall from the inner rotunda of the private quarters. The guards, including the one carrying the book from the Sorting Hall, were behind us. The goddess glanced at them, and they moved back, giving us more room.

"According to the Norns, you will take over Helheim after Ragnarok. I didn't plan to tell you on your first day, but I'm a strong believer in getting to the point. When the time is right, I will share that information with the Grimnirs. For now, I don't see why you shouldn't know the truth. You and your consort will take over for us," she added.

My consort. I saw a glimmer of hope. "And I can take anyone as a consort?"

The goddess chuckled. "As many as you want."

I didn't want many. Only one.

"But we hope you will have one who will stay by your side at all times," Baldur said. "No matter how many women your grandfather slept with, your grandmother Frigg was his official consort and she was accorded the respect that came with it."

I'd already found my one. The invisible line I'd imagined between Echo and me blurred. Grinning, I kissed Baldur on the cheek.

"Thank you, Father." I turned and kissed the goddess. "And you, too, Mother. Now I'm going to see Eirik and force him to take a break."

"We'll stop by later to wish you goodnight," the goddess said.

"Can I take the book with me?" I indicated the large book with notes from souls still needing closure. A guard was carrying it. "I have an idea, but I want to pass it by Eirik first. It might take his mind off Celestia."

"The book is yours," the goddess said while Baldur waved over the guards.

"Thank you," I told the guard and reached for the book.

"I'll be honored to carry it for you, my goddess," he said, bowing. His eagerness was sweet, and I remembered him from when I'd arrived.

"It's Creed, right?"

"Yes, my goddess."

"Thank you, Creed."

The goddess smiled with approval when our eyes met. "I'll see you later."

I left with Creed trailing me and glanced back once. The goddess and Baldur were watching us. I waved and disappeared into the rotunda, the inner sanctum guards bowing. I was never going to get used to that. We hurried past them and heard Eirik's voice before we entered the bedroom. He was reading to Celestia. He looked up and frowned.

"I'll take over while you rest," I said, going to stand beside his seat. "Get in beside her, and I'll keep an eye on both of you."

"No, you'll fall asleep and—"

"I just learned how to will fatigue away, Eirik," I fibbed. "The magic in this place is amazing. Mother showed me how to will things. Knots. Fatigue. Sore feet. I helped welcome the souls and even found some that needed closure." I didn't let his disinterest slow me down. "Creed, can I have that?"

The guard placed the book in my hands and stepped back, his eyes going to Celestia. "How is she doing?"

"She'll be fine, Creed," Eirik said.

"The villagers want to know if they can come and keep vigil.

Sometimes the love and positive energy from many helps," he said.

Eirik stared at him strangely, and for a brief second I thought he'd bite his head off.

"That's fine," Eirik murmured. "I know she'll appreciate that."

Creed bowed and exited the room. It was obvious Celestia was loved.

"What's that?" Eirik asked, staring at the book.

"The book of unfinished business." I explained how it worked. "I think it would be nice to have students at Mystic Academy help families needing closure. It could be part of their weekly assignments, choosing someone from the book and finding ways to get the message to them from their dead relatives."

"Are you thinking of teaching there?" he asked.

"No, silly. I'll be attending it as a senior. I think students would get a kick out of actually helping people. Do you think it's a good idea? I mean, it's better than having the reapers do it. Echo, Andris, Syn, Nara, and Rhys have been helping them find closure when I couldn't. Instead of having reapers do it, the students could. Maybe under the supervision of a teacher."

"Like who?"

"I don't know."

"Andris is interested. Torin talked to me about him. Syn is also interested." Life flashed in his eyes. "Can I see that?"

We went through the requests. I hadn't asked for their addresses, yet they were there. The goddess had probably put them there.

"Man, that's fucked up," Eirik said.

"What?"

He tapped at the page. "This asshole wants his ex-wife to know he slept with her sister. What kind of a shitty message is that from a dead person?"

"Check the footnote. His wife had left him for his best friend."

"Ah. Well, it's still a shitty thing to tell someone when you are dead. Are you going to tell her?"

"No. I agree with you. It's a crappy thing to pass on." As I stared at the page, the words faded away. Nice.

Eirik turned the page and read the next one. "Damn, some are sad. Her stepfather belongs behind bars."

"I know."

He frowned and threw me a look. "How can you stand listening to such sob stories? I'd want to hurt someone."

I told him the story of the girl who was bullied at a prep school and ended up dying. "Making the guilty pay and apologize makes the anger go away. Maybe Syn and Andris could be in charge of these field trips. They enjoy making Mortals squirm."

Eirik nodded. "I think it's a brilliant idea." He yawned. "Lavania is open to suggestions, so she might go for it."

"Get in bed with Celestia and hold her," I said.

He scowled. "I don't want to crush her."

"Do you know why Bald... Father is warm when most souls here are so cold?"

"I didn't know their skin was cold. Celestia was warm when she astral projected here." He reached out and stroked her cheek.

"Well, he is warm because of Mother's touch and love, so crawl in bed and keep your woman warm." My reasoning was warped, but I wanted him to rest. "I'll be here, and if I get tired, I'll will it away. Mother and Father also promised to stop by."

He still seemed reluctant.

"Listen, Eirik. I trust you. When you came to me and told me I was your sister, I believed you because of that trust. When you told me Celestia could heal Dev, I put my faith in her hands because of that trust. Now I'm asking you to trust me to watch over her while you sleep. If anything goes wrong, I'll wake you up."

He sighed and nodded. Without saying a word, he got up, pulled off his shirt, and crawled under the blankets.

"Do you want me to dim the lights?"

"Do you know how?" he asked, sounding too much like the old Eirik.

"No, but I know I can will it." I stared at the nearest crystal and watched the light dim. Man, magic was cool. Eirik's eyes were already closed when I reached out to stroke Celestia's forehead. His eyes flew open.

"She's fine," I whispered.

"No, she's not. I want her back to normal now, laughing and driving me crazy."

He was impatient like Echo. I returned to reading the requests in the book. I was almost done when the goddess and Baldur arrived with a blanket for me. Without saying a word, they took the lounge across from mine. Watching them, I wished Echo were with me. I kicked off my shoes, tucked the blanket around me, and leaned back.

I must have dozed off because when I woke up someone had moved me to the lounge and all I could see was Eirik's broad back. Syn was snoring on the chair I'd sat on earlier. I became aware of the warmth against my cheek and the familiar scent of the man I loved. I turned my head, and my eyes met Echo's.

"Hey," he said.

"Hey back to you." I palmed his cheek where he still had a bruise. "You okay?"

"For now. Sorry for earlier."

"You are a drama queen."

He smiled. "I should be insulted, *my goddess*, but since I happen to adore you, I'll let it pass. Go back to sleep. I'll keep watch until Mr. Snores wakes up."

Then something else occurred to me. "Were they here when you two arrived?"

"They as in the goddess and the Golden One? Yes. I told them we were here to help you keep watch."

I grinned. That was the Echo I knew. He must have decided to stop acting like an ass. "And?"

"They said thank you and gave up the lounge. Your father didn't even offer to carry you to bed. They just smiled and moseyed out of here."

"They know about us," I said.

"I hope so. Have they told you anything?"

"No, but she returned my blanket the last time you spent the night at the farm. She must have seen you. I wonder why she's not saying anything. Even after the gym, she just asked if you were doing okay. I told them you were being your usual self, stubborn and melodramatic."

"You told my goddess I'm melodramatic?"

I grinned at his disgruntled tone. "I thought I was your goddess. I searched for you in the halls earlier during my introduction but didn't see you."

"I was the first to kneel and pledge to protect you."

I settled against his chest, grinning. "Then you'd better treat me right. I now have a hall full of reapers and guards to kick your ass if you don't."

"And I'd take it because you, Cora Einmyria Jemison, daughter of Hel and Baldur, are mine." He dropped a kiss on my forehead and tucked me under his chin. "Even when the damn hall drops to its knees and shows allegiance to you, you are mine."

"Could you two keep it down or get a room?" Syn growled. "Some of us are trying to sleep here."

Smiling, I closed my eyes and went back to sleep. My Echo was back.

~*~

When I woke up, I was in a bed, and it wasn't mine. *Please, let it be Echo's.* I looked around while stretching. There was nothing on the walls, and the décor was bland. Blue everywhere. There was what appeared to be an outline of a mural, but that was it. Blue wasn't Echo's color. Voices filtered from outside the room. The second I opened the door, disappointment coursed through me. I was still at Eirik's.

"Morning," Trudy called. The others—Jessica, Hayden, and Zack—scrambled to their feet.

"Don't, guys. Is that coffee?"

Jessica handed me a cup. "Echo told us how you take it."

"Thanks. I'm starving." I glanced at the closed bedroom door. "Are they awake?"

"Still asleep," Trudy said. "If Eir doesn't come today, I'm offering to go to Asgard and get her."

"I'm coming with," Hayden offered.

Trudy scoffed at the idea. "You just want to see Asgard."

"Red, you are annoying. This is about Celestia, not Asgard," Hayden retorted.

"Can I come, too?" Jessica asked.

"No one is going anywhere," the goddess said, sweeping through a portal and into the room. I hadn't seen the portal open. "We have to get rid of the people out there first."

The others scrambled to their feet again, and she pinned them with a glare. "Get your mother, Trudy. She's not answering my summons."

"Who is out there?" Trudy asked instead of leaving.

"Villagers from Eastern Gjöll Pass," the goddess said. "They are here to keep vigil now that word is out about Celestia. I want them gone."

"Creed asked Eirik if it was okay for the villagers to come and keep vigil, and Eirik said yes," I said.

Surprise flickered across the goddess' face. Then she sighed. "Okay. Fine. They can stay for a day. But no more talks about going to Asgard"—her glance swept the faces of the three girls—"until the emissaries I sent return. Trudy, find your mama and tell her we need breakfast. She also needs to make food to feed the villagers."

The others disappeared, leaving me with the goddess, who still looked slightly annoyed.

"I hope they won't be a bother," I said.

"Oh, the villagers are always a bother. I never had visitors until your father came here. And even then, they had to send an emissary asking for an audience first. Then Eirik returned home, and they all wanted to meet him and challenge him. We hosted hundreds of guests for weeks. I tried to ignore them, but some came with little children who went everywhere and asked incessant questions. I couldn't turn around without bumping into one." Her expression said she'd thoroughly disliked it.

"Why did they need to challenge Eirik?"

"Because he is a dragon and there are so few of them, he had to prove himself." She smiled. "That's the official story I told him. But we knew they all heard he was the future leader of the gods, and everyone with a dragon daughter came to see if he was worthy of marrying their daughter. Some had babies who couldn't even walk, yet they wanted to offer them to him."

I laughed. "He must have hated that."

"He refused to attend the party until I sent Echo to bring Celestia. She was the only one he'd listen to then. As soon as he told them he wasn't interested, they left." She frowned. "Getting rid of the villagers won't be easy because they don't want anything from me. They're here for her."

"So why don't you like visitors. Your hall is beautiful."

"Thank you. It does have a certain appeal, doesn't it?"

"Yes, it does. The columns are gorgeous, and the details on the ceilings and murals are breathtaking."

"I do love the architecture, but I tried to make it as unwelcoming as possible."

I laughed, liking her bluntness. She had a dry sense of humor. "Why unwelcoming?"

"To discourage visitors. I do not have time to receive guests and listen to their silly prattle. They interfere with my work. The souls are my first priority, not entertaining people who are curious about my work or me. Then there are those who want favors. It's not my job to awaken souls from their rest just so someone can talk to their dead relatives. Unfortunately, your father loves a good party, and I find it hard to deny him anything."

Litr and Astrid arrived with our breakfast. Once again, I ignored the apple juice even though the goddess insisted, and I focused on the eggs and bacon. The bacon pieces were long.

Afterward, while the goddess attended to souls, I disappeared into my bedroom to shower and change. The long-sleeved, gray knit dress I changed into was new and gorgeous. I added warm leggings and wool socks that came to just above my black, low-healed boots. A quick sweep of the brush through my hair and light makeup, and I was ready. Astrid was waiting for me when I came back to the living room.

"The goddess wants to finish your tour when you are ready, young goddess. She wants you to wait for her here while I get her."

"My name is C… Einmyria, not young goddess."

"Yes, young goddess."

Somehow I didn't think she'd listen to me. I planned to keep trying until they stopped bowing and used my name. The goddess joined me, and we left to check on Celestia first. Guards trailed behind us the second we left the family quarters. I was surprised when she stopped to ask one of them how his wife was feeling.

"Much better, my goddess. She is in the hall with the villagers. They all hope the young healer recovers soon."

"Celestia saved her pregnancy last week," the goddess explained as we crossed the rotunda to Eirik's quarters.

Eirik looked much better than he had yesterday. He'd even eaten breakfast and changed. We left his room and picked up the tour of the halls from where we'd left off. We headed east to the Banquet Hall and Guest Halls. We went through a tunnel then down the stairs to the dungeons. The goddess didn't hide the fact that she'd kept Eirik in the dungeon when he first arrived.

"Do I regret it? Yes. It was drastic, but I was petrified his grandfather had suppressed his dragon forever." She showed me the eastern Resting Halls. They were smaller and each soul was actually in a private room, where they could relive their memories in peace. It didn't matter that the rooms were the size of a shoebox.

"Would you like to see Mr. Cooper's room?"

"Yes." I could tell Raine I saw her father.

She flicked her scepter, and runic writings appeared in the air and floated to the door. When it opened, Mr. Cooper was reliving memories of his family. Some had Eirik, and I was in one of them. I couldn't have been more than twelve. I didn't realize I was crying until the goddess waved her scepter and the doorway closed.

"Don't cry," she said, rubbing my back. "He is very happy. You saw that."

"I wish Raine could see him."

"Invite her to visit."

"Really?"

She nodded. "She is like a sister to you, according to Tristan. He and your father spoke at length about the two of you and your friendship with Eirik." A frown chased the smile off her face. "If I had known you were my daughter, I would have moved every obstacle to bring you home, Einmyria." Regret laced her words. "But you are here now, so no regrets. Tell me about Raine."

I talked as we walked back to her quarters to see more pictures and watch videos. She had questions about my work with souls and the dying, Raine's interaction with the Norns and Maliina, and how I'd blamed Maliina for my ability to see souls.

"I'm so sorry you had to go through that alone, *dýrr mín*," the goddess said. "The runes Maliina etched on you only stabilizes a possession so the two of you can coexist within one body, which is what she wanted. They are very unique, so she must have learned about them from evil Norns. The locator runes I etched on you when you were a baby are the ones that attract souls. Your grandmother etched them on me, so she could always find me, but I'd forgotten to use them on Eirik. I thought he was safe here in the hall. They are harder to bring to the surface because you don't really need to, except when someone with them needs to track you down. But if you want to learn to engage them, I'll teach you."

She engaged hers, and mine appeared.

"See? They are the same ones I have and the ones Maliina etched on your brother when I was trying to find him before she switched allegiance to the evil Norns and started adding others." She pointed out the one I should focus on first and how the others follow. There were about five bind runes, but the first one was the most complicated.

I studied it and engaged it on and off. "Just continue working on it until you can do it without thought. One day, you can etch it on your husband and children so you never have to go through what I endured."

"Is there a way I can expel a soul once I allow it to possess me? I always worry one would refuse to leave, especially when Echo is not around." I realized what I'd said, but I couldn't take it back. "Or Syn and Andris. They are the other reapers who tend to keep an eye on me when I have a session." Now I was blabbering. "Are there such runes?"

"I was going to discuss that with you. Warding runes can be engaged to stop a soul from possessing you and expel it when it stays too long. We'll work on those."

# CHAPTER 13. NEW SUITORS AND BODYGUARDS

Days went by fast as I got to know the goddess and Baldur. They wanted to know about everything—my teachers, my life on the farm, my likes and dislikes. I explained every picture and video. I loved seeing them together. He teased her a lot and made her laugh. They reminded me of Mom and Dad. They answered every question I had about them, and slowly, I started seeing them not as a god and a goddess, but as a loving couple, people I could relate to. I learned from Baldur that the goddess could have easily entered my mind and seen all my memories. Instead, she'd chosen to sit through hours of videos and pictures, and listened to my version of events. Only a mother would put up with that.

In the afternoons, I learned how to engage my locator runes without locking on to my medium runes. She taught me warding runes, which I added to mine.

"We can test it with souls here when you are ready."

"But they are solid here," I said.

"Yes, but they switch back and forth from physical to energy form based on your will. Think of them as newborn babies, completely dependent on you. If you want them to be in their physical form, you force your will on them. If you want them to be pure energy, you will it. Your father, for instance, has stayed in his physical form for so long you can't force your will on him. Even I can't do it. He controls the form he takes, and he's chosen the physical. Working with souls will help you test your warding runes."

We often ate breakfast and lunch with Eirik after checking on Celestia. He no longer looked like a hobo, but he wasn't the old Eirik either. Celestia meant everything to him, and his world wasn't going to be right until she came out of the coma.

Maera fed Celestia some green liquid stuff that looked like blended spinach. It kept her healthy and hydrated. Twice a day, Eirik kicked everyone out, except Maera. I didn't know what they were doing until Trudy explained that they massaged Celestia's body.

The emissary to Asgard hadn't yet returned. I wasn't sure whether the goddess would go there as she'd threatened or whether Baldur had convinced her not to go.

Trudy, Hayden, and Jessica spent so much time in the pool I rarely saw them, but when I did, Jessica still couldn't look at me without turning pink. I'd catch her glancing at me from the corner of her eye. I tried to make her feel at ease, but something about me kept her on edge. I hoped she'd talk to me about whatever was bothering her. Zack was often with them or at the Grimnirs' gym working out.

Nighttime was my favorite because I got to see Echo. Like clockwork, he never failed to come to Eirik's to check on Celestia. He often stayed until I fell asleep. I'd wake up in the middle of the night to find his arms around me. The lounge became our bed, just like the chair had been ours when we'd kept vigil by Dev's bed while Celestia treated him. Unfortunately, Echo was often gone by morning.

Sunday morning—or was it Monday?—I woke up disoriented. I wasn't on the lounge or in Eirik's guest room. Someone had finally carried me to my own bedroom.

The scent of bacon and eggs reached me, and my stomach growled. I followed the smell to the dining room, where breakfast was laid out on the side table. Litr was issuing instructions to Astrid like a drill sergeant. He stopped when he saw me.

"Morning, Litr, Astrid."

They both bowed, despite me repeatedly telling them not to.

Litr pulled out a chair for me. "I hope the young goddess slept well," he said.

I couldn't get rid of the title "young goddess" either, but I was determined. "Einmyria, Litr. You too, Astrid. Where is everyone?"

"The goddess has joined Baldur in the Throne Hall. They are deciding on what to do about the new arrivals." He placed a plate of eggs and bacon in front of me.

"More villagers?" I'd only seen them from afar.

"No, the ones arriving in my realm without permission," the goddess said from behind me. As usual, I hadn't felt the portal open. "The nerve. They've come because of our Celestia, or so they say. I'm sure some had never even met her."

"Where are they from?" I asked, cutting the bacon.

"All the other realms. I have sons of kings and their entourages, young gods and their mothers, men of noble and not so noble birth outside my gates asking for entrance. I will not allow it. I can understand those she's dealt with in the Eastern Gjöll Pass and Jötunheim worrying about her. Thank you, Litr." She took the chair he'd pulled out and picked up the goblet of apple juice he'd set by her hand. He always anticipated her every demand. "Pour Einmyria some apple juice, Astrid," she ordered and waited while the girl did.

I sipped the juice and tried not to grimace. It wasn't that bad. I knew all about the special apple for the gods and how it kept them young. Still, that didn't stop me from hating the fruit or its products. I'd avoided drinking the juice since I arrived. I focused on the bacon instead.

"I know the person responsible for this fiasco," the goddess continued. "Eirik's annoying friend Lavion. He must have said something at the market in Nidavellir. It's where people from the realms go to trade goods." She glanced over her shoulder. "Trudy?"

A portal opened, and the redhead peered inside. "I've told Mama you want to see her."

"Then why are you looking guilty?"

"Who? Me?"

The goddess harrumphed. "Do not go outside to look at the tents or the new arrivals."

Trudy made a face.

"Not without guards," the goddess added.

Trudy pouted. "Why?"

"It's not safe."

Trudy sighed. "Okay."

The portal closed, and Litr served the goddess. She tasted a piece of bacon and put it back on the plate. "That's cold. Take the food back to the kitchen and ask Maera to prepare it again. Even my meal is suffering because of them."

I stared longingly at the remaining bacon on my plate as Astrid whisked it away. It had tasted perfect to me. The goddess didn't speak until they were gone.

"I don't like discussing Trudy in front of them. She's not a servant here just because her mother is my housekeeper. She's under my care and tutelage because of what she is, and I'd hate for anything to happen to her."

"What is she? I mean, I know she can manipulate memories." I had yet to ask her and Hayden to get my memories back. Spending time with my parents had been a priority.

"And she has the power of premonition, but she's much more than that," the goddess said. "Remember we were talking about your friend Raine announcing Ragnarok and alerting the gods?"

I nodded.

"Trudy is an announcer, too," the goddess explained. "She'll do it from Jötunheim. The prophecy said there would be three of them—one in Asgard warning the gods, a second one here waking my warriors, and a third alerting the Jötnar. I've always known Trudy would alert the people in Jötunheim," she explained. "It annoys the Norns that she is a member of my household."

"And Eirik will announce from here."

She chuckled. "Who told you that?"

"Raine. Isn't that why the Norns were after him?"

"No. I haven't figured out why the Norns tried so hard to keep him from me. I even thought he might be the third announcer, but he's not a seer. All the announcers must be able to see into the future. I'd even thought Celestia might be the third one. It would make sense, since she lives here and she has the ability to see into the future, but I don't think she's the one." A thoughtful expression entered her eyes. "Norns can be hypocrites. The Wise Ones weave destinies and their minions seal them, yet they're doing everything they can to lure your friend,

Raine, to their side. At least they haven't tried to take Trudy because she's under my care."

"She's been to Earth. Weren't you worried about her going there or other realms?"

"I was, but Eirik promised to take care of her, and my son always keeps his word. As long as she is with him, I never worry."

What if Trudy fell in love and moved away from Eljudnir? "I had no idea she was that special," I said.

"She is, which is why I keep her close. Had she been raised in Jötunheim, she'd be dead by now. Possible announcers are born every few centuries, but they never survive to adulthood. All three must survive for Ragnarok to take place. I wouldn't be surprised to learn that the Norns weave their destinies with that in mind, deliberately delaying Ragnarok until they have the right announcers. Ones who are also Norns. It might explain why they want your friend, Raine, to join them."

If Celestia was the third announcer, could the Norns be behind her coma? Maybe the hags wanted all the three announcers to be like Raine, all would-be Norns.

A loud howl reached us, and the goddess sighed. "My poor hound. Modgie had to tie him up the moment he caught the scents of the animals drawing the carriages of our unwanted visitors. You do know why they are here, don't you?"

I was still thinking about Celestia, so the switch in subject threw me off. "Who?"

"The new arrivals. They are here because of you."

I blinked. "Me?"

"Yes. A few are here for Celestia because she is a healer, while others came to show Eirik their support because he is the most powerful dragon in all the realms and they are loyal to him. But the majority of the sons of minor gods and kings are shamelessly using the situation to meet you. Their arrival is interrupting the order of things in my hall. The Grimnirs do not need strangers gawking at them while they escort souls."

I'd already concluded she cared about her reapers, guards, and servants, and this confirmed it. No wonder they were loyal to her. She was protective of them.

"I will throw that annoying Dwarf with the damned on Corpse Strand and let him rot there for a few weeks."

And she was melodramatic. "Lavion?"

"Yes. He was supposed to bring back a healer. Instead, he's spread news about your arrival. I will not have them in my hall, not when you don't have any interest in them." She gave me a pointed look, and my cheeks warmed.

"You know why," I whispered.

"Yes. Echo?"

I nodded.

"I saw you together when I returned your blanket. He's spending a lot more time here than on Earth, and he holds you while you sleep every night. Do you love him?"

"With all my heart. We thought you wouldn't approve of our relationship."

"Why wouldn't I? He is a man of moral convictions and a hard worker. He's also very handsome. Whether he loves you as deeply as you love him is another story. He's not done anything to prove himself worthy of you."

My jaw dropped. "He doesn't need to prove anything. He is very supportive and loving. Without him, I never would have overcome my fear of souls or started helping them. As far as I'm concerned, he is more than worthy."

She smiled. "We'll see."

Thoroughly annoyed, I glowered. "So refusing to listen to him was a test?"

"I wouldn't call it that."

Of course she wouldn't. She'd been so nice that her attitude now completely blindsided me. This was the mother who'd thrown Eirik in the dungeons to awaken his dragon. I didn't like this side of her one little bit.

"Mother, I will not have you test Echo. He truly loves me."

"My dearest daughter, if I wanted to test him, I would have thrown him in the land of the fire Jötnar and let him fight his way home to you. Or I would have had Trudy scramble his memories and see if he could fall in love with you again. No, your father suggested we should wait and see what Echo is willing to do to show he loves you. He suggested…" A frown creased her brow. Actually, half her brow, the normal side, while runes on the other side appeared and disappeared. She made a disgruntled noise and shook her head. "Oh, that impossible man. This entire mess is not Lavion's doing. This is *his* doing."

She was hopping from topic to topic so fast and confusing me. "What mess? Whose fault?"

"The arrival of the young gods and princes from other realms. Your father must have sent Lavion to spread the news of your arrival. Shake the tree a little bit and see what falls off. Very clever and totally unacceptable. I need to have a long conversation with that father of yours." She stood while I stared at her in confusion.

"What does he hope to gain by inviting them here?"

"He is about to test your young man by giving him a chance to prove himself in the oldest way known in all the realms. He knows possible suitors will challenge Echo to show their prowess and to impress you. Jousting and sword fighting to win a maiden's hand. The whole thing is ridiculous and barbaric." She shook her head while I tried to pick my jaw off the floor, again. "I have no idea what goes on in your father's head sometimes. No wonder he is walking around with a big smile on his face. Maybe we will sneak off to Asgard to get Eir while they pound on each other." Her gaze went to my goblet. "Drink your apple juice, Einmyria. It's good for you."

I didn't see her leave because the dining room disappeared to be replaced by a fighting scene so bloody I gagged. The vision disappeared as fast as it had appeared, but I'd seen enough. Echo was going to fight a giant, and from the looks of things, he was going to lose.

No, I wasn't going to Asgard. If Echo was going to fight for me, I had to be by his side. A family that stands up for each other survives.

Echo was my family.

~*~

I tried to open a portal to wherever Echo was and failed. Disappointed, I disappeared into my bedroom to shower and hopefully cool down. Dad would not have pulled this crap on me in Kayville. It was ridiculous and barbaric, like the goddess had said. Just because Baldur was my biological father didn't give him the right to test Echo. From the vision alone, Echo was not going to survive this. If he got seriously hurt, I was leaving Helheim for good. Let's see how Baldur felt about having no daughter to dangle in front of suitors like a prized mare.

I stepped out of the bathroom to find Astrid waiting in my bedroom. She'd been doing that since day one, but I always told her I didn't need her help—until today.

"Can you find Echo for me, Astrid?"

She left and returned a few minutes later. "He's not in the hall, but I told the guards you are looking for him. They'll find him."

"Find Syn and Rhys, and tell them to find Echo."

She left. She was so eager to please me I felt bad for my grumpiness. So when she returned and asked about the rollers I was using, I showed her and she helped with my hair.

"Now what?" she asked.

"I wait for it to dry while I eat breakfast. Back at home I use a hood to dry it." When she frowned, I explained what the hood did.

"Or you can just will it." She touched my hair and removed one of the rollers. The lock was dry and the curl perfect. No wonder the goddess' hair was always perfect. There were perks to living in a magical place.

"Thank you, Astrid."

"What dress and shoes would you want to wear? I'll get them for you."

For the next few minutes, she and I worked together. She got my clothes and shoes and even helped me remove the rollers. Then she excused herself to get my breakfast since the goddess had rejected the first one. I changed into the long-sleeved aquamarine dress with a built-in hoodie she'd picked and added heeled ankle boots.

"What would you like to eat, young goddess?" Litr asked when I joined them and lifted the dome lids. Once again, there was bacon, eggs, and pancakes. "These are fresh off the gridle."

"Everything, except apple juice."

Confusion flashed on his face. "But your father insists that you drink some."

Baldur was not my favorite person at the moment. "That's too bad."

The shocked expression on Litr's face made me feel terrible. "I hate apples. My parents grow apples. The ones in Midgard," I explained when he frowned. "I grew up eating apples and apple pies, drinking apple juice, and eating dried apples. So now I hate everything to do with apples."

"But the apple is the fruit of the gods. They all eat it."

Litr looked so distressed I caved. "Okay, I'll have some."

He beamed and indicated for Astrid to pour some.

"Is Eirik awake?"

"Yes. I've already given him breakfast. He's eating right now." He took the tumbler from Astrid and offered it to me while she picked up a plate and started scooping food. When he stared at me expectantly, I took a sip and tried not to make a face.

"Hmm, it's good," I fibbed. He grinned with approval. "Can I ask you something, Litr?" He nodded. "Have you ever seen jousting?"

His eyes lit up. "Oh, yes. Challengers fight and compete for a prize. It is exciting."

Like hell it was. "What if they are fighting for the hand of a maiden?"

"Then the rules are different. Everyone fights the one who claims to be the maiden's favorite. The same way they'd challenged Baldurson for dominance as the dragon leader." Astrid whispered something in his ear, and he smiled. "Most suitors come with their clan. Sometimes the challenger uses his clansmen to weaken their opponent before facing him."

"But that's cheating," I protested.

"When dealing with the gods or kings, they don't consider it cheating because his men belong to him."

Damn it. Echo could not fight a line of people without help. Eirik might help. "Can you open a portal to Eirik's place? I'll eat with him."

Astrid heaped food on a plate while Litr opened a portal. I could see Trudy, Hayden, and Jessica. Trudy saw me first and waved. Maybe they could help. No one would ever suspect them.

"Don't forget your apple juice," Litr said, and I almost groaned. So close. I took it and thanked him. The three girls studied me with varied expressions. Hayden smiled, Trudy scowled, and Jessica still refused to hold my gaze, her face turning pink. She and I needed to talk sometime. Right now, I needed to know things from these two girls.

"Have you guys eaten?" I asked while still standing inside my parents' living room.

"Not yet," Trudy said, sounding annoyed. "Mama said to wait here. It's crazy out there with more people are arriving, and I'm starving."

"Come in here and get food."

Hayden and Trudy didn't hesitate. Jessica did. Getting irritated, I waved her through the portal. They crowded around the platters of food and served themselves. I caught Jessica staring at me from the corner of her eyes. She gave me another shy smile when our eyes met.

As we ate, Trudy talked about everything: the people camping on the grounds, the villagers in the hall, the Goddess' frustration, and her mother loving every second of it. Listening to her, you wouldn't know she'd announce the end of the world. But then again, Raine was like her. Just a regular girl.

"Damn, Trudy. Do you ever stop talking?" Hayden finally said.

"Bite me, Hayden Ferrand. Until Celestia came here… No, until Eirik came here we never had visitors, so I'm enjoying it. Don't ruin it for me."

"Do you guys know why they are here?" I asked.

"For Celestia. Everyone loves her," Trudy said.

"Some of them are here for a different reason," I said and got their attention. I explained what I'd learned from the goddess and watched their expressions. They were shocked. "So you've never attended anything like this before, Trudy?"

"Nope. I've never seen anything this exciting until now. Not that this is exciting. Jousting and sword fights. It is terrible." Despite her words, her eyes sparked with excitement.

"And barbaric," Hayden chipped in.

"What if I asked you to help?" I asked.

"Help how?" Trudy and Hayden said in unison.

"Eirik told me how you helped him fight at some market place by using your minds."

Trudy and Hayden exchanged grins.

"Can you do it again?" I asked.

"Yes, we can help like we did in Nidavellir." Hayden glanced at Trudy, who nodded.

"We got inside their heads, and they forgot to fight because they were busy reliving their worst nightmares," Trudy said. "I've even done it to the goddess' warriors when they pissed me off."

Feeling better, I sighed with relief. "Thank you, guys. I was thinking of getting Raine, too. I don't have active powers and"—I glanced at Jess—"you?"

Jess shook her head. "Me neither, but Eirik could help if you ask him."

"No, I can't. He should only focus on Celestia. We have to deal with this." We ate in silence, everyone lost in thought. I kept imagining the worst things that could happen to Echo. I needed to be distracted. "Can you guys retrieve my lost memories now?"

A muffled sound came from behind me, and I glanced over my shoulder to find Litr and Astrid. I thought they'd left. Litr looked panicked. I swear the Dwarf had more facial expressions than Dev as a soul.

"We can," Trudy said, and Hayden nodded.

"You won't mess with my other memories, will you?"

"Nope. We are really good," she bragged then glanced at Hayden. "Ask Echo or Eirik. We kicked ass in Nidavellir."

"Of course you did," Baldur said, entering the room through a portal. Litr followed him. He must have left to get him. "My girls eating breakfast without me?" He dropped a kiss on my temple. "Morning, Daughter."

"Morning." I'd just started thinking of him as a father, and he had to go and screw that up with his betrayal. That was how I saw it. Echo could die or worse—lose a challenge to some faceless, all-powerful giant. I glared at Baldur as he moved to Trudy and leaned down to study her face.

"Morning, child. I hope you're not up to mischief."

"Me? Never." She gave him a wide-eyed look, and he laughed.

"You've worn that innocent look often enough while doing something unconscionable, so you're not fooling me. Behave." He kissed her temple and moved to Jessica. "Morning, Daughter Number Two." She turned red. He placed a finger on her chin and tilted her to study her face. "What's this? Tears?"

"No, Father," Jessica whispered.

"You are a precious child, but Baldur sees all." He kissed her temple and moved to Hayden. He squeezed her shoulder. "Always nice to have you around, Hayden Ferrand. I still say you are related to an Asgardian. It will come to me."

"Hopefully never," she mumbled.

"Don't say that." He sat on the chair Litr had pulled out. He was between Hayden and me. "Family is important and must be cherished." He tucked a napkin under his chin and picked up his utensils. "So, girls, what is this about retrieving Einmyria's memories?"

"They suppressed my memories weeks ago," I said.

"Is that so?" Litr placed a plate piled with food in front of Baldur, who dug in, the honey on the pancakes dripping down his chin.

"It was for a good reason. You have some honey on your beard," I said. He tried to lick it with his tongue, and laughter erupted around the table. I even found his antics funny despite being angry with him. He was such a goofball. I wiped it off with my napkin. "There. It's gone."

He patted my hand. "Thanks, *dýrr mín*. Now about these memories, what can I do?"

I explained about Raine's wedding. "I just want those back. Celestia said Trudy and Hayden could retrieve them."

He studied Trudy and Hayden. "You can do this without harming her in any way? We just found her and don't want her forgetting about us."

He would wish he didn't know me if Echo got hurt.

Trudy nodded, her direct gaze not wavering.

"Okay. Give me your hand, *dýrr mín*." I did and watched him close his eyes. When he opened them, he smiled. "Nothing bad will happen."

I shot him a dubious look. "How do you know?"

"I am one of the best seers in the universe, Daughter." He gave me a sheepish grin. "At least I was. I even saw my own death. Since I knew it was my destiny, I didn't try to stop it. Your grandmother tried. Okay, look at me. Everything will be okay."

*Yeah, try telling that to Echo.* "Will it, Father? I know what you are doing, and I do not approve."

He caught on fast. "It's my job as your father to make sure he's worthy of you."

"What if something happens to him?"

He frowned. Bet he hadn't thought of that. If anything happened to Echo, I would never forgive him.

"Do you believe in him?" Baldur asked.

"Yes."

"Then he will prevail. Remember, he won't just be proving himself to me and your mother but to the people in this hall."

Damn. I should have known this was bigger than a father trying to make his future son-in-law sweat. I sighed. If he had to fight members of each group before some pompous son of a god or a king, I was getting him back-up. I needed Raine here.

"Fine," I said.

"Good. Trudy and Hayden, go ahead." His eyes didn't waver from mine, and he continued to grip my hand. I had a feeling it was his way of reassuring himself I was okay. I gripped his larger hand and waited.

Trudy and Hayden leaned forward to look at me. At first, I didn't feel anything. Then I felt a slight pressure in my head, and I tensed. I brought my other hand and placed it on top of Baldur's, happy he was here.

He smiled. "You are doing great."

How did he know? The thought barely flashed in my head when new memories drifted into my mind. There was one of me walking along the hallway toward the attendance office. Seeing three girls, a short one with a cloak. One in a semiformal dress that hugged her body, gorgeous red hair perfectly styled. And a third who downplayed her looks in a simple outfit. I smiled at my initial reaction to them. The scenes moved faster. The walk to the upstairs bathroom, arriving at the castle in England, and watching Raine come down the stairs.

"She was such a beautiful bride," I said, laughing.

More memories of Celestia and me talking rushed through my head. Asking Dev to help Mr. Cooper. Taking pictures with them. And finally, walking with Raine and her father to join Torin. Their vows were beautiful. The pressure eased, and Baldur dabbed my cheeks with a napkin.

"Are you okay, *dýrr?*" he asked.

A loud knock on the door stopped me from answering. Litr went to answer it, and a familiar voice reached me.

"Is Einmyria okay?"

"She is fine, Echo." Litr sounded like he was ready to slam the door on Echo's face. "The family is having a private moment."

"I need to see her," Echo insisted.

I stood, grinning.

"Let him in, Litr," Baldur bellowed. "Sit down, Einmyria." It was an order, and I found myself obeying. "Girls, go help Maera distribute food to the visitors."

Trudy and the others took their time standing up. Echo entered the room, and his eyes flew to me.

"You've been crying," he said in a gruff voice.

I nodded, grinning.

He scowled and stepped closer. I had a feeling he wasn't aware of anything or anyone in the room, except me.

"You're now smiling," he added, sounding confused.

"And crying. I just got back the memories of Raine's wedding. Trudy and Hayden retrieved them." I indicated the girls with a wave of my hand. Trudy had already opened a portal, but instead of leaving, they were deliberately taking their time. Echo's focus shifted to the others in the room. He went a little pale when he saw Baldur. Yep, he definitely hadn't noticed their presence.

He stepped aside and smiled sheepishly at the girls as they went through the portal. "Thank you for getting them back."

The girls grinned. Something in Trudy and Hayden's expressions when their eyes volleyed between Echo and me said they'd seen a lot more in my head than the wedding. I didn't care.

"Girls, close that portal now," Baldur ordered and waited until they did before waving to a chair. "Take a seat, Echo."

Wariness entered Echo's eyes, but he walked confidently forward and sat. He must have been in the gym because he wore a tank top and sweatpants, his perfectly sculpted arms glistening with sweat. He smelled so good, and I wanted to lean closer and inhale him. Kiss him. It had been almost five days since we kissed, and I missed the taste of him.

He kicked my leg under the table, and my eyes flew to his face, but he wasn't looking at me. His focus was on Baldur, and I realized I'd been staring at him. I was probably drooling. I sat up straighter. Baldur was studying Echo with narrowed eyes.

"Have you eaten breakfast, young man?"

"No, Golden One. I just got back and went straight to the gym when I felt... I was in the gym."

He was nervous. A first since we'd met. He swallowed and glanced at me. When he nudged my leg, I realized I was staring at him again. My face warmed, and I forced myself to look away.

"Litr, prepare a plate for our guest," Baldur said. He lifted his tumbler and chugged apple juice while still staring at Echo. For the first time, I saw how intimidating he could be. He had a presence that was easy to ignore when around my mother because she tended to dominate everyone whenever she entered a room. But without her, he became the center of attention.

"You do know these chambers are off-limits to Grimnirs."

*Oh brother.* I glanced at Echo to see if he was shrinking, but his eyes didn't waver.

"I didn't stop to think. She was in distress, and I felt she needed..."—*me* was implied, but not said—"help."

"So, you knew my daughter was in distress and charged in here to investigate?"

"Yes, Golden One," Echo said without hesitation.

"And how may I ask did you know this?"

"It's hard to explain, sir."

"I have time."

Crap! My instinct to protect him kicked in. "We've been working together for almost a year, Father," I explained. "I help the souls needing closure, and Echo reaps them. We make a good team."

Baldur studied me. Then he smiled. "That's good to know, Daughter." He focused on Echo. "How did you know my daughter was in distress?"

"I just do. It's a connection I still don't understand myself. When she is sad or hurt, I always know."

"Interesting. How did you get past the guards?"

Echo frowned. "I think they stepped out of my way."

The corners of Baldur's lips twitched as though he was trying not to smile. "Litr!"

"I'll check on them, Golden One." The Dwarf placed a stack of hot pancakes in front of Echo and hurried out of the room.

"Eat your food. You're going to need your strength," Baldur said and drained his drink.

Echo paled again.

Litr returned, walked to Baldur's side, and whispered in his ear. I tried to hear what he was saying with little success. Litr took Baldur's plate away and replenished his cup. Then he came to collect my plate.

"Are the guards okay?" I asked him, but Baldur answered instead.

"They'll live," he said, and I knew Echo had probably barreled through them.

"The goddess is going to need help keeping order around the hall, Echo. I'm pulling you off reaping duty and putting you in charge of Einmyria's protection."

Panic flashed in Echo's eyes. I was in the process of sipping my drink, and some went the wrong way. I started to cough. Echo and Baldur both stood to pat my back.

"Protection?" Echo asked, going back to his seat. "Is she in danger?"

"Yes." Baldur stayed standing. He wiped his lips and handed the napkin to Litr.

"Who would dare want to hurt her?" Echo asked.

"The suitors lining up outside the hall could easily kidnap her." This time, Echo choked on his drink. I thumped his back while Baldur watched with a smug smile. My father had a cruel streak in him. "The only people here to keep vigil are the villagers and the clans from Jötunheim. The rest of them, erecting larger and fancier tents in our front yard, are here for Einmyria." The paler Echo got, the broader Baldur's grin grew. He even gripped Echo's shoulder. "The word is out about her arrival, and more will be coming from all over the realms to ask for her hand. I expect many marriage proposals the second they catch a glimpse of her. But none of them is good enough for her. Not a single one until they prove themselves worthy."

Baldur rubbed his hands and grinned gleefully as though looking forward to denying every request. I guess I should have been happy, except he was being mean to Echo in the process.

"So eat, shower, and report here to be her bodyguard since you've shown that a dozen of my well-trained guards cannot stop you when you believe she is in danger." Baldur pressed a kiss on my temple. "Go see your mother when you are done, *elskr mín*. I believe she was hoping you'd join her in the Sorting Room again."

# CHAPTER 14. MY MOTHER, MY CLAN

"Suitors?" Echo growled when we were alone.

"He knows about us," I said.

"How in Hel's Mist did they hear about you? If they think they can waltz in here and propose to you—"

I shoved a piece of bacon in his mouth. He glared at me. "You're not listening to me. My parents know about us. Mom told me. My father invited the suitors."

Echo frowned. "Why?"

"There's going to be a tourney so the men can show me how manly they are. Anyone I favor will be challenged by the others and beaten to a pulp. Namely you. My father invited them here so you could prove to him, the hall, and all the realms that you are worthy of me. I tried telling my mother you've already done that, but she wouldn't listen until she realized my father's grand plan. She was livid."

"Oh." Echo grinned. "Good. I saw a few showing off their sword skills earlier, and I wasn't impressed. I can take them all."

"No, you can't. It's barbaric, and I will not be a part of it. Neither will you. I had a vision, and it doesn't end well."

"For them or for me?" He chuckled. I kicked him under the table. "It doesn't matter what you saw, Cora-mia. Any cuts and bruises I acquire along the way, I'll wear with pride. I'm going to enjoy knocking deities and princes on their asses."

Muffled laughter came from Litr. When I looked at him, he wore a straight face. I liked the Dwarf, but this was not a laughing matter.

"You need to take this seriously, Echo. I'm going to talk to Eirik about it." I got up, but he caught my wrist. "What?"

He tugged me closer. "This is my fight, not your brother's."

He was acting like it was fun and games while I kept seeing the vision of his bloodied face. If he thought I was going to let this go, he was out of his mind. No one was messing with him while I was around.

"Okay, Echo."

His eyes narrowed. "Why are you agreeing with me?"

I leaned down and kissed him. "Because you are right. This is your battle. Later, warrior. I'll be at Eirik's."

"Don't try and solicit his help," he warned.

"I won't."

"And don't leave his quarters until I get there."

"Okay."

He continued to scowl. "Now I know you are up to something. You're downright scary when you agree with me."

"Apologize to the guards."

Litr opened a portal to Eirik's living room. Echo was still staring at me when the portal closed. I headed to the bedroom, but Eirik wasn't there. Instead, I found Celestia's father reading to her. He stopped reading and started to get up when he saw me.

"Don't get up, Chief Deveraux," I said, walking to the other side of the bed. "How is she doing?"

"The same. I've never understood magic, but what if magic can't help her this time?"

"It will. We just need to find what works."

"One of the kitchen maids gave me this," Celestia's aunt Genevieve said, entering the room with a tray containing a basket covered with a cloth, a pitcher of mead, and two glasses. The smell of fresh loaf filled the air. Since she used her shoulder to open the door, she didn't see me until the door swung open, and she turned. "Your, uh, Your Highness. I didn't know—"

"Don't, please. My name is Cora. Einmyria actually. I have to get used to the name while here. I'm just a simple girl raised by two farmers."

Genevieve chuckled. "Simple? I don't think so, but I'm happy you are down-to-earth because I have no idea how to address you or your parents." She placed the pitcher and the glasses on top of the coffee table by the sofa, poured the drink into a tumbler, and gave it to Celestia's father. "It's a mad house out there. I think Eirik is ready to go full dragon on them. He's too worried about Celestia to care that they are here for her. I do love that boy. So protective."

"He is a nice young man, your brother," Chief Deveraux said. "At first I didn't approve of her getting involved with him, but he's proven himself. Even here, he understands her need to help people and encourages it. She's only been here a few months, and she's already touched so many people."

I didn't want to burst their bubble; so instead, I sat on the edge of the bed and took Celestia's hand. The guilt still ate at me. I kept hoping to find her alone, so I could apologize for the part I'd played in her coma.

"Talk to her," her aunt encouraged.

I glanced at her. Had she read my mind?

"I'm a nurse and know how therapeutic it is to hear the voices of loved ones while in a coma. Richard has been reading to her."

"I used to volunteer at an assisted living facility. My charges loved to have me read to them even though they'd act like my presence bothered them."

"How sweet. We need more young people helping the elderly at such facilities and nursing homes. Why did you stop?"

"My work with souls made that impossible." I stroked Celestia's hand and focused on her. "Listen, Celestia. I know we just met, but I've come to see you as my sister. You are strong, funny, and unstoppable, so I know you can beat this. Please, fight and come back to us. Not just for my brother, but for our family. The goddess and Baldur miss you. She's told me so many stories about you and how you've helped her people. You should see the hall and the grounds. It's packed with people who want you to get better. My brother is miserable without you. I haven't seen him smile since I got here, and he's walking around like a piece of him is missing. And I want a chance to really get to know you, so please come back." I leaned down and kissed her.

Everything went black, but this time, I knew what was coming. Black gave way to the snowy landscape and the crowd of onlookers yelling for blood. Two fighters in the arena were beating the crap out of each other while we watched from the hallway behind the glass wall. Once again, I recognized a bloodied Echo. Wincing, I averted my eyes and found Raine standing beside me, her hazel eyes glowing. What was she doing in my vision? Beside her was Trudy, her eyes glowing, too. On my other side was Hayden and… Celestia?

The scene faded, and I stepped away from the bed, grinning. Celestia was going to be okay.

"She's going to be okay," I told her father. He and Genevieve studied me with doubtful expressions. "Sooner than you know it. You'll see."

"We'll be leaving later today, but we'll be back," Genevieve said. "My shift starts tomorrow morning, and Zack's father doesn't know about realms and the gods. He thinks we are in Europe somewhere, visiting Celestia and her fiancé. And Richard"—she indicated Celestia's father with a wave of her hand—"has a department to run. We'll return later in the week. Celestia's vitals are normal, and they are keeping her hydrated with that concoction Maera feeds her. I don't know what's in it, but she's in good hands." She stroked Celestia's hair. "She's loved here."

"She is, and she'll be okay," I added again, wishing I could tell them about my vision. I bade them goodbye and left the room. The guards saw me coming and bowed. I recognized Creed.

"Morning, Creed," I said.

"Morning, young goddess. How is Celestia doing?"

"The same, but she's going to be okay. She'll wake up soon."

He nodded. "Thank you. Can I open a portal for you somewhere?"

"Yes, to Eirik. I need to talk to him." A portal opened before I finished talking. "Thank you."

"I didn't do it," Creed said.

Had I just opened my first portal? Grinning, I went through it and entered a room that looked like a den, except it was done in ivory and gold. Gilded reliefs bordered its marble walls and picture frames. Eirik and Baldur sat by the fireplace, talking, and both got to their feet when they saw me.

"She's going to be okay, Eirik. I saw a vision of her at the fight, and she was fine."

"Vision?" he asked. "Since when do you get visions?"

"Since Kayville. I saw Mother take my blanket. I didn't know she was the one, but I guessed from Celestia's reaction."

"Your mother did what?" Baldur roared.

"It's okay. She returned it, and I kind of understood why she needed to confirm I was the real Einmyria. We even discussed it when I got here."

Baldur was still scowling.

"She apologized," I added.

He frowned. "Your mother apologized?"

"Yes. It's in the past."

"About your visions," Eirik said impatiently.

"Yes, I, uh, had some of the scenes from the wedding before you guys told us what happened. They could have been just memories, but they were so vivid I'm convinced they were visions. And I've had two since I came here."

I was surprised when Eirik believed me without question. "How did she look?"

"Worried."

His eyebrows slammed down.

"No, I mean she looked okay, but she was worried about Echo, who was being crushed by a giant." I gave Baldur a pointed look. "Has our father told you what he's planned for Echo?"

Unease flittered across Baldur's face while Eirik's mouth twitched.

"It's not funny," I snapped.

"We're talking about Echo, Sis," Eirik said. "He's like a cat with nine lives. He'll be fine."

"Not according to my vision. It is a barbaric practice, Father." I glared at Baldur.

"I can call it off if it makes you happy, Daughter," he said.

"No," a familiar voice said from behind me, and I whipped around.

Echo stood in the doorway. "May I come in, Golden One?"

Baldur nodded, but he threw me a worried glance.

"What do you mean by no?" I asked. "You haven't seen my visions, Echo. I will not have you reduced to ground beef while I watch."

He closed the gap between us and cupped my face, not caring that my father and Eirik were in the room. He peered at me. "I'll be fine, sweetheart. I promise you. The parts you didn't see are when I'll be winning." He smirked, and I punched his chest. He didn't even have the decency to wince. "I need to do this."

"No, you don't. You don't have to prove anything to anyone. I know you. I know you're worthy of my love and I'm worthy of yours."

"The rest of the realm doesn't know that. I'm doing this for them, so they can leave us alone for the rest of our lives. Don't you want that? Just you and me in our happy bubble, everyone else looking in and wishing they could be us."

"You are silly."

"But right because I'm going to make you the happiest woman in all the realms."

"I know."

He kissed me right in front of my father. "You don't have to watch me fight if you don't want to."

"Of course, I have to watch you. What kind of a fiancée would I be if I'm not out there cheering for you?" Shaking my head, I turned and focused on the Throne Hall. "I'm going to check out the competition."

The portal opened to the Throne Hall, but it was empty, except for the guards. Creed appeared and led the way once I explained where I wanted to go. A wide doorway led to the Waiting Hall, where a crowd was gathered, some seated on benches and others on the floor. Most of them were Dwarves from Eastern Gjöll Pass, Creed explained. The regular-sized ones were Jötnar. Unlike the Throne Hall, this room had more benches and mirrors on the inner walls, which made the crowd seem even larger. The first ones to see me nudged the ones next to them.

"Einmyria," whispers spread across the room. One by one, they dropped to one knee and bowed.

"Tell them not to do that, please," I said.

Creed yelled something in a language I didn't understand, and the people rose. They still stared and whispered. Some inched closer, cutting us off. Creed and his team tried to stop them, but they were determined. I told him to stop.

"You are Einmyria," one Dwarf said.

"Yes, I am. Thank you for coming to see Celestia. She will be okay because she can feel how much you love and need her."

A woman of regular size with a baby in her arms walked around the crowd. The guards moved as though to intercept her, but once again, I stopped them.

"My baby would not be alive if it weren't for Celestia. She healed her when she was still in my belly," she said.

"Are you also from Eastern Gjöll Pass?"

"No. I'm from Ironwood Forest, Jötunheim." She nodded at a group of about ten adults and children. "That's my family. Chief Skavnir will be coming, too. We couldn't wait. The second the traders came with the news, we left." Her chin trembled, and tears filled her eyes. "Celestia must get better. She's a gifted healer. We only have one like her in the south, and he is old."

"She will be fine." I touched the baby's soft hair. "Your daughter is beautiful."

"Thank you." An older girl came from their group and showed me where Celestia had healed her. She was her older daughter, Laufey. She was almost as tall as Celestia but sounded like a child.

As though a floodgate had opened, more came forward. Pregnant mothers, old men, children. The more I commented on their babies, the more they wanted to talk. Some of the visitors were asking about Celestia, while others wanted to know where I'd been all these years. I avoided answering questions about me and focused on Celestia. In minutes, I was surrounded. Creed and his guards wore helpless expressions as they were pushed out of the way.

"Back up, please," Echo called out, and the questions stopped. He hadn't come alone. Syn, Nara, and Rhys were beside him. The four towered over the Dwarves, who stepped back.

"You didn't have to scare them away," I told Echo and received a scowl.

"Creed, I got her."

The guard nodded and walked away with his partners.

"We should be heading that way, Goddess. Your mother is expecting you."

I glanced toward the Sorting Hall. The windows facing the east, where the visitors had erected their tents, were in the opposite direction.

"Just a second. Like I said, I'm checking out the competition." I took off. The goddess had brought me to this side of the building to show me the Banquet Hall and the Ballroom. It led to the eastern Resting Halls. The room curved and disappeared around the bend. Ahead were the unstained east windows. Several staff members were pretending to clean them while studying the people outside. They moved away when they saw me.

Beautiful, colorful tents were erected everywhere, their colors stark against the white snow on the ground and the outer wall. Some of them were huge and gaudy with gold frills and embroidery. Surrounding them were smaller ones of similar colors. All had flags at the highest point.

Echo slid beside me, while the other three spread out as though creating a no-walking zone around me. I didn't know how the goddess did things here, but I didn't think it was necessary for me to have guards, suitors or not. What could they possibly do? Kidnap me? The guests in the Waiting Hall hadn't seemed dangerous, just eager to meet me and ask about Celestia.

Ignoring Echo, I focused my attention on the craziness outside. "So the colors of the flag represent a realm?"

"A clan," Echo said. "The ones with single colors are for various Light Elves families from Álfheimr. That belongs to a minor god from Vanaheim, and so do those two. The black with snarling saber tooth tiger belongs to a *Dokkalfr*."

"A what?

"*Dokkalfr* means Dark Elf. They are a warrior race, like Asgardians. They left Álfheimr after a civil war and couldn't find a home anywhere else. The Dwarves allowed them to settle in Svartalfheim. They live on the surface while the Dwarves build their homes underground."

Back at home, I had shown zero interest in other realms, except Helheim. Now I wish I'd read more or asked Lavania.

"Do you know any *Dokkalfr*?" I asked.

"No, but Eirik is friends with one," Echo continued. "Niorun. She has silver eyes, lots of tattoos, and an attitude. You can't miss her. I saw her around earlier. Like Lavion, she has an open invitation to Ejudnir and shouldn't be camping out there, but I saw her out there. She and her maiden warriors must be guarding a prince from their land. The tents to our left belong to shifters from southern Jötunheim," Echo continued, adding anecdotes whenever he mentioned different clans. He pointed out the different flags and banners of the Cat, Bear, and Raven Clans, ice giants, and the water giants.

"The fire Jötnar rarely bother with other realms, but you never know." He inched closer and took my hand, threading our fingers together. "You might be the one to make them leave their homes."

He was trying to be funny, but I wasn't amused. I didn't understand the customs of these people and hated that he was being forced to participate in them. More carriages were still arriving at the gates.

One had a huge red and yellow flag with an animal in the center, but that was not what had me gawking. Two dragons—one gray and the other white—circled above them. They flew over the castle, bellowing and causing a ruckus. They disappeared out of sight.

"Is that the Dragon Clan?"

Echo chuckled. "The dragons are Karle and his sister, Olea. They are from Ironwood Forest Wolf Clan. Your clan."

I blinked. "Mine?"

"Yes. They are your mother's people, so that means they are yours, too."

I'd been an only child with Mom and Dad as my only living relatives for so long it was strange imagining an extended family. When Raine had come into my life, I had considered her an honorary sister. Now, I had two sets of parents, a brother, an almost sister-in-law, an adopted sister who couldn't look me in the eye, and a clan. A clan. My people. It was surreal.

"One of the mothers in the Waiting Hall said she was from the Wolf Clan. Celestia saved her baby."

"Eirik and Celestia often visit them. I'll take you if you'd like."

It was the first time he'd included himself in what I might do in other realms. "They are giants?"

"Jötnar, yes," Echo said. "But they can shift to regular sizes. Some, like your mother and you, don't have the ability to shift back and forth."

"Isn't that why Angr... uh, my grandmother didn't keep me and left me in Ironwood Forest?" Home of my clan. It was going to be a while before that sank in, but I liked it. I belonged to a freaking clan. "Because I couldn't shift?"

"Yes. I know you are discovering your roots, and I'm happy for you, but we would never have met had she not left you in that forest."

I glanced at him and grinned. "I don't know, Echo. I'd like to think you and I would have found each other somehow. We were meant to be together. All this crap my father started is not going to change the fact that my destiny is linked to yours."

"When you say things like that, I want to open a portal, take you to my quarters, and make love to you," he said while staring straight ahead.

"Why don't you?"

Chuckling, he lifted my hand to his lips and kissed my knuckles. As though he remembered we were not alone, he glanced over his shoulder. For whatever reason, he returned to his old, spontaneous self. He cupped the back of my head and kissed me hard and possessively in full view of the hall and anyone staring at our window.

"I hope the prancing peacocks out there saw that," he whispered when he lifted his head. It took a few seconds for my world to right itself and for my senses to come close to resembling normal. Then, what he'd said registered, and I glanced outside.

I'd been so busy staring at the spectacular tents I hadn't paid attention to the people sitting or standing in front of them. Some were warming themselves by fire barrels, while others didn't appear bothered by the cold. One giant didn't even wear a shirt. He wore a robe, his masculine chest bare. His face was hairless, and even from where I stood, I could see his striking features. He was the giant from my vision. Could Echo take him?

"Stare hard enough and he'll know you are interested," Echo mumbled.

I chuckled. "I can still look at a man and marvel at his perfection."

"No, you can't. I'm the beginning and the end for you. Your destiny is with me."

Was that jealousy in his voice? I lifted my hand and brushed the back of my arm against his. "It is. Doesn't change the fact that all this is new to me and I'm allowed to stare."

"What if they misunderstand and think you are interested in them."

I scoffed at the idea. "Then that's their problem, not mine. No, that's your problem since you insist on fighting them. Now, stop scowling and take me to your goddess."

"You are my goddess." He stroked my cheek. Then he went back to scowling at the people outside. "And no one claims what's mine," Echo vowed. "Elves, Dwarves, or Jötnar. No one."

The thought of him fighting that giant filled my heart with dread. But since there was no point venting about it, I walked away. When my eyes met Nara's, she gave me a broad grin. I didn't return it. I had enough on my plate without adding her ever-changing moods to it.

Echo led the way across the hall. He walked ahead and to my left while Syn was to my right. Nara and Rhys took the rear. I saw my clanswoman and waved. I should sit down with her sometime and learn about my people.

I continued past the empty Throne Hall to the entrance to the

Sorting Room. The goddess was inside, talking to Baldur. The number of souls was unusually high. I hurried to their side.

~*~

"Sorry, I was distracted by the tents."

"I'd love to kick out the whole lot, but your father will never forgive me."

Baldur chuckled. "Your mother is joking. She is a gracious hostess, and once she gets over her annoyance, she'll open the doors and let them inside."

"Doesn't mean I have to like it," the goddess said. "They'll be underfoot, eavesdropping when I forbid people from being near the Sorting Hall." She kissed Baldur's cheek. "Go. We have work to do."

"I will need your decision soon, *elskr mín*. We can't have sons of every prominent person, god, and king from all the realms freezing outside our hall."

She grinned as though that was exactly what she hoped for. "Maybe they'll pack up and go home."

"Soon, Hela," Baldur added, then he kissed my cheek and walked away.

"Are you really not going to let them in?"

"I will. Your father enjoys entertaining, and I find it hard to refuse him anything. He tells me Echo plans to face anyone who challenges his right to court you."

I glanced toward the entrance at Echo. "He explained in his charming way why he needs to do it."

She sighed. "And you found yourself agreeing with him even though you don't like it?"

"Exactly." I gave her a sheepish grin.

"Irresistible men are the bane of women's existence."

I laughed. I hadn't expected her to say something so normal. "That's so true."

"Now tell me about your visions. I heard you've had several."

I glanced at the souls. "But the souls."

"Can wait. I want to hear about your visions. It's an ability that's making me rethink a lot of things. Your brother inherited the berserker powers from your grandfather, but you might have your father and grandmother's ability. Both are gifted clairvoyants."

I told her what I'd seen, and she dissected it, easing my fears about Echo. "I'll be there, too. Nothing is going to happen to him if I can help it."

Her voice and the look in her eyes said she meant it, and I believed her. Just like that, she stopped being the goddess and became my mother.

"Are we going to cheat?" I whispered.

"No, Einmyria. Goddesses don't cheat." She lifted her chin, and I stood straighter, imitating her. "We direct the outcome of events because we can."

"*Noblesse oblige?*"

"More like deity oblige."

I hugged her. "Thanks, Mother. I was really worried about Echo."

She kissed my temple. "No need to thank me, Daughter. It's a mother's duty to watch out for her children. I'd be remiss in my duties if I didn't look out for him when you love him. Now about the souls. Are you sure you want to do this? You don't have to right now."

"It's okay." Despite her words, I could tell she really wanted me with her. Doing the same thing over and over again for thousands of years must get boring and lonely. Now she had me. "I don't mind, and I really do want to practice. So first, I engage medium runes, will them while they are in energy form, and blend with them, listen to them. Then, when they are done, I engage warding runes to expel them."

"That's right. Do you want a chair? I don't want you getting tired."

She was a worrywart, too. Just like Mom in Kayville. "I'm fine, Mother. Besides, you are standing. If you can take it, so can I."

"Are you making fun of my age, young lady?" The eyebrow above her blue eye shot up, and she didn't crack a smile, yet I heard the teasing in her voice.

"No, I'd never do that. You look fabulous, but the fact is"—I wrinkled my nose and grinned—"you are old. Ancient."

She laughed out loud, drawing the attention of the guards and the Grimnirs, including Baldur who was talking to Echo and his team. The surprise on their faces was baffling.

"That's a good one. I'll have to tell your father. If I'm old, what is he?"

"One-foot-in-the-grave old?" I added without thinking. "I, uh, I didn't mean to say that."

"Because he died and came here?" She chuckled. "I don't care about his previous life. We got the best part of him. His soul. Did you know that his body was burned on a pyre on top of his ship? The most beautiful and largest ship in all of Asgard. Thor, despite his strength, could not push it. They had to use a Jötun. Our people." She sobered up, reached out, and tucked a lock of my hair behind my ear. "I'm happy you are home."

"I'm happy I'm home, too." And it was the truth, despite the unwanted suitors.

"Okay. Let's get to work."

For two hours, we welcomed souls, and I used my runes to help those who needed closure before sending them to their Resting Halls. Twice, there was some commotion by the entrance, but no one disturbed us. When we were done, it was lunchtime. Baldur was waiting for us when we left the room. He didn't look happy. He whispered something to Mother and whisked her away.

"What's going on?"

"The guards your mother sent to Asgard returned without Goddess Eir," Echo said. "Your father is pissed."

"Why didn't they bring her back?"

"They weren't allowed past the gate. Heimdall was gone, so his guards placed them under arrest while waiting for his return. It's been over a week. They were lucky a certain Valkyrie overheard the guards talking about spies from Helheim and asked what was going on. Somehow he got them released."

"Which Valkyrie?"

"Andris."

"I told you he wasn't bad. Man, Eirik is going to be devastated by this."

The number of people inside the Waiting Hall had nearly doubled. And since they weren't dressed fancily, I assumed more villagers had arrived to keep vigil.

When we arrived at Eirik's, it was too quiet. Usually, I could hear his voice from the door. Imagining the worst, I rushed into the bedroom, but he wasn't alone. The room was packed.

Lavion was back, and with him were two elderly healers. One had a hand on Celestia's forehead while the other touched her chest. Tammy watched them with narrowed eyes. She was never far from Celestia's side. Zack, seated on the lounge, had been scarce, but I'd seen him with the other three girls. Hayden, Jessica, and Trudy stood at the foot of the bed while Eirik was in his usual seat. They all looked up when I entered. I went to sit on the arm of Eirik's chair.

"What do you see?" Eirik asked the healers.

The Dwarf touching Celestia's head had been staring at me. She shifted her attention to Celestia. "I see memories of her healing the villagers, then a man in a white robe. There are memories of possession and tormenting people." She glanced at Eirik. "Has she ever done anything like that while in the astral plane?"

"No," Eirik, Hayden, and Tammy said at the same time.

"Celestia is a healer," Eirik added sharply. "She'd never possess anyone."

"I'm only telling you what I'm seeing, Rising Star," the Dwarf said. "I didn't mean to offend."

"There's also a very strange energy coming from her, but it's not hers," the second Dwarf said. "It is weak."

"Is it my grandmother's?" Eirik asked.

The Dwarf shook her head. "No. I'd recognize hers from what she did to the orphans in my village."

A hollow feeling settled in my stomach as I listened to them. There could be another explanation for what they were seeing. Dev. He'd possessed people and messed with their heads, and his memories and energy could have transferred to Celestia when she'd helped him.

"Can you compare the different energy inside her with another?" I asked.

The Dwarves studied me.

"Yes," the one touching Celestia's head said. "Do you know where it's from?"

"Yes." I couldn't tell them how Celestia had helped Dev. Echo had said those with her kind of gift kept it a secret. "She treated a friend of mine. Maybe his memories and energies were transferred to her. If I brought him here, could you check his energy and compare it with hers?"

"I've never heard of anything like that happening, but then again, I've never met a healer like this young lady," the first healer said. "So young yet so powerful. Yes, I can compare their energies."

I glanced at Eirik. He wore a bleak expression. "We need to bring Dev here."

He nodded and called out, "Echo?"

Echo entered the room. He must have been in the living room. "I'll get him."

"No, send Rhys and Nara. Father wants you to keep an eye on Cora." Eirik went to Celestia and dropped a kiss on her forehead. Then, ignoring everyone, he headed for the door.

"Eirik," I said when he brushed past me.

"I need to be alone," he murmured and continued out the door.

I saw the pity on the others' faces. They didn't have to say it. They all knew helping Dev had messed up Celestia, and Eirik was pissed about it. He was probably blaming me for it. Without speaking to anyone, I left the room.

Echo was talking to Rhys and Nara in the rotunda. I walked past them without slowing down and headed straight to my parents' quarters. I dropped on my bed and went back to the place where I'd been when I'd first arrived in Eljudnir, blaming myself for what was happening to Celestia.

# CHAPTER 15. I'LL DIE FOR YOU

A knock at the door announced Echo. Without saying a word, he crawled beside me and tucked me under his chin, not caring that my mother might walk in on us.

"It's not your fault," he whispered.

"It is."

"Do you want me to talk to Eirik?"

"No. In his present mood, he might barbecue you." I sat up. "The weirdest thing is I know she'll be okay. I saw it in a vision. She was with me in the glass hallway, looking down at you fighting one of the giants. Raine was there, too."

"When did you see this?"

"This morning after breakfast. I don't know how Celestia wakes up, but she does. In the meantime, I have to find a way to help her. We'll start by exonerating Dev."

"Rhys and Nara went to get him. I don't think memories are transferable. Energy, yes, but not memories." He stroked my arms. Then he reached down and laced our fingers. "I'm supposed to ask Litr to bring you lunch."

"I'm not hungry."

"I am. You want to come with me to Grimnirs Hall for lunch?"

I lifted my head to study his face. "Seriously?"

He nodded.

"Okay."

"Good. May I carry you there?"

"Is that your way of telling the entire hall we are together?"

"Eating lunch together does that. Kissing you does that. Carrying you is my way of keeping you close to my heart."

I grinned. No wonder I was crazy about him. He said the sweetest, corniest things ever. "I like the thought, but I'd feel ridiculous. I don't want my people to think I'm the kind of woman who needs to be carried around. However, I'll eat lunch with you in the hall. So put me down, please."

"Can't I at least carry you to the door? Hold you just a little longer?"

Really corny. A knock on the door interrupted him, and I wiggled from his arms. Litr was on the other side of the door when I opened it. He didn't even blink when he saw Echo.

"The Rising Star wants to see you outside the dragon's room. He sent Karle, but he got lost."

"Dragon's room?" I asked.

"It's where he changes, but we are going to lunch first," Echo said.

"No, we're going to see him first," I said.

Echo groaned. "If he does or says anything to hurt your feelings, he'll have to deal with me," he vowed, and Litr chortled.

"It's not funny, Litr," I reprimanded him.

"No, young goddess. But you need these before you go outside." He gave me a green fur-lined cloak with a hoodie. The inside was warm and so soft I sighed. The gloves, also fur-lined, came to my elbows.

"Thank you. They fit perfectly. Whose are they?"

"They are your mother's."

My mother's. I might not have known her for most of my life, yet I felt a closeness to her that was hard to explain. Maybe it was because she took such pride in my work with souls and was excited about my abilities, while Mom and Dad in Kayville had tried to hide them.

"Okay, Mr. Hothead. Let's go." I took Echo's arm. "And you cannot pick a fight with my brother. He's hurting, and we both know he would not have asked Celestia to help Dev if it weren't for me. So I'm responsible for her situation." Echo opened his mouth, but I shook my head. "Not a word. Let's prove that Dev didn't contaminate her energy, and I'll stop blaming myself."

We followed Litr to the rotunda, then through a portal to a hallway with high small windows. Mother hadn't shown me this side of the hall.

"He is outside." Litr pushed open a side door, and cold air drifted into the hallway.

Echo went ahead of me and growled. "We have a problem."

"What?" I asked, trying to see around him.

"Some of the preening buffoons are coming this way. Litr, get Syn and some guards. I don't know what Eirik was thinking asking you to join him. I have a mind to go out there and give him a lecture on your safety."

"Do you really think I'm not safe, or is my father just being overprotective?"

"I'll take overprotective over a mob knocking you down in their eagerness to meet you. When they present you, it's going to be in an orderly, stately manner. You are a goddess and deserve to be treated like one."

I didn't know how to respond to that, so I kept quiet. Litr returned with Syn and two other guards. They went to intercept the guests while Echo and I trudged through the snow to where the golden and the gray dragons stood, hot breath blowing from their noses and turning the air foggy.

"I'll help Syn keep them away," Echo said and left. I tilted my head to study the dragons. They were huge, but Eirik towered over the gray dragon, his scales gleaming. I wondered why he didn't have his chipped horn fixed. He lowered his head and stared at me with his big eyes. Everything about him was huge. His jaws. His teeth. His wings.

"I'm sorry for storming out like that." His voice was a low rumble that was both familiar and strange.

"Don't be."

"No, I shouldn't have. Trudy just chewed my ears for doing it. I didn't know you thought I did it because I blamed you for Celestia's situation. Far from it. If anyone should take the blame, it's me."

"Why? Celestia helped Dev because of me, not you."

"No, I asked Celestia to help him because I felt he deserved it. He helped Raine's father down that aisle, he helped save you from dark souls, and he brought Echo and Rhys back together, which meant no tension around the hall. Mother was getting tired of their rift. Helping Dev was for everyone, but the decision was mine. If he contaminated

Celestia's energy, it's because something went wrong and laying blame is not going to fix it. Are we good?"

Every second I spent in his company showed me how much Eirik had grown and changed. "Of course."

"You haven't met Karle, have you?"

I waved at the gray dragon. "No, but I saw him and his sister when they arrived. Echo said you are from Jötunheim. Nice to meet you, Karle."

Karle stared at me slack-jawed without responding.

Eirik groaned. "Ignore him. If his sister were around, he'd get his act together. What? Why are you staring at me like that?"

How could I not stare at him? He was a dragon. A freaking talking dragon. My brother. "Damn, you are huge."

He chuckled, the sound rumbling through him. "Don't say it like it's a bad thing. Thanks for sharing your vision. When Celestia is up and about, I'll take you up and show you the entire realm."

"Uh, let's take it one step at a time. I have to get used to you as a dragon first, not the annoying guy who used to tease me." I glanced at Karle. "He used to be so mean to me when we were young, there were times I actually thought I hated him." Karle bobbed his head without speaking. So as not to embarrass him, I focused on Eirik. "May I touch your scales? I'm dying to find out how they feel."

He lowered his head. "Go ahead."

"They are smooth," I said, touching his cheeks. The images that followed didn't surprise me. I didn't tell Eirik about them, but I grinned and asked, "Why the chipped horn?"

"A badge I wear with honor. One day, I'll tell you the story. We have to go, Sis. Keep an eye on Celestia for me while I'm gone, okay?"

"Okay." I waved to them and backed away. Karle was still staring at me with a dopey expression. Eirik chuckled and bumped him. "Let's go, Casanova."

Karle turned, but I still heard him say, "She is—"

"My sister, so stop drooling," Eirik retorted. "It's embarrassing."

"I don't care. She's beautiful."

"Next time, try telling her that while looking at her."

I watched them take off, their massive wings sending snow flying in the air. I tried to cover my face, but the blast of air they created nearly knocked me off my feet.

"I got you," Echo said, steadying me. "Let's take you back inside before we have a riot on our hands." I saw what he meant when I turned around. The people he, Syn, and the guards had been detaining had tripled in number and were getting closer. Some were pointing at me. I heard them yell out my name as Echo ushered me inside the hall. He slammed the door shut.

"Damn opportunists. Lavion must have described you, because the second the blast of wind knocked off the hood of your cloak, they recognized you."

"I don't care. I had a premonition." I hugged him. "That's the third one today, Echo. Third. It took Raine forever to get hers. The magic here probably has something to do with it, but a touch triggers it. I touched my ring, and I got one about you." I removed the gloves and cupped his face. "Come on. Show me his future. Something. Anything." Nothing. I went to Syn and gripped his hands. He'd just walked in from outside, and they were cold.

"Not that I mind the love, but what's going on?" the Nubian asked.

"She's trying to get a premonition," Echo said with a resigned sigh.

"So I'm going to touch everyone until I get one." They stared at me as though I'd lost my mind, but I didn't care. "Hey, don't judge me. I come from a line of powerfully gifted people, and my grandmother dumped me in a forest because she thought I was worthless. Her loss. I didn't even realize how I felt about not being gifted until now." I stared at my hands and grinned. "I belong. I didn't feel it at first because I thought everyone in my family had a gift, except me. Mother can move things. She lifted her hand and the scepter flew into it. She can read minds. Father has the power of premonition. I mean, I was happy helping souls, but this is different." I hugged the guards, who looked both shocked and amused. No premonition. I kissed Litr on his ruddy cheek. "Damn, nothing."

Syn and Echo exchanged grins.

"Cut it out, you two. I will find what triggers it. Come on. Let's check on Celestia, then go to lunch."

Tammy was with Celestia, so I knew she was in good hands. From there we headed to Grimnirs Hall. The sheer number of men and women from every walk of life stuffing their faces was mind-boggling. Echo led the way to a table. It wasn't until we sat that I noticed the silence and the stares.

"Want to say something, Goddess Einmyria?" Syn asked.

"No, ignore them," Echo said.

"At least order them to stop staring," Syn countered. "They'll listen."

"Go sit somewhere else, Syn. She doesn't need to say anything to anyone. Here comes Maera."

The Dwarf hurried toward us, and behind her was a female in a driven cart. "Do you think she'll boot me out?"

Syn grinned. "Absolutely."

"No, she won't. Eirik eats with us all the time. Syn, stop being an ass."

Maera stopped at our table and paused to catch her breath. She glared at Echo. "Is this your doing?"

"I'm supposed to watch over her, so where I go she goes."

"It's where she goes, you go, you impossible man. What are you doing in the Grimnirs Hall, young lady?" Maera asked, pinning me with a glare. I guess I'd been demoted from "young goddess" to "young lady."

"Getting ready to eat. I'm starving." I looked behind her at the cart. "Is that lunch? It smells good."

"Litr already took food to your quarters."

"But I'm here, Maera. I don't mind. I get to hang out with Echo." I hugged his arm. Syn whistled and raised his hand. "And Syn, too," I added, grinning. "Do you want everyone in the hall to think I'm too good to eat the food they're eating?"

"Of course not." Maera sighed. "First, your brother and now you.

I don't understand young people anymore. There is bending rules, and there's outright rebelling. Next thing I know, it will be your father and mother in here."

"Now that's a wonderful idea," I said.

Maera paled.

"I was just kidding. Thank you for letting me stay." I leaned forward and kissed her cheek. Images flashed through my head. I blinked, and they were gone. Maera was walking away.

"I just had another one," I whispered to Echo. "Maera is not going to be happy, but Trudy will be going to Mystic Academy with us."

Lunch turned out to be fun. I even forgot about the other Grimnirs in the hall. I didn't realize I was holding on to Echo's arm as we walked out until I reached the front hall and saw Trudy and the other girls. They stared at our linked arms, but I didn't pull away. My parents knew about us, so I was done hiding our relationship from everyone.

I joined the girls, and we walked back to Eirik's. "Thanks for talking to Eirik, Trudy. I thought he was angry with me, but he wasn't. He was just having a moment."

Trudy scoffed. "A moment? I know he is your brother, but I swear he can be very unfeeling sometimes."

"More like often," I corrected her. "I grew up with him. Well, practically grew up with him. I'd ask him to help me with school stuff, and he'd say no in the mean, uncaring voice, then add that I should look it up myself. But he could be so nice and sweet afterward, and I'd find myself forgiving him."

"Did you really have a crush on him?" Hayden asked.

I glanced back at Echo and caught the smirk on his face. He'd heard the question. "I thought I did. He and I bickered like siblings. He thought all the guys I dated were losers and that I used my looks to get my way."

"Did you?" Jessica asked and turned pink.

"Uh, yes. Shamelessly." The girls laughed, even Jessica. "Wouldn't you?"

"I've never attended a school," Jessica said, and uneasy silence followed. She'd lived in an institution all her life because no one had wanted to adopt her. I stopped, and they did, too.

"My parents in Kayville put me in an Immortal institution for a month when I started seeing souls. They tried to suppress it." From their reaction, they hadn't known about it. "I hated it. Seeing souls was traumatizing enough without being trapped in that home. But I was only there for a month, and it was a nightmare. I can't imagine just how terrible it must have been for you all those years, Jess."

"It was horrible," she whispered.

"I'm going to attend Mystic Academy in the fall. You should come with me. As my sister, no one will mess with you."

She stared at me with shiny eyes. "You think of me as, uh, your sister?"

I chuckled. "I should be asking that question, seeing as I'm the new one around here. Do you think of me as your sister?"

"I impersonated you," she whispered.

"You were manipulated. You are my sister now, Jess, and that's all that matters." I gave her a hug. When I stepped back, she was fighting tears. "Now all we need to do is convince our parents to let you come with me to Mystic Academy. We need Eirik on board too, of course, and Celestia."

"And my mother because I plan to go, too," Trudy said.

I hid a smile because I already knew the answer to that. We reached Eirik's place and found Tammy with Lavion's two Dwarves. The one that had kept staring at me hopped down and took my hand.

"Hel's daughter, how befitting that you are one of the roosters. I never thought I'd see the three of you in one place. Where is the third one? The one with dark hair?"

I didn't understand what she was saying. "Who?"

"She's talking about Raine," Trudy said.

"She's back on Earth."

"No, I just saw her with the goddess. I never thought I'd live to see the three of you together. The end is near."

I still had no idea what the woman was talking about, but I smiled and nodded. I took off the second she turned away. Raine was here? Just like in my vision. Echo was with Syn in the living room and stood.

"Raine is here," I told them.

"Cora!" Trudy called, and I glanced over my shoulder. She'd followed me out of the bedroom.

"I'm going to find Raine."

"Are you clairvoyant?" Trudy asked.

"Uh, yes. I just started having visions. How did you know?"

"Lavion's aunt said you are one of the roosters."

"I heard her." But I didn't believe her.

"That means you are one of the seers who will announce Ragnarok. Me from a forest in Jötunheim, Raine from Asgard, and you from Helheim."

I shook my head. "No, I'm not."

"Ask the goddess. We thought it was Eirik, but he doesn't have the gift to see into the future. You do. The healer, Lavion's aunt, recognized you."

Frowning, I turned to face Echo. His expression said he was shocked, too. It couldn't be true. There was too much happening too fast. First my visions; now this.

"It makes sense, sweetheart," he said.

"No, it doesn't. I just barely started having visions."

"Your parents used runes to suppress your ability to see souls, so they must have suppressed your other gifts. You could still have more. Telekinesis and mind reading like your mother. Shape shifting like your grandfather. Like you said, you come from a family of powerful Witches. You could be the most powerful of them all," he added, words dripping with pride.

He was no longer intimidated by who I was or my family. Instead, he was celebrating me, my abilities. I pulled his head down and kissed him. When I stopped, his eyes were glowing.

"What was that for?" he asked.

"You keep reminding me why I love you, Echo Maidrid. Now I need to find Raine."

Still wearing a puzzled expression, he opened a portal to the Throne Hall, where Raine, Torin, and Dev were talking to my mother by the steps.

"Raine!"

She started toward me, paused, and curtseyed to my mother, who waved her off. I met her across the room, and we hugged. Her hands were freezing. I shrugged off the cloak Litr had given me and draped it around her shoulders.

"What are you doing here? I told you I'd be fine."

"We brought Dev. He was wary of coming with Rhys and Nara, so we offered to bring him." She stroked the top of the cloak. "Ooh, this feels amazing. I was out there for only a few minutes, yet the cold crept to my bones. This"—she hugged the cloak—"is exactly what I need. Look at you. You look amazing. Oh, and I just met your mother." She glanced over her shoulder. "She's intimidating."

"It's all a front. Look at her." The goddess was laughing with Torin while Dev looked like he couldn't wait to escape. "Poor Dev. Should we rescue him?"

"Not yet. I want to hear about Celestia. Rhys said she hasn't recovered since last week and they are trying to find a way to help her, but he didn't say how."

"Her energy dropped so low after she healed Dev she went into a coma."

"Oh no."

"My mother has brought healers from all over the realms and beyond, but no one has been able to help her. She even sent emissaries to Asgard, but that didn't pan out. Eirik is taking it hard, but I saw…"

"Yes? What did you see?"

I didn't know where to begin. "I've been seeing things before they happen."

Raine laughed and hugged me. "Finally. It's been so hard not telling you I'd seen you do much more than help souls." She leaned back and added, "But the scenes I saw were from the new school, so I wasn't sure when you'd start having visions."

"Are you saying you've known I'd be clairvoyant?"

She nodded. "Since two weeks ago."

I yanked my hand from hers and pinched her.

"Ouch. What's that for?" she screeched.

"For not telling me. Some best friend you are. You could have warned me."

"Rule number one of clairvoyance is never tell people what you've seen or they'll try to change it or fight it. Your gift had to come naturally, and you needed a trigger. Mine was the dying Seeresses. What was the first thing you saw?"

"My mother visiting my room and taking the blanket," I said. I explained what I'd seen in my vision.

"Why didn't you tell us?"

"I wasn't sure what it meant or whether it was a one-time thing. If someone had told me she'd seen visions of me doing clairvoyant things, I would not have been so afraid or conflicted."

"No, seriously, ask your mother. She'll tell you the same thing. Never reveal visions to the person they affect."

"Is that right, Mother?" I asked.

Raine paled. Before she could turn around, the goddess placed a hand on her shoulder. "I'm afraid Raine is right, Daughter. You never tell anyone what you've seen or they'll do something to change it. Why do you think the Norns have been working hard to lure Raine to their side?"

"To change the outcome of Ragnarok," Raine said, her shyness forgotten.

"Exactly. They must be gnashing their teeth right now because I have all three of you under my roof." Mother touched Raine's cheek, then mine.

"Is it really true about me? Lavion's aunt said it, but I didn't want to believe her."

She grinned and palmed my cheek. "Yes, my beloved daughter. I was going to tell you after our guests left, but the healer beat me to it." She sighed. "Why don't you two run along while we move the villagers to one of the other halls and let the preening peacocks inside?"

"Preening peacocks?" I laughed. "You sound like Echo."

"I stole the description from him. Show Raine around, and tell your brother as soon as he returns that I want both of you ready to receive our guests."

"How are we going to help Celestia now that Goddess Eir is not coming?"

"Raine's husband offered to get her. They won't refuse a Valkyrie entrance." She smiled at Raine. "I hope you two will stay and visit for a while."

"Thank you, ma'am." Raine watched her glide away. "She's an interesting person."

"I thought you were scared of her."

"Intimidated, not scared. She's fascinating."

"I know, and amazing. So are you going to Asgard with Torin or staying?"

"After what you told me about Celestia, I'm staying. My presence in Asgard would only disrupt things. I'm not ready to go there." She slipped her arm through mine and grinned. "My best friend is the second rooster. I love it. It's like we gravitated toward each other. Who is the third one? Eirik?"

"No. Trudy. You'll announce Ragnarok from Asgard, I will from here, and Trudy from Jötunheim forest. Mother said every few centuries a rooster is born, but they never live long enough, so there are never three of them alive at the same time. She has a theory about that. She thinks the Norns have been manipulating the fate of roosters for a long time until they had one who was one of them."

"Me?" Raine asked.

"Exactly. Come on. Let's get Dev."

"You get Dev."

He was talking to Rhys and Nara but kept glancing at us.

"He's been morose since you left," Raine continued. "I'm not sure whether it's because he misses you or he really does feel whatever Celestia is feeling. Don't leave without me. I need to talk to Torin before he leaves. He's not going to believe what you just told me. My best friend is one of the roosters. Wow." She hugged me again then took off.

~*~

\ The second we entered Eirik's room, Dev rushed to Celestia's side. Tammy still kept vigil from the other side, and the same healer who'd mentioned the three roosters stepped away from the bed and walked to Raine. She kissed her hand and bowed.

"It is an honor to meet you," she said.

"Thank you." But Raine's focus was on Celestia. "Have you figured out what's wrong with her?"

"No," she said sadly. "But the young goddess said a friend she healed was coming."

"That's him." I introduced Dev to the healers. "Celestia healed him before she lost consciousness, so compare his energy to the one you felt inside her."

Dev's aquamarine eyes clouded. "Celestia's a giver, not a taker. Remember how she checked my energy before she healed me? All I felt was the flow of her life force toward me. I would never harm her or contaminate her energy. If I did, I'd willingly give up my life to save hers."

The anguish on his face said he was suffering with Celestia, but I had to confirm it. "I understand what you are saying, Dev. But we need to confirm it because the healers detected another energy and memories that cannot be hers."

"Memories? Her memories didn't blend with mine, or I would have some of hers."

I sighed. "Dev—"

"Okay. If it eases your mind, doll-face, I'll let them check." He sat on a chair and smiled at the two healers. Raine and I stood behind his chair as the two Dwarves pressed their pudgy hands on his forehead and chest.

Eirik returned wearing some outfit that looked like a scuba suit. He frowned when he saw Dev.

"Did he?" he asked.

I shook my head. "They are still comparing?"

"They're inside my head," Dev grumbled. Raine and I exchanged a glance. Dev had done terrible things, the same things the healers had seen in Celestia's heads. On the other hand, he'd recently done so many amazing things. The Dwarves mumbled in their language.

"What are they saying?" Raine asked.

"I don't know." Eirik marched off to the living room, then we heard him yell to the guards to find Lavion. When he returned, his Dwarf friend was with him. "Translate what they are saying."

We waited while Lavion talked to the healers. "They've never seen energies so alike. They want to know if Celestia and Dev are twins."

"She healed him. That's all they need to know," Eirik said. "Is the other energy his?"

"I'll tell you what they find out, Eirik," I said. "You need to shower and change. Mother expects us in the Throne Hall as soon as you are ready."

He nodded, stared at Celestia one last time, then disappeared into the bathroom.

"Enough," Dev said firmly in a voice I'd never heard him use before. He pushed the hands of the Dwarves away and stood. "I didn't do this to her, but I'll find out what's wrong with her even if I have to die again to do it."

"Dev," I protested.

"If I have to be a soul again to help her, I will. Rhys. Nara." The Grimnirs entered the room. He spoke rapidly in Druidic language. All I got was a brief sentence here and there, but they were enough. The shock on their faces must have mirrored mine.

"What's going on?" Raine whispered.

"He just asked Rhys and Nara to find a way to… to kill him," I said, my voice breaking. Celestia had sacrificed herself for him, and now he was doing the same for her.

"What? But his soul can't really replenish her life force," Raine muttered.

"He wants us to find a way to drain his life force and give it back to her. That's something some healers can do," Nara said, fighting tears. "They take from one and give to another, killing the giver in the process."

Rhys looked furious, but he didn't speak. Objecting to what Dev was suggesting meant agreeing to sacrifice Celestia. Besides, Dev's expression said he'd do it whether they agreed to help him or not.

He walked around the bed, sat on the chair, and took Celestia's hand. He closed his eyes. "Celestia, *mon mhuirnín*. Thank you for the best two weeks of my life. You gave me a chance to reconcile with my brothers and sister, talk, eat, and drink with them. I would not have had this opportunity if it weren't for you."

Tears filled my eyes.

"I can feel you struggle to break free, but you can't without my help, so I'm going to freely give you what you've given me." He opened his eyes and looked at the two Dwarf healers. "You will transfer my life force into her. You both have the gift."

The two Dwarves watched him with stricken expressions. Rhys and Nara were having an argument by the door and moved closer. No one could stop Dev. Giving up his life for Celestia's was his decision.

"This is crazy," Raine said.

"It can't be"—my voice shook so much I had to stop and clear my throat—"the only solution."

"What solution?" Eirik asked, stepping into the bedroom in a bathrobe, his hair wet. No one spoke. We were all fighting tears.

"I've decided to give back what she gave me," Dev said. "It will be enough to jumpstart her healing. Whatever is stopping her from regenerating her life force will no longer be there. I don't care about my life. I will not let her fade away while I live."

"Neither will I," Tammy said. She'd been quiet, until now. "If Dev and I both gave her some of our life force, we could all survive. She will not forgive herself if you sacrificed yourself for her, Dev. But between the two of us, we might help her and still survive."

"No!" Everyone turned to look at me, but I was looking at Eirik. His expression said he couldn't believe I was choosing Dev over Celestia. "Dev, you said something is stopping her from regenerating her life force. The evidence has been there all this time, and I didn't see it."

"See what?" he asked.

"Celestia generates more life force than most people, yet she's in a coma. That's what I'd expect from someone like me after I'm possessed. Do you remember, Raine, when I'd let a soul possess me without medium runes? My energy would drain, and I had to nap to rejuvenate. Even with medium runes, I still get drained. Imagine a soul staying inside me indefinitely."

"It would drain your energy or drive you crazy," Dev said.

"Exactly, except we are dealing with Celestia, who is like an Energizer battery. She keeps generating more."

They all continued to stare at me like I was crazy.

"Celestia is possessed. Something or someone is inside her right now, constantly draining her energy. The memories the healers saw are not Celestia's. They belong to whoever possessed her. The same with the energy the healers detected. It belongs to the thing inside her."

"But the energy inside her is weak," the Dwarf healer said.

"I can't explain that. All I know is she's displaying classic symptoms of possession."

"Do you remember when we were at your place and she astral projected to find the person who'd stolen your blanket?" Raine asked. "She said something powerful and dark had chased her."

"And when she healed the villagers in Jötunheim and Gjöll Pass days later, she'd grown tired quickly," Eirik said. "That's why I was worried about her healing Dev."

"When she healed Dev, her energy dropped so low, but the sucker is still mooching off her and barely keeping her alive." I was getting really pissed. Why hadn't I seen it before? I'd been so caught up with meeting and learning about my parents, and the drama with Echo, I'd stopped thinking. I engaged my medium runes and locator runes, and moved closer to Celestia.

*Come out of her, you son of a bitch.* Nothing happened. From the expression on Eirik's face and the others, they were wondering what I was doing. "I'm trying to draw out the bastard."

The others crowded around the bed, watching me.

"Do you feel anything?" Eirik asked.

I was so frustrated I wanted to scream. "No."

"Do you remember how I blended with you to stop Maliina?" Dev asked. "A soul can force this other being out of her." Dev's eyes moved from face to face. "I need my life force drained now until my soul separates from my body. I'm willing to die for her. It's the only way to help her. I'll push this other soul out and give her a chance to survive. She could always heal me again."

Somehow I doubted Eirik or even Mother would allow Celestia to help Dev again.

# CHAPTER 16. THE IMP, THE PEACOCKS, AND THE GODS

"No. You are not going to die, Dev. We need my mother's warding runes. I'll be right back." I raced out of the room, almost bumping into Nara and Rhys. "I need to find my mother."

"She is in her quarters," Rhys said.

I raced across the rotunda and pushed open the door to my parents' quarters. "Mother? Mom!"

A portal opened, and the goddess appeared on the other side. Trudy was brushing her hair. Mother got up. She'd changed into a long-sleeved emerald green dress that hugged her curves and flared at her feet. On her waist was a bejeweled belt with green stones and embroideries, which continued up her chest in a V-shape and became a neckpiece. The same jewels were on the braces around her wrists. A sheer green cloak around her shoulders appeared to be attached to both the neckpiece and her wrist braces.

"Wow, you look amazing," I said.

She chuckled. "Thank you, *dýrr mín*. Why haven't you changed?"

"I'm supposed to?"

"Of course. We might be forced to host the most eligible bachelors from all the realms, but it's also your introduction. The dress you are wearing is lovely, but it won't do for the evening."

"I'll worry about that later. Right now, you need to come with me." I grabbed her hand. "I know what's wrong with Celestia, and we need your help. She's possessed."

Her scepter flew into her hand. At the same time, a portal opened straight into Eirik's bedroom. Trudy and I followed her. Everyone stepped back.

"I don't know why I didn't think of that," I said, feeling guilty. "I've been possessed so often I should have seen it, but it never crossed my mind that was the problem."

"We don't have or allow possessions in my realm," Mother said. "Whoever did this is heading straight to Corpse Strand." She pulled the blanket off Celestia and used her scepter to etch warding runes on her arms and legs. She stepped back and pointed the glowing rock at Celestia's chest.

"Come out," the goddess ordered. "I command you to come out of her."

Nothing happened.

The runes on her side moved faster while more appeared on her normal side. She tried again and again. Eirik and I joined her. We both engaged our locator runes. The same runes appeared on Celestia, but the soul inside her refused to come out. The green crystal on Mother's scepter changed color, becoming black.

"Mother!" Eirik gripped her arm and shook his head. "That's Celestia you're pointing that thing at."

"I hate souls who refuse to obey me." The crystal went back to being green.

"I can help her, Goddess," Dev said, bowing. "I need to die for that to happen. As a soul, I can push out the one draining her."

The goddess shook her head. "You have a good heart, Druid, but that won't be necessary. My daughters worked hard to bring you back, so you must honor them by staying alive. I have billions of souls at my command." She looked at me. "Come with me, *ástin mín*." She opened a portal to the eastern Resting Hall. We stopped outside the first entrance. "Do you remember how to retrieve a soul?"

"Yes, Mother."

She handed me her scepter and rattled off a birth time.

"Why him?" I asked.

"We need someone we trust."

Using the scepter, I created the air runes like she'd taught me and added the dates. They floated to the door, and it opened. Tristan Cooper stepped out, looking more alive than I'd ever seen him. His eyes volleyed between my mother and me.

"Cora, what are you doing here? You're not...?"

"Dead? No, Uncle Tristan." I hugged him. "I'm home. I'll tell you the story later, but right now, Mother and I need your help."

"Mother?" he asked.

"Yes, Tristan. Cora is my daughter. She and Raine will fill you in later. Right now I need your help with Eirik's Celestia. She's possessed by a very difficult and evil soul, and we need you to push it out." She opened a portal to Eirik's bedroom.

My eyes went to Raine when I entered, but she was staring at her father with wide eyes. She teared and whispered, "Dad."

"Sweetheart." He opened his arms, and she ran to him.

"I can't believe you are here," she said, laughing and crying.

"Tristan, you two can sit down and catch up for as long as you want. Right now, we need you," Mother said impatiently. "The warding runes I etched on Celestia are not working because she can't engage them. I need you to blend with her." She was like a drill sergeant. Mr. Cooper followed her instructions, and we all crowded around the bed and waited.

Mother gripped her scepter, and Raine had hers ready. She must have brought it just in case. Eirik carried his mace. The soul wasn't going to escape.

"Einmyria, go stand by the door. You too, Raine and Trudy," Mother added. "Lavion, I didn't see you there. Escort the healers to your quarters. This soul is tenacious, so I don't want her jumping from Celestia to one of you. Everyone. Tammy, Dev, even you, Son, move back."

"But I have my warding runes," I protested.

"I know, Daughter. But I do not want to put you in harm's way, so humor me."

I moved to where the others stood and gripped Raine's arm. Mr. Cooper separated from Celestia first and floated above her, but his hand stayed inside her. What was he doing? Dev mumbled something I didn't catch, but I was sure he and I were thinking the same thing. Mr. Cooper was supposed to push out the soul. Then I realized he was pulling out one, but the soul's hand was tiny, like a child's.

First came the arm, then a lock of curly hair followed with a cherubic face belonging to a baby in a pink dress, white tights, and pink shoes. She couldn't have been more than a year old. Her eyes were droopy as though she'd been asleep. She yawned and looked at the faces of the people around the bed. I hadn't even realized we'd moved closer to the bed, where she floated and still gripped Mr. Cooper's hand.

"A baby?" Mother said with so much annoyance we laughed. "No wonder she didn't listen to me. Children are impossible."

The little girl's blue eyes locked on Mother, and she wiggled her hand from Mr. Cooper's. She extended both hands toward Mother.

"Mama," she said.

"No, I'm not your mother!"

The girl giggled, showing a few baby teeth. She floated toward Mother. I'd never seen someone move so fast. We all watched with morbid fascination as Mother pointed her scepter at the child.

"No," came from around the room, but we might as well not have spoken. She engulfed the baby in a green glow and suspended her in midair, where she rolled and giggled.

"All this trouble over a baby," Mother mumbled, studying her.

"She's so cute. Is she a soul?" I asked.

"No, that's not a soul, Einmyria," Mother said. "Judging by her clothes, she's Mortal, a gifted Mortal baby with the power to astral project, and I want her out of my realm." She reached out, and chubby fingers grabbed hers. "She solidified quickly."

"How did she do that?" I asked, moving closer to examine the baby.

"Astral images are like souls. While on Earth, they are in energy form, but the second they enter my realm, the magic here makes it possible for them to become solid. Like this little one. You just have to will it. She wanted to touch my hand, and she did, shifting from energy to solid." Mother tried to free her finger, but the baby thought it was a game and giggled. "The last time a female Mortal astral projected here, my son ended up falling in love with her. I'm out of sons." She said it calmly while still trying to get her hand back, and we laughed. The baby continued to give her toothy giggles. "Troublesome imp."

"She's adorable," Trudy said. "Can I carry her?"

"Not yet," Mother said, and Trudy made a face. "Do not get attached to her. She's only staying here until someone finds her and transports her astral image back to her body. I'm sure her parents are worried about her. They're probably keeping vigil by her body." She glanced at Raine, who was inching closer to her father. "Raine, Einmyria tells me you help Mortals."

"Yes, Goddess."

"When you leave here, find this baby and ease her parents' pain. I can imagine what they are going through."

Raine nodded. "I can do that."

"Good. Go spend time with your father. One of the guards can escort you to a guest room." She finally freed her fingers and placed her hand on the baby's head. "I can access her memories and see what she's seen." She frowned and tsked. "This poor child had latched onto some very wicked souls in her short life. Too many. Trudy, tell your mother we need a crib, food, and clothes. Then find Jess. The two of you will be in charge of her until her family is found. You and Hayden should suppress these horrific memories in her head, too."

Trudy raced out of the bedroom while Raine took her father's arm, a broad grin on her face. Dev and Eirik were with Celestia. Only Tammy stayed by the baby. I watched Mother. She closed her eyes, furrows appearing between her brows.

"Strange," she said. "The child's memories show her at home, not a hospital. Her name is Hannah, and she has an older brother, Wes, and two sisters, Talia and Lana." She harrumphed. "Interesting. They all look different. Is that normal on Earth?"

"Depends. If the children are adopted, they won't look like their parents or each other, but they're still a family."

"Is that enough information to track down her family?"

"Is there a family name? The father's or mothers?" I asked.

Mother shook her head. "No. Mom and Dad. Pops. The old man.

Why would they refer to their father as an old man?"

I laughed. "People do that sometimes. I'll tell Raine everything." Raine had already left with her father. I touched the baby's locks. "Poor thing. Your family must be worried about you."

"They probably don't know she's gifted," Tammy said. "Someone needs to tell them and have them bind her powers until she's ready."

"Then you work with Raine to help educate her family," Mother said and went to join Eirik. Trudy returned with Hayden and Jess. Hayden rushed to Celestia's side.

"Look at her. Isn't she adorable?" Trudy picked up the baby, and the green glow disappeared. "We'll take care of her," she called out. She tapped Jess' arm and waved Hayden over. "Let's go. We'll come back to check on Celestia." Rhys and Nara followed them out of the room.

"Her name is Hannah," I heard Nara tell Trudy.

"Rhys," Mother called out, and the Grimnir stepped back into the room. "Keep an eye on them. Don't let Trudy get too attached to that baby. And if Raine needs help finding the family later, help her."

I went to join Mother. Eirik was back in his favorite seat. Tammy and Hayden were on the lounge with Dev.

"How is she doing?" I asked.

"She'll get better now," Mother said. "Both of you need to get dressed. We have guests."

"Do I have to go?" Eirik asked, his focus on Celestia.

"Yes, Son. Your sister needs you by her side."

"I'll send Dev to get you if she needs you," Tammy said.

"Good idea, Tammy. Come along, Einmyria. You need to get ready. Son, find us when you are ready."

I followed Mother through a portal to their quarters.

"Maera has been working hard to make some gowns for you, so you should have your pick." She pushed open the door to my bedroom, where Maera and Astrid were busy straightening three gowns on forms. One was an off a shoulder gold, trumpet dress with green accents and a sweetheart neckline. If someone were to ask me,

I'd say the dress was haute couture.

"It's gorgeous. Maera, how did you make them so fast?"

"I'm actually behind because of the guests. We'll make more," Maera said reassuringly. "Some will be short and some casual."

The woman would be a celebrated designer if she lived on Earth. I moved to the second dress, a cream with gold embroidery on the bodice, sleeves, and along the hem. The same gold embroideries were on the wrist braces. The butterfly sleeves almost looked like a cloak because they were the same length as the dress and had an opening for hands. I couldn't really describe it, except to say it was gorgeous.

The third dress was hunter green like mother's, the design vintage with gold floral detailing. Two cloaks, one gold with green lining and the other green with gold lining and protection runes along the edges.

I hugged her. "I don't care about the length. I love them, and I'm looking forward to wearing each and every one of them. I'll wear the first one and the green cloak with gold lining."

Mother chuckled. "Good combination. Gold is your father's color, and green is mine. Find me when you are ready. I have a necklace that will compliment that dress. Show her the shoes."

~*~

I felt like a princess. The dress, the cloak, the emerald necklace, the shoes. Ohmigod, the shoes were to die for. Crystal-embellished mesh pumps in nude. I fell in love when I first saw them. I had no idea how Maera had done it. I was sure she'd gotten my dress and shoe size from my clothes, but to work wonders this fast? Magic or genius? I didn't care.

"Prince Revan Anoreth of Alarian, Álfheim," the court announcer said.

I forced myself to focus on the next handsome prince or son of a god being introduced. And they were handsome. The pale-haired man bowed, his flowing robes sweeping the floor. He lifted his head and smiled. Damn, he was gorgeous. Pretty, really. I nodded and smiled, wishing I had a watch. This was beyond boring, and I was getting tired of smiling.

He went to join his entourage as the next son of a king or a minor god strutted forward. I was on the left side of Mother's throne while Eirik stood to the right of Father's seat. Eirik had mastered the art of keeping a straight face even though I knew he couldn't wait to be with Celestia. He looked like an Asgardian, fancy outfit, vest, and cloak. Father was in his element, smiling and nodding. I was fidgety. I wanted Echo, but there were no Grimnirs in the Throne Hall. Had Echo lied to me about parties including Grimnirs? Although this couldn't be described as a party. It was a parade of beefcakes and their proud mamas and papas checking me out. So far, I was impressed and a little intimidated but not really drooling.

Mother reached over and covered my hand. She'd already placed it on the arm of her throne to make me focus.

"Bored?" she asked.

"Very. How can you stand it?"

"I usually can't. That's why I don't entertain." She stared down her nose at the next guest. She didn't smile, just nodded curtly. She knew how to draw a line between her and her guests. I tried to be as calm and indifferent as her, but some of these men were comical in their attire.

"Preening peacocks" Echo had called them, and they did look like the exotic birds. Over the top cloaks, fancy clothes, jewelry, and swords strapped to their waists. I didn't catch the names. It didn't matter whether they were Dwarves, Elves, or Jötnar. None matched up to Echo. Where was he anyway? I wanted him here so he could see that none of their glitter and glam impressed me. Yes, I liked my clothes, but I wanted to shine for him.

I tried to see how many more guests were waiting to be introduced. They were entering through a different entrance by the Waiting Hall, not the door the Grimnirs usually used. Each guest walked to the foot of the stairs to be introduced, his entourage waiting on the side.

The staff served drinks and food, but I doubted the guests

appreciated Helheim's lavish offerings. They stood in groups with their entourages, whispering in low voices, and staring at me. Mother hadn't introduced me yet, but they knew who I was. I'd heard the whispers.

The next one marched like a drill sergeant and wore a black uniform of some kind with medals. His skin was grayish, and his tattoos covered one side of his face and shaved head. Unlike the all-male entourages of the other peacocks, this one had an equal number of male and female guards. They all had skin with the same grayish hue, Mohawk white or pitch-black hair, black cloaks with silver designs on the shoulders, and sleeveless shirts. Their arm braces almost reached their elbows, and tattoos covered the visible skin to their shoulders.

He was introduced as Dorac, son of a *Dokkalfr* general. Mother waved over one of his guards after the introduction. She stepped up to the throne and bowed. She had serious body piercings, several on her ears, and a stud on her nose. Her tattoos covered her neck and the shaven sides of her head, and her eyes were silver. They stood out against her dark skin. Was she Eirik's friend Niorun? Unlike the other guards, she wore a leather duster like a Grimnir.

"Niorun, since when are you part of an entourage in my hall?" Mother asked.

The girl made a face. "My father ordered me to bring Dorac to Helheim, and I couldn't say no." It was obvious she considered the task a chore. She glanced at me and nodded. "I'm Niorun, your brother's friend." She glanced at Eirik and added, "Hey, Baldurson. Can I visit Celestia while here, Goddess?"

She talked to Mother without fear, yet I'd noticed wariness in the eyes of the others when they were introduced.

"Of course. Try not to start a fight while in my hall," Mother warned.

Niorun grinned. She was beautiful. Exotic. "I'll try, Goddess, but I can't make any promises. If they insult me, my guards, or my people, I will be obligated to defend our honor."

"Not in my hall, Niorun. I mean it."

"Outside the hall?" she asked, and Mother smiled. It was obvious she had a soft spot for the girl.

"If you must. However, your father will have to be informed if you destroy my property."

Niorun groaned. "Yes, Goddess."

Mother lifted her scepter and brought it down. Silence spread across the hall. "Thank you for coming to my hall. I know you came here to keep vigil with us while my son's consort, Celestia, fought for her life. You'll be happy to hear that she is doing better and is expected to fully recover within the next forty-eight hours. You are welcome to stay until she is back on her feet."

She paused as though daring them to say anything.

"For now, drink. Eat. Enjoy our hospitality. Let's see which ones are bold enough to ask about Einmyria," she added softly to Father, but I heard her. She was tough as nails, baiting them even though we knew they were here for me.

The conversation in the room rose until Lavion stepped forward and bowed. "Goddess, may I have the honor of talking to your daughter, Einmyria?"

Instead of answering him, Mother glanced at Eirik. "Rescind the invitation to that little man." She glared at Lavion. "About what, Lavion, son of Drathyn?"

"Life, Goddess. Her dreams and mine, and a way to make them merge," Lavion said, grinning. "She is more dazzling than the sun, yet more delicate than the *benga* flowers that bloom at midnight under the full moon in my homeland. It would be an honor to have her as my consort."

I fought hard not to smile. He was bold and funny.

"Lavion, my daughter will one day rule this realm. Any man she favors with her affection and devotion will be her consort, not the other way around." The conversation level shot up. Apparently, they hadn't known I'd rule Helheim.

Revan, one of the Elven princes, stepped forward and bowed. "If it pleases the young goddess, I would like a chance to win her approval."

The blue-eyed Jötun, now in human size but still towering over the Elf, rose to the challenge, too. "I would love a chance to court the young goddess and will meet any challenges to prove I'm worthy of her."

"I will challenge anyone for a chance to prove I'm worthy of the young goddess," another claimed and more followed. *Oh brother.* I glanced at Father from the corner of my eye. He wore a broad grin. It was obvious he was enjoying himself.

There was commotion at the entrance of the Waiting Hall, and one of the guards ran up the steps to whisper something in Mother's ear. She exchanged a glance with Father, then said, "Let them come inside."

The guard hurried out. Silence swept across the hall, and necks craned to see who had arrived. Mother wasn't even looking. She was busy whispering to Father. I was about to ask her who had arrived when they entered.

No, they made an entrance.

Echo led the way, and behind him were Rhys, Nara, and eighteen Grimnirs I'd never met. Dressed simply in the reaper uniform—leather pants, black shirts, fingerless gloves, and leather dusters—they looked badass. Had he finally reunited with his Druid brothers and sisters?

"No one in here is worthy to win the young goddess' affection, except me," Echo said. "And that's why she already favors me."

I wanted to clap. The goddess sighed and muttered, "He didn't even wait to be introduced. Should I kick him out?"

"Mother!" I sputtered. Eirik chuckled, and I glared at him. "It's not funny."

"Who are you?" came from the lined-up suitors.

"I'm Echo Mairid, Druid of Eljudnir, soul reaper to Goddess Hel." Laughter rippled among the people assembled in the Throne Hall. Echo smirked. "Laugh all you want, but no one courts Einmyria without going through me. I will accept any challenges, because when I'm done with you, you will pack up your tents and leave our hall, and she'll stay here with me as my goddess, the love of my life, and the woman I cannot live without." He glanced at me and winked. I grinned. Now he was showing off.

"I challenge you," rang out from the line, and with each challenge, Echo's smile broadened. I had a feeling he would have enjoyed facing each and every man that challenged him. Luckily, Mother had promised to intervene, and I trusted her. There would be no fighting Echo. Some didn't volunteer to fight him. Maybe they figured anyone bold enough to claim me in front of all of them and my parents had to be legit.

"Who wants to start now?" Echo asked and pulled out two swords from the belt around his waist. "I'm ready."

Mother's staff connected with the floor, and I could swear a pulse of energy spread across the room. Silence followed its wake, and everyone's attention shifted to her.

"There will be no fighting in my hall. My daughter is not a prize to be handed over to the winner like some toy. She is her own person, strong, independent, and gifted. She has already chosen a mate, and her decision is final."

*Deity obliges.* I loved her. She didn't take crap from anyone. She'd promised to nix this nonsense in the bud, and she just did. The disappointed faces of our guests made me grin.

"Enjoy our hospitality until Celestia is back on her feet," Mother added, "or feel free to leave whenever you wish. Thank you for coming." She glanced at Father, who stood and waved Echo closer.

"What I'm about to say is something the rest of the guests don't need to hear," Father said. "You have a year to court my daughter."

"Father," I protested.

"Humor me, Daughter. I know you are an honorable man, Echo, respected by your peers, and you have the loyalty of your people. What I don't know is how you treat my daughter. As her father, I have a right to observe you and see if you are worthy of her." His eyes met mine before he continued. "You must wait until you turn eighteen before you take him as your consort. We will never get back the years we missed out on, but we could build quite a few memories from now on.

Your mother and I have a lot to teach you and to learn from you. Should you change your mind during the year, I will throw a ball and invite every eligible bachelor in all the realms for you, including the group here tonight. Is this acceptable to both of you?" The look he gave Echo said he'd better not argue. I didn't mind waiting because I knew my feelings were real and true.

"Yes, Golden One," Echo said. "I agree. And thank you for accepting me."

Baldur looked at me. "Daughter?"

I moved to where he stood and hugged him. "I love him, but I will wait like you suggested. And I like that I can come to you if he is not acting right."

Eirik snickered. He knew I could take care of myself, but sometimes a father loved to know his daughter still needed him. Mine had missed out on a lot.

"I love you, Father." I stepped back and looked at the goddess. "Mother?"

"I know you will give him hell if he misbehaves, but you always have us if you need to figure out your next plan of action."

Laughing, I kissed her on the cheek. "Love you, Mother."

Pink tinged her normal cheek. She patted my arm. "We have more visitors. Take your rightful place by my side. Echo, take your place, too." Echo started down the steps, but Mother called him back. "Your place is by my daughter's side."

My throat closed. I had the best parents ever. I took my place, and Echo stood beside me, the back of his hand brushing against mine. I hooked my pinky with his just as Torin entered the room. Was Goddess Eir finally here? He made his way to Mother's side and whispered in her ear.

I glanced toward the entrance, but I didn't see any new arrivals. Instead, I found Raine with her father. Grinning, she gave me a thumbs-up. Trudy, Baby Hannah, Hayden, and Jess were also around. I wondered if they had witnessed Echo's dramatic entrance. Dev and Tammy were missing, so I knew they were with Celestia.

The announcer went to the archway separating the Throne Hall from the Waiting Hall and yelled, "Welcome Alfadir, Goddess Frigg, and the *Ásynjur Court* to Eljudnir."

Six warriors in black uniforms, gold capes, and horned helmets marched into the room. None carried a weapon, and I noticed why. They'd handed them over to Mother's guards.

One by one, everyone faced the doorway and dropped to one knee. An old man with a patch over one eye entered the room. Dressed like an aging military general, he commanded attention even though he looked frail with his white beard and hair. Beside him was a middle-aged redhead, and trailing behind them were at least a dozen women in flowing gowns and capes. Behind the women were two hound dogs. Two ravens flew around the room and disappeared from view.

Odin and Frigg. My grandparents. They walked past the Grimnirs and the suitors and climbed the stairs, stopping a step below the throne.

Frigg came up the last step, her eyes moving from my parents to Eirik, then back to my parents, her expression apologetic. Mother stood, and they gripped arms in a weird hug.

"I'm very sorry we just heard about Celestia," Frigg said. "There was a misunderstanding at the gate, but we left the second the young Valkyrie told us what was happening."

"Then welcome to Eljudnir." While the woman moved to hug Father, then Eirik, Mother faced the old man. For one brief moment, they had a staring contest, neither one speaking.

"I should have sent an emissary," Odin said.

"You are here now," Mother said, her voice neither angry nor welcoming.

"When I learned that Frigg and her court were traveling to your realm because our granddaughter was ill, I bade them a safe journey and wished the child a speedy recovery. Then I heard about another granddaughter, one I didn't know existed, and I forgot protocol and decided to join Frigg. I hope my presence won't inconvenience you."

"I try not to let anyone inconvenience me. This"—she indicated me—"is your granddaughter, Einmyria. Einmyria, these are your grandparents from Asgard and the members of *Ásynjur Court*." She didn't give anyone a chance to speak, her focus not shifting from my grandfather. "I'll give you a moment with Baldur and your grandchildren while I escort Eir to Celestia's bedchamber." She didn't smile, and I noticed she didn't welcome Alfadir Odin.

"I'll go with you, Mother," Eirik said. "Grandpa." He clasped his right arm with Odin. Then they hugged. "This is a nice surprise."

"It's a start."

"I'll be back. I want to be there when Celestia wakes up." Eirik bowed to the women accompanying our grandparents, then cocked his arm to one of them, a woman with wavy gorgeous reddish-blond hair tumbling down her back, clear blue eyes, and pale freckled skin. Wearing a red dress and a blue cloak clasped with a leafy brooch, she reminded me of Aunt Svana. She wore a lot of red jewelry—necklaces and a forehead piece. "I'll escort you to our chambers."

As Eirik, Mother, and Eir walked away, my grandmother enveloped me in a perfumed hug. "I want to hear all about you."

# CHAPTER 17. STUPID FIGHT

For an hour, I answered questions about my life, starting with what Eirik had told them about my disappearance. Then how he'd found me, which got me talking about my life, locator runes, how they attracted souls, and my decision to help them. They exchanged glances when Father told them I was the third announcer of Ragnarok and what the Norns had told Mother about me taking over Helheim after Ragnarok.

"I want you to meet the man who helped me when I was struggling with my ability to see souls," I said.

Echo, who'd stood to the side while I talked to my grandparents, once again stepped forward to claim his place by my side. I took his hand.

"He is also my future husband," I added.

"How wonderful. You must bring him to Asgard, so we can get to know him better," Grandmother said, eying Echo.

"I know you," Grandpa added, searching Echo's face. He'd taken Mother's chair, and I couldn't help but wonder how she'd react to that. I had a feeling Mother would never forgive him for the past.

"He was one of the Valkyrie rebels who turned his dying race into Immortals, *dýrr mín*," grandmother said. "I never forget a face. And if I remember correctly, your sentence to serve Hel was over centuries ago. Why didn't you return to us?"

"I chose to stay out of my loyalty to my goddess, Goddess Frigg, but it seems this is where I was meant to belong." Echo took my hand. "It is my destiny to be with Einmyria, and she is the future of Helheim."

"So it seems," Grandfather added. "I guess everything I did led to this moment."

Grandmother chuckled. "I told you, didn't I? No matter what we did to reshape the future, we cannot change the threads the Norns have weaved. Is it possible you could travel with our granddaughter and her young man to Asgard, Son?"

And just like that, the conversation shifted to my father, and I learned something interesting—this was the first time my grandparents had visited Helheim and their first glimpse of Father since he'd arrived here.

Instead of answering Grandmother, Father urged me to mingle with the guests. "Let them know you. Echo, you stay here and keep watch. As you can see, you won't miss a thing from up here."

My father had a cruel streak, and I had a feeling he meant to make Echo prove himself in more ways than what he'd said. I wasn't worried. From Echo's expression and the smile he gave me, he didn't seem bothered by our temporary separation. He knew he had me.

He escorted me to the foot of the steps and paused to say, "I love you."

"Love you more."

He chuckled.

"Rescue me if you see me drowning," I said.

"No, you're going to shine like you've been doing since you got here. I'm so proud of you."

He knew exactly what to say to make me feel good. Still smiling, I joined the men stuffing their faces and drinking Mother's wine and mead. Sure they'd ignore me now that they knew I was unavailable, I was surprised when they flocked around me and tried to outdo each other.

"May I send you an invitation to visit my realm?" someone asked, followed by a description of his realm.

"Yes, I'd love to visit sometime." More invitations followed, and I gave the same answer. Someone must have told them Echo had a year to prove he was worthy of my love, and I knew the culprit. My eyes met my father's and caught his grin. He was going to make Echo sweat. I just knew it. I was tempted to tell Mother. No, what Echo and I had was strong enough to weather any storm.

Once again, I had to answer questions about where I'd been all these years. I gave them a shorter version of what I'd told my grandparents. Some wanted to know about life on Earth. They found things we did on Earth peculiar and were laughing at something I'd said when Goddess Eir returned to the hall with members of the *Ásynjur Court*. I'd wondered where they'd disappeared to. I excused myself.

"How is Celestia?"

"She is up and will join us shortly," the Asgardian healer said. She introduced members of Frigg's court, but not a single name stuck. They were all goddesses in their own right and unmarried. They regaled me with stories of their work until silence filled the room, and I saw why.

Mother was back with Eirik and Celestia, who wore a gorgeous hunter-green gown with a Victorian collar and trumpet sleeves. A sheer shawl with lace around the edges completed the outfit. It was Boho and elegant, and it was the same dress she'd worn in my vision when Echo fought the Jötun.

Damn!

Echo was still by the throne, a half smile on his lips. He didn't seem ready to kill anyone. In fact, he'd worn a benign expression ever since I joined the disappointed suitors on the floor. Raine had said I could alter a vision if I told those in it, and I assumed I'd done just that. Where was she?

The rest of the evening was a blur. I ate and talked, but the worry that I might not have prevented the scene in my visions ate at me. Our grandparents left first, and the hall cleared soon after.

"Are you really okay?" I asked Celestia as we left the hall. I hadn't had a chance to talk to her since she'd joined us, except for the brief hug.

"Oh, yes. Eir helped a lot by speeding up my energy production. I hope one day I can be as good as she is. I even met the cute little girl responsible for my coma."

"Baby Hannah," I said.

She chuckled. "Baby Hannah. She is so adorable and powerful for one so young. I remember hearing baby giggles while in the AP, just before the dark energy reached me."

"The day you went looking for whoever stole my blanket?"

She gave me a sheepish grin and nodded. "Yes. I think they were chasing her."

"You knew it was Mother who took my blanket, didn't you?"

"Yup. I was with her outside your school several times, but she came to the farm on her own to confirm you were the one. Sorry I couldn't tell you the truth at the time. Even Eirik didn't know we'd sneaked out to see you. And I'm sorry I messed up your homecoming."

I chuckled. "You made it memorable. Because of you, our grandparents finally visited Helheim. Because of you, I had to tell would-be suitors not to bother because I'm already taken."

"I'll accept the suitor thing, but Alfadir didn't come to see me." She stifled a yawn. "Have you seen the guys? I'm a bit tired, but I'm scared of going to bed alone. I know it's stupid, but I want Eirik around when I do."

"No, that makes perfect sense, especially with Baby Hannah still around. The last time I saw them, they were with the Asgardian group."

"Can we ask the parents?" We stopped and looked behind us. My parents were coming toward us, but they didn't seem to be in a hurry. I caught the knowing gleam in Celestia's eyes. "What?"

"I love that you've embraced them. Eirik was worried you might not because your parents back at home are awesome. His were lacking, so it was easy for him to open his heart to the goddess and Baldur."

I guessed Mom and Dad would always be my first parents, but I didn't see why I couldn't have two sets of them. "They aren't perfect, my Kayville parents, but they are loving. And the ones here are pretty awesome, too, and also imperfect. It's easy to love them."

"Who is easy to love?" Baldur asked, having heard the last sentence.

"You and Mother." Surprise flickered across their faces. "This evening would have been a disaster if it weren't for you two. Thanks for making sure everything went smoothly and for accepting Echo."

Father shook his head. "We haven't—"

Mother backhanded his chest and cut him off. "Echo is an honorable man, and you two are perfect together."

Father chuckled, placing one arm around my shoulder and the other around Celestia. "The success of this evening rests solely on your shoulders, beloved daughter. You accepted invitations from every single suitor on the floor and made them feel like they still have a chance with you."

"Oh no." I covered my face. "I was trying to be polite."

"Next time, tell them you'll discuss it with me," Mother said. "That should stop them cold. Otherwise, the evening wasn't bad."

"They finally came," Father reminded her.

"Doesn't change a thing," she retorted.

I knew they were talking about the Asgardians.

We reached the rotunda, and Father dropped a kiss on my temple and Celestia's. "Are you two waiting up for your boys?"

"Yes. Where did they go?"

"They escorted your grandparents home," he said. "They used a different portal, not the one at Gjöll Pass."

"We'll wait for them." I hugged him. "Goodnight, Father. Don't give Echo a hard time, or we'll elope."

The look on his face was priceless. I could have threatened him with moving back to Earth and never coming back, but I couldn't be that cruel. Besides, I knew I could never walk away from them. They were my parents as much as Mom and Dad back in Kayville.

"I'm just messing with him," I whispered to Mother. "When I marry, I want your support one hundred percent, my two dads walking me down the aisle and giving me away, and my two moms playing matrons of honor."

"I will?" she asked, pink tinging her normal cheek, and the runes on the other sped up.

"Absolutely. Matron of honor is reserved for mother of the bride. That means you will manage everything. Echo doesn't have parents, so you'll have to make sure he and the gentlemen are dressed and ready. You have to make sure everything goes smoothly, flowers done perfectly, the correct music selected, food for all the guests done to perfection, seating arrangements, and, above all, take the stress off me. You will be the second most important person at the wedding."

"I think you should elope," she said with a deadpan expression. Celestia and I laughed. She had a dry sense of humor, but this time, I wasn't sure whether she was serious or not. I wanted a wedding. The bigger the better.

"Are you serious?" I asked.

She chuckled. "No, Daughter. I'm joking."

"But we'll give you our blessing in a couple of centuries," Father said.

"Our daughter wants a wedding *a year* from now, Baldur, so we will give her one. The bigger the better."

"Mother! Did you get that from my head?"

"No, *dýrr mín*. I promised your father I'd never read your thoughts or your brother's. I just knew you'd want a big wedding."

"I do." She was an enabler. It was not bad having one mother who was. I gave her a hug and a kiss. "Love you, Mother. Father, you have one year to get used to sharing me with Echo." I kissed his cheek and took Celestia's arm.

"I'm so happy I didn't have a wedding. Once our parents accepted our decision, we moved in together and Eirik gave me this." The ring looked ancient. "Grandma Frigg gave it to him just before we left Asgard."

She really didn't know they were planning a wedding for her? I couldn't wait to see her face when she found out.

~*~

Raine, Trudy, Jess, and Hayden were in the living room, talking. Baby Hannah was missing.

"Where's Celestia's baby?" I asked, and the others laughed.

"Mother is taking care of her," Hayden said.

"And mine is helping so she doesn't shift into energy and float away

274

until Raine finds her body and her family," Trudy added.

"She is powerful. I carried her and felt a tug," Raine added.

Celestia nodded. "She attached herself to my astral image when I was trying to find the person who stole Cora's blanket."

"Einmyria," Hayden and Trudy chorused.

"She likes to use Einmyria here and Cora when she's back in Kayville," Trudy explained, and Hayden nodded.

"I didn't say that," I protested. Then I remembered these two sifting through my memories. "Never mind. You two are never getting inside my head again." The grins they traded said they'd seen more than enough. "What did you two see in the head of Celestia's baby?"

"Hey," Celestia protested. "She's not my baby. The little imp hijacked me. I've never seen a child that powerful."

"Says someone whose powers manifested themselves when she was a baby," Hayden cut in. "Mom says there are powerful orphans out there who lost their parents when you guys fought the Immortals in Kayville, Raine. Their parents didn't tell them they were fighting or supporting Lord Worthington or who they really are, and some are younger than others. This baby could be one of them."

"Mother said she has a brother, Wes, and two sisters, Lana and Talia," I added.

"We saw them while hiding her memories," Trudy said. "Her older sister looked and acted just like Hayden."

"No, she didn't," Hayden shot back, but her words lacked heat.

"Same know-it-all attitude," Trudy continued.

Hayden grinned. "The bratty younger sister acted just like you. And she's boy crazy. Just like you."

"Enough, guys. What about her dark memories?" Jess asked. She tended to be quiet, so it was nice to see her participate. In fact, I had a feeling she often mediated disputes between Hayden and Trudy.

Trudy shrugged. "They were there, but we don't know if they are hers or if they belonged to someone she's possessed. I mean, the Dwarf healers said memories are rarely transferred."

"Maybe the dark forces I thought were chasing me were actually with her," Celestia added. "We might need to do more than find her parents. We might have to protect her. Grandmother Frigg protected me when I was a baby. When she heard about Baby Hannah, she said we should think about protecting gifted younger kids, too."

"We could start some type of organization and work together to find the lost orphans," Raine said. "Summer starts soon, and I have time. Who is game? We could bring them here."

Trudy laughed. "Did you see the goddess' reaction to Baby Hannah? She's not going to start an orphanage in Helheim anytime soon, unless she gets grandkids and gets used to babies." Trudy wiggled her eyebrows at Celestia and me.

"Don't look at me. I have no intention of starting a family yet. I'm keeping Eirik to myself for the next century or two." She didn't crack a smile while everyone laughed. "I mean it. We both have some nasty genes, and the last thing I need is a child asking me about their grandmother."

Silence followed.

"Your mother is still with Crazy Granny?" I asked, and Celestia nodded.

Raine pointed at me. "That leaves you and Echo to provide the grandbabies, chica."

I laughed and explained about waiting for a year. "So in the meantime, I'll just sneak into his quarters without anyone knowing," I added.

"Nothing happens in Eljudnir without the goddess knowing," Trudy and Jess said in unison.

"On the other hand," Trudy added, "you will be at Mystic Academy in the fall."

"And Echo has homes all over the world," Raine piped in.

"Okay, enough about me. We were talking about rounding up orphans. Where can we take them? According to Mother, the Norns recently stopped relocating orphans, so unless we search for relatives in other realms, we have to keep them with Mortals."

"We could talk to Lavania about them," Raine suggested.

"Or my mom knows some amazing Immortals who wouldn't mind fostering the children until they were ready to attend the Academy," Hayden said. "You tired, Celestia? That's the second time you've yawned."

"No, I'm okay. I'll wait for Eirik. Raine, you and Torin can take one of our guest rooms, unless you prefer using one in the guest hall."

"It all depends on Torin. I mean, I wouldn't mind staying for a few days and maybe visiting with my father again. Seeing him was amazing. As long as your mother's invitation is open, Cora, I'll be visiting and sharing my life with him. Children. Grandchildren. Don't look at me like that," Raine added when I glanced at her stomach. "I'm not pregnant. I'm talking about the future. Mom is going to flip once she hears about this." While Raine gushed about her visit with her dad, my thoughts drifted to Echo.

For the first time since I arrived in Helheim, I should be relaxed. Celestia had regained consciousness and my parents were awesome, yet I was worried. Maybe having the ability to see the future wasn't going to be as cool as I'd thought. A loud rumble from outside reached us, and we looked at each other.

"What was that?" Raine asked.

"Probably Garm," Trudy said. "He's been locked up because of the visitors, and he doesn't like it."

"No wonder we didn't see him."

"That wasn't Garm," Celestia said, standing. "That's my Eirik, letting out steam. I could recognize his bellow from anywhere. Come on." She opened a portal to the Waiting Hall.

We followed her and ran to the window to look outside, but nothing was happening. Despite the crystal lights inside and outside the tents, there was nothing unusual going on.

"There's no movement out there," Hayden said.

"Heimdel hearing?" Celestia teased, then explained about Hayden's possible connection to the God Heimdel.

"Yeah, that was a joke when I didn't know about my connection to the other realms. Now that I do, I'm not claiming anything or anyone."

A roar rattled the glass windows.

"I know where they are," Trudy yelled and took off. A portal opened into the glass hallway connecting Grimnirs Hall to the west Resting Halls.

"Holy crap!" someone whispered, and my stomach dropped to the bottom of my soul.

The macabre scene from my vision was playing out right before my eyes. Echo was in the middle of the arena, wielding two swords and facing off with a man almost twice his size, his shirt bloodied. He wasn't the only one fighting. His Druid buddies were also facing off with some of the men while the rest of the guests cheered.

"Un-freaking-believable," Raine whispered, so I followed her eyes to where Torin was busy wielding a sword like a Samurai alongside the Druids. "I'd forgotten what an amazing fighter he is." She laughed.

Raine could be bloodthirsty. While she cheered her man, I studied Echo. He moved like a dancer, parrying, jumping, and whipping around to block an attack. He laughed and attacked, blades moving so fast they blurred. He locked his opponent's sword with both of his, swung it out of the way, and caught him in the gut with a sidekick. The man stumbled back. Echo stepped back to give him a moment, then beckoned the man to step forward. He was having fun.

"Aren't you going to tell them to stop?" Trudy asked.

"Not yet. Raine?" When she didn't respond, I glanced at her.

Her eyes glowed, and one of Torin's attackers lost his footing, leaving him with two. She grinned with each punch and kick he landed on his opponents. When he went low and wrapped his legs around the knees of one of the men, and he came crashing down, she cheered.

"Raine!" I called again.

"My man is kicking ass," she said. "Let me enjoy this."

"Look at Niorun and her guards," Trudy said. "They are fighting with the Grimnirs."

"And so are the rest of the Druids," Jess added.

The Dark Elf was armed with two swords, but she used her body, dropping low to sweep her leg under the Elven prince, who danced away, easily evading her. From her expression, she was getting angry.

"Ouch," Raine said. "Echo just landed on his back. Do you want me to help him?"

Echo's opponent was trying to hack him into tiny pieces. *Come on, Echo. Get up!* I cringed when the blade barely missed him and sank into the snow. He twisted his legs, spun on one shoulder, and used the momentum to lift himself to his feet.

"Holy shit," one of the girls said. Yep, that was impressive.

The giant rushed him, but Echo was ready, attacking left and right, ducking and coming from below. He came from the left and kicked the man on the side of his knee. The giant's knee buckled, and he went down. Echo unleashed a roundhouse kick and caught him on the side of the head.

The second the man went down, three of his men went after Echo. These were regular size, and they didn't carry swords. I might love to see my man mow other men down, but I couldn't let those bastards gang up on him.

"Guys, do something," I said.

"I got it," Raine said. One of the men tripped and landed on his back, but another swept the snow and plowed into the crowd.

"Whoa!"

"I didn't do that." Raine pointed at Celestia, who was peeking through her fingers.

"I hate fighting," Celestia mumbled. "It's stupid."

"Not when your man is winning," I said and high-fived Raine, as our men ducked and threw punches, dominating their opponents. More men started from the sideline, but fire shot from above and cut them off, forcing them to step back.

"No ganging up on one person," Eirik bellowed from above.

I looked up at my brother, refereeing from above. Rhys and Nara joined Echo, and the three fought like parts of a well-oiled machine. I grinned, watching them. For a spiritual people, they sure knew how to fight.

Raine pinched me.

"Ouch. What's that for?"

"It's time to stop this. My man is bleeding and so is yours, and the giants keep shifting forms. Tell them to stop. You are the only one right now who can walk down there and make it happen. Instead, you are grinning like you get off watching your man kick ass."

"I do. He's kicking ass. I didn't see the whole picture in my vision. I didn't see Torin, his Druid brothers, or Niorun."

"Torin is fighting a giant right now, and that won't do. Walk down there and do your goddess thing, because if I go down there, roots will shoot through the snow and your mother won't be happy with the mess I'll leave behind on her landscape." Her expression said she would do it.

"Party pooper," I grumbled.

"Bloodthirsty bitch."

"Goddess to you," I corrected her.

"Still a bitch, Goddess."

"And don't forget it." The others laughed. I opened a portal and could see Echo on the other side. There was something about a man in his element that was hot, and I loved a good sport. Despite the blood on his shirt, he didn't have any cuts or wounds. I wondered what had brought on the fight.

I stepped onto the field and the fight stopped as though someone had thrown a switch. I got bows, some stiffer than others.

"Thank you for the entertainment, but it's time this stopped." I looked up at Eirik and waved him over. "Celestia needs you."

Eirik whooshed down and landed, snow flying everywhere. The bands on his legs and neck shifted and became a suit, covering him from neck to toe—the same outfit I'd thought looked like a scuba diving suit. He ran to a doorway and disappeared into the glass hallway. Torin followed him.

The rest of the guests drifted away, leaving behind the Druids, including Dev. They were smirking and backslapping each other. I turned my focus on Echo.

"Had fun?"

"Oh, yes. They'll never forget who I am. Can I have a hero's kiss and a hug?"

"I don't think so. You are bloody, and I'm wearing a one-of-a-kind gown." He started to close the gap between us. "Echo, don't you dare."

He laughed. "Sweetheart, never dare a man on an adrenaline rush, especially when it's about what he needs." He reached me and gripped the back of my head. "And right now, I need to kiss you, Cora-mia."

I forgot about his bloody clothes when our lips touched. His kiss was addictive. When he lifted his head, I was clinging to him.

"Want to see my quarters?"

I nodded. We were the last to leave the field using the same door Eirik had used. "Why don't you just create a portal from out there?"

"Because of the magic in this realm, a portal outside the halls can shift to any place. That's why we use the caves. Don't ever create a portal to leave the hall or enter it."

I kept the information for later. He created a portal to his quarters. His place was smaller than Eirik's and consisted of a bedroom and living room. On the walls were murals of stone henges and another of an old man in a white robe and a flowing dress cinched around the waist with a sash. He held a staff in his hand. I didn't need to be a genius to know he was a Druid. On the table and in display cases were more Druidic collectables. The bedroom had a giant bed and an enlarged photograph of me on his wall.

"Where did you get that?" I asked.

"I took it when you first bought me my cell phone, and I had it enlarged." He pulled off his shirt and glanced at me. "I'll be out as soon as I can. Unless you want to join me."

"Really?"

He laughed. "Just kidding. Your parents know you are here."

"No, they don't."

"Oh, yes, they do."

He disappeared into the bathroom. While he showered, I studied his Druidic knick-knacks. When he returned to the living room, he had pulled on pants and a T-shirt. He wrapped his arms around my waist and nuzzled my neck. I leaned against him and sighed.

"I've missed you," he whispered.

I turned to face him. "Then do something about it."

He shuddered. "I would, but your father scares the crap out of me. Come on. I'll walk you back to your quarters." He linked our hands, and we left his place. Instead of using a portal, we walked.

Each door had a runic symbol instead of names. We passed Grimnirs heading to their quarters. Some stopped walking and bowed. I told them not to, but after the first hallway, I gave up and just smiled.

When we reached the rotunda, Echo stopped, completely ignored the guards, and cupped my face. The kiss he gave me was both sweet and hot.

"I'm going to wish you goodnight now, sweetheart. Can you have breakfast with me in the morning?"

"At your place or in the Grimnirs Hall?"

He chuckled. "In the hall. We'll have all the time in the world to be together. For the next year, I'm courting you and winning your father's approval."

"You have Mother's."

"I know, but he counts, so I have to win his, too."

I sighed and laid my head on his chest. "Why were you fighting out there?"

"A few princes said I was hiding behind your skirt, that I wasn't a man enough to accept their challenges, so I showed them."

"Mom said no fighting in her hall."

"We were outside."

"Semantics. I was very impressed and proud of you tonight. You kicked some serious ass, and you are going to teach me how to pull those moves, too. But now, I gotta go to bed." I kissed him. "Love you. I'll see you tomorrow for breakfast."

He waited in the hallway until I entered the room.

There were no sounds from my parents' bedroom, yet the door opened before I was halfway across the room. I turned and faced my parents.

"How bad was the fighting?" Mother asked. Trudy was right. Nothing happened in her hall without her knowledge.

"Not that bad. They seemed to enjoy it. It wasn't Echo's fault," I added quickly. "They insulted his honor, and he had to defend it."

"Unfortunately, our people can be unstoppable when they want something. They will continue to challenge him until the two of you are officially married," Father said.

"He will rise to the challenge, and his brothers have his back." I grinned, remembering the way the Druids had rallied behind him.

"Don't forget your brother. He will never let anything happen to him because of you," Mother added.

I noticed that. Eirik was an amazing brother. "And he has me. I'm going to start training tomorrow."

Mother grinned with approval, but Father looked worried.

"What about your work with souls and your abilities?" Father asked.

"I'll train when I'm not on soul duty. Right, Mother?"

"Right, Daughter. She'll be fine, *dýrr mín*. I'll work with her, too, when Echo is busy. Goodnight, Daughter."

"Night, Mother, Father."

I couldn't wait for the next year to pass so Echo could officially be my consort, but I was also looking forward to learning more about my new family, other realms, Mystic Academy, and exploring my abilities in the coming months. My life was as perfect as it could possibly get.

## EPILOGUE: A WEEK LATER

"Where are they?" Mom whispered.

I rubbed her arm reassuringly. She was tense, and Dad was wiping his glasses, a sign that he was nervous. Echo had brought them to the hall from Kayville and left to find my other set of parents.

"They'll be here, Mom. Dad, your glasses are clean." He gave me a sheepish grin, put his glasses back on, and studied the ceiling.

"This is fascinating. Just fascinating. Will you show us around?"

"Of course, Dad. We have the whole weekend after the wedding."

I wasn't sure what Dad found fascinating, the architecture of the hall or the wedding decorations. Strings of crystal lights formed a canopy along the ceiling, and silk bows decorated every column. Pink-ice protea plants and assorted tropical plants in full bloom lined the walls and continued through the Waiting Hall to the Banquet Hall, where the wedding would take place. Maera told me she'd found the plants in Álfheim. According to her, the realm had lush vegetation and fertile soil.

Mother and Father's voices reached us from the hallway leading to our private quarters, and I blew out a breath. I was nervous. I wanted my two sets of parents to like each other. Bond. They all shared an equal place in my heart, and I wanted them to get along.

"Here they come," I said, and Mom gripped my hand. Dad adjusted his glasses.

Father wore his signature gold and white clothes while Mother's moss-green gown had a dropped waistline and intertwined runes in gold along the hem and sleeves. They didn't wear cloaks, which would have made them look even more intimidating. Echo walked behind them. Mom released another deep breath beside me, and I glanced at her.

"She is striking, nothing like I'd imagined," she whispered.

"I know. You'll like her," I reassured her.

The last week had passed quickly. Eirik had taken Celestia to visit friends in Jötunheim and Vanaheim while we prepared for their wedding. They were coming back tonight. Raine, Torin, and Dev had left, but were returning for the wedding with the rest of the entire Kayville crew—Svana, Lavania and her husband, Femi, Hawk, Blaine, Ingrid, and Andris. Raine was still looking for Baby Hannah's family. They'd moved, and someone was stopping her from opening a portal to wherever they were.

Helping with the wedding were Celestia's aunt Genevieve, Tammy, and Hayden. Celestia's uncle wasn't going to make the ceremony, but Zack was already here. Tristan and the Grimnirs had been invited, too. The setting was in the Banquet Hall and, the last time I'd checked, everything had looked perfect. I didn't think the people from Asgard would show up since this ceremony was really for the benefit of Celestia's family, but Mother had hinted at a surprise visitor.

"Welcome to Helheim," Mother said, shaking Mom's hand and then Dad's. Father hugged Mom and kissed her on the cheeks, making her blush. He even surprised Dad with a manly hug. His warmth eased the tension. Echo came to stand beside me, and I inched closer.

It was amazing to see both sets of parents smiling and comfortable with each other. For the next hour, Echo and I stayed with them as they toured the hall. They included us in their conversations. I had to stop the dads when they started on Echo.

When we reached the gym and headed upstairs to watch the Grimnirs, the men bonded over sports. They settled on seats to watch a basketball game.

"They're not going to leave, are they?" I asked, and both my mothers shook their heads, looked at each other, and smiled. I loved seeing them bond over the similarity in their husband's behavior.

We left the men, including Echo, and went toward the Sorting Hall.

The goddess explained to Mom what I'd been doing with souls, and when a soul reached out and touched me, I listened and reassured her.

"Isn't she something?" I overheard the goddess whisper.

"Yes, she is," Mom said. "From when she was baby, she was drawn to them. It scared us so much, and that was why we used special warding runes to stop her from seeing them. I'm sorry if that stopped you from feeling her."

"No, it's not your fault, and I will not allow you to blame yourself," the goddess said firmly. "I didn't know she was alive, so I didn't look. What did you think about Echo when she brought him home?" she asked, smoothly changing the subject.

And that was my cue to leave. I went in search of the girls and stayed with them until Maera came to announce that dinner was served. Echo and I ate with my parents. The conversation flowed effortlessly. Each hour I spent listening to them get to know each other meant the world to me. My world was perfect.

Eirik and Celestia arrived right after dinner. We'd already told Modgie to warn us when they entered the realm. I got the girls and ran to the front entrance to wait for them. Genevieve, Tammy, and even the parents joined us.

The look on Celestia's face when she saw the decorated hall was priceless. She teared up and punched Eirik's chest when she realized he'd known all along. Then she kissed him. We whisked her to the guest room where Maera had been closeted for days. She'd refused everyone entry, including Trudy.

Maera pulled Celestia into the bedroom and told everyone to wait in the living room. It took forever before she opened the door, and Celestia stepped out in an exquisite, white princess gown made with illusion netting and shimmering floral appliqués.

Our jaws dropped, and awe filled the room. Now I knew why Maera had refused to show anyone the gown. It was one of those creations that made you sigh and tear up when you first saw it. Celestia grinned as she watched our reactions.

"What do you think?" she asked, turning.

No one spoke, but we got up to admire her from all angles. The bodice came to just around her belly button, but the naked-illusion pattern extended along the sleeves to her wrists, except the back, which had a single row of pearl buttons. Because it didn't have the floral appliqués, it looked like she wore pearls along her spine. The full, frothy skirt made with sparkle-flecked tulle flowed down to the floor, making her look taller and ethereal.

Every one started talking at once, but I went to Maera and knelt to look her in the eye.

"Please say you'll design my wedding dress," I whispered. "Something like hers. I mean, not exactly alike, but just as unique and gorgeous and amazing."

Maera laughed and cupped my cheeks. "It will be an honor, young goddess."

We made Celestia tear up again, but that was nothing compared to the next day when Mother entered her changing room with Celestia's grandmother, the surprise guest. According to Hayden, Celestia's grandmother had raised her and nurtured her gifts, taking the role of mother when hers had disappeared.

The wedding was just like in my vision. Echo, Rhys, and Torin were groomsmen, and Karle was Eirik's best man. Hayden was the maid of honor, and Jess, Trudy, and I were the bridesmaids.

We stood together, a close-knit family, and listened to Celestia's vows.

"From the moment we met and I thought I was meant to help you, I knew you would change my life," she started. "I didn't realize then that you'd end up helping me. Before you, I'd been blind to my potential and strength. I can now see. Before you, I'd merely existed, but now I can feel. I can hear the right words that encourage, support, and uplift, and not those that hurt and destroy. I can touch love, because you embody that word. You have helped me triumph over challenges and encouraged my personal growth. You've chased away my demons and fought dragons for me. You've gone without sleep and food for me. You've hurt when I've hurt, shed tears when I've cried, and laughed with me. You've shown me what true love really is, and that I'm worthy of it."

There was not a single dry eye when I glanced at Raine and the others.

"Remember that I love you and value your opinion, even when I don't take it," Celestia continued. "Remember that I love you and never keep score, even when I'm winning." Laughter trickled through the room. "Remember that I love you when I'm angry and throw things at your head or when I complain about your arrogance. Remember that I love you when I cringe as you kick ass, because on the inside, I'm cheering for you. You are my rock. My dragon. My best friend. There's no place I'm more content than by your side, and I'll always love you."

Eirik cleared his voice, and we expected him to be a goofball. He surprised everyone.

"In the presence of our families and friends, I take you, Celestia, to be my mate, my love, my consort, and my wife. Together, we can accomplish more than I could ever do alone. I will never let the pressures of the present and uncertainty of the future stop me from loving you, because you are my partner in mayhem, my enabler in trouble, and my companion in a life full of unexpected, strange adventures. I will encourage you to try new things and revisit the old to refresh your memories. I promise to celebrate our love daily, snuggle with you often, and make you laugh out loud. I vow to lend you my strength only when you need it, and to cheer you on from the sideline and support you when you don't. I pledge to nurture and be respectful of your talents and quirks even when they involve dead animals." He glanced at a raven in the back of the room, which I'd assumed was one of Odin's. "You have a huge, kind, and giving heart, and I'm the lucky man you've given it to for safekeeping. I promise to never give you a reason to doubt my love for you, because this is just the beginning of our journey together. We have forever, and I will love you always."

The entire time, Echo's eyes were on me, so I knew his vows to me would be just as moving and sincere because he and I were two halves of a whole.

I had a year to work on my vows, and I planned to make them perfect and unique, just like he was.

## THE END

# THE RUNES SERIES READING ORDER

Thank you for reading RUNES Series. If you enjoyed it, please consider writing a review. Reviews can make a difference in the ranking of a book.

The links are available here:

Runes Series: http:// bit.ly/ RunesSeries-ByEdnahWalters

Check out the other books in the Runes series (See below). I still have one more Torin/ Raine book to release in 2017/18.

*To be updated on more Runes exclusives, giveaways, teasers, and deleted scenes, join my newsletter. http:// bit.ly/ EdnahWaltersNewsletter

*For the discussion about the series, join my private page on FB: http:// bit.ly/ EdnahsEliteValkyries

**READING ORDER**
Runes: http://bit.ly/RunesbyEdnahWalters
Immortals http://bit.ly/ImmortalsbyEdnahWalters
Grimnirs http://bit.ly/GrimnirsbyEdnahWalters
Seeress http://bit.ly/SeeressbyEdnahWalters
Souls http://bit.ly/SoulsbyEdnahWalters
Witches http://bit.ly/WitchesbyEdnahWalters
Demons http://bit.ly/DemonsbyEdnahwalters
Gods http://bit.ly/GodsByEdnahWalters

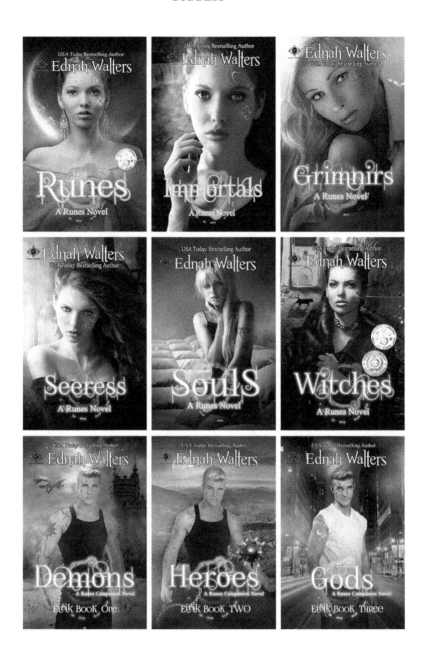

# DISCOVER THE NEXT IN THE SERIES

**STORM (Phantom Islanders Book 1 Part I)** at www.ednahwalters.com

A journey of discovery, adventure, and unforgettable Love
**Pirates no longer roam the seas.**
**Phantom Islands don't exist**

Nanny to a wealthy family, eighteen-year old Alexandria "Lexi" Greendale sends home most of what she earns to support her disabled brother. She is determined to help him get the surgery he needs to walk again. Her dreams come to an abrupt halt when she rescues a man from drowning.

How does he repay her? Captain Storm Orath abducts her, claims her as his chosen mate, and takes her to a magical island that is centuries behind times with barbaric customs.

For Lexi to make it home to her family, she must fight the lure of the man and the island he controls, and escape, or stay trapped forever.

**Pre-Order Today!** Coming May 2nd 2017.
Storm: Phantom Islanders Book 1 Part I

## NOTES FROM THE AUTHOR

I have had so much fun writing Runes series, and I hope to write the last Torin/Raine story and Runes spinoff focusing on Mystic Academy. We'll see how it goes.

I am also about to launch Runes Kindle World, so make sure you signed up for my newsletter. You don't want to miss this. The Runes Kindle World will launch April 18th 2017. There will be thirteen amazing stories by authors you know and love, but these stories will be based in Runes World. So, expect to meet your favorite characters and hear their stories before you met them in Runes or afterwards. There will be new additions to the Runes World. Witches, Valkyries, Grimnirs, Immortals, regular girls and guys.

I'm also about to start a new mythology-series featuring pirates, swordsmen and shieldmaidens. So as not to spoil the surprise, I won't mention the mythos in the series. However, I'll say there are shifters and phantom islands, gutsy heroines, and some amazing captains.

I hope you've enjoyed Cora's journey as much as I've enjoyed writing them. I've listened to her and chronicled her growth form the feisty, boy-crazy girl in Runes to a Goddess. She and Echo deserved happily ever after. Please, don't forget to write a review

# ABOUT THE AUTHOR

Ednah Walters holds a PhD in Chemistry and is a stay-at-home mother of five. She is also a USA Today bestselling author. She writes about flawed heroes and the women who love them.

Her award-winning YA Paranormal Romance—Runes Series—started with Runes and has a total of 9 books to date. The next one, Goddess, will be released in 2017. Her last book in Raine Cooper and Torin St. James' story, Witches, was a Readers' Favorite Awards winner.

She writes YA Urban Fantasy series—The Guardian Legacy Series, which focuses on the Nephilim, children of the fallen angels. GL Series started with Awakened and has a total of 4 books. The latest book in the series, Forgotten, was released in June 2015. The GL series is published by Spencer Hill Press (Beaufort Books)

Ednah also writes Contemporary Romance as E.B. Walters. Her contemporary works started with The international bestselling series The Fitzgerald Family, which has six books, and her USA Today bestselling series, Infinitus Billionaires.

Whether she's writing about Valkyries, Norns, and Grimnirs, or Guardians, Demons, and Archangels, or even contemporary Irish family in the west coast, love, family, and friendship play crucial roles in all her books.

To stay up to date with her work, exclusives, giveaways, teasers, and deleted scenes, join my newsletter.

## EDNAH WALTERS' LINKS:

YA/Ednah Walters': http://bit.ly/EdnahWNewsletter
For the discussion about her series, join her private pages on FB:
RUNES and GL: http://bit.ly/EdnahsEliteValkyries
Ednah Walters' Website: http://www.ednahwalters.com
Ednah Walters in Facebook: http://bit.ly/EdnahWFans
Ednah Walters on Twitter: http://bit.ly/EdnahTwitter
Facebook Fanpage: https://www.facebook.com/AuthorEdnahwalters
Instagram: http://bit.ly/EdnahW-Instagram
Blog: http://ednahwalters.blogspot.com

**E.B. WALTERS' LINKS:**

E.B.'s mailing list.
http://bit.ly/EdnahsNewsletter
For the discussion group about her billionaires, join her private page:
http://bit.ly/LetsTalkBillionaires
E. B. Walters' Website: www.author-ebwalters.com
Facebook Fanpage: https://www.facebook.com/AuthorEBWalters
Twitter: https://twitter.com/eb_walters
Blog: http://enwalters.blogspot.com

GODDESS

.